CLAIRE TURNE... ...LOWING
FACE TOWARD TYLER.

"If I didn't thank you before, Tyler, then I do now. You don't know *how* frightened I was. Do you realize you've come to my rescue once again? You truly are a hero!"

Tyler gritted his teeth and kept driving. If it meant so much to Claire, he wanted a kiss for it, not a damned knighthood.

"I just don't know how to thank you," Claire continued, seeming oblivious to his testy mood.

"You don't need to thank me." What he needed was a good swift kick in the pants. His plan had been to seduce Claire, not to keep rescuing her. But his plan kept getting all twisted around, so that sometimes he wasn't sure what his motives were anymore.

She put her hand on his arm. "I want to make it up to you, Tyler."

At last! Tyler pulled up on the reins. His gaze targeted her lips, his manhood already thickening with desire. "How?" he asked huskily.

Other **AVON ROMANCES**

THE DUKE'S RETURN *by Malia Martin*
A KNIGHT'S VOW *by Gayle Callen*
LOVING LINSEY *by Rachelle Morgan*
THE MACKENZIES: JAKE *by Ana Leigh*
THE MEN OF PRIDE COUNTY: THE PRETENDER
by Rosalyn West
NEVER TRUST A RAKE *by Eileen Putman*
NIGHT THUNDER'S BRIDE *by Karen Kay*

Coming Soon

MY LORD DESTINY *by Eve Byron*
THE TAMING OF JESSI ROSE *by Beverly Jenkins*

And Don't Miss These
ROMANTIC TREASURES
from Avon Books

THE BRIDE OF JOHNNY MCALLISTER *by Lori Copeland*
MY BELOVED *by Karen Ranney*
TO TEMPT A ROGUE *by Connie Mason*

LINDA O'BRIEN

Courting Claire

AVON BOOKS ◆ NEW YORK

AVON BOOKS, INC.
1350 Avenue of the Americas
New York, New York 10019

Copyright © 1999 by Linda Tsoutsouris
Inside cover author photo by Edda Taylor Photographie
Published by arrangement with the author
Library of Congress Catalog Card Number: 99-94800
ISBN: 0-380-80207-4
www.avonbooks.com/romance

First Avon Books Printing: September 1999

AVON TRADEMARK REG. U.S. PAT. OFF. AND IN OTHER COUNTRIES, MARCA
REGISTRADA, HECHO EN U.S.A.

Printed in the U.S.A.

WCD   10 9 8 7 6 5 4 3 2 1

To Jim, my soulmate and my support
in this crazy and wonderful occupation.

To my dear ones, Jason and Julia,
and the other VIPs in my life,
Natasha, Lacinda, Tamara,
Damian, and Wolfgang.

To my family and my uncles
for their valuable assistance and support.

To my dear friend and oftentimes my muse,
Cindy, for keeping me grounded.

Chapter 1

SEND TO: MISS CLAIRE CAVANAUGH,
C/O SPRINGDALE COLLEGE

YOUR FATHER HAS DIED. STOP.
BELLEFLEUR TO BE SOLD. STOP.
COME QUICKLY. STOP.

Paducah, Kentucky, 1897

Thunder reverberated up and down the river as Claire hurried her young sister along the dock. Fierce gusts whipped the girls' long skirts around them, binding their ankles and slowing their progress. Claire's grip tightened on her heavy leather valise as she glanced up at the turbulent gray clouds. Within moments the storm would break. She prayed it would not prevent the boat from leaving.

But what if it did? Although the harbormaster had assured her the *Lady Luck* could make the trip, Claire's frantic mind sought solutions. Could she hire a hansom cab to take them such a distance? Was there a train they could catch, instead?

"Cee Cee, I can walk alone," her twelve-year-old sister insisted in a frustrated voice, trying to shrug off Claire's arm.

"Please, Em, it's dangerous. See that? The rain has started."

As she spoke, heavy raindrops broke from the clouds and battered the wooden planks, quickly soaking through the girls' light spring clothing. Beneath the dripping brim of her hat, Claire squinted at the white paddlewheel steamboat ahead, where passengers were disembarking. Umbrellas unfurled as throngs of people scurried along the dock, seeking shelter. Claire clutched Emily closer so they would not be separated.

"You're squeezing me!" Emily complained, trying to wriggle free.

The protest barely registered; Claire's thoughts were on the telegram she had received from their housekeeper yesterday: three brief lines that had turned her safe, insulated world upside down. How she wished the telegram had given her more information! But of course, Mrs. Parks had been distraught when she'd sent it. The elderly woman had worked for her father for twenty years, and had been in complete charge of the household since Claire's mother had died four and a half years ago. Her father had always said, "Thank God for Mrs. Parks. I don't know what we'd do without her."

But it wasn't Mrs. Parks they would have to do without. Once again Claire experienced that feeling of disbelief she had felt when she opened the telegram.

YOUR FATHER HAS DIED.

Claire had immediately taken a leave of her studies, then set out to fetch Emily from her school, praying they would make it in time for the funeral.

Yet although the impact of her father's death had not fully registered in Claire's benumbed brain, the second and third lines of the telegram had.

BELLEFLEUR TO BE SOLD. COME QUICKLY.

The thought of losing her home paralyzed Claire with fear. She remembered too well what it was like to have no home, to huddle under bridges, sleep in barns and take refuge in alleyways. She had known the indignity of digging for food in the dead of night in someone else's garden, the humiliation of begging for scraps, and the degradation of being so dirty even dogs shied away. And she had vowed never to suffer such indignities again.

The telegram was a mistake—it had to be. The estate was not just their home, but their security for the future. Claire tried to assure herself that the message was just the product of an old woman's fears. Nevertheless, she was frightened.

Emily took that moment to declare her independence. "I'm going to walk by myself!"

"Don't be a goose, Em. We're almost there," Claire replied, as they drew near the boat ramp.

Emily twisted out from under Claire's arm, straightened her yellow bonnet, and righted the slender white cane she had been gripping. "I can walk alone!" she stated, taking a step forward.

But Emily couldn't see the immediate danger before her. As Claire reached for her, the toe of Emily's shoe caught the edge of the ramp and tripped her. She cried out as she fought for balance against the ferocious wind.

"Emily!" Claire lunged but wasn't quick enough to catch her sister as she pitched over the edge of the dock. "Someone help, please!" she screamed over her shoulder, as she dropped to her knees. Clinging to the slippery wooden planks, Emily dangled some ten feet above the dark, churning waters of the Ohio River.

Claire wrapped her own fingers tightly around the small wrists, praying for strength. "Hold on, Em. I'll try to pull you up."

Emily's face was white as she gasped for breath. "I—can't—hold on. I'm slipping."

"Yes, you can!" In horror, Claire saw the small fingers

slide closer toward the edge. "Help, please!" Claire
screamed desperately.

In danger of being pulled over herself, Claire stretched
out flat to gain leverage. A vicious gust of wind tore her
hat from her head, but she barely noticed. Her hands
ached; her arms felt as though they were separating from
her shoulders. She couldn't hold on much longer and Emily was too heavy to lift. Had anyone heard her cries over
the roar of the wind?

"Cee Cee," her sister sobbed, "I don't want to die."

Claire choked back a sob. Emily was the only family
she had now. If something were to happen to her . . .
"Don't be afraid, Em," she cried over the wind. "You're
not going to die—I won't let you. Help will be here soon,
I promise."

Standing under the protective shelter of the *Lady Luck's*
promenade deck, Tyler McCane was talking with his assistant when he heard a woman's cries for help. He turned
quickly, his keen gaze scanning the dock. Stepping to the
rail, he saw a slender figure lying on her stomach near the
edge.

"Grab a life rope, Jonas," he called, pounding down
the deck toward the ramp.

Within moments he was kneeling beside the woman.
"Here, I've got her," he said, leaning over to grip the
child's forearms. The woman seemed reluctant to release
her hold, as though she was in shock. "I've got her—let
her go!" he thundered, and she obeyed.

Wind-driven rain pelted his face, and the heavy muscles
in his arms shook from his efforts. Tyler blinked hard to
clear his vision and gritted his teeth as he hauled the girl
up. With a cry the woman clutched the girl to her, mur-
muring into her ear and stroking her head.

Jonas stepped forward and wrapped a blanket around

the child's shoulders. "Let's get you both to shelter," he urged.

The woman stepped back and put a hand over her mouth; her eyes overflowed with tears as Jonas ushered his new charges up the ramp. When they reached the safety of the deck, she covered her face with her hands and sobbed.

Purely by instinct, Tyler put his arms around her, tucking her head under his chin. She was soaking wet and shivering in the May winds. "It's all right," he said with a tenderness that surprised him. "Your daughter is safe."

"I nearly lost her," the young woman wept. "I wasn't vigilant. I have to be vigilant. Emily is my responsibility now. *Everything* is my responsibility now. How will I ever manage?"

Some distant memory within Tyler responded to the anguish in her voice. "The child is safe, and so are you. Now, let's get out of this rain."

The woman raised forlorn eyes to his. Her eyes were of such a startling cobalt blue that his breath was momentarily taken away. "Thank you for saving her life," she said in a choked whisper. "Emily is all the family I have now."

Tyler studied her small oval face. She was much younger than he had at first thought, certainly too young for the child to be her daughter. Her skin was as smooth and as clear as fresh cream, her bow-shaped mouth pale from fright. Her hat had apparently blown off in the storm, and her hair, freed of pins, draped like sodden black curtains around her face and down the back of her white blouse. Her eyes, framed by long black lashes, spoke of sorrow and anxieties. Yet underneath, he saw a steely determination that he knew all too well.

At a loud thunderclap, Tyler picked up her valise and led her up the boat ramp. "Let's see about a hot drink to warm you."

"Do you know when the boat will leave?" she asked through chattering teeth.

"In this storm?" Tyler asked. "It won't."

She stopped abruptly, her dismay evident. "Then I must speak with the captain. It's imperative I reach Fortune as soon as possible."

The coincidence surprised him. Fortune, Indiana, a small town on the Ohio River, happened to be his destination. But Tyler had no intention of setting out until the storm blew over and the river calmed. He hadn't made a name for himself by being reckless. "We'll leave when the danger has passed."

"Are you the captain?"

"No," he began, "but—"

"I need to see the captain." She started to move around him.

"I do own the boat."

She stopped and turned, her guileless blue gaze piercing his thick shell of indifference. The hairs on his arms and neck prickled as a strong feeling of presentiment washed over him: this woman was going to destroy him.

Tyler let out his breath slowly. "Why don't we find your Emily?" he suggested, keeping his tone matter-of-fact, "and then we'll get you some hot coffee." He headed down the narrow inner passageway, telling himself he was crazy. No one could predict the future. And no woman would ever again have the power to destroy him.

"Please," she called from behind, "I have to get home. Mr. Galloway assured me you would be able to take me tonight. I'll pay whatever it costs."

Tyler gritted his teeth in annoyance. Abe Galloway, who worked at the harbormaster's office in Paducah, was a longtime friend. "Mr. Galloway had no business making assurances he couldn't keep. I won't leave at the risk of people's lives. We'll embark in the morning."

"You don't understand—"

"No, *you* don't understand," he said, swinging to face her. "There are nineteen people on this boat. What reason could you possibly have that would make me risk their lives?''

The woman's lower lip trembled as she spoke. ''I'm sorry. I wasn't thinking. My father—'' she let out a shaky breath ''—has just passed away. We wanted to be home for his funeral in the morning.''

Tyler stared at her dispassionately. Her father wouldn't *know* if she made it to the funeral—the man was dead, for God's sake. But as she wiped a stray tear from her cheek, he found himself envying her father for inspiring that kind of devotion.

What harm would it do to help her out? The storm would blow over soon; they could leave in the middle of the night and reach Fortune before morning.

Then what the hell is the problem? Tyler had no answer. He had never believed in fortune-tellers, prophecies, or divinations. He used his head to make decisions. Yet for some reason, that premonition had shaken him to the core. He snorted. He was not going to be controlled by an illogical notion.

''I'll confer with the captain,'' he said irritably. ''We'll try to have you home by morning.''

Reginald Boothe gave his hand-tooled boot a last buff and pulled it onto his right foot. ''So he's really dead,'' Boothe remarked to the big man sitting on the other side of his desk.

''I talked to Doc Jenkins yesterday,'' Sheriff Wilbur Simons replied, his hands resting placidly on his protruding belly. ''And I saw the undertaker's wagon coming back from Bellefleur.''

With a smirk, Boothe leaned back, clasped his hands behind his head, and propped both booted feet on his desk. ''The timing couldn't be better. I wonder if that little talk I had with Arthur had anything to do with his sudden demise?''

The sheriff scratched the back of his neck, shifting uneasily in the chair. "I couldn't say."

"And who *is* there to say?" Boothe replied in his meticulous British accent. "That antiquated, feeble-minded housekeeper? She can barely remember her own name."

"I give you credit for your patience, Mr. Boothe," the sheriff said. "You've wanted that land a long time."

The banker's smile flattened and his expression grew hard. Yes—too long. But Arthur Cavanaugh was dead at last, and his two brats certainly weren't going to be an obstacle. "I intend to move forward quickly. Tomorrow I'm meeting with Tyler McCane, the owner of the Lady Luck, hopefully to sign our partnership agreement. With McCane's gambling license and the Cavanaughs' land as an operating base, I'll be a millionaire within two years, mark my word." Boothe pointed his finger at the sheriff. "I won't forget your help, either."

Sheriff Simons's heavy face flushed with gratitude. "I appreciate that, sir. But what if McCane doesn't like the agreement?"

"He'll like it—he's as eager to make a deal as I am. After all, look what he's getting: prime riverfront land; an adjoining piece of property on which to build his own house, if he chooses; the money to build a fleet of steamboats; and a prominent businessman as his backer. And all he's putting in is half-ownership of his boat and a gambling license."

"Seems to me that's a lopsided deal."

"Perhaps on the surface," Boothe replied calmly. "But McCane knows the value of his gambling license, and I guarantee you that he knows I've tried unsuccessfully to come by one through other sources. We must never forget, Sheriff, with whom we are dealing. McCane has a reputation for being a clever, ruthless man."

"He can't be more clever or ruthless than you, Mr. Boothe."

The banker smiled smugly. "Then let's just say McCane

and I both know how to get what we want."

Simons opened his mouth to speak, then shut it again, as though fearful of broaching a sensitive subject. Boothe chafed impatiently, tapping his fingers on the desk. "If you have something to say, Sheriff, say it."

"What will happen if Arthur Cavanaugh's daughters decide to fight for their land?"

Boothe took pleasure in the sheriff's apprehension. Wilbur Simons knew full well how far he would go to get what he wanted. "Cavanaugh was so heavily in debt that they can't possibly afford to keep it. A loan without collateral is out of the question, and an extension of time is simply not possible—since I hold the lien. We're dealing with a pair of females, and mere children, at that. Do you really think they'll pose a threat?" At the sheriff's shamefaced look, Boothe said, with a lift of one eyebrow, "And if they should, do you have any doubts about my handling them?"

"No, sir," the sheriff responded unhappily.

"Any other questions?"

With a heavy sigh, Simons lowered his gaze. "Looks like you thought of everything."

Boothe leaned back in his chair and formed a temple with his fingers. "Wilbur, something is on your mind. Out with it, man."

The sheriff nervously scratched his mustache. "I've known the older girl since she came to Fortune. I hate to think of her losing her home, especially with that blind child to look after."

Boothe eyed him over the tips of his fingers. "You feel sorry for her, do you? Even though her father nearly cost you your job? Well, Sheriff, here's a solution: marry her."

"Marry Cee Cee?" The sheriff looked stunned. His full face reddened and his hands clasped together, twisting and wringing, as though he were waging an inner war with himself. "But I'm twenty-seven years her senior."

"How long have you been a widower now? Five

years?'' Boothe gave him a knowing wink. "A mature man may be just what she needs."

Simons rubbed the back of his neck. "I don't know. She probably wouldn't have me."

"You can offer her a home, security, a place for her sister—things she'll be desperate for. Think about it, Wilbur. You could ease your conscience and get yourself a young bride to boot."

Boothe watched as the sheriff scratched his mustache and shook his head, contemplating the suggestion. Wilbur Simons was incompetent—the whole town knew it—but Cavanaugh had been the only one to try to do something about it, until Boothe had stepped in.

Wilbur Simons made a perfect lackey—a simple man with a simple mind, yet smart enough to know where his loyalties belonged. And they belonged to the man who had saved his job: Reginald Boothe.

"I see your point," the sheriff said at last.

The bank president's thin lips arched into a smile. "I knew you would."

After the sheriff had departed, Boothe swiveled his chair to look out the open window, where the smell of fresh fish wafted through on a spring breeze. From his second-story office of the Fortune Farmer's Bank, he had a clear view of the Ohio River. For a moment, he watched a barge move slowly past. Another barge was being loaded at the docks directly in front of him. From below he heard the jingle of horses' harnesses and the shouts of men unloading heavy crates from flatbed wagons.

Boothe turned his gaze downriver, where he could see the rise that signaled the beginning of Cavanaugh land. Soon, he thought with a contented smile, his riverboats would be plying the Ohio from that land—*his* land—raking in those lucrative gambling dollars.

Thinking back to all the years he had fought and plotted

against Arthur Cavanaugh, Boothe began to chuckle. He would have the last laugh after all. "You can rot in hell, Arthur, and your brats with you. You may have had Marie, but *I* will have your land—one way or another."

Chapter 2

$\sim\!\!\infty\!\!\sim$

As Tyler halted before his cabin, the young woman put out a hand to steady herself against the wall. "Are you all right?" he asked.

"I'm just a little woozy. I'll be fine."

She didn't look fine; she looked like she was ready to drop. Keeping a close watch on her, Tyler opened the door and followed her inside.

The child sat at the table, talking quietly with Jonas, sipping a cup of hot chocolate and shivering under the brown wool blanket draped around her shoulders. Her black hair hung in damp braids down the back of her sodden dress, and her small face was very pale, making for an altogether pathetic sight.

"Cee Cee?" the girl called, looking around. "Cee Cee, is that you?"

"It's me!" The young woman hurried across the room and hugged the child to her. "I've never been so frightened in all my life, Em. Promise you'll listen to me from now on."

"I was frightened, too, Cee Cee."

Tyler watched the two, puzzled, as Jonas rose and came toward him.

"Emily is blind," Jonas whispered. "That's her sister, Claire, also known as Cee Cee."

Blind! Tyler couldn't believe he'd been so stupid. He should have noticed the girl's unfocused stare. Her sister

12

certainly had her hands full, and he didn't envy her.

"I'm going to the pilot house," he informed Jonas. "See to them, will you?" He glanced back at Claire and saw her watching him. For a moment he was tempted to stay, but he talked himself out of it.

Claire felt a curious sense of disappointment when their rescuer left the cabin, but she smiled politely as the older man came forward and took her hand. "Jonas W. Polk the third, at your service, Miss Cavanaugh. Let me get you some coffee to warm you up."

"Thank you, Mr. Polk. You're very kind."

She accepted a cup of the steaming beverage and thanked him again. He was much older than their rescuer, with a long, narrow, weathered face, sun-bleached brown hair, and an accent of some kind—British, Claire guessed.

"Have you ladies eaten recently?"

At the mention of food, Claire's stomach rumbled. "Early this morning."

"We'll remedy that soon enough. Come with me, Lady Emily. You can help with the menu while your sister warms up." Jonas left the cabin with her sister in tow.

Pulling a blanket around her shoulders, Claire sat down on the narrow bed that hung from the wall and propped her chin in her hands. Hunger seemed the least of her problems. Tomorrow morning she would be attending her father's funeral.

How could it be possible? Arthur Cavanaugh was too powerful and certainly much too ornery to have succumbed to death. Claire hadn't even known he'd been ill. He hadn't indicated anything about it in his letters to her; he'd always been in robust health.

In the letter she had received only ten days ago, he had expressed his excitement over a discovery on the estate, something that would secure Claire's and Emily's future. Surely he hadn't meant that he was going to sell Bellefleur for a huge profit. The land had been in her father's family for generations. It was their home, the only real home Claire could remember.

But what if she and Emily were turned out onto the streets? How would they survive? She began to tremble as those unwanted memories flooded back, trying to drag her once again into the past. Jumping to her feet, Claire paced rapidly, her hands balled into fists. She was no longer that frightened child. And she would sell her soul to the devil before she would ever subject Emily to what she had endured.

Outside the storm raged on, and for the twentieth time that day Claire wished her fiancé had come with her. She had never felt more alone, more in need of a strong shoulder. But Claire understood Lance's reasons for staying behind. It was bad enough she had to leave a week before finals, and right before graduation, too; she couldn't expect him to do the same. But she wished he'd at least offered to come.

The door opened suddenly and her sister's rescuer walked in. He stopped when he saw her, as though he'd forgotten she was there, then a look of irritation crossed his face. He settled himself at his desk on the opposite side of the cabin and delved into some paperwork. Claire stared at him uncertainly. Should she go? Stay? She smoothed her skirt, then cleared her throat.

Without looking up, he asked, "Has the dizziness passed?"

"Yes."

"Has Jonas gone to get food?"

"Yes."

With a nod, he resumed his work. Stewing, Claire pulled out a chair at the table. Some gentleman he was! Drumming her fingers, she glanced around the cabin. Everything from the mahogany paneling and dark red-and-brown wool carpet to the built-in bookcase and cherry desk seemed neat and orderly and masculine—like him. She took it to be an indication of his character.

"Must you?"

Claire blinked in confusion. "Must I what?"

"Tap your fingers on the table."

"I hadn't realized I was doing it."

"Do you realize it now?"

Did he take her for a dolt? Claire fumed. "I beg your pardon," she said stiffly. After all, he *had* saved her sister.

With a rustle of paper, he returned to his work.

At least he'd stopped scowling. He was handsome when he wasn't scowling.

He appeared to be about thirty years old. He had a lean, chiseled face with penetrating, gold-rimmed brown eyes and a cleft in his chin. Dark wavy hair framed his strong features, and his white shirt and slim black pants emphasized his powerful build. His shirt sleeves had been rolled back, revealing tanned, muscular arms.

For some reason, he reminded Claire of her father—though not in looks or dress. Perhaps it was his somber expression. Or perhaps it was his bravery and generosity: like her father, this man had proved himself a hero.

He was also potently masculine.

Claire felt her cheeks warm. Why did she find him so attractive? He was the complete opposite of her fiancé. Lance had a beautiful face, with a wide, bright, dimpled smile that was boyish and endearing. His short hair, which he wore combed straight back, was more blond than brown, and he stood only half a head taller than Claire—unlike Emily's rescuer, who towered over her.

Somehow, this man seemed intimidating. Claire didn't want to think of him as dangerous, yet she sensed a restlessness in him, like that of a panther on the prowl, which made her feel vulnerable. Lance, on the other hand, was solid, sensible, and safe. Above all else, Claire craved safety.

The man looked up and caught her staring. Not knowing what else to say, she blurted, "I'm sorry, but I don't believe I've heard your name."

At first, Claire thought he was going to ignore her. But then he rose and came over. "My fault." Unsmiling, he held out a strong, wide hand. "Tyler McCane."

At the firm grip of his long fingers, a tingle of electricity raced through her, starting at her fingertips and ending somewhere deep inside, leaving her suddenly breathless. "Claire Cavanaugh," she replied, blinking up at him.

"Not Cee Cee?" A bare flicker of a grin appeared on his darkly handsome face. Claire sensed that he was not accustomed to smiling. For some reason, that bothered her.

With a blush, she slid her hand from his warm grasp. "Actually, those are my initials. My father started that years ago. He gives everyone a nickname, though not all of them are complimentary."

Claire looked down as tears stung her eyes and her throat tightened. How long would it take her to remember to refer to her father in the past tense?

"Do you have a night robe with you?" Tyler asked abruptly, breaking into her thoughts.

His question stunned her. "I beg your pardon?" she replied stiffly, suddenly fearing he had ulterior motives for bringing her to his cabin. She glanced quickly at the door. Was it locked?

Tyler opened a cabinet in the wall and took out a lady's wrapper. "It may be a few hours before we can leave, so you and your sister may as well sleep until we reach Fortune. If you don't have a night robe, you can wear this."

Longingly, Claire eyed the beautiful rose-patterned silk wrapper. She had only one change of clothing and some personal necessities in the leather valise—Emily's clothes consumed the bulk of the space—but she could not wear such a scandalous outfit in front of him. She was shocked that he had even suggested it—unless she had misunderstood? "Thank you, but I'll be fine," she said coolly.

"Suit yourself. If you want to wash up, there's a small privy behind that door."

Claire hadn't noticed the second door in the cabin. Stepping inside the tiny, paneled closet she found a portable commode, a porcelain washbasin attached to the wall, and several towels hanging from rings.

She unbuttoned the cuff of her damp sleeve and rolled it up, thinking again about the silk wrapper. Did it belong to his wife? *How silly even to wonder!* she chided herself. What difference could it possibly make to her if Tyler McCane was married?

While Claire washed, Tyler busied himself at his desk. He knew he should be in the pilot house conferring with the captain, checking the weather, or doing any number of tasks that awaited him—yet he stayed, though he felt foolish for doing so. He assured himself the reason for his interest was purely carnal; after all, he hadn't offered her the wrapper solely for charitable reasons. He regretted that he wouldn't see her with only that thin layer of silk covering her body. Hearing the click of the door handle, Tyler looked up.

Claire had plaited her damp hair into a thick braid which now hung over one shoulder, brushing the tip of her breast. Tyler's gaze moved down the damp white blouse to her narrow waist, down the curve of shapely hips. She was a comely woman, and his blood grew thick and hot as he imagined what she would have looked like in the silk wrapper. He imagined untying the sash and parting the robe, revealing the glorious body beneath. He could see himself carrying her to his bed, laying her back so that he could feast his hungry gaze on her, unbraiding her black hair so that it fell around her naked shoulders.

She met his eyes warily, and there were bright spots of color in her cheeks, as though she knew the direction of his thoughts and was embarrassed. In a fluid, graceful motion, she raised one hand to tuck a wisp of hair behind her ear. Her unbuttoned cuff fell back, revealing a slender ivory forearm. Tyler's groin tightened. Her movements were both innocent and sensual, a potent combination he found difficult to resist.

His earlier, instinctive fear returned, but he shoved it aside. He'd long ago taught himself rigid control over his emotions. She was just a lovely woman, and his physical response was natural and meaningless.

"Was that your wife's wrapper?" she asked suddenly, as though to either divert his attention or remind him of proper conduct.

"My wife's?" he repeated blankly. "I'm not married."

Jonas entered at that moment, balancing a tray of food on one hand and holding onto Emily with the other. "Here we go, ladies," he sang out cheerily. "Time to eat."

Tyler's gaze met Claire's for just an instant and saw her relief. Was it because Jonas had arrived or because he wasn't married?

With his assistant in charge now, Tyler left. Still, he couldn't stop thinking about Claire—her intriguing eyes, her beguiling smile, her sensuous body. In light of her recent bereavement, he was almost ashamed of his base thoughts.

When he returned to the cabin three hours later, he found the sisters fast asleep on his bed. Leaving the lantern outside, he quietly crossed the room to gather a few personal items and a change of clothing. He paused for a moment to gaze down at Claire. What a shame she wasn't alone.

"They're sound asleep," he told Jonas, as he prepared to bunk down in his assistant's cabin across the hall.

With a yawn, Jonas climbed into one of the two wall-hung beds. "They should be pleased when they wake up and discover themselves nearly home. Poor things—received a telegram right out of the blue. What a dreadful way to find out about their father. And then having to rush home for the funeral, and Claire only weeks away from graduating from college."

"You're certainly a fount of knowledge," Tyler muttered dryly.

"Emily's quite a little chatterbox."

"That explains why you hit it off so well." The bed squeaked as Tyler rolled onto his side. "But their problems are not our concern."

"But you see, they're orphans now. Their mother died four years ago, and they've just lost their father, too."

Tyler sighed. "They'll be fine. There's money in the family."

"Perhaps we should see them all the way home."

"Perhaps you should stop talking so I can catch some sleep. I've got that meeting with Boothe later today."

"Ah, yes. Our new partner." Jonas doused the lantern near his bed. "Still, Tyler, about the girls, I think—"

"Damn it, Jonas," Tyler ground out, rising on one elbow, "stop thinking! You're getting soft. And by the way, Boothe is not a partner until he signs on the dotted line."

"And if he balks?"

"He won't. He wants this partnership as much as I do. With Boothe's backing, we'll have the biggest operation on the Ohio. We'll all be wealthy beyond our wildest dreams. How do you like the sound of that?"

"It's music to my ears," Jonas admitted. "I just hope there aren't any hitches."

"Hitches are merely temporary interruptions—nothing to fret about."

"I know," Jonas said with a sigh, "like women."

"Exactly. Neither will stop me from getting what I want."

"Time will tell," Jonas murmured, "and so will the right woman."

Tyler pretended not to hear him. It was Jonas's firm conviction that he needed a wife. Though a confirmed bachelor, the feisty Englishman was nevertheless quite sentimental about the state of holy matrimony. Tyler, however, had no such sentiment. He'd learned early on that women could be enjoyed, but never trusted.

Draping an arm across his forehead, he found himself thinking of a certain woman with intriguing blue eyes, and he smiled. He would enjoy an opportunity to get to know Claire better. He'd been too long without female companionship.

It wasn't that he'd lacked opportunities; the glamour of riverboats attracted women. But since he'd bought *Lady Luck* he'd been too busy establishing a name for himself to devote much attention to them.

Her slender form flitted across his mind once again. He wouldn't mind devoting some attention to Claire, so long as it didn't interfere with business.

Reginald Boothe winced at the heavy, persistent knocking on his front door. Whoever was waking him at this ungodly hour had better have a damn good reason for it. Tying the sash of his robe, he yanked open the door to find Sheriff Simons on the other side, his hat in his hand.

"Yes, what is it, Sheriff?" he asked impatiently.

"I thought you'd want to know that Cavanaugh's daughters are coming back for the funeral. Abe Galloway, from the harbormaster's office down in Paducah, reported that they'll be arriving this morning by boat."

What did he care that the girls were coming home? About to slam the door in Simons's face, Boothe had second thoughts.

"Why don't you meet them at the docks?" he suggested. "Welcome them back, express your heartfelt sympathy, and find out what their plans are. I'm sure you'll impress the older one with your consideration—what was her name?"

"Cee Cee." The sheriff blushed bright red as he said it. "What about their housekeeper? She'll probably send someone to meet the boat."

Boothe suppressed an exasperated sigh. "Offer to pick

up the girls *for* her. In fact, why don't you keep an eye on them for as long as they stay in town?''

With a big grin, Wilbur Simons bobbed his head once and turned to leave.

"And Sheriff," Boothe called, "don't forget to send Mr. Galloway a generous token of my appreciation." He shut the door and returned to his bedroom, where his mistress, Daphne Duprey, the wickedly delectable daughter of the town council president, awaited him. Even so, he wasn't too angry with the sheriff for disturbing him. It was good to keep abreast of what Cavanaugh's daughters had planned—in case more serious efforts were required.

Claire awoke with a start. They were moving! She heard gears grinding deep in the belly of the boat and said a quick prayer of thanks. They would be home in time for the funeral.

She and Emily washed and dressed quickly in the dim cabin and emerged onto the deck as the first rays of the sun skimmed the horizon. At that moment, the *Lady Luck* rounded a bend in the river, bringing their hometown into view. "We're almost there," she told Emily, giving her sister's shoulder a reassuring squeeze. It would be good to be home again, regardless of the circumstances.

"Good morning, ladies."

The deep bass voice sent a disturbing thrill of excitement through Claire. She noted the trim cut of Tyler's figure in a dark serge suit and white shirt as he approached. "Good morning," she and Emily said in unison.

"We should dock within the hour," Tyler told them. "If you'd like some breakfast, the dining room is at the front of the boat. Just follow this deck straight ahead."

Claire gave Tyler a grateful smile. "Thank you for all your help. I can't tell you how much we appreciate what you've done for us. You're a brave, generous man."

Uncomfortable with her praise, Tyler muttered a response. His actions had been automatic, not heroic. He didn't want to be held in such high regard.

Emily held out her hand, which Tyler took. "If it weren't for you, I wouldn't be here. Cee Cee is very lucky you heard her calls for help." Almost as though she could see him, she gave Tyler a wink and turned. "Coming, Cee?"

With a look of amused exasperation, Claire followed.

Tyler allowed himself the pleasure of studying her as she took Emily's hand and led the way to the dining room. Claire's braided hair revealed a slender neck and small, shapely ears. Her outfit was typical, demure college fare: a full-sleeved white blouse and a long, slim navy skirt. Even so, he felt the surge deep in his groin that signaled impending arousal.

Perhaps he could invite Claire to dine with him one evening. Alone.

"How very kind of you to take us home, Sheriff," Claire said to the large man seated next to her sister in the buggy.

"It's an honor, Miss Cee Cee," he replied in an earnest voice, gazing at her with puppy dog eyes over Emily's head. "I'm just glad I was there to help you out."

Claire felt Emily punch her gently in the ribs. The sheriff was one of Emily's favorite targets. Behind his back she referred to him as "Simple Simon," after the nursery rhyme. Giving Emily a discreet nudge back, Claire smiled briefly at the sheriff, then turned away. Her gaze swept the familiar sights of her hometown as they made the journey to Bellefleur. She hadn't been home since Christmas, but nothing in Fortune had changed.

They traveled down Grand Avenue, which ran parallel to the Ohio River, slowing at the intersection of Main Street to let a large wagon pass. One block up Main sat the mayor's house, where his seventy-year-old mother would be knitting in her rocker on the front porch. Next to the mayor lived Minnie Pennywhistle, on whose wide verandah the Fortune Ladies' Society met every Tuesday morning. Across the street lived the judge, and behind his house the steeple of the Presbyterian church was visible. The familiarity of it all gave Claire a feeling of security.

"I'm sorry about your—uh—recent loss," the sheriff said awkwardly.

"Thank you." Claire turned when someone called a greeting to her from the sidewalk. "Hello, Mrs. Gardner," she called back with a wave.

Her smile dissolved when Reginald Boothe stepped out of the bank on the corner and paused to settle his derby on his head. Though he was quite distinguished in manner and dress, Claire found him repulsive. He wore his light brown hair combed back from a high forehead and gazed out at the world through eyes that were narrow slits in a smoothly shaven face. His nose was long and bulbous at the tip, his mouth narrow-lipped and humorless, and his long chin curved forward, giving him a haughty air.

Boothe stared at her as their buggy passed, a faint sneer on his face. With a huff, Claire lifted her chin and looked away.

"Who was that?" Emily wanted to know.

"Reginald Boothe," Claire leaned close to say.

"The snake?" Emily whispered, using the nickname she had given him. "He's the one who—"

Claire gently squeezed Emily's arm in warning. "Yes," she whispered.

As Emily knew the story, her mother, the beautiful ebony-haired Marie Reneau, had been widowed and penniless with a ten-year-old daughter to care for. Reginald Boothe had hired her as his cook, only to dismiss her without pay two months later. With no money and nowhere to go, Marie and Claire had lived by their resources until the prominent landowner Arthur Cavanaugh took them in. He had fallen in love with his new housekeeper and married Marie a short four weeks later. Emily had been born the following summer. The story had been given an almost fairytale quality in order to shield Emily from the truth.

For Claire, the story was anything but a fairytale. The night she and her mother had left Boothe's house, as well as the weeks that had followed, would be forever etched in her memory. Had Arthur Cavanaugh not taken pity on them, neither she nor her mother would have survived.

Although twelve years had passed, the horrors Claire had endured still brought on nightmares that left her in a cold sweat. She would never forget the panic in her mother's voice when she had awakened Claire and told her to dress quietly so as not to rouse the household. Nor would she forget the bruises that had marred her mother's beautiful face, or the fear and loathing in her eyes. Claire had known something terrible had happened, but she had been too timid to ask about it.

It wasn't until her mother had died that Claire had uncovered the truth. While entering the date of her mother's passing in the family Bible, she'd noticed that Emily had been born a mere seven months after her mother's marriage to Arthur Cavanaugh. Great care had been taken to hide the fact of Emily's early arrival, and she now realized that it had been done to cover a horrible secret: Reginald Boothe had raped Claire's mother. Emily was Boothe's daughter.

When Claire told her father what she'd discovered, he'd told her his greatest fear was that Boothe would find out and try to take Emily away from him, or worse, try to destroy the child.

She turned to gaze at her sister's delicate face. While Emily didn't look much like either Marie or Arthur, she thankfully bore no resemblance to the banker. Claire loved Emily with all her heart, and she would do whatever was necessary to keep Boothe from finding out the truth.

There was only one thing that puzzled her. Though she understood her father's reasons for hating Boothe, she didn't understand why Boothe had taken every possible opportunity to defame the Cavanaugh name. But with her father gone, hopefully Boothe's vengeance would be gone as well.

She felt Emily's hand grip her arm. "We're almost home! I can smell it."

As they turned onto River Road, the long dirt road that led to Bellefleur, Claire sat forward on the bench, her heartbeat quickening. "There it is, Em," she said, tears blurring her vision. "Home."

"Oh, do describe it, Cee Cee," Emily said excitedly.

"The pear trees are in bloom," Claire began, "and Mrs. Parks has set pots of petunias, white and pink, on the sides of the steps. The grass is thick and long, and the sky is cloudless—"

"I hear the birds chirping," Emily interrupted, "cardinals, jays, robins—oh, they sound so beautiful!"

"And the house," Claire continued with a lump in her throat, "the house looks the same, Em, like a stately old gentleman welcoming his family home."

The enormous limestone home sat high on a hill. The estate boasted a roomy carriage house, stables, two huge black drying barns, a cornfield, and a tobacco field. Their land extended down to the Ohio River, where they had built a dock for shipping their crop.

Claire had found her haven there, with a man who had loved her as if she were his own blood. Although Arthur Cavanaugh had a longstanding reputation for being obstinate and stubborn, for which many in town had resented him, he had opened his heart to Claire and her mother. He had become her father; Claire could remember no other. Her own father had been a soldier who had died from malaria when she was a baby.

Now, the thought of stepping into Arthur Cavanaugh's shoes terrified her. How would she ever manage Bellefleur without him?

"I can't imagine Pa not being there," Emily said in a quiet, mournful voice.

"Neither can I, Em," Claire answered, swallowing the lump in her throat.

As the buggy drew nearer, Claire saw Mrs. Parks step out onto the wide, covered porch to greet them. The elderly housekeeper leaned on a cane, and even from that distance Claire was alarmed to see that she was stooped and painfully thin, appearing ill.

When the buggy stopped, Claire stepped down and gave a hand to Emily. "Mrs. Parks is on the porch, Em," she said. "But be careful. She looks very fragile."

As Emily set off toward the porch, the sheriff bounded out of his seat and hurried around to offer Claire a hand with her valise.

"Can I carry your bag to the house for you?" he asked, his full face flushing deep red.

"Thank you, but I can manage," Claire said, as she took it from him.

"What are your plans now, Miss Cee Cee?" Wilbur Simons held his hat before him, his meaty hands crushing and releasing the brim as he shot a shy glance at her from beneath bushy brows. "I mean after the funeral. Are you going back to college?"

Claire glanced at him curiously, wondering what was causing his nervousness. "I hope to, Sheriff." When he stood shuffling his feet, she said, "May I get you something to drink?"

"Oh, no," he replied. "I wouldn't put you to the trouble. I'll just be on my way."

"Then, thank you again for the ride." She felt his eyes on her as she climbed the steps. Claire had known the sheriff for years, but suddenly he seemed more a stranger than a friend.

"My dear child," Mrs. Parks said in a tremulous voice, enfolding Claire in her embrace. Claire felt the tremors in her hands and pulled back to look at her. She had aged drastically in the five months Claire had been away. Thinning white hair had been pulled crookedly to the top of her head. The once crystal blue eyes were cloudy, and the skin around them purplish and wrinkled. Her cheeks were sunken, and her mouth, lined by age, trembled.

"How are you, Mrs. Parks?" Claire asked in concern.

Tears filled the foggy blue gaze. "Oh, my dear, where do I begin?"

"Tell me what happened to my father." Claire felt Emily reach for her hand and she gave it a reassuring squeeze.

Mrs. Parks shook her head. "Your father had been feeling fit as a fiddle only the day before he died. Indeed, for the past few weeks he'd seemed happier than I'd seen him since your mother, God rest her soul, passed on. That morning he was up early and out of the house before breakfast. Sometime later I heard him moving about in his study, slamming drawers and talking to himself as though he was greatly disturbed. Then I heard a sound like something heavy falling, and I went to see what it was. I found him lying on the floor. The doctor said it was a stroke."

"Poor Papa," Emily whispered.

"Let's go inside and I'll make us some tea," Claire suggested, her voice thick with emotion. "Em and I will need to change for the funeral soon." Eager to see the house again, she put an arm around Emily's shoulders and they stepped into the spacious front hallway together. But as Claire took in her surroundings, her eagerness turned to dismay.

"Does it look the same?" Emily asked excitedly.

Claire couldn't find the words to answer her. The condition of their home was shocking. A feeble effort had been made to sweep the dark oak floor, but it had merely moved the dust around. Tea stains marred the pale green carpet runner on the oak staircase, and the Turkish rugs needed a good beating. A thick coating of dust covered every surface in the parlor to the left and the dining room on the far right. It was plain to see that Mrs. Parks was too feeble to maintain the home. "Yes, Em, the house looks the same."

"Why don't you girls sit down in the parlor," Mrs. Parks suggested, "and I'll go back to the kitchen to heat some water."

"No, please, Mrs. Parks," Claire said, ushering the housekeeper into the parlor. "You sit down and I'll heat the water."

"I'm going up to my room," Emily announced. "Call me when the tea is ready."

As Claire started toward the kitchen, the housekeeper motioned her back. "There's something you must see before Emily returns," she said in a whisper.

A shiver of apprehension slithered down Claire's spine as Mrs. Parks reached a shaking hand into the pocket of her dress and pulled out a folded piece of paper. The woman's chin quivered and her eyes filled with tears as she held out the paper. Claire's legs suddenly felt too unsteady to move. "What is it?" she asked reluctantly.

Tears began to roll down Mrs. Parks' lined cheeks. "It's the bank's foreclosure notice, Claire. We have five days to move out of the house."

Chapter 3

The room spun dizzily as Claire gripped the paper, trying to make sense of it. The notice had been sent *two weeks* ago. Why hadn't her father taken care of it? "How can they foreclose? We *own* Bellefleur!" At the housekeeper's silence, Claire looked up. "Isn't that true?"

"Your father, God rest his soul," Mrs. Parks said, pausing to dab her eyes, "took out a mortgage to pay his debts. But he hadn't made a payment in six months."

"There can't be any debts," Claire argued. "He had money. He always had money."

Mrs. Parks shook her head. "There hasn't been any money for a long time, dear."

"Then how could he afford to pay for my college, or Emily's school?" Claire demanded. "How could he afford to pay the farmhands?"

"From the loan, but that money is long gone."

Mrs. Parks had to be wrong. Claire marched straight to her father's study, sat in his leather chair, and began to rummage through the desk drawer. Pulling out his ledger, she opened it to the last page and scanned the entries. "This can't be right," she said aloud.

She found his bank book and opened it, then let it drop into her lap. Closing her eyes, she took slow breaths, forcing herself not to panic.

When she opened them again, Mrs. Parks stood in the

29

doorway, leaning on her cane. "What are we going to do, Claire?"

"There has to be a mistake," Claire said. "Surely he has money someplace."

"He lost it all," the housekeeper replied sadly. "Promoters came through last summer looking for investors for oil wells. That's when your father took out the mortgage, even though he knew it was purely speculation. When they didn't find oil, he lost the money."

"It's not possible," Claire stated, trying to stem her rising hysteria, "that he lost *all* his money that way. He was too smart to invest everything he had on mere speculation."

Her strength waning, Mrs. Parks found a chair and sat down. "Your father was never the same after your mother died. And when you girls left home, it was like losing Marie all over again. He was lonely, and he took risks he shouldn't have."

"But he had to have known the bank would foreclose if he didn't make payments. Surely they sent him letters warning him about missing payments."

"They did, but he wouldn't open them. You know how he hated that Reginald Boothe. He said the banker was plotting against him." Fresh tears began to fall. "Where am I going to live, Claire? I'm too old to find a new position."

"You won't need a new position," Claire insisted sharply. "Your home is with us. And our home is *here*. *No one* is going to take it away from us."

"But how are we going to keep it?"

Claire propped her elbows on the big cherry desk and rested her aching head in her hands. She couldn't think what to do. Why wasn't her father there? How dared he leave her this mess!

The letter! Claire lifted her head to stare out the window, trying to remember what her father had said in his last letter. But all she could remember was that he had discovered something that would secure their future. She began to search through the papers scattered about his desk. There had to be a document that would tell her what the discovery was.

An envelope caught her eye, but it was from Emily's school. "What is this about?" she asked, and pulled it closer.

The housekeeper looked confused. "I don't remember."

Claire pulled out a letter, scanned it, then looked up at Mrs. Parks in shock. "Hawkins won't take Emily back unless we pay her tuition. Wasn't it paid?"

"Oh, mercy me. Emily's tuition was paid only through last December. Your father hasn't been able to make a payment since then."

"Then Emily can't go back to school." Claire stared blankly at the window. Hawkins School for the Blind had been a life-saver for Emily. Though she loved her sister dearly, the girl was a handful. Blindness did not deter her once her mind was made up. But at Hawkins, Emily was safe. There she was studying Braille, learning to be self-sufficient and to behave like a lady. What would she do if she couldn't go back?

Claire pushed up on unsteady legs and headed for the kitchen. "I'll make tea," she said numbly.

Sitting across the desk from the bank president, Tyler studied Reginald Boothe's plans for a private dock. So far he liked what he saw, as well as what Boothe had to say. He glanced at Jonas, who seemed unusually dour.

"Gentlemen, what do you think?" Boothe asked.

Tyler let his gaze move slowly from the rolled out blueprints to Boothe's face. Though the banker appeared quite calm, Tyler's skill at poker had taught him how to read eyes, and right now he knew Boothe was nearly panting for his approval. But Tyler held all the aces and he intended to keep it that way.

"It seems adequate," Tyler replied in a noncommittal voice. "When do we get to look at this property?"

"Right now, if you'd like," the banker told him.

Tyler glanced at Jonas, got his nod of approval, then rolled up the plans and got to his feet. "Let's go."

Outside, they had to wait for a funeral procession to pass before they could cross to Boothe's buggy. It occurred to Tyler that the funeral was probably for Claire's father— but he was about to make the most crucial business decision of his life; Claire's problems did not concern him.

As they drove north through town, Tyler noted that most businesses were situated along Grand: the bank, a pawnshop, a telegraph office, the general store, a barbershop, a ladies' clothier, and two churches. Smaller businesses were located on the two main cross streets. On the outskirts of town they turned west on River Road, heading down to the river.

"I own this parcel of land on the left," Boothe explained. "It used to be part of the Bellefleur estate, but the owner sold it to pay off debts. As you can see, the land doesn't extend down to the water. Per the deal, I'd deed it to you. You can build a house on it, if you'd like."

Most of Tyler's time was spent on the *Lady Luck* since he had never been able to tolerate being tied to one place. Yet he wouldn't mind having a winter home, and one close to the new docks would be handy. "I'll take that into consideration," he replied.

Boothe stopped the buggy at the river and stepped down. Tyler and Jonas followed him onto a small dock used for shipping crops. "Imagine, if you will," Boothe said, turning to face them, "what you saw in the plans: slips for twenty boats, a large dock, and plenty of space for buggies to park or turn around."

Tyler studied the terrain. The flat bottom land stretched for a good half mile along the river, perfect for his needs. From there it rose steadily in a sweep of green to a summit where a large, elegant limestone house stood. "What about the house?"

"It would make a perfect inn," Boothe declared. "I'd put a fine restaurant in it, too. Down here, near the docks, I'd build a row of shops for the tourists."

"Does anyone live there?"

"Just an old woman and two girls," Boothe assured him, "but they'll be moving out soon."

Tyler turned back to the water, envisioning his boat moored along a new dock. He'd never felt so close to fulfilling his dream. His excitement bubbled just below the surface, where no one could see it.

"Do we have a deal?" Boothe asked.

Tyler looked at Jonas, keeping his tone casual. "Any questions or comments?"

Turning slightly, Jonas said in a low voice, "I've got an uneasy feeling about this, Ty."

"Boothe is a savvy banker," Tyler quietly assured him. "He wouldn't sink his own money into a frivolous pursuit." Then again, all Tyler really knew about the man was that he had the money to put into the project and that he ran the most profitable bank in the county. He had heard the banker was ruthless in his business dealings, but what successful businessman wasn't? Tyler looked back at the large home on the hill. His common sense told him to sign the agreement. Yet he knew if he didn't heed Jonas's warning, he'd never hear the end of it. Turning to the banker, Tyler said, "We'll need another day. I want to look over the agreement again."

Boothe's thin lips stretched into a semblance of a smile. "I'm afraid I'll need to know today. I have someone willing to accept the deal right now as it stands. I'd hate to lose him while you're trying to make up your mind and then have you back out."

Tyler returned the smile. "I'll let you know tomorrow before noon."

Boothe rubbed his chin, as though pondering the offer.

Tyler calmly held his ground. The banker was too eager for this deal to haggle over a few more hours.

"All right," Boothe said at last. "I'll wait until noon. Shall we head back?"

Tyler took a last look around and, with a smile of satisfaction, started back for the buggy. Bellefleur was perfect. If all went well, he'd realize his dream before the year was over.

Claire heard the cocks crowing and slowly came awake. For a moment she half expected Mrs. Parks to come in and tell her that her father was already at the breakfast table. But then she remembered: he had been buried yesterday.

She turned her head toward the dressing table against the wall, where she kept a portrait of her mother and father. They were together now. Her father was happy at last.

But she was alone, with a blind sister and an elderly woman depending on her to save their home. And if she managed to save it, how would she run it? She pressed her fingers to her temples. *Why didn't you teach me, Papa? Didn't you trust me?*

The truth was that Arthur Cavanaugh had trusted very few people. He had run the entire estate himself, including the bookkeeping, refusing to rely on foremen or land managers.

Yet Claire knew it wasn't that her father hadn't *trusted* her. He had merely wanted to take care of her, to insulate her from ever having to worry about finances again. Indeed, the sum total of her responsibilities had been to graduate from college. After that it had been presumed she would marry, when her husband would assume the role of provider.

Ask Lance for help, she could hear her father saying. *He'll take care of you.*

That thought should have reassured her. Instead, it

stirred something inside her, something foreign and rebellious, that felt oddly like resentment. But Lance was her fiancé. Why shouldn't he help her?

She recalled the conversation they'd had before she'd left to go home. After packing hurriedly, Claire had rushed to see Lance, holding the telegram tightly in her hand.

"What happened?" he'd asked in alarm.

Claire had showed him the message. She'd spoken quickly, her throat aching from holding back her grief. "My father has died. I have to leave."

"Before finals? You won't graduate."

"I'll have to come back for the summer session. It doesn't matter if I graduate in May or in August. I have to go home."

"What does this mean?" Lance had pointed to the second line. *"Is your house to be sold?"*

"That has to be a mistake."

"Your inheritance isn't in jeopardy, is it?" he'd asked.

"No! My father has always provided for me, and always will."

He had seemed to relax then. "That's a relief—for you."

"I wish you could come with me."

Lance had smiled and put an arm around her shoulders. "You'll be fine; you're a strong woman. And as soon as graduation is over, I'll come out."

Claire frowned at the ceiling in her bedroom. For the first time, she began to wonder whether it was she or her inheritance that had attracted him.

Startled, she flung back the covers and slid out of bed. Why was she questioning Lance's feelings now? She had no time to waste on such foolish doubts. Only four days remained in which to stop the foreclosure. Her first priority was to find a document or letter that would tell her what her father had discovered. She chose a serviceable gray plaid dress, washed and changed quickly, and headed downstairs to the kitchen.

The coldness and emptiness of the once-cheerful room stunned her. Yellow-and-white calico curtains still hung at the windows, and a yellow checked cloth still covered the long table in the center of the large room. But no fire crackled in the big black stove, no slices of juicy ham sizzled in the frying pan, no pungent coffee permeated the air. Instead the stove was cold, and the chill morning air smelled only of rain.

Claire looked around. Where did Mrs. Parks keep the coffee? She opened the pantry just as the housekeeper hobbled slowly into the kitchen, leaning heavily on her cane.

"I'll see to breakfast," the woman assured her. "Sit yourself down, dear."

From years of habit, Claire started to pull out a chair. But Mrs. Parks was in no condition to wait on her. "I'll help you." She would have to see about hiring kitchen help.

After a quick breakfast, Claire began a thorough search of the study. When that proved futile, she investigated her father's bedroom. Finding nothing in his bureau, she opened the door of his closet and stepped inside. Standing on her toes to see the very top shelf, Claire spied the mahogany jewelry box she was looking for. Stretching as high as she could, she inched it off the shelf and took it to the bed. Inside she found the four gray cases containing her mother's jewelry: diamond earbobs, a long strand of pearls, an amethyst brooch, and a large emerald-and-diamond pendant on a glittering gold chain.

Claire dangled the pendant between her fingers, watching the diamonds sparkle in the morning light. A lump of sadness stuck in her throat. Her father had given it to her mother as a gift when Emily had been born. The diamond earbobs had belonged to her Grandmother Cavanaugh, and Mama had worn the pearls at her wedding.

Now they were hers—but she had to be practical. The emerald-and-diamond pendant alone would provide enough money to pay off the mortgage. The other pieces would keep the farmhands paid until after the crops were in. If she couldn't find out what her father had discovered, she would have to sell the jewelry.

"Cee Cee, what are you doing?" Emily asked, as she came across the room.

"Looking at Mama's jewelry," Claire replied guiltily.

Emily picked up each piece, examining it with her fingers. "They must be very beautiful." She rubbed the smooth stone of the brooch against her cheek. "How cold this stone feels," she said with a shiver. "It makes me sad. Why are you looking at them?"

"I—I'd forgotten what they looked like."

"I wonder why Pa never showed them to me?" Emily asked.

"Perhaps it was too painful a reminder." Claire packed the jewelry away, hoping to put an end to the subject.

"I'll bet Pa would want you to wear the pearls and earbobs at your wedding," Emily said, "as long as Rancid Lanced keeps his paws off them."

Claire shoved the box onto the closet shelf. "Stop calling him that."

"He reminds me of a skunk."

"You haven't given him a fair chance. Lance is charming and handsome and—" She turned around, only to find her sister had gone.

Although Emily had insight far keener than most people's, Claire disagreed with her assessment of Lance and chalked it up to jealousy.

She agreed with her sister about one thing, however. She *should* wear the pearls and earbobs at her wedding, and Claire hoped she wouldn't have to sell such treasures. Hoping for a clue to her father's mysterious discovery, she returned to her room and took his letter out of her valise. Her eyes welled with tears as she read it.

My dearest Cee Cee,
How I wish you and Emily were here now to share the

joy of my discovery with me. I dare not share it with anyone until I confirm it, so I will save the news as a surprise for your graduation, for it directly benefits your future. I will only say that the discovery is incredible good luck. Little did my forefathers know how fortuitous their land acquisition would be. God bless you and keep you safe until I see you again.

Your loving father

She was *sure* his discovery was connected to their land. After another search of the house proved futile, all Claire could think to do was to plead with the bank for more time. She prayed she could do it without having to see Reginald Boothe.

"I'm sorry, Claire." Charlie Dibkins, a clerk at the bank, gave her a sympathetic smile. "Once the notice of foreclosure is sent out, there's no reprieve. It's Mr. Boothe's policy."

Of course it would be Mr. Boothe's policy, Claire thought angrily. The man had a heart of stone. She sat in the straight-backed wooden chair opposite Charlie's small desk in the enormous lobby of the Fortune Farmers' Bank and tapped her shoe against the oak floor. What would her father do in such a situation? He wouldn't give up, that was for sure—especially when Reginald Boothe was involved. She studied Charlie, thinking hard.

She and Charlie had been schoolmates; he'd even had a crush on her at one time. Surely a little feminine persuasion could convince him to intercede on her behalf. "Charlie," she said softly, "you know I came back for my father's funeral yesterday. If the bank takes away our home, Emily and I will have nowhere to go. Won't you please help us?"

The young man gazed at her with large, limpid eyes. "I wish I could, Claire, but I don't have the authority. The most I can do is get you in to talk to Mr. Boothe—though it won't do any good.'' Charlie leaned close to whisper, "A colder man I've never met.''

The last person she wanted to see was Reginald Boothe, yet she *had* to have more time. "I'd like to see Mr. Boothe now, please.''

"Now?'' Charlie ran a finger underneath his collar. "I don't know if he can see you right now, Claire.''

"It has to be now.'' *Before I lose courage.* Rising, Claire sailed toward the staircase.

"Wait!'' Charlie called, scurrying after her. "You can't just walk into Mr. Boothe's office!''

Claire started up the stairs with her former schoolmate on her heels. He passed her at the top and barricaded her from his employer's door with outspread arms.

"I can't let you do this, Claire. He'll be furious with me for letting you up here.''

"Stand out of my way, Charlie.''

"All right, all right! I'll ask him if he'll see you.''

"Don't ask, *tell*. It's imperative that I see him now! And I won't take no for an answer.''

Charlie put out both hands as if to ward her off. "Stay right here, Claire. And promise me you won't do anything rash.''

She nodded, then let out her breath, proud of herself for taking a stand. *I'm not the only Cavanaugh who can be ornery,* she thought, lifting her chin high in the air.

She hoped her newfound courage worked as well on Reginald Boothe.

Chapter 4

Tyler sat opposite Boothe's desk, looking over the revised partnership agreement. At his insistence, the document now contained a clause to protect his ownership of the *Lady Luck* and his gambling license. If either of the partners wanted out, the partnership agreement would be terminated and possession of both the boat and license would revert to Tyler. Boothe hadn't been pleased about the addition, but he'd done it.

"All seems to be in order," Tyler said, pushing the document across the large cherry desk.

"Good." Boothe dipped his pen in the inkwell, signed his name at the bottom, and handed the agreement back, along with the pen. "Where is your assistant today?"

"He sailed this morning with the *Lady Luck*." Tyler took the pen and poised it above the document. Something made him hesitate. He glanced up at the man who was about to become his partner. Boothe had the same driving ambition he had, as well as money. The deal was good for both men, but better still for Tyler. He would at last have the opportunity to get everything he'd ever dreamed of. Yet something nagged at him.

Tyler blamed it on Jonas. To allay his assistant's fears, they had gone over the agreement several times the previous evening, until finally Jonas had to concede that there was nothing in it that could harm Tyler. Yet he had maintained his wariness, much to Tyler's annoyance.

40

"Is something wrong?" the banker asked.

Tyler saw the panic in Boothe's eyes. What the hell—he'd studied the man, the land, and the agreement. He'd done everything right. Jonas was just a worrier and always would be. He couldn't let that affect his thinking. Putting pen to paper, Tyler scratched his name and slid the document back across the desk.

There was a quick knock on the door and then a young red-haired man put his head in.

"Mr. Boothe?"

"Yes, Dibkins? What is it?"

The clerk hurried across the spacious office and said in a low voice, "There's a customer outside, a lady, demanding to speak with you right away, sir."

"Have her wait," Boothe replied in a bored voice.

"But sir," the clerk countered timidly, "she's very insistent. She says she *must* see you immediately."

Before Boothe could reply, Tyler stood. "We're finished here. I won't keep you from your business."

The bank president came around his desk to see Tyler out as the clerk scurried ahead of them to open the door. Boothe offered Tyler his hand. "I'll be in touch with you in a few days."

As Tyler stepped outside the office he caught sight of a young woman standing at the window, gazing through the pane. Though her face was hidden by her black hat, there was something familiar about her.

"You wanted to see me, madam?" Boothe inquired in his stuffy British accent.

The young woman turned, tilting her head to reveal a pair of cobalt blue eyes gazing out from beneath the wide brim of her hat. Tyler felt his stomach gallop as those eyes fixed on him. Claire looked every inch a lady in her fine dress—very different from when Tyler had last seen her.

"Good morning," he said, cocking an eyebrow.

A slight blush colored her complexion, but Claire did not smile at him. Her delicate oval face looked strained and her hands clutched the neck of her drawstring hand-bag. "Good morning," she replied. She immediately turned her attention to his new partner. "I must speak with you," she said in a clipped tone.

With a puzzled frown, Tyler watched Claire march into Boothe's office after the banker. He decided to wait around until their meeting was over; then he'd escort her downstairs. Maybe the delectable Claire would join him for dinner this evening.

"Young lady," Tyler heard Boothe begin in a haughty tone, "if each customer in the bank came charging up to my office demanding to speak to me at every turn, I'd scarce be able to fulfill my duties, wouldn't I? However, since you are here," he said, returning to his desk, "be seated and be brief. State your name first, please, and then the reason for your rude interruption."

Tyler couldn't resist the chance to eavesdrop. He told himself it was merely out of curiosity, and not out of any concern for what was troubling Claire. He glanced around and saw the young clerk hovering nearby, obviously with the same intentions. With a wink at the clerk, Tyler leaned against the wall opposite the door, where he could see inside.

"My name is Claire Cavanaugh," she stated proudly, standing in front of Boothe's desk. "I'm Arthur Cavanaugh's daughter. I doubt I need explain the reason for my interruption."

"Well, well!" There was a slight tone of surprise in Boothe's voice. "I should have guessed. You look very much like your mother. *Very* much." Tyler saw Boothe's gaze slide slowly over her, and he caught her slight shudder, as though the man repulsed her. "I assume you've come about the foreclosure notice," Boothe said.

"I need an extension of time, Mr. Boothe. Four days are simply not enough for me to come up with the money."

"We don't give extensions," the banker said in a monotone, turning his attention to a stack of papers on his desk.

"But I just learned about this notice yesterday."

Boothe opened a walnut case and removed a cigar. "Your father should have told you."

"My father was *buried* yesterday!" Claire protested angrily.

"Your father was *warned* four months ago that we would foreclose on Bellefleur unless he made a payment."

Tyler moved closer to the door. He was positive the banker had called *their* land "Bellefleur." He waited impatiently as Boothe paused to light a cigar.

"Considering the time that has passed, Miss Cavanaugh," the banker said, "we were more than generous with your father."

"Generous?" Claire spluttered. "You're nothing but a vulture waiting to feed off my father's misfortune!"

Boothe gave her a disdainful glare. "This is a business decision."

Claire knew he was lying. "Perhaps I'll take my story to the newspaper and let everyone know what a mean-spirited man you are. How do you think it will look when the story comes out that you've put two young women, one who's blind, and an elderly lady out of their home?"

"Will you also tell the newspaper how your father lost his money?" Boothe blew a stream of cigar smoke into the air. "Or shall I?"

Claire glared at him with hatred. Reginald Boothe wouldn't think twice about humiliating her family, just as he hadn't thought twice about turning Claire and her mother out onto the streets nearly thirteen years before. "Give me two months," she bargained.

"Impossible."

"The crops will be in by then, and—"

"No, Miss Cavanaugh."

Panic rose inside her like a tidal wave. She was going to lose her home—she and Emily and Mrs. Parks would be homeless. Her breath came in shallow bursts, making her lightheaded. *I need you, Papa. Help me!*

But there was no one to help her.

Clenching her hands at her sides, Claire tried again. "Give me thirty days, then. "

"Our meeting is over."

"But Mr. Boothe, you can't—"

"Good day, Miss Cavanaugh!"

For a long moment, Claire was so horrified that she couldn't move. Boothe sat at his desk calmly puffing on his cigar, a glimmer of a smile on his face as her world collapsed. He truly *did not care*. He was a monster.

Feeling the sting of angry tears, she fought them back and turned away. She would not give Boothe the satisfaction of seeing her break down.

But as she approached the door, determination stiffened her spine and made her look back. "I won't let you steal my home from me, Mr. Boothe! You'll have your mortgage payment in four days."

"In full," Boothe warned, his snake eyes glittering with triumph.

Claire's fingers curled into fists. "You'll have the full payment, Mr. Boothe, in four days. I wouldn't want your bank to fall into ruin on my account."

Clearly irritated, Boothe scraped back his chair. "Good day, Miss Cavanaugh," he repeated brusquely.

She gave him the coldest, most contemptuous glare she could muster, then marched out of his office, holding her head high. She nearly collided with Tyler, and looked up in surprise as he gripped her shoulders to steady her, gazing down at her with his piercing eyes.

Too distraught to speak, Claire moved around him and walked straight down the stairs. Her thoughts in a frightening whirl, she left the bank and began walking, oblivious to her direction. At the corner of Grand Avenue and Fifth Street she stopped for a passing buggy and noticed she was standing in front of the church where her parents had been married, and where she and Lance were planning to be married before fall.

Claire's heart began to race. That was it! She would ask Lance for the money! She knew he would help.

With renewed hope, she turned back toward the telegraph office.

With a frown, Tyler strode into Boothe's office and slammed the door behind him. He was furious as hell at the man behind the desk, and more than a little upset with himself for believing the banker's lies. "What's going on?" he demanded.

Boothe looked perplexed. "Is something wrong?"

But for the terseness of his reply, Tyler's rigid self-control gave no indication of the fury raging inside him. "Why did you tell me you owned that riverfront property?"

Boothe sat back with a tolerant smile. "So *that's* what this is about. I gather you heard my conversation with Miss Cavanaugh. Let me assure you, then, Mr. McCane, that I would have told you had I thought there would be a problem. But there won't be. This bank has handled many, many foreclosures. I know precisely what I'm doing. That property is ours."

"That's what you told me before."

"Then let me say it again: there won't be a problem."

The banker's matter-of-fact attitude reassured Tyler slightly. Still, he wasn't about to let the man play games with him. "I hope the hell you're right, Boothe. If you lose that land, the partnership is off."

"As it should be," Boothe replied smoothly. "Trust me, Mr. McCane. Everything is under control."

"I'll *trust* that you'll do whatever is necessary to get that land."

"Of that you can be sure, Mr. McCane," the banker replied with a tight smile.

Somewhat mollified, Tyler turned and walked to the door. Though he hadn't been pleased to learn that Bellefleur was Claire's property, he wasn't about to let his dream be destroyed by a woman he barely knew.

The narrow two-story building that housed the telegraph office sat between the barber shop and the Fortune Pawn Shop. Smelling of machine oil and beeswax, the telegraph office was quiet when Claire opened the door and stepped inside. Ned Barry, the spry seventy-two-year-old operator who lived in an apartment above the office rose from his stool and came toward her, a pencil tucked behind his ear. "Hello, there, Claire. Good to see you and Emily back, but sorry to hear 'bout yer pa."

"Thank you, Mr. Barry."

"Need t'send a wire?" He removed the pencil and readied his tablet.

"Yes, please, to my—" For some reasons, her next words stuck in Claire's throat. What was wrong with her? She had to contact Lance. She *should* contact Lance. As her intended, it was his duty to help her.

Mr. Barry looked up expectantly. Claire gave him a sheepish smile. "This is to my fiancé, Lance," she said quickly. By the time she finished dictating her message, she found herself gritting her teeth.

"By the way, Mr. Barry, I'm posting a notice that I'm looking for kitchen help. Room and board are free. Would you spread the word, please?"

"I'll see what I can do," he promised.

Claire felt better when she left. Lance would no doubt wire money within the next two days, and Mr. Barry could always be counted on to disperse news.

Wilbur Simons stood in Boothe's doorway, hat in hand, and cleared his throat. "You wanted to see me?"

"Come in, Sheriff," Boothe replied, replacing his pen in its holder. "I know you've been keeping your eye on Claire Cavanaugh, but for the next four days it is imperative that I know exactly where she goes, what she does, and who she sees. Understand?"

"Sure. I just passed her coming out of the telegraph office," Simons volunteered.

"Very observant, Sheriff. Now you need to find out whether she sent or received a wire, and what it said." He watched the conflicting emotions play across the sheriff's heavy face. What he was asking Simons to do was illegal. However, the sheriff knew better than to disobey an order. And it would be a simple matter to get a copy of the wire: Ned Barry wouldn't dare refuse to cooperate with the man who owned his building.

With a nod, the sheriff turned and walked out.

Ned Barry rose from his stool as Wilbur Simons lumbered into the office. "Can I help you, Sheriff?" he asked.

"Mornin', Ned." Simons hunkered down to talk through the cage. "You send a wire out for Miss Cavanaugh?"

Eyeing the sheriff warily, Ned nodded.

"You still got the message, Ned?"

"Who wants to know?"

"Mr. Boothe."

Ned glared at the man opposite him. "I got it."

"I need to see it."

Ned Barry stared hard at the sheriff. "You know I can't do that."

The sheriff rose to his full height and hitched up the waist of his pants. "I need to see it, Ned," he repeated firmly.

With a furious sniff, Ned retrieved Claire's message from the stack and shoved it through the opening in the cage. Simons took the piece of paper and left, stopping at the door to add, "Mr. Boothe would be real appreciative if you'd keep an eye out for the reply to that wire. Understand?" He liked to add that last part, just as Boothe always did. It made him feel as powerful as his boss.

"I ain't no idiot," Ned snarled. "Wish I could say the same for you."

"Sorry you feel that way, Ned. Good day to you." The sheriff closed the door behind him.

At the sheriff's return, Boothe sat forward expectantly. "Well?"

"She sent a wire to her fiancé in Springdale," the sheriff reported, out of breath from his climb up the stairs. "She asked him to wire her money." He placed the message on Boothe's desk.

Boothe calmly perused the paper. "You told Ned Barry to watch for the reply?"

"Yes, sir, I did."

"Good work. Perhaps it would be wise for you to pay a social call on Miss Cavanaugh today."

Simons's face flushed as he grinned. "I'll do that right away."

Claire returned home to find a buggy hitched up in front of the house. For a brief moment she thought Tyler McCane might have come to call, then she chided herself for having such ridiculous thoughts. She was engaged.

Still, a tingle of excitement traveled down her spine when she thought of Tyler. That sense of danger about him drew her like a magnet.

Stop it! she scolded herself. *You're an honorable woman!* Recalling that Tyler had been outside the office during her meeting with Boothe, she hoped he wasn't here: if he had heard any of their conversation, it would be too humiliating.

"Cee Cee," Emily called out, as Claire removed her hat and hung it on the hall tree, "Jonas came to see us!"

When Claire walked into the parlor, Jonas Polk rose politely from the blue sofa. He was dressed in a white linen suit and held a white derby in his hands. "Good morning, Miss Cavanaugh," he said cheerily, taking her hand. "I hope this isn't a bad time to call."

"Not at all, Mr. Polk. May I take your hat?"

"Jonas brought me a surprise," Emily announced, as Claire carried the hat to the front hall. When she returned, her sister held up one hand. On it was a white sock puppet of a rabbit, with long floppy ears made of red plaid flannel, shiny black buttons for eyes and nose, and whiskers made of starched black thread.

Claire would have thought the gift too young for her sister, but Emily didn't seem to mind. "How kind of you, Mr. Polk," Claire offered.

"Made it myself," Jonas told her proudly, resuming his position on the sofa. "I grew up in a traveling show back in England. My parents were Punch-and-Judy puppeteers. Thought I'd teach Emily here how to make puppets so she can put on her own shows."

Emily slipped his creation off her hand. "Isn't it wonderful? When can we make another one, Jonas?"

"Tomorrow, after the *Lady Luck* docks—if your sister approves."

"That would be fine," Claire replied. She clasped her fingers together nervously, wanting to ask about Tyler, but fearing to appear interested in him.

A knock on the front door spared her the dilemma. Claire excused herself and went to answer it.

"Afternoon, Miss Cee Cee," the sheriff said, ducking his head shyly. "Hope I'm not interrupting anything." He shifted from one foot to the other, his hat pressed to his chest, looking at her expectantly.

"Is there something you need, Sheriff?" Claire asked curiously.

"I just wanted to see how everything's going." He

craned his neck to peer inside the house. "Mind if I come in and sit a spell?"

Claire groaned inwardly, hoping the sheriff didn't feel obligated to look out for them, now that her father was gone. She showed him into the parlor, which, to her dismay, was now empty. The sheriff sat on her father's overstuffed brown-and-blue print chair, put his big feet up on the ottoman, and heaved a big sigh of contentment. Claire perched on the edge of the sofa and waited.

"How's everything coming along?" he asked.

"Very well," Claire lied. The last thing she wanted was for word of their hardship to get around town.

The sheriff nodded approvingly. "How are *you* doing?"

"Just fine, thank you."

"And your sister?"

"Fine." Claire saw him about to speak again and quickly added, "Mrs. Parks, too."

"Good, good." He balanced his hat on one knee, brushed the crown with one hand, then looked around the room, as though suddenly interested in the decor. Claire looked around, too, noticing the heavy layer of dust on the black marble mantelpiece and tabletops, the dinginess of the tasseled gold lamp shades, the faded draperies, and the worn upholstery. There was no hiding that money was in short supply, but a good cleaning would help. She would have to tackle that problem soon.

"Would you care for some lemonade, Sheriff?" she asked, forcing a smile.

"That'd be real nice, Miss Cee Cee."

Claire hurried to the kitchen, where she was surprised to find Mrs. Parks and Emily listening to one of Jonas's stories.

"How's Simple Simon?" Emily asked. "He didn't bring you a pie, did he?"

Ignoring her sister's gibe, Claire took a glass of lemonade and returned to the parlor, only to find that the sheriff now sat on the sofa. When he saw her, he moved his bulk to one side, obviously intending for her to resume her seat there. With an inward sigh, Claire obliged, handing him the drink.

He took a long pull. "You're looking mighty fine today, Miss Cee Cee," he said, wiping his mouth with the back of his hand.

"It's kind of you to say so," Claire said, with little conviction.

He glanced around the room again. "Are you going to be able to keep up this place?"

"I'm certainly going to try."

"It'd be a whole lot easier on you and your sister if you had a man to help you out."

His condescending attitude annoyed her. "We're managing just fine on our own, Sheriff," she said firmly.

"It's got to be rough on you, though, being such a young, delicate—" he inched closer, giving her a yearning look, "—purty little thing."

Claire stared at him in surprise The sheriff was *flirting* with her! Good Lord—how could she tactfully get him to leave?

A rabbit's face popped up over the back of the sofa. "Hello, there," the sock puppet said, in a voice higher than Emily's. "I'm Fluffy. Who are you?"

"Wilbur Simons," the sheriff answered dutifully, setting the glass of lemonade on a table.

"What are you doing here, *Wilbur*?"

"Emily," Claire said in a warning tone.

"No, I'm Fluffy. Want to hear a nursery rhyme?"

Claire cringed. "If you're really smart, Fluffy," Claire said in a stern voice, "you'll hop off to your den before you get yourself in trouble."

"But Mrs. Parks needs your help in the kitchen."

"I see." Claire gave the sheriff a helpless look. "I'm sorry. I hate to rush you, but I have duties to attend to."

"I'll come another time," he promised. With a groan,

he got to his feet and lumbered to the door. "Thank you for your hospitality, Miss Cee Cee."

"You're quite welcome." Claire shut the door and leaned against it, then pushed herself away and went to thank the rabbit.

Tyler turned as Jonas sauntered up the deck toward him. His mood hadn't been good since his meeting with Boothe earlier, and his assistant's absence had only made his disposition worse. "Where have you been?" he snapped. "The boat docked hours ago."

Jonas looked at him as if he'd suddenly sprouted horns. "If you must know, I was visiting little Emily. I took a puppet to cheer her."

"What did you do that for?"

Jonas gave him a reproachful look. "I shouldn't have to remind you, but her father just passed on. What has *your* knickers in knots? Didn't you sign the agreement?"

"I signed it," Tyler growled. "Afterward, I found out the property in question belongs to the Cavanaughs."

"Why, that slimy Londoner!" Jonas declared. "I hope you tore up that agreement on the spot. The nerve of him, foreclosing on helpless women and a blind child!" He paused to look hard at Tyler. "You *did* tear it up, didn't you?"

"Do you think that will stop the bank from foreclosing?" Tyler asked, his anger stronger than the situation warranted. He took a deep breath and forced himself to a calmer state. "I told Boothe if he didn't get the land, I'd tear up the agreement."

"What?" Jonas cried indignantly.

"The simple fact is, Jonas, that with her father gone, Claire can't afford the house." Tyler turned toward the river, bracing his arms on the rail. "Her financial state has no bearing on me or my plans."

"For God's sake, Ty, she's a young woman struggling to keep her home. Where is your heart?"

"This is a business matter, Jonas," Tyler ground out, feeling his control slipping.

"Your business matter is affecting two young women I've grown quite fond of," Jonas argued.

"That's *your* mistake." At Jonas's silence, Tyler glanced around to find his assistant glaring at him. "Look," he said, "I don't like the fact that Claire and Emily are losing their home, but it's not my concern, and neither is it yours. I've got too much to accomplish to worry about anyone else's problems."

Jonas shook his head sadly. "You know I care about you like you're my own son, Ty, and that I've always admired your determination. But this is different. You've locked away your heart, and *that*, lad, is a sad way to go through life."

For a moment, Tyler remembered the look of fear and panic in Claire's eyes as she'd left Boothe's office, but he hardened himself against it. He didn't want to feel anything for her. "You're wrong, old man," he lashed out. "It's the smart way to go through life. You can't be hurt if you use your head instead of your heart."

"You can't be loved, either," Jonas replied.

Tyler stalked to his cabin. He poured himself a jigger of whiskey, more stung by his assistant's blunt words than he cared to admit. He didn't need Jonas to tell him how to live his life. He downed the whiskey and poured himself another, until he felt the soothing heat spread through his veins, dulling his senses, and with them, the sharp edges of a wound he had thought long buried.

Rising, Tyler found his legs unsteady and carefully made his way to the privy. He stared at his blurry reflection in the mirror above the commode. He didn't need to be loved. He didn't *want* to be loved. He was, in fact, unlovable, and preferred it that way.

He opened the wall cabinet to put on a fresh shirt and

saw the lady's silk robe hanging inside. At once, an image of Claire wearing the robe burned through the fog around his brain and he suddenly realized what he needed, what had drawn him to her in the first place. It had nothing to do with love. It was lust, pure and sweet and satisfying.

He put on a clean shirt, combed his hair, and went to find some black coffee. Then he was going to find Claire and ask her to join him for dinner.

"Mr. Boothe? The reply came back."

Reginald Boothe glanced up from his paperwork to see Sheriff Simons standing at his door. Simons handed the wire to Boothe, who read it carefully, then gave a sharp bark of laughter. "Take it to her yourself," Boothe ordered, slipping it into the envelope, which Ned Barry had conveniently left open. "I'm sure she'll need a shoulder to cry on after she reads this."

Chapter 5

Claire was surprised to find Wilbur Simons at her door for the second time that day. He seemed agitated, so she stepped out onto the porch. "What is it, Sheriff?"

"This wire came in for you while I was talking to Ned at the telegraph office. He said it was important, so I thought I'd better bring it right out."

With a hasty thanks, Claire tore open the envelope and removed the telegraph, turning her back to read it. Her eyes flew over the few lines, her heart racing at a dizzying speed as she absorbed the news.

> UNABLE TO SEND MONEY. STOP.
> SORRY COULDN'T MAKE FUNERAL. STOP.
> WILL SEND LETTER EXPLAINING. STOP.
> LANCE.

"No!" she whispered, clutching the paper to her chest. Lance couldn't help her. She was right back where she had started. What was she going to do?

"I can't sell the jewelry!" she said aloud. "I *won't* sell it!"

"Bad news?" the sheriff asked, startling her. She had forgotten he was there.

Claire could feel his breath on her neck. Numbly, she folded the telegram and turned, taking a discreet step back. "It's a note from my fiancé. He—won't be able to join

55

me as I'd hoped. Thank you for bringing the wire out, Sheriff.''

Realizing that he'd been dismissed, Simons's face turned an unflattering shade of red. ''Glad to be of help, Miss Cee Cee. Let me know if you need anything. I'll be more than happy to oblige.''

As soon as he'd gone, Claire paced the length of the covered porch, too worried even to cry. Where was she going to come up with the money to pay the bank? She had less than *four days*. She had no savings, no valuables of her own to sell. She had no relatives to whom she could apply for help. She had no recourse but one—and that one tore at her heart. Her only hope was that she could some day buy back her mother's precious treasures.

''Claire?'' Mrs. Parks called from the front door. ''Why was the sheriff here?''

''He brought a telegram from Lance.''

''Lance?'' she asked, stepping onto the porch.

''My fiancé,'' Claire reminded her.

The housekeeper looked chagrined. ''How could I have forgotten that?''

''It's all right, Mrs. Parks. We all forget things.''

''I forget too often.'' Her eyes watered and her chin trembled. ''I don't know what to do about it.''

''Perhaps you need to get more rest,'' Claire suggested, putting her arm around the woman's frail shoulders. ''Trying to keep up with this house must be a chore. I'm going to see about having someone come out to help you.

''Mrs. Parks, I'm going to have to take Mama's jewelry to the pawnshop. Will you keep Emily away from the bedroom while I pack it? I don't want her to know.''

''Oh, my, a pawnshop? I surely hate to see you sell off her things. Those pieces should go to you girls.''

''I don't have a choice!'' Immediately Claire regretted her sharp tone. Mrs. Parks had always treated her with patience and loving kindness. Having lost her husband and two children to disease, she had regarded Claire and Emily as her substitute family. Claire owed her the same kindness in return.

"You know, dear," the housekeeper called, as Claire started upstairs, "I remember a friend of your papa's asking to buy some of those pieces a long while back. Maybe you could see if he's still interested."

Claire stopped. It *would* be better to sell to a friend of her father's rather than to a pawnshop. "What was his name?" she asked, hurrying back down the stairs.

The housekeeper's forehead wrinkled. "Let me see, now. It was Tom something. Neeley? No, that was Ed Neeley. Handlon? Turner? Oh, horsefeathers!" she said in frustration.

"*Try to remember,* Mrs. Parks," Claire pleaded.

The woman wrung her hands in agitation. "The harder I try, it seems the less I remember." She hobbled back toward the kitchen on her cane, muttering to herself.

Claire packed the jewelry cases in a small satchel and headed downstairs, still in shock over Lance's reply. She had thought he, of all people, would find a way to help. After all, what affected her future also affected his. He must have had a very good reason. She would just have to wait for his letter to find out what it was.

Reginald Boothe strolled into the Fortune Pawn Shop and glanced around the dingy room. Dust motes floated on a shaft of sunlight streaming in the front window, lighting a glass-topped counter filled with timepieces, cheap jewelry, weapons, and an array of odds and ends. "Walter?" he called.

A moment later, a faded blue curtain parted and a short, heavy, gray-haired man came out from the back room. "Oh, hello, Mr. Boothe," Walter Greene said in his heavy German accent. "It is always a pleasure to see you."

"Thank you," Boothe said with a nod, pleased by the way Greene showed the proper respect.

"What is it I can do for you? Does your watch need cleaning, perhaps?"

Boothe patted the timepiece he kept in his vest pocket. "No, no. The watch is fine. I need a favor."

"*Und* what is that?" he asked.

"Claire Cavanaugh, Arthur's oldest child, might come to see you about selling off some jewelry. Don't buy it. Tell her you have too much inventory. Understand?"

"Why would I not want to buy her jewelry?" Greene asked, as his wife, Anna, came from the back room to stand at his side. "She would not come here unless she needed money badly."

"You don't need to know why, Walter," Boothe cautioned.

For a long moment, the pawnshop owner stood staring at the banker, his fingers clenching and unclenching at his side, as though he couldn't decide whether to take issue with the order or not. Finally, his heavy shoulders sagging, he gave a nod.

With a satisfied smile, Boothe paid his respects to the man's wife and left.

Tyler tied up the horse and buggy he had rented, grabbed the lady's straw hat from the seat and strode up the steps of Claire's front porch, knocking sharply. Through the screen he saw Emily moving cautiously up the hallway.

"Who's there?" she called.

"Tyler McCane."

As Emily drew closer, she sniffed the air. "It's you, all right. Your smell can't lie."

Tyler scowled at her, then remembered she couldn't see him. "I don't smell."

"Everyone smells—some just smell better than others, that's all." She opened the door and let him in. "You smell good. Rancid Lanced smells like a skunk."

"Who's Lanced?" he asked, glancing around for Claire.

"Lance Logan is my sister's fiancé. She went to town, if that's why you're here. Do you want to come into the parlor and wait?"

Claire had a fiancé? "Thanks. I think I will."

Glancing around, Tyler noted the poor condition of the furnishings in the once-magnificent room—more proof that the house was too much for Claire.

"Want some lemonade?" Emily asked, as he settled in a chair in the parlor, the hat beside him.

"Got anything stronger?"

"I'm not allowed to pour it." She made her way to a small sideboard, felt for a glass, and set it down in front of a decanter.

Tyler followed her to the table, removed the stopper, and took a whiff. "Whiskey. Not bad."

"It was Papa's. No one else drinks whiskey in this house. I would, but Claire would chop off my fingers."

"That's a pretty harsh punishment. Tell me about Rancid Lanced."

"Don't call him that in front of Claire," Emily warned. "She met him at college and thinks he's sweeter than apple butter." Emily paused to make a gagging sound. "She got a telegram from him today. I don't know what it said, but she was pretty unhappy about it."

Tyler took a sip of the whiskey. Claire's father had good taste. "So when is Claire supposed to get married?"

"Hopefully, never. Say, are you interested in her?"

"Answer the question."

"I will if you will."

Tyler studied her earnest little face and had to grin. "It's a deal."

"They plan to marry this fall. Your turn."

"Maybe I am."

"*Maybe* you are?" Emily repeated in disbelief.

"Maybe you are what?" Claire asked from the doorway.

Tyler swung around in surprise, feeling his ears redden.

Claire gave him a glance that was at once pleased and curious as she crossed the parlor toward him. She wore a trim brown skirt and an ecru blouse with full sleeves. The blouse had a low V-shaped neckline, revealing her smooth ivory neck and a tempting glimpse of shadow between her breasts.

"Good afternoon," he said.

"Good afternoon." Claire tried to appear composed, but the sight of Tyler's handsome face had sent her heart skidding out of control.

He snatched a bedraggled hat from the chair and proudly offered it to her. "One of my men fished this out of the river."

It was the straw hat she had lost in the storm, the once-pert cluster of daisies on the front now hanging like limp noodles, the black ribbon at the crown puckering, and the wide brim drooping beyond redemption. "How very thoughtful of you," she said with a smile. "Would you care for some coffee or tea?"

His intense gaze never leaving her face, he said, "No, thank you, but there is something you can do—have dinner with me tonight."

His invitation stunned her. "That's very kind, but I—"

"You really didn't have time to sample what our chef can do."

Claire caught sight of her sister standing quietly by the sideboard, hoping not to be noticed. "Emily," Claire said, "would you excuse us, please?"

"Drat," her sister muttered, as she made her way out of the parlor. " 'Bye, Tyler."

"Mr. McCane," Claire corrected. "I'm sorry," she said to him. "My sister knows better."

" 'Tyler' is fine." He lifted Claire's hand and held it between his own, gazing down into her eyes. His own were hooded, as though masking deep secrets. "So, will you say yes?"

Claire swallowed. His deep voice, with its hint of a

southern twang, his penetrating gaze, and his warm touch made her knees grow weak and her stomach flutter. She stared into his eyes, wondering what secrets he was hiding, and wishing she could probe further and find out.

That was insane. And she couldn't justify having dinner with Tyler, especially when the attraction was so powerful. With all her worries, she doubted she'd be good company, anyway. She gently slid her hand from his grasp. "I'm sorry, but I can't," she said, trying to keep the regret from her voice.

"Care to tell me why? Maybe I can help."

Claire briefly considered telling him her troubles, but couldn't bring herself to admit the sorry state of their finances to a stranger. "Thank you, but there's really nothing you can do."

"You're wrong, you know. There *is* something I can do. I can give you the best dinner you've ever had. There's no better way to take your mind off your troubles than with an excellently prepared meal and a bottle of good wine."

"It's very tempting," she admitted, "but—"

"But?"

Claire studied him thoughtfully. She *did* owe him for saving Emily's life, and for getting them both home. And she would certainly love to take her mind off her worries, if only for a short time. Yet a tiny part of her remained frightened of him—or of the attraction she felt for him.

He picked up her hand again, turned it palm up, and brought it to his lips. "There's one thing you should know about me," he said huskily, pressing a soft kiss into her palm. "I never take no for an answer."

Claire's heart did a flip, but she forced herself to say evenly, "Then you should know that I always make up my own mind."

His eyes crinkled at the corners as he again kissed her palm. Tyler radiated virility and danger, making Claire's stomach tense with excitement.

"Forgive my impertinence," he said.

"I accept your invitation."

"I'll pick you up at seven o'clock."

Wordlessly, Claire watched him stride from the room, then she ran to the window and peered out as he climbed into the buggy. "What in heaven's name have I done?" she said aloud.

"At least he smells good," Emily said from behind her. She was wearing the ruined hat.

Exasperated, Claire snatched it from her head. "You were eavesdropping!"

"*I* won't tell Rancid Lanced if *you* won't."

"There's nothing to tell," Claire said defensively. "I'm just repaying Mr. McCane for saving your scrawny little neck. And stop calling Lance that horrid name! Where is Mrs. Parks?"

"Hanging out the wash. Whatever are you going to do with that hat?"

"Make you wear it to church, if you don't stop listening behind doors."

"Did he really think you'd wear it?"

"That doesn't matter. It's the thought that counts," Claire reminded her.

"Does that mean he thought you'd look good in a drowned hat?"

"Brat!" Claire called back, as she opened the door and hurried to find the housekeeper. Tyler hadn't really come to bring her the hat; it had been his excuse to ask her to dinner. He was interested in her!

Claire's stomach fluttered excitedly, but her excitement instantly turned to guilt. And yet . . . she couldn't resist the attraction.

"Mrs. Parks," she called, lifting her skirt as she made her way through deep grass, "I was going to take care of the laundry."

"You've got a lot on your mind, dear. It's no problem."

Claire picked up a sheet and pinned it to the line. "Have

you remembered the name of Papa's friend?''

The housekeeper took a wooden clothespin out of her mouth. ''For what, dear?''

''For the jewelry,'' Claire reminded her.

''Mercy me, that's right.'' Mrs. Parks picked up a pillowcase from the laundry basket. ''No, dear. I can't seem to remember. Did you have any luck at the pawnshop?''

Claire shook her head. ''The shop closed early today, for some reason. I suppose it will reopen in the morning. Please, Mrs. Parks, could you try to concentrate on the man's name? I don't want to take Mama's jewelry to the pawnshop.''

Her thin shoulders hunched. ''I'll try,'' she said with a sigh.

After shooing Mrs. Parks into the house to rest, Claire finished pinning up the rest of the laundry and carried the basket inside. There wasn't anything more she could do until morning. In the meantime, she was dining with Tyler McCane that evening and she hadn't begun to think about what she would wear.

That thought struck her as absurd. She was fretting over a costume, when in less than four days she might not even have a home. Feeling suddenly agitated, she took her hat from the peg at the door and slipped outside to walk down the long slope to the river's edge, her place of solace.

How many times had she stood in that same spot, gazing across the Ohio River at the verdant hills of Kentucky? A lump came into Claire's throat as she turned to look back at the magnificent house on the hill behind her. There wasn't a more beautiful sight in the whole world. Although she had seen it nearly every day of her life for the past thirteen years, she never tired of it. Closing her eyes, she drew in a deep breath and let it out, feeling the tenseness in her muscles drain away. A sense of inner peace filled her. This was where she belonged. No one was going to take it away from her. Somehow she'd find a way.

*   *   *

Tyler escorted Claire to the dining room, and introduced her to the chef who came out to greet them. Claire gazed around her in delight as she took her seat. The room was as elegant as any fancy hotel dining room in Springdale or St. Louis, with plush rose-and-green carpeting, walnut wainscoting, white linen-covered tables with green upholstered chairs, and beautiful artwork everywhere. She knew Lance would appreciate a room as elegant as this. He loved fine things.

She was glad she had worn one of her best evening toilettes, a mint green silk gown with a heart-shaped neckline and a wide sash that trailed down the back.

Suddenly aware that they were alone in the room, she asked warily, "Are we the only ones dining this evening?"

Tyler opened a bottle of champagne, the pop of the cork jarring Claire's already taut nerves. "We closed the dining room early." He paused to pour the sparkling wine into two glasses. "I prefer privacy."

Nervously, Claire watched dozens of tiny bubbles float to the top of the golden-colored liquid. Tyler raised his glass and waited until she did the same, then touched the rim of his flute to hers. "To a beautiful dinner companion," he said in a low, husky voice, his dark eyes gleaming with intensity, "and a beautiful evening together."

Trying to keep her hand from trembling, Claire took a larger sip than she intended and nearly coughed when it went down too quickly. Holding the white linen napkin to her mouth, she glanced at Tyler, who looked like a hungry wolf ready to feast on his prey. It had been stupid to accept his invitation—she was tempting fate. Perhaps she ought to talk about Lance; that would cool his ardor.

"What do you think of the dining room?" Tyler asked, watching her carefully.

"It's lovely. I've certainly never seen anything like it,

not even in Springdale, Illinois, where I attended college.''

Tyler sipped his champagne. ''Then I'm sure you'll enjoy the meal I've chosen. I hope you don't mind that I've taken the liberty of ordering in advance. I want you to have only the best.''

She'd never met anyone who behaved as gallantly as Tyler McCane, even though she knew he was doing it only to seduce her. Lance had never treated her with such courtesy. But then, Lance had never tried to seduce her.

Lance! Good heavens, she still hadn't worked him into the conversation.

''Were you and Emily traveling from Springdale?'' Tyler asked, giving her the perfect opportunity to mention her fiancé. Instead, she found herself wondering *why* Lance had never tried to seduce her. Hadn't he found her appealing?

At that moment, a waiter appeared with a tray on his shoulder. Claire glanced up to find Tyler waiting for an answer to his question. *What was his question?*

''St. Louis,'' Claire quickly replied as a covered plate was set before her. ''Emily attends—attended—a school for the blind there. I had to leave college to pick her up . . .'' Her sentence died as she watched the waiter remove the lids from both her plate and Tyler's at the same time, revealing a juicy brown standing rib roast underneath covered with a dark mushroom sauce, surrounded by crispy brown potato slices. Her mouth watered. ''I'm sorry. What was I saying?''

''Something about leaving college.''

''Oh, yes. I had to leave just before finals.''

Tyler shook out his napkin and placed it across his lap. ''Will you be able to go back to take them?''

''I hope so.'' Claire quickly followed his example, then tried a bite of potato. A piece of succulent meat followed. She closed her eyes in ecstasy. It was pure heaven!

He held out a silver basket. ''Bread?''

''Thank you.'' She took a thick, warm slice, broke it in

two, and sampled a bite. "M-m-m! Delicious."

Tyler's eyes darkened as he watched her. "I agree." He didn't seem to be referring to the bread.

Claire's pulse raced. She reached for her wine and took a steadying drink.

"Do you like the wine?" he asked.

"It's very smooth, like velvet. I like it."

Tyler stroked the stem of his glass. Claire watched, hypnotized.

"Like women, every wine has a unique blend of characteristics—texture, bouquet, taste. Some are soft and compliant; some are robust and independent." He took a sip, watching her over the rim. In a deep, sensual voice, he said, "I prefer the former."

She *knew* he wasn't referring to the wine. Raising her glass, Claire ran the liquid over her tongue. She was actually enjoying his little game.

"I rather think if I were a wine, I'd be robust and independent."

"Interesting."

Claire raised an eyebrow. "How so?"

He reached across the table and ran his hand down the side of her face. "Because your skin is like silk, and your mouth supple—compliant." He let his hand linger for a moment as he gazed at her, then he reached for his wine and lifted it in a toast. "Here's to your robust independence."

Claire touched her glass to Tyler's. Her coquettish behavior shocked her. Was it just that she missed the attentions of a handsome man, or was it this man in particular who drew her?

She feared it was the latter, but didn't understand why. Tyler McCane was as far from the safe, secure man she desired as anyone could be. And why hadn't she mentioned Lance? She'd certainly had the opportunity. She put down her glass, determined to end the game.

"If you're finished," Tyler offered, "I'd like to give you a tour of my boat."

Claire hesitated, her conscience needling her even as his voice sent shivers of excitement down her spine. Was she purposely courting danger?

She took his arm and allowed him to lead her straight into what she was sure was the wolf's den.

Chapter 6

❧◖◗❧

As they left the dining room, Tyler noticed how stiffly Claire held herself. Even her hand on his arm felt tense. He would have to put her at ease. "You should have seen the *Lady Luck* when I first bought her," he began. " 'Dilapidated' would be too kind a word for her. This boat was so bad that I had a hard time finding men to repair her. Jonas was the only person who believed I could get her to float."

"My sister certainly seems taken with Jonas," Claire remarked. "And she doesn't trust people easily."

"Jonas is my right hand," Tyler confided. "He sees to the daily operations of the boat. I have absolute trust in him, and I don't trust people easily, either."

When they came to the stairway to the upper deck, Claire gathered her skirt in one hand and started up the narrow steps in front of him, providing Tyler the perfect opportunity to enjoy the charming sway of her hips. He had long been an admirer of the female form, and this one was a fine example. The challenge was to uncover it—and Tyler loved a challenge.

"This is the promenade deck," Tyler said, as he stepped onto the upper level. "If you will accompany me around to the other side, I'll show you the view."

As they strolled along, her arm hooked through his, Claire noted the immaculate wooden planks underfoot, the shiny white railing surrounding the deck, the rows of padded white benches with backs for sitting in the open air, and the pilot house at the rear. "You certainly keep it clean," she remarked. She turned to find Tyler watching her. His eyes had deepened to the color of rich coffee and his gaze was warm, caressing, almost frightening in its intensity.

Claire quickly looked toward the shore, her cheeks on fire, her stomach aflutter. What was he thinking as he studied her? What made his gaze so warm and his eyes so dark? Certainly she had not encouraged him—had she?

Guilt flooded her with shame. She hadn't discouraged him, either. She could have refused his dinner invitation; she could have turned down the tour. And she most certainly should have told him about Lance by now.

Claire suddenly became aware that her arm was still linked through Tyler's. Even worse, she was stroking the smooth linen of his coat, pressing her palm against sinewy muscle, sending tiny currents of electricity from her fingertips to her toes. Shocked, she abruptly drew her hand away.

"Is something wrong?" he asked.

Claire opened her mouth to confess her fraud, but the words died as her gaze locked with his. For a moment, neither spoke or moved. Then Tyler reached out to stroke a finger down her cheek, pausing to trace her bottom lip. His gaze moved down to where his fingertip rested, then he leaned forward and gently replaced his finger with his mouth.

Claire's heart raced as she felt his firm, warm lips against hers. Though it was only a fleeting kiss, her body responded with strong, primitive desire. She suddenly yearned to run her hands up his arms to his shoulders and feel the strength there, to weave her fingers through the thick brown hair that fell to his collar and pull him down to her level.

Then Tyler slipped his arms around her back and his lips captured hers again, powerfully, hungrily, stoking her desire until it was a fire out of control. His taste intoxicated her; his smell heightened every sense; his touch melted her bones, until she felt as pliable and as compliant as clay in the hands of a master sculptor. His arms tightened around her, bringing her body snugly against his. She heard him groan, as though he found her delicious. And when he coaxed her lips apart and probed the hot insides of her mouth with his tongue, she nearly swooned from the shocking desires that whirled through her brain.

Suddenly, horrified, Claire stepped back, breaking the kiss. She pressed the back of her hand against her swollen lips, her body throbbing still with passion that could go nowhere. What was she thinking? She didn't even know this man! She had no excuse for her appalling behavior.

"I don't know what came over me," she said breathlessly, her face hot with embarrassment. "Perhaps it was the wine. In any case, I apologize deeply. You see, I—" Claire stopped short. Tyler was watching her closely, waiting for her to go on. Why couldn't she tell him? "I—think we should move on and pretend this didn't happen."

There was a pause, and then, with a hint of frustration, Tyler replied, "Whatever you wish."

Once again Claire was assailed by guilt. She couldn't let him think she found his behavior offensive; it was her own that offended her. She averted her gaze. "The truth is, Mr. McCane, that I'm engaged to be married."

He merely said, "Congratulations. Shall we finish our tour?"

She glanced at him surreptitiously as she took his arm, astonished by his lack of emotion. They finished the tour and Tyler took her home, saying nothing more about her engagement.

In the late hours of the night, Claire wrote a long letter to Lance, telling him how much she missed him, hoping to convince herself.

*   *   *

Tyler sat at the desk in his cabin, thumping his pen distractedly on the desktop. Except for the one lamp turned low on the corner of the desk, the room was dark. It matched his mood.

As soon as he'd taken Claire home, he'd returned to the *Lady Luck* and dove right into the ledgers he'd planned to work on the next morning. It was a feeble attempt to put the disastrous evening out of his mind; he couldn't quit thinking about Claire.

With her in his arms, kissing him with a passion that surprised and excited him, he'd had a hard time thinking rationally. For Claire to suddenly back away and ask that they pretend it hadn't happened was not what he'd expected. Damn that Rancid Lanced!

Conversation after that had been strained. He wasn't used to being rebuffed, and it had put him in a testy mood. If she was so deeply committed to her fiancé, why had she let him kiss her in the first place?

He didn't know what kind of game Claire was playing, but *she* didn't know that Tyler was a master at games.

He looked up when Jonas appeared with the customary tray and two glasses of whiskey.

"Time to put the ledgers away," the Englishman announced, setting a glass in front of Tyler.

"Thanks." Tyler rubbed his eyes and yawned as his assistant sprawled in a nearby chair, his lanky legs stretched out before him.

"How did your dinner go?" Jonas asked casually.

"I'll sum it up in two words," Tyler said, as he reached for the glass. "She's engaged."

"You knew that beforehand. Or had you conveniently forgotten?"

"I was hoping *she* had. And don't tsk-tsk me, damn it! For an engaged woman, she's mighty free with her kisses."

"From your sour disposition," Jonas said, pausing to

take a sip of whiskey, "I'd guess your evening was ruined by a guilty conscience."

"Claire's, or mine?" Tyler snapped.

"Claire's, obviously. You seem to have lost yours."

Tyler gave him a warning glance. "I'm not in the mood for your barbs, old man."

"Then I'll tell you straight out: leave Miss Cavanaugh alone. She has quite enough to manage without you panting after her *and* her land."

Tyler drained his glass, banged it down on the desk, and stalked to the door. "Thanks for the advice." He opened the door and waited.

The wily Brit rose, straightened his clothing, and walked out with dignity. He paused to look back. "I believe I erred. Perhaps it *is* your conscience that's bothering you."

"Go to hell." Tyler slammed the door and began to undress with quick, angry movements. Jonas was wrong on both counts. It wasn't his conscience or lack of it that bothered him; it was his pride.

But he wasn't about to give up, not when he was so close. He'd read the desire in Claire's kiss as clearly as if she'd said it aloud.

After a sleepless night, Claire rose early, a feeling of foreboding hanging over her like a black cloud. Her evening with Tyler had ignited desires she didn't dare explore. The telegram from Lance had left her puzzled and disheartened. And the uneasy feeling persisted that something else was about to happen.

She was standing in front of the pawnshop when the owner raised the shade at the door and turned over the OPEN sign. He saw her, hesitated a moment, then opened the door. The bell overhead tinkled merrily as she walked inside. "Good morning, Miss Cavanaugh," he said, as he turned and shuffled slowly back to his counter.

"Good morning, Mr. Greene," she returned. "How are you today?"

"I could be better," he said with a shrug.

"I'm sorry to hear that," Claire said, studying his forlorn expression. "Have you seen Doctor Jenkins?"

"Sadly, a doctor cannot fix this problem. What have you got there?" he asked, pointing to the satchel.

Claire set the bag on the counter, took out the gray cases, and opened one. "I'd like you to look at this pearl choker, Mr. Greene."

Walter Greene walked around behind the counter and picked up the necklace, running it through his fingers and holding it up to the light. "Very good quality."

Claire opened the case with the diamond earbobs. "What about these?"

He picked one up, put an eyepiece in his right eye, and examined it closely. "Very nice. Virtually flawless."

Claire took a deep breath. "I'd like to sell them."

The pawnshop owner slowly placed the earbobs back in their case and closed the lid. "I cannot buy them, Miss Cavanaugh. I have too much inventory."

Claire's heart began to race in apprehension. He *had* to buy the jewelry. What would she do if he didn't? "Won't you just take a look at this piece, Mr. Greene?" She removed the diamond-and-emerald pendant and held it out. "It's beautiful, isn't it?" she asked in a wavering voice.

Claire saw his eyes widen and took hope from it. Greene took the pendant from her and stared at it, letting his breath out between his teeth in admiration. But when he handed it back, he shook his head sadly. "I wish to *Gott* I could help you, but I cannot."

Claire's stomach knotted. "Please, Mr. Greene, please consider buying at least one of them. Surely you have room for one more piece of jewelry."

He shook his head again, dropping his gaze. "I cannot."

Tears blinded Claire's eyes as she packed up the jewelry. "I hope you feel better soon, Mr. Greene," she said softly, as she walked to the door. The bell over the door tinkled once again.

"Miss Cavanaugh!" he called.

Claire paused to look back. The shop owner started to speak, but stopped suddenly, his eyes darting nervously toward the window, as though something had distracted him. He hung his head. "I'm sorry."

As Claire left the shop, she heard Sheriff Simons call out to her, but she didn't acknowledge him. She climbed into the buggy and drove home at breakneck pace, her throat aching from holding back her tears. It suddenly seemed imperative that she reach the safety of Bellefleur. Once there, she ran up to her room, flung herself on her big featherbed, and sobbed.

"I can't go through it again!" Claire cried, her voice muffled by the pillow. She drew in huge gulps of air, remembering the terror she had felt at being left alone while her mother went in search of work, the hours of hiding while she waited for her to come back, the dread of thinking that her mother might not come back at all. Other, more frightening memories crept into her thoughts, and Claire clapped her hands over her ears to block the sound of the nightmarish voices that had haunted her from childhood.

"Say, what do we have here? Why, it's a purty little filly. Here now, don't pull away. You're scared, ain't ya? Has your ma left you all alone? Well, you just stay here with ol' Will and Bob and we'll take care of you just fine. Easy now, little filly. Don't you kick me, now, or I'll whup your ass. Hey! You come back here!"

Claire's heart hammered against her ribs as if she were still running and running. Curling up in a ball on the bed, she let the painful memories wash over her until she was empty of every emotion—every thought but one. She would die before she let the same thing happen to Emily.

* * *

Reginald Boothe leaned back in his chair and puffed on a cigar. "I had a friendly little chat with Walter Greene," he told the sheriff. "I think it's safe to say there is no possible way Claire Cavanaugh can make that payment now."

"Not unless Walter changes his mind and buys her jewelry," Simons cautioned.

"He won't change his mind."

The sheriff rubbed the back of his neck, his expression doubtful. "I don't know, Mr. Boothe. Walter is different, being foreign and all."

"He's also my tenant, Sheriff. He knows what's good for him."

"If you say so," the sheriff conceded unwillingly. "Do you want me to stop following Cee Cee now?"

Boothe blew out a stream of smoke. "Not yet. If she's half as cantankerous as her father was, she'll keep trying. You *did* contact the jewelry and pawnshops in Mt. Vernon, didn't you?"

"Yes, sir. I told them the jewelry was stolen merchandise and to call me if Cee Cee tried to sell it."

"That's using your head, Sheriff." Boothe swung his chair to look out the window. "Now may be a good time to push a marriage proposal."

"It don't seem likely she'll want to hear it," Simons said sadly, "being engaged, and all."

Boothe looked around at him. "Think about this, Sheriff. If this Logan fellow was truly her fiancé, wouldn't he have come back with her for her father's funeral? Wouldn't he be here in her time of need?"

"I suppose so."

"But he's not, is he? It's something to check out, wouldn't you say?"

"You're right, Mr. Boothe," the sheriff replied.

With a smug smile, Boothe leaned back in his chair and put his feet on the desk. "I'm always right."

*   *   *

Claire woke up with a start, and for a moment, thought it was morning again. Her confusion disappeared as she slowly uncurled her stiff limbs and sat up. A glance at the clock on her bedside table showed that she had missed the noon meal, yet she felt no hunger. Her thoughts were focused on one thing only: saving Bellefleur. If she only knew what her father had discovered. It was her only remaining hope for saving their home.

Claire washed her face with cool water, dried her eyes, smoothed back her hair, and straightened her clothing. It wouldn't do to let Emily and Mrs. Parks know how worried she was.

"Cee Cee?" Emily called, tapping softly on her door. "Are you ill?"

"I was just resting, Em," she said, opening the door to admit her sister. "I had a headache."

"Ben wants to speak to you," Emily told her. "Mrs. Parks sent me to fetch you. He's waiting on the front porch."

Claire found Ben Walsh, their longtime farmhand, waiting quietly at the base of the porch steps. He stood with battered felt hat in hand, his white shirt and canvas work pants permanently stained from toiling in the fields, his face downcast. "Howdy, Miss Cavanaugh," he said somberly.

"You wanted to see me, Ben?"

"I hate to bring this up, miss, seein's how your pa just died and all, but me and the boys, we gotta know." He looked up at her from under shaggy eyebrows. "Are we gonna get paid our wages?"

Claire's heart went out to her father's loyal worker. Ben and his wife Martha had raised three children on the wages earned at Bellefleur. Claire knew he would soon need to save money for his retirement. Claire didn't want to lose him, but neither could she give him false hope. "I don't have any money to pay wages right now, Ben. I'm trying my hardest, but I can't guarantee anything. I don't even know if I'll be able to stop the bank from foreclosing.''

"We was afraid something like that was gonna happen. We seen that Boothe feller out here last week and we knew it meant trouble.''

"Reginald Boothe came here?'' Claire asked in surprise.

"Yes'm. Real early one mornin'. Came driving up in his fancy buggy. I saw him talkin' to yer pa out by the east barn. He left real quick, though, when yer pa went to fetch his shotgun.''

"That was last week?''

"Yes'm. 'Bout nine days ago, I'd imagine.''

"Did you talk to my father afterward?''

"No, ma'am. After Boothe left, your pa went straight up to the house, cussing up a storm.'' The farmhand paused, then looked down and shook his head. "I never saw him after that, until the day of the funeral.''

Claire's jaw clenched. She knew instinctively that Boothe's visit had precipitated her father's death. Boothe had probably brought the foreclosure notice in person just to harass him. The man was not only a monster, but a murderer as well.

"Thank you for coming to me first, Ben,'' Claire told him. "I'll understand if you want to find work elsewhere.''

The farmhand sighed as if the weight of the world was on his shoulders. "I'd like to finish out the week, miss, if you don't mind.''

"Thank you,'' she said, in a voice thick with tears. She was about to turn away when she remembered her father's letter.

'Ben,'' she called, hurrying down the steps after him. "Did my father mention anything to you about a discovery?''

"I don't quite get your meaning, miss.''

Claire didn't know how to explain her dilemma without revealing too much. Her father hadn't felt safe in telling anyone what he had found. "Is there anything new or different going on with the land?"

"New?" Ben scratched his head. "Well, this ain't exactly new, but round about last fall your pa had a wildcatter out here, checkin' for oil."

"A wildcatter?"

"A driller, or roughneck, as they call themselves. They're fellas that work on crews, drillin' for oil."

Claire was puzzled. Her father had never mentioned it in his letters. "What made him think there was oil on the property, Ben?"

The farmhand shrugged. "Could be all the rumors goin' round about this part of the country bein' oil-rich. Myself, I think they're a bunch of hogwash, but your pa musta thought there was somethin' to 'em. I never saw that fella again, so I'm supposin' he just gave up." Ben paused to take out a handkerchief to wipe his face. "Then there was another fella out here 'bout two weeks ago, doing some kinda surveyin'."

Claire looked down the hill to the river beyond. A land surveyor? Had someone made an offer to buy Bellefleur? "Do you know who this fellow was?"

He shook his head. "No, miss. I truly don't. Miz Parks might, though. I seen her talkin' to him."

Claire sighed dispiritedly. Mrs. Parks probably wouldn't even remember that a surveyor had been out there. "If you think of anything else, will you please tell me, Ben?"

She stood in the shade of the porch and watched him walk back toward the tobacco field. Had her father been referring to oil in his letter? Had he expected to find oil on the property? But why would he have needed a survey done? Lost in thought, she jumped when Jonas Polk came around the opposite corner of the porch.

"Didn't mean to frighten you," he said. "You've got enough to deal with, without me adding to it."

Claire was mortified. "You heard our conversation?"

"Couldn't help it," Jonas said with a sheepish shrug,

as he climbed the steps of the porch. "I was coming up that way when I heard the two of you discussing matters. I didn't want to intrude, so I waited around the side of the house."

"This is a very difficult time for us, Mr. Polk. I hope I can count on your discretion."

"You have my word on it, Miss Cavanaugh," he vowed, marking a little "X" with his finger on his linen suit. "Just don't give up. There's always a way."

"I can't give up, Mr. Polk. I'd rather die than lose my home."

"I understand." He showed her the bag he had slung over one shoulder. "I had a few hours of free time this afternoon, so I thought I'd bring over material for Emily to make more puppets. She seems to enjoy it."

"Very much so. She doesn't have enough to occupy her time."

"Poor little tyke." Jonas shook his head sadly. "She reminds me of my sister, Anne. She was four years younger than me and much better looking—if you can believe it. She had a lame foot, but she got around well enough. Always had a soft spot in my heart for her, and the little imp knew it, too." He sighed regretfully. "I left England when I was twenty and never got back home to see her. She died last year."

"I'm so sorry," Claire said quietly.

"That's life, I suppose. You never know what lies ahead. Well, I won't take up any more of your time. Is Emily in the house?"

"She's down at the stables."

"I'll just take a walk down there, then, if you don't mind," Jonas said, tipping his hat. He started to walk away, then paused and turned around. "A question, if I may. Did I hear correctly that Reginald Boothe came out to see your father shortly before he passed away?"

"You heard correctly." Claire didn't even try to hide her dislike of the man.

Jonas rubbed his narrow chin. "Makes a bloke stop and think, doesn't it?" He stared down at the ground for a long moment, as though contemplating the matter. "Well, I'll just be off to the stables, then."

Claire started to go back inside the house, but suddenly a walk in the bright sunshine sounded like a very welcome break. "Mr. Polk," she called, lifting her skirts to hurry down the porch steps, "I'll go with you."

After they had walked along in companionable silence for several moments, Jonas asked, "Enjoy your dinner last night, did you?"

Claire glanced at him, wondering how much he knew. "The food was delicious."

"And the company?" he prodded.

Claire hesitated, trying to frame her answer as tactfully as possible. "Well, there was a slight misunderstanding. Mr. McCane wasn't aware that I'm engaged."

"I see."

"It's my fault, really," she added. "I should have told him when he issued his invitation. I feel terrible now that I misled him."

"Don't blame yourself for a moment. Ty should have guessed that an attractive young lady like you would be promised to someone."

"You're very close to him, aren't you?" Claire observed.

"Like the father he never had," Jonas said proudly. "Well, he *had* a father, in the strict sense of the word. But the bloke never acted like a father, if you know what I mean. From what I've heard, he was a cruel bastard, pardon my language."

"Mr. McCane's mother raised him, then?"

"Tried to, for a brief period of time. Unfortunately, the poor lady had her own demons to battle. She wasn't mother material, it seems. An uncle in New Orleans is who Ty ended up with. But the lad didn't stay land-bound for long. When he was twelve, he talked his uncle into letting him work on his riverboat and eventually became quite a card sharp. That's how he earned enough to buy the *Lady Luck*. He hasn't been off the water for more than a day or two since."

As they drew near the barn, Jonas gave Claire a wary glance. "Ty wouldn't be too happy if he knew I was discussing his past."

"I won't say a word," Claire replied.

They were just about to enter the big fieldstone stable when the clatter of wagon wheels drew their attention to the road alongside the property, and Claire saw the sheriff approaching Bellefleur.

"Oh, no! Not again! That man shows up at least twice a day."

"Duck inside the barn," Jonas urged. "I'll tell him you've gone to town."

"He'll only come back later," Claire said with a sigh. "I may as well see what he wants."

Mrs. Parks met Claire at the back door. "Sheriff Simington is here to see you, dear. I put him in the front parlor."

"Do you mean Simons?"

Mrs. Parks blinked in confusion. "What did I say?"

"Simington."

"Now, why on earth would I say that?" she muttered to herself. "How silly of me." Hobbling to a chair, she lowered her thin frame onto it and covered her face with her hands.

"Are you all right?" Claire asked, concerned.

For a long moment Mrs. Parks was silent. Then she whispered, "Sometimes I fear I'm losing my mind."

Claire's heart went out to her. She put an arm around her shoulders and pressed her cheek against Mrs. Parks' wrinkled one. "Perhaps you were thinking of someone else. Please don't worry about it. I'll come back and make tea for us as soon as the sheriff leaves." Giving her a gentle hug, Claire left the kitchen and headed up the hallway.

Wilbur Simons was standing beside the fireplace, one foot on the raised hearth, one hand holding the front of his vest, his double chin raised high, as though he was getting ready to deliver a speech. When Claire walked into the room, he abandoned his stance and lumbered toward her, beaming.

"Afternoon, Miss Cee Cee. I brought you these."

Claire reluctantly took the daisies that were thrust at her. "Thank you, Sheriff."

"I'd greatly appreciate it if you'd do me the honor of calling me by my given name."

"I—I don't know, Sheriff," Claire stammered. "I wouldn't feel comfortable . . . It wouldn't be seemly . . ."

"Now, Miss Cee Cee," he said in a stern voice, "there's no reason for you to feel uncomfortable calling me by my given name. After all, we're old friends."

Old enough for you to be my father! Claire thought, with a shudder of distaste.

He took her hand between his meaty paws. "In truth, Cee Cee, I was hoping we could become better friends."

Claire stared at him, appalled. Dear Lord, now he wanted to *court* her.

"Ow! Owwwww!" Claire heard her sister cry from outside the house.

She whirled around and dashed to the front door as Jonas came in carrying Emily. "Poor tyke's in a bad way," the Brit said. "Might be her appendix."

"Her appendix?" Claire stared in horror at her sister's pain-riddled expression.

"Or it might be something she ate."

"Owwww!" Emily cried again, holding her midsection. "It hurts, Cee Cee. Make it stop."

Claire's own stomach clenched in fear. "I'll send for the doctor. Would you carry her upstairs, please, Mr. Polk? Her room is the second door on the left." Claire turned to the sheriff, who had followed her to the hallway. "I'm sorry, but I have to take care of my sister."

"Want me to fetch Doc Jenkins for you?"

"Thank you, but I'll send one of our farmhands."

Simons's frustration showed on his face, though he tried to disguise it. "I hope your sister is okay, and I hope you'll consider what I said." He turned and walked to the door. "I'll be back another time."

"That's what I'm afraid of," she muttered, as she dropped the flowers on a table and hurried upstairs.

She turned the corner and found Emily and Jonas standing in the upstairs hallway waiting for her. Emily covered her mouth with her hand to suppress her laughter.

"You're not ill at all!" Claire cried.

"We thought you might need a bit of assistance getting rid of Simple Simon," Jonas explained with a wink.

"You've frightened me out of a year's growth!" Claire exclaimed in relief, then began to laugh with her sister. "Bless you both for coming to my rescue." She pressed a quick kiss on each of their cheeks. "It seems the sheriff has decided to court me."

"Doesn't he know of your engagement?" Jonas asked.

"He does. That's the odd thing."

Suddenly, Claire heard Mrs. Parks cry her name from the kitchen.

"Looks like someone else is trying to rescue you," Jonas offered.

Fearing the woman had injured herself, Claire dashed downstairs to the kitchen. She found Mrs. Parks sitting in a chair, fanning herself.

"What happened?" Claire asked breathlessly.

"Simington!" Mrs. Parks cried. "I know why I said it! I remembered the man's name!"

"Sheriff Simons?" Claire asked, sure the woman was confused again.

"No, dear. The friend of your father's who wanted to

buy the jewelry," she explained. "His name is Roger Simington!"

Claire's mouth fell open in surprise. "You remembered! That's wonderful!" she cried, giving Mrs. Parks a hug. "I remember Mr. Simington. He used to come out to see Mama and Papa. Does he still live in town?"

"I don't know, dear. Mr. Bailey down at the post office would know."

"I'll go to the post office right away!" Excitedly, she hurried to her room to pick up the satchel with the jewelry cases inside. With any luck, she would be able to visit Roger Simington before dinner and have the money for the bank by morning.

She'd beat Reginald Boothe yet!

Chapter 7

~~~~OQC~~~~

Driving the buggy down River Road, Claire glanced up at the sky, which was dark gray with the threat of a storm. She pulled up hard on the reins as Tyler McCane, leading a chestnut mare, stepped into the lane ahead of her.

"Mr. McCane, what are you doing way out here?" she asked in surprise.

"I was on my way to see some property when my horse threw a shoe. Mind if I hitch a ride with you back to town?"

"Of course not," she told him.

He tied his horse to the back of the buggy and climbed in beside Claire, setting off a flock of butterflies in her stomach. She clicked her tongue and the horse started up. "I'm surprised you didn't see Sheriff Simons pass by," she said, keeping her tone casual.

"I did. He was too far away to hear me yell."

"What property were you looking at?"

"The land across the road from yours."

Claire glanced at him curiously. "The bank owns that land."

"Not anymore."

She suddenly remembered that Tyler had been in Boothe's office the day she had gone to ask for more time, and recalled overhearing them talk about doing business together. Now it made sense. Did Tyler know how the bank had acquired it? She hoped Boothe had kept it confidential, but she wouldn't put anything past him.

"Do you know the history of that property?" she asked, keeping her eyes on the road.

"Not really."

Claire relaxed. "It belonged to my father at one time. He bought the land with the intention of raising racehorses."

At Tyler's silence, Claire glanced his way. He was watching her with the same intense light in his eyes that she had seen just before he had kissed her. She quickly looked away as her face flooded with heat. The taste of his potent kiss lingered with her still, haunting her dreams and filling her with an ardent longing to be held in his arms once more, to be kissed with the same passion that she had tried so hard to forget.

But she *had* to forget. Tyler McCane was a threat to her future. Claire tried to call up an image of Lance, but failed miserably. What was happening to her? Why was she so attracted to this man? He had no permanent home, no ties, and no roots—and worse, seemed not to need them.

"What are you going to do with the land?" she asked, trying to steer her thoughts in a safer direction.

"I'm still deciding." He shifted his position, moving closer to her. "About last night . . . I didn't mean to put you in an awkward spot. If I offended you, I apologize."

Claire kept her eyes fixed on the road. "I feel bad for misleading you, no matter how unintentional it was." *Or was it intentional?*

Tyler rested his arm on the bench behind her, his hand lightly brushing her back, sending tingles of electricity through her skin. Claire straightened to keep from touching him again, frightened by the desire he aroused.

"Your fiancé is a lucky man to have such a captivating woman as his future bride," he told her. "I hope he knows just how lucky he is."

Claire had always thought she was the lucky one to have

attracted Lance's attention, since she did not find herself particularly pretty. Indeed, Lance had been considered the catch of the year, and she knew the other girls in her dormitory had envied her. For a long time, Claire had worried that it would be her father's wealth that would end up attracting a man. But Lance had changed all that. As the third son in a prosperous farming family, Lance would have only a small inheritance, but he had ambition and charm enough for two men. His professors had predicted he would go places. He didn't need Claire's inheritance to be a success.

But why hadn't he journeyed to Fortune to be with her? And where was the letter he had promised?

She became aware that Tyler was watching her again, as though waiting for her to respond to his statement. "Lance is an extraordinary man," she said, with more conviction than she felt.

"Will he be joining you shortly?"

"I don't know," she admitted. "I'm waiting for a letter."

Neither one spoke for a few minutes. Then, as they approached the bank, Tyler said, "You can let me out here."

Claire guided the horse to the side of the street and waited for Tyler to step down. Instead, he turned to her again. "I'd like to have dinner with you tonight, just as friends, as my way of making amends."

She gazed at him wordlessly. Could they be friends and nothing else? Could she ignore the stirring of desire his nearness caused?

"I promise, no tours." A slight grin lifted one corner of his mouth and made him irresistible.

Claire nibbled her lower lip. Perhaps she should give him the opportunity to make amends. Besides, if her plans went well and she was able to pay off the mortgage, she would have something to celebrate. "All right."

Tyler smiled broadly, something Claire had never seen before. "I'll see you at seven o'clock."

An intense longing filled Claire as he untied his horse and strode away. She suddenly couldn't wait until evening—and she knew that was very wrong.

Trying to put aside her thoughts, Claire hitched the buggy by the post office and went inside to talk to Mr. Bailey, the postmaster. There she learned that Roger Simington had moved up river to Mt. Vernon, where he owned a thriving feed and grain business. It would take several hours by buggy to get there, but only half that time by ferry.

Claire glanced at the turbulent sky. She might get to Mt. Vernon before the storm broke, but she didn't want to take a chance on being delayed again overnight. She would just have to leave early the next morning. Her stomach churned uneasily. She had only two days before the bank foreclosed.

"Cook tells me you're having a guest for dinner again tonight," Jonas remarked, standing in the cabin doorway with his arms folded.

Tyler didn't look up from the papers on his desk. "That's right."

"If at first you don't succeed, et cetera, et cetera."

"That's right."

"A bird in the hand, et cetera, et cetera."

Tyler glared at his assistant. "Did you want something, Jonas?"

"Interesting question, that," the Brit replied, strolling into the room. "Do I want something? Hmmm. If we interchanged 'want' with 'wish,' then I could say honestly that I do, indeed, *wish* something."

Tyler leaned back in his chair and waited. He had long ago learned that Jonas knew things Tyler would never have found out on his own, and would reveal them only when it seemed prudent to do so. "What do you wish?" he asked, playing along with him.

"Have you ever promised not to tell a secret, then wished you could because what you learned was very important?"

Now Tyler understood the game. "I suppose you couldn't be blamed if someone guessed the secret."

Jonas stretched out on Tyler's bunk, his arms folded behind his head. "I would think not."

"Did you go anywhere this morning?"

"I did. I went to see Emily."

Tyler wasn't pleased about that. Jonas was growing much too attached to the child. "I suppose you talked to her quite a bit."

"Right after I talked with her sister, who had just finished talking with a farmhand."

"I don't imagine this has anything to do with overhearing their conversation."

Jonas rubbed an eyebrow. "Not that I intentionally listened, mind you."

"And what you happened to hear, was it something that affects our agreement with Boothe?"

"Oh, for pity's sake, Ty." Jonas threw his legs over the edge of the bunk and sat up. "All you think about is that bloody agreement. This young woman is struggling to find a way to keep her home, and she can't even pay her farmhands. What will she do? Where will they go? Don't these things weigh on you?"

"If I had to assess how each business deal I made affected everyone's lives, I'd still be working as a hand on my uncle's boat."

"So you don't care that Claire and Emily may be homeless, yet you feel no remorse in inviting Claire to dinner in order to seduce her?"

Tyler clenched his jaw. He'd been in a good mood since he'd convinced Claire to have dinner with him, the best mood he'd been in since . . . hell, he couldn't remember when. Why she affected his mood so didn't concern him too much. The potential for seducing her was clearly the cause. He needed a physical release and she was the handiest, and comeliest, means to it.

Yet Jonas's words nettled him. He both remembered and recognized the panicked look in Claire's eyes after her meeting with Boothe. She was losing her home and she was frightened. Well, he'd been in the same situation, and it had made him a stronger person.

Tyler lowered his eyebrows, his stubbornness coming to the fore. "Claire's personal problems and her agreement to see me this evening are two separate issues, Jonas. Besides, in the financial bind she's in, I'm sure she'll appreciate an expensive dinner."

Jonas threw up his hands in disgust. "Do what you want. Just don't involve me."

Tyler was sure he'd made the right decision when he glanced at Claire sitting beside him in the buggy that evening. She had put her long black hair up in a twist, except for a few curls at her nape. She wore simple pearl earbobs, and her cheeks were faintly pink, as were her soft lips. Her dark blue dress emphasized her cobalt eyes and creamy complexion, and the rounded neckline enhanced the long line of her slender throat. His body responded with a surge of desire.

As he seated her in the dining room of the *Lady Luck*, Tyler leaned down low enough to detect the softest of floral scents in her hair and on her skin. And when Claire smiled at him across the table, he could almost taste her kiss. But he had to proceed slowly. He had, after all, promised to make amends.

Tyler had planned the seduction carefully. The first step was to disarm her, to make her believe he was not an enemy but an ally.

"Tell me about your fiancé," he said, sipping his wine.

He saw her cheeks grow pinker. "Lance is from Springdale, Illinois, where we both attended college."

"Has he graduated?"

"He will shortly," Claire answered hesitantly.

Tyler leaned over the table, his face a mask of concern. "I don't mean to be forward, but you've just gone through a trying ordeal. Shouldn't he be here with you?"

Looking chagrined, Claire toyed with her napkin. "I don't know why he hasn't come, but I'm certain he had good reason—perhaps a family emergency. He has promised to send a letter explaining why he couldn't—" she paused, as though she realized she was about to reveal something, "—come. But it hasn't arrived yet."

The waiter brought their food and Tyler let her eat a few bites before continuing. His plan was going well, although the ease with which he was carrying it out didn't give him as much pleasure as he'd expected. She was too naive. Either that, or she had her own game plan—perhaps *he* was the one who was being naive.

"I'm certainly grateful to Mr. Polk for the attention he's paying Emily," Claire said, shaking Tyler out of his musings. "I know my father's death has been hard on her, but she's so good at hiding her feelings that I forget how lonely it must be for her. Mr. Polk seems to sense her loneliness and respond to it. He's a very good man, Mr. McCane."

"Call me Tyler, please," he said, forcing a smile. The last person he wanted to discuss, let alone praise, was the man who had decreed himself Tyler's conscience.

"How did you meet him?" she asked, lifting her glass to her invitingly parted lips.

"Jonas worked for my uncle," he replied quickly, wanting to move the conversation back on track. Before he could do so, however, she spoke again.

"What did your uncle do?"

"He owned a riverboat in New Orleans."

"Of course! As I recall, that's where you came by your love for the river," she said, then immediately looked aghast. She quickly reached for her wineglass and took another sip. "So you and Jonas decided to buy the *Lady Luck* and start your own business. You've done quite well for yourself, it seems."

Tyler eyed her warily. He didn't remember ever mentioning his uncle to her. "Yes, I've been fortunate," he said cautiously.

"And so have we. Because of your bravery, my sister's life was spared." She gazed at him admiringly. Tyler shifted uncomfortably.

"What brought you to Fortune, Mr. McCane?"

"It's Tyler," he reminded her. "I came here to expand my riverboat business."

"And do you plan to operate your business from downtown?"

Tyler studied Claire's earnest face, certain she had no inkling as to what lay in store for Bellefleur. "The docks downtown aren't large enough to accommodate my plans," he replied, with deliberate ambiguity. "I'm looking at another piece of land."

"Sometimes I wish I were a man," Claire said with a heavy sigh, gazing somewhere beyond him. "Men can do things like that: start a business, buy a boat, get a loan. What can a woman do if she needs money? Who will lend it to her if she has no means of income, no assets? What can she do to protect herself from greedy men?"

Her vulnerability made Tyler unexpectedly hesitant to take the next step.

"But other times," she continued, "I'm glad I'm not a man. Men can be so cold and selfish!" She leaned toward him as if to share a confidence. "I know you had a business dealing with Mr. Boothe from the bank, but you should be warned that he is as greedy and as cold as they come. Don't trust him, Mr. McCane, not a bit."

"Call me Tyler," he said. He looked around, wishing the waiter would appear and divert her attention.

"You've done so much to help me," Claire told him, gazing at him with those innocent blue eyes, "that I feel

I owe you that warning. What he's done to my family is unspeakable. I wouldn't wish anything so dire to befall you."

Tyler filled up his wineglass and took a deep gulp. Miserable didn't begin to describe how he felt at that moment. His plan was in a shambles, his conscience had finally been prodded into existence, and he was beginning to doubt his new partner—and all because of this beguiling young woman. He remembered the premonition he'd had when he'd first met Claire, and wondered if it could be true. Was she going to destroy him?

Setting the glass down with a firm *thunk,* Tyler fixed her with the penetrating gaze he knew women loved. Damn it, she was not going to do anything to him but satisfy his desire. He was going to stick to his plan and let the consequences fall where they would. "I appreciate your candor, Miss Cavanaugh. For someone in my profession, it's refreshing to find a woman who isn't out to use a man to her advantage."

"Use a man to *her* advantage?" Claire looked stunned. Tyler wondered if it was just a ruse.

He leaned forward and took her hand. "I've never had a dinner with a woman just as friends. Women expect seduction."

Claire pressed her free hand to her throat. "They *do?*"

"Indeed they do." He sighed with exaggerated suffering. "Ah, well. Did you want dessert?"

"I really should be going," she told him, glancing at the watch pinned at her waist. "I have to leave early tomorrow for Mt. Vernon." Claire started to rise, and Tyler jumped up to assist her. She walked with him to the buggy, where, before he handed her in, she turned to look up at him. "I can't thank you enough for your kindness, Mr.—er—Tyler."

"I was just wondering," Tyler said, gazing down into her eyes, "if you would mind if I kissed you—just a friendly parting kiss."

He saw the hesitation in her eyes and wondered if he had moved too quickly. But then a blush colored her cheeks and she looked down, as though suddenly shy.

"A friendly kiss would be all right, I suppose."

It was Tyler's turn to hesitate. Did she really believe he could kiss her as a friend and feel nothing, or was this part of her game? Putting his hands on her arms, he dipped his head down and met her lips with a gentleness that astounded him.

Claire opened her eyes and blinked at him, her lips parted slightly in wonder. "That was very nice," she said in a surprised voice.

Tyler's blood ran hot as he gazed down at those soft, luscious lips, remembering Claire's passionate response the last time. But now she merely turned and climbed into the buggy. He shook his head. Perhaps she *did* believe they could just be friends. Perhaps she truly was an innocent.

The harsh reality hit him as they drove up to Bellefleur. Claire wouldn't feel so friendly when she learned that he and Boothe were partners in a plan to take over her land. For just a moment, he regretted getting involved with Boothe. Then he reminded himself that he had worked hard to get where he was. He could not let a woman keep him from reaching his ultimate dream.

"Tyler," Claire said shyly, when he pulled to a stop in front of her house. "Could I—that is, do you think we could—" She stopped and looked down at her hands, obviously embarrassed. "Oh, never mind."

Tyler came around to help her down. Putting his hands on her waist, he lifted her, gazing into her eyes as he slowly set her down. By the way she kept her hands on his shoulders as she looked up at him, he knew what she had intended to ask. But he wanted to hear it from her. He left his hands at her waist. "Ask me," he said huskily.

He saw her throat move as she swallowed. Her eyes were huge and her fingers clasped his shoulders tightly. "I just thought perhaps we could try another friendly—"

Tyler didn't wait for her to finish. She rose on tiptoes to meet him as he dipped his head. His fingers tightened on her waist as his lips touched hers, gently at first, then with more passion, until he forced himself to step back. Drawing an unsteady breath, he gave her a semblance of a smile. "How's that?" he asked, keeping his tone casual.

Her voice shook when she answered. "Fine. Just fine. I'll say goodnight now. Thank you again for everything." But instead of turning and walking up the steps to her house, she stood still, staring at him. And instead of turning away and walking back to the buggy, Tyler did the unthinkable. He kissed her again.

This time it was Claire who kissed with more intensity, and Claire who stepped back first, staring at Tyler as though stunned. And he knew if he did not turn away at that moment, he'd kiss her in a way that would be much more than friendly.

Why, when his plan seemed to be moving along so perfectly, did it seem like she was the one in control? Or had she planned it that way? He climbed into the buggy, needing suddenly to put distance between them.

As he pulled away, however, Tyler couldn't help but look back. The porch was empty. Claire had slipped quietly into the house, leaving him with an aching loneliness he hadn't felt since he was five years old.

For the first time, he began to believe Claire *could* destroy him, just as his mother had, twenty-five years ago.

But only if he let her.

Chapter 8

Claire closed the front door behind her and leaned against it, smiling dreamily as she remembered the taste and feel of Tyler's firm lips on hers. "Just a friendly kiss," she said on a sigh, as she started up the stairs. "That's all it was."

Then how was she to explain the trembling that seized hold of her when she was near him, or the butterflies in her stomach, or the exquisite ache throbbing right now between her thighs? How was she to explain the fierce yearning deep within her for a man she barely knew?

She locked her bedroom door, stripped off her garments, and stood before her cheval mirror, aware of herself as a woman as she had never been before. Running her hands slowly over her breasts, down the planes of her ribs and stomach to the apex of her thighs, she closed her eyes and sighed, imagining Tyler's hands touching her, stroking her, in ways she had never imagined with Lance. Had she ever felt this way after Lance had kissed her?

Pulling her nightgown over her head, Claire sat down on the edge of her bed. What was she to do? Betraying Lance would go against everything her mother had taught her about love and commitment.

Claire removed the pins in her hair and began to brush out her locks in long, smooth strokes. She had to be up early in the morning to make it to Mt. Vernon and back before the bank closed. Only after she had stopped the foreclosure would she think again about Tyler McCane.

She assuaged her conscience further by writing another letter to Lance.

While Claire dined with Tyler, Walter Greene and his wife Anna sat in the kitchen of their modest home eating their evening meal. Walter sopped up salty beef broth in his bowl with his bread, stuffed the bite in his mouth, and shook his head sadly. "I feel sorry for them, Anna," he said. "What are those poor *kinder* gonna do if they can't raise money? Live in the street?"

"Hush, Walter," his roly-poly wife admonished, wagging a finger in front of his face. "Don't make trouble for us. You did as you were told. That's good enough."

"Yah, I did as I was told—like *ein Kind*, Anna. Like a child. Now I ask myself, am I a man or am I a child?"

"You're a wise man, Walter, who knows not to cross Herr Boothe."

"I don't feel wise, Anna," he said with a weary sigh. "I feel old and tired and sick."

"What can I do to help, Walter?" she asked, wringing her broad hands in concern.

"Nothing. I have a sickness in here," he said, tapping his chest. "In my soul."

"Have some more soup," his wife encouraged, dipping the ladle into the heavy pot. "Soup is good for the soul, too."

The pawnshop owner finished his dinner in silence. He had always been a law-abiding man and a good Christian, as well. He knew in his heart that he would get no rest unless he did what was right. What Mr. Boothe had told him to do was not right.

He looked at his wife of thirty-seven years and remembered the beautiful young girl he had married. He thought of the fine children he had brought into the world, and of the values he had taught them. They would not be proud of him now.

Wiping his mouth with his napkin, Walter Greene pushed back his chair and got up with a groan. "I have to go out for a while, Anna."

His wife looked up in concern. "So late?"

He reached for his hat and settled it on his head. "Yes, Anna, so late."

"You're going to buy Miss Cavanaugh's jewelry, aren't you?" his wife fretted.

"I'm going to do what I should have done this morning."

"Walter, I'm afraid. What if Herr Boothe finds out? He's an evil man. The devil himself hides when that man is near."

"Now, Anna, don't worry. It's dark outside. No one will see me go." He paused, and impulsively leaned down and kissed her cheek. "You are still a beautiful woman, Anna."

"Hush, Walter." Her plump cheeks turned pink with embarrassment, but he knew she was pleased by the compliment.

"I'll be back later," he said.

"Walter!" his wife called, scurrying after him. She grabbed his shoulders and kissed him hard. "Take care of yourself."

"Of course, Anna," he said, scoffing at her concern. "I'm a wise man, remember?"

Hitching up his ancient black buggy, Walter set the old horse at a comfortable trot heading west to Bellefleur. He felt relieved, now that he'd made a good decision. But as he drove up the long road to the Cavanaughs' house, a shadowy figure stepped out of the dark and ordered him to stop.

Walter pulled up on the reins, his heart thumping in fear. "Stand out of my way!" he cried with a courage he didn't feel.

"You shouldn't have come out here, Walter."

"My business is not with you!" He rose as the man stepped up to the buggy.

"I thought you understood, Walter."

The pawnshop owner turned to reach for his buggy whip, only to feel a thick rope around his throat. With a cry of fear, he turned to struggle with his captor, but the man was taller and stronger. "You're a devil!" he called in a hoarse whisper, struggling with fumbling fingers to keep the cord from cutting off his breath.

"Then that makes you a foolish man, Walter. For only foolish men go against the devil."

"I curse you!" the pawnshop owner cried with his last breath, clutching his killer's coat. "You will never win."

Walter's murderer released his hold on the rope and watched as the man's limp body slumped to the ground. "You still don't understand, do you, Walter? I always win."

As Claire drove through town early the next morning, she was hailed by Anna Greene. She pulled the horse and buggy to the side of the street as the short, stout woman scurried toward her, spots of bright red in her cheeks.

"Miss Cavanaugh, please, have you seen my husband?" she cried, wringing her hands.

"No, I haven't, Mrs. Greene," Claire replied, surprised by the question.

Anna looked back toward the shop, clearly in distress. "He told me he was going to see you last night." She turned back toward Claire, tears in her eyes. "Something has happened to him."

Claire was puzzled. "Why would he be coming to see me?"

"To buy the jewelry you tried to sell him yesterday. He told you he could not buy it and he was very upset all evening. Walter does not like to tell lies."

"He told me a lie?"

"He had to!" The poor woman wrung her hands and glanced uneasily over her shoulder before whispering, "Herr Boothe told him to lie!"

Claire pressed her lips together angrily.

"Please, don't think poorly of Walter!" Anna pleaded. "He is a good man, but Herr Boothe is our landlord. If we don't do as he says, we will be evicted. I tried to stop Walter from going last night, but he had to set things right for you."

"I wish I could help you, Mrs. Greene, but your husband never came to my house. I haven't seen him since yesterday morning."

"*Gott in Himmel!*" the woman moaned. "Something happened to him; I know it here." She clutched her hands to her chest. Catching sight of the sheriff coming up the street in his buggy, Anna gasped. She turned back to Claire, a frantic look on her face. "Say nothing about Mr. Boothe to anyone, please!" she begged Claire. "If something happened to Walter, then I am in danger, too." She clapped her hands to her face as though another idea had just occurred to her. "Miss Cavanaugh, *pass auf!* Watch yourself! You may also be in danger."

As Claire stared at her in stunned silence, Anna turned and waved her arms. "Sheriff, Sheriff!" she called.

Claire watched as Anna ran up to him. "Please, you must help me. Walter is gone. He didn't come home last night."

"Now, Miz Greene, calm down," the sheriff replied in a condescending voice. "He probably got drunk and spent the night in a barn."

"No," she said stubbornly, shaking her head, "he would not do that to me. Walter is a good man."

"Miz Greene, your husband is probably sleeping on a cot in the back of his shop. You run along and check. If he's not, I'll see what I can do to find him."

Anna started to argue. "Please, Sheriff, you must believe me—"

"Go home, Miz Greene," Simons told her sternly, "and wait for him to show up."

The poor woman stared at him for a long moment, then turned and started toward home, muttering to herself, her hands clasped in front of her as though she was praying. As she passed the buggy, she glanced at Claire and quickly put her finger to her lips as a reminder.

Claire was still shocked by her warning. She knew Reginald Boothe was capable of many things—but cold-blooded murder? Would he kill just to be able to foreclose on Bellefleur? She didn't think it was likely.

The sheriff walked toward her, smiling broadly. "Morning, Cee Cee. You're out bright and early this morning."

"Sheriff, I think you need to help Mrs. Greene look for her husband."

Seeing several ladies walking up the sidewalk toward them, Simons stepped close to the buggy. "Take my word for it," he said in a low voice, "this has happened before. They get into a little spat, he goes off, she frets, and then he comes back and they make up."

Remembering Anna's frantic plea, Claire studied him skeptically. "Are you sure?"

"Course I'm sure. Just let me handle this."

Claire shook her head uncertainly. "I certainly hope you're right about Mr. Greene."

"Where are you off to?" Simons asked in a friendly tone.

His nosiness was beginning to annoy her. "Mt. Vernon," she said, without elaborating.

"Is that a fact? I have to go there myself this morning."

Claire gathered the reins and looked down at him. "Then perhaps I'll see you there. Good day." With a flick of the reins, she guided the horse down the street.

Claire made the trip in two and a half hours and located Roger Simington at his feed and grain store with no trouble. He was a pleasant looking man in his fifties, with thick salt-and-pepper hair and a neat beard. She waited until he had a break in customers, then introduced herself. Simington was surprised to see her, and even more surprised at her reason for coming. He invited her back to the store room, where she opened the cases of jewelry.

"I've admired this emerald-and-diamond pendant for years," he admitted, lifting the necklace from its container. "I tried to buy it after your mother passed away, but your father wouldn't part with it. I know it must have had great sentimental value to him. I'm truly sorry you're being forced to sell it now."

"Saving my home means more to me than the jewelry does," Claire told him.

Simington examined the other pieces one by one as Claire crossed her fingers and said a quick, silent prayer. He was her last hope.

"How much do you want for them?"

Claire took the piece of paper with her calculations on them from her drawstring handbag, and showed him the total. "I can sell them all to you for this amount and no less."

She watched anxiously as Simington studied the figure, slowly stroking his beard. "That's a steep price."

"They're valuable pieces."

Claire held her breath and waited. After what seemed like an eternity, he looked up. "I'd like to help you out, but just I can't go that high."

Claire felt her knees grow weak. "Then would you make me another offer?"

He looked over the jewelry once more. "I can give you five hundred less."

Five hundred less! Though she would be able to pay off the mortgage, there would be nothing left over for expenses. But she didn't have a choice. "I'll take it."

"I won't be able to get to the bank until first thing tomorrow," he explained. "But I should be able to bring it to you by mid-morning. Is that all right?''

Claire sawed at her lower lip. That would be pushing it very close to the deadline. ''As long as I have time to get to the bank before closing tomorrow.''

Simington put an arm around her shoulders. ''I'll be there. And I'll even throw in a dozen bags of feed for your inconvenience. I'll load them up for you now.''

Claire felt as though a heavy weight had just been lifted from her shoulders. ''Thank you so much.''

''Thank *you*, Miss Cavanaugh. You're going to make my wife one very happy lady.''

Standing on the far side of his store, Roger Simington saw a large man walk in and look around. The man looked familiar, but Roger couldn't immediately place him. One of the clerks stepped forward to help him, then pointed in Roger's direction.

''Something I can do for you, mister?'' he asked, as the stranger approached.

The man extended a beefy hand. ''Sheriff Simons from Fortune.''

Roger remembered him then. Wilbur Simons—probably the most incompetent lawman he'd ever met. He also remembered that Arthur Cavanaugh had campaigned relentlessly to get him out of office, but had never succeeded. ''What can I do for you, Sheriff?''

Simons was studying him curiously. ''Didn't you used to live in Fortune?''

''A few years back.''

''I thought I saw a friend of mine come in. Claire Cavanaugh.''

Roger was instantly cautious. Why would he be looking for Claire in Mt. Vernon? ''She's been here and gone. Bought a few sacks of grain, I believe. I'm surprised you didn't run into her.''

Simons rubbed the back of his neck. "Guess I missed her."

As the sheriff strode out of the store, Simington made a mental note to tell Claire.

The rain fell in torrents as Tyler stood in the pilot house with the captain, watching as the *Lady Luck* docked at Fortune. He opened his pocketwatch to check the time and shook his head. Two in the afternoon and they had left that morning at eight o'clock. Because of the storm, they were behind schedule.

"Man overboard!" he heard one of the deckhands shout.

Tyler dashed down to the deck to where several of his men were gathered. One pointed into the water just beyond the boat, where Tyler could see what appeared to be a body wrapped in a wool blanket bobbing up and down with the current. He turned away, feeling his stomach heave. "Pull him in, boys," he said tersely. "Rob, you go tell the sheriff we've got a dead man out here."

His forehead beaded with cold sweat, Tyler walked back to his cabin, shut the door, sat down in his chair, and dropped his head into his hands. At a knock on the door he muttered, "Come in, Jonas."

His assistant walked in and sat across from him. "I hear we have a body on our hands."

Tyler couldn't reply. His mind was reeling, filled with images from the past, painful remembrances, flashes of another body floating in the water. He pressed the heels of his hands into his eye sockets to block out the pictures, but it didn't help. Pain knifed through him as sharply as it had that day fifteen years ago. He clenched his teeth, willing it away.

"Tyler, are you all right?"

He felt the hand on his shoulder and looked up, half expecting it to be his uncle, pulling him away from the edge of the dock. "I could use a drink," he said hoarsely.

In a minute, Jonas handed him a whiskey and he downed it. Leaning his head back, Tyler closed his eyes and pressed the cool glass to his forehead. "I thought they were all gone."

"Who?" Jonas asked.

"Not who—what. The memories."

"Care to tell me about them?"

It was a long moment before Tyler could reply. "My father drowned."

"I thought he'd abandoned you and your mum."

"He did. I only saw him once afterward, when he turned up dead—drowned and full of alcohol."

"Ah. Now I see."

"The man treated his horse better than he did people," Tyler said through clenched teeth. "He deserved to drown." Why, then, Tyler asked himself, was he so upset? What had his father ever done for him? He rose with a jerk, banged his glass on the table, and strode out of his cabin. He had a dead body on his hands. He might as well take care of it.

By the time the sheriff arrived, the rain had stopped. Simons walked down the dock to where Tyler's men had laid the blanket-draped body. Standing silently nearby, Tyler watched as Simons squatted beside the body and lifted a corner of the blanket. Less than a minute later, he dropped the blanket over the dead man's face and stood with a groan.

"Who is he?" Tyler asked.

"Walter Greene, the pawnshop owner," the sheriff replied. "Wife's been looking for him all day. He must've gotten drunk and walked straight into the river."

The undertaker arrived just then, and took a long sling from the back of his wagon. Tyler helped him lift the body onto the sling and load it into the back. As he did so, he sniffed, but he could detect no odor of alcohol. Tyler knew from experience that if the man had been drinking, it would be noticeable.

"I think you're wrong, Sheriff," he said. "This man wasn't drunk."

"Now, what else would make him walk into the river?" the sheriff asked with a scoff.

"How do you know he walked in?" Tyler asked.

Simons hitched up his pants. "I appreciate your help, McCane, but why don't you let me handle this?" He turned away to help the undertaker close the back of his wagon.

Jonas came to join Tyler. "What was that about?" his assistant asked.

Tyler nodded in the sheriff's direction as he rode away. "For a man with such a big body, he has a *very* small mind."

"Mr. McCane, sir?" one of Tyler's crew members called, hurrying over to him. "I forgot to show you this." The deck hand pulled a watch and fob out of his pocket and held it out. "I found it on the dead man's body. He had the watch clutched in his hand and the chain was wrapped around his wrist."

Tyler took the watch and examined it, then handed it back. "Donny, when you've finished here, take it to town and give it to the widow. Her husband owned the pawnshop. Someone in town can direct you to her house. I'm sure she'll appreciate having her husband's watch back."

As the deck hand returned to the boat, Tyler turned to Jonas. "I'm heading for the bank. Boothe and I are meeting to go over the architect's plans. You're welcome to come."

Jonas gave him a dark look. "No, thank you. I've made other arrangements."

Tyler didn't have to ask what they were. Jonas was off on another mercy visit to Emily. As he headed toward town, Tyler felt a melancholy settle over him. He and Jonas had been friends since he was seventeen years old, and in all that time they had never had a serious row. Now he feared they might end up going their separate ways over the Cavanaugh land.

The trip back to Fortune had been long and jarring and wet, but once she reached Bellefleur, Claire could not contain her excitement. She hopped out of the buggy, hitched the horse at the iron ring, and ran up the steps of the porch. "Mrs. Parks, Emily, where are you?"

"In here, Cee Cee," Emily replied from the kitchen.

"Mercy, dear," the housekeeper cried, hobbling down the hallway on her cane. "Whatever is the matter? Oh, gracious, you're wringing wet."

Claire met her halfway and gave her a hug. "We've done it, Mrs. Parks. We're not going to lose Bellefleur! I found Roger Simington this morning and he's agreed to help me. He'll bring the money tomorrow morning." Claire looked around as Emily made her way toward her.

"What happened, Cee Cee?"

Claire threw her arms around her sister and swung her around in glee. "I'm happy, Em! With Mr. Simington's help, we're going to keep our home."

"May I join in the congratulations?" Jonas asked, stepping into the hall from the kitchen.

Claire gave him a hug, too. "Yes, you may, Mr. Polk. This is a wonderful day, and tomorrow will be even better."

Jonas waited until Claire was alone to tell her about the pawnshop owner. "I hate to spoil your excitement, but I'm afraid I have some bad news." At Claire's startled look, he said, "Walter Greene's body was found this morning in the river."

The hairs on Claire's neck rose. Anna Greene had been right! Claire remembered her plaintive cry: *"Something has happened to him, I know it. Now I am in danger, too."*

Claire shivered, a feeling of foreboding creeping over her. "Do you know how he died?"

"Sorry, I can't help you there," Jonas admitted. "Tyler was talking to the sheriff about it, but I came into the conversation too late."

"This is dreadful!" Claire said. "Poor Anna. I'll have to go see her." She started upstairs to change out of her wet clothing, but slowed as she remembered Anna's words of warning: "*Watch yourself! You may also be in danger.*"

Claire shivered. Were Anna's fears correct? Had Reginald Boothe murdered Walter Greene because of her land? Were she and Anna both in danger? Claire was just about to run to her father's gun cabinet and take out a rifle when logic took over. Boothe wasn't going to murder her just so the foreclosure would go through. He hadn't built up his bank by killing people who got in the bank's way. He used money and intimidation to get what he wanted. Besides, when she paid off the mortgage tomorrow, she would be rid of him forever.

Nevertheless, she decided to stay safely at home until Roger arrived with the money. She would have to postpone her trip to see Anna until tomorrow.

"What do you think, McCane?"

Tyler looked up from the architect's plans toward Boothe, sitting across the table from him. They were seated in a small conference room on the second floor of the bank late that same afternoon. "I like them."

"We'll start next week." Reginald Boothe leaned back and lit a cigar. "I think we can safely say we're well on our way."

"When does the foreclosure take place?"

"The deadline is four o'clock tomorrow. That gives us—" Boothe reached for his watch, only to remember he'd misplaced it. "—Approximately twenty-four hours."

"And if Miss Cavanaugh comes up with the money?"

Boothe blew out cigar smoke in little puffs, as though chuckling. "She won't."

"Why didn't you just buy the land from the Cavanaughs to build your boat docks?"

"For three reasons," Boothe said, squinting over the smoke haze. "First, Cavanaugh wouldn't sell. Second, I hadn't found a partner I wanted to do business with. Then, when I knew the land would be going into foreclosure, it didn't make sense to pay an inflated price for property I could get for a song."

"We'll still have to bid on it."

"Naturally, but I've checked around. There won't be any other bidders. Trust me."

Tyler watched the banker blow a smoke ring. He was coming to realize he didn't much like Boothe's way of doing business, yet he had to trust his partner to get the job done. He pushed back his chair and stood. "Let me know when the work begins."

On his way down the second floor hallway, Tyler passed Sheriff Simons, who was so preoccupied he didn't even nod a greeting. Tyler paused at the top of the staircase as the sheriff charged into Boothe's office.

"Sorry I'm late, Mr. Boothe. Mrs. Greene was down at the office making a fuss about her husband's death. She keeps insisting that I investigate it."

Tyler shook his head. How in the world had Wilbur Simons come to be sheriff?

"What did you think she'd do?" he heard Boothe snap. "I trust you're doing all you can to convince her it was an accident?"

The sound of footsteps blocked the sheriff's reply, and then Boothe closed his office door. Tyler stood where he was, pondering their odd conversation, then he headed out and across the street to where the *Lady Luck* was moored. Before he reached the riverboat, he stopped and turned to look back at the bank, Boothe's words echoing in his head.

"I trust you're doing all you can to convince her it was an accident."

On a whim, he changed direction and headed for the undertaker's.

Reginald Boothe closed the door and sat down at his desk, his jaw clenched in anger. "I specifically told you to make sure the body didn't turn up. Now you're going to have to devise a damn good explanation for those marks on his neck."

"I don't like this," Simons said, shaking his head. "You didn't have to kill him."

"It seemed the best way at the time," Boothe said dismissively.

"But I don't know how I'm going to explain those marks."

Boothe glared at him. "Use your head, Sheriff. You're the law, for God's sake. Did you at least find out where Claire was headed this morning?"

"I tracked her all the way to Mt. Vernon, but all she did was buy some sacks of feed."

"That doesn't make much sense, does it?" Boothe asked testily. "She could have purchased grain here in town."

"I know it, Mr. Boothe, but I saw her leave with the feed. I talked to Roger Simington and he told me the same thing himself. And then she came straight back to Fortune. No stops."

"Roger Simington?" Boothe sat forward. "He's an old crony of Cavanaugh's, and quite well off, from what I've heard. I wonder why Claire went out to see him?"

"Maybe it was a social visit, since he was a friend of her pa's."

"More likely she asked him for money." Boothe's long fingers drummed the desk top. Claire Cavanaugh hadn't made that long trip for a few sacks of feed. "I suppose we won't know if she was successful unless she shows up today with the money." He slammed his fist on the desktop. "*Damn* it!"

Swivelling his chair, Boothe stared out the window in the direction of Bellefleur. Tomorrow was supposed to be his day of victory. He'd be damned if that little bitch would keep him from it. He reached for his watch to check the time and scowled as he remembered again that he'd lost it. He'd checked his carriage, his home, his office, even his mistress's home. Where in bloody hell could he have left it?

"Mr. Boothe?" the sheriff said hesitantly. "What do I do if Miz Greene keeps on making a fuss?"

"Thanks to your bungling, the only thing you can do at this point is to assure her you're looking into the matter." Boothe rose with a frown. "I've got to see about getting another watch. Is that all you wanted?"

"Yes, sir." Simons walked out of the bank muttering to himself, his stomach a mass of jelly. What his boss had done made him sick, but what could he do about it now? Arrest him? When he himself had disposed of the body? Legally, that was aiding and abetting a criminal. Shaking his head, the sheriff returned to his duties. He had no choice but to keep quiet and hope that no one ever found out.

Anna Greene opened the door of her small cottage to find a young man standing on her porch. "Yes, what is it?" she asked listlessly, her eyes swollen from weeping.

"I have something for you, Mrs. Greene," the young man told her, handing her a cloth-wrapped bundle.

Anna unwrapped the bundle and stared at the watch and chain inside. "Where did you get this?" she asked, suddenly alert.

The young man ducked his head sadly. "We found it on your husband's body, ma'am. It was in his hand. Mr.

McCane thought you'd want it back." He lifted his cap politely. "My condolences to you, Mrs. Greene."

"Thank you," Anna replied automatically. She shut the door and stared at the timepiece, one hand covering her mouth. "*Gott in Himmel*," she whispered. The unique gold pocketwatch had been made in England—an old, valuable piece that Walter had come across. On the decorative front, the letter "B" had been engraved. On the back was a hunting scene of two hounds standing over a felled buck. Walter had sold the watch only two months ago to Reginald Boothe, who had been fascinated by it, especially because of the engraved letter on it.

Now she knew positively that Boothe had murdered her husband. Anna looked around in alarm. What if he found out she had his watch? "What should I do, Walter?" she cried, clasping her hands together and gazing upward.

She heard his voice as clear as a bell. *Get out, Anna, before he murders you, too.*

"Something I can do for you?" the tall, slender white-haired man asked Tyler as he looked around the furniture shop called Gasoway's. Tyler recognized him as the man who had come out to collect Mr. Greene's body.

"Tyler McCane," he said, shaking the man's hand. "Are you Mr. Gasoway?"

"That's me."

"You're the undertaker?"

The man eyed him skeptically. "Didn't I see you down at the river this morning?"

"The *Lady Luck* is my boat. My crew discovered Mr. Greene's body." Tyler paused when a pair of women entered the shop, and stepped closer. "I'd like to see him."

Gasoway's eyes registered his surprise, but then he shook his head. "Sorry, son. Can't let you do that. It's being prepared for burial."

Tyler took out five dollars and tucked it in the man's vest pocket. "It won't take long."

Gasoway looked over at his customers. "I'll be right with you, ladies," he called out, then said quietly to Tyler, "Step through those curtains and take the steps down. I'll give you five minutes. And don't breathe a word to a soul that I let you in."

While Gasoway assisted the ladies, Tyler slipped through the curtain and down the stairs to a cold, dimly lit cellar. A sheet-draped body lay on a table in the center of the room. Tyler lifted the sheet to look, but at the sight of Walter Greene's white, bloated features, he had to turn his head away. Taking a deep breath, he tried again—and saw dark bruises ringing the man's throat. He dropped the sheet and stepped back.

Walter Greene had been strangled. Why was it being called an accident?

Chapter 9

When Tyler returned to the *Lady Luck*, Jonas was absent. Tyler had half a mind to go out to Bellefleur to fetch him, but he realized he was just looking for an excuse to see Claire again. Damn it, he couldn't get her out of his mind. He had relived her kisses all night and had awakened painfully aroused. He knew he could find some willing female in town who'd enjoy a good roll in the hay, but for some reason that didn't sound appealing at all—he'd only be thinking of Claire, anyway.

He strode out onto the deck as Jonas walked up the ramp.

"You look like a man with a lot on his mind," his assistant commented.

"Remember the body we found this morning?" Tyler asked, leaning on the rail.

"Ah, yes, the pawnbroker. Funny you should mention it. I wanted to talk to you about that very subject."

"On a hunch, I went to the undertaker's today," Tyler informed him. "Guess what I found? A ring of bruises around Mr. Greene's neck. He was strangled, Jonas."

"Bloody hell!"

Tyler ran his hands over the railing, feeling the smoothness of the wood. "I overheard Boothe tell the sheriff to convince Mrs. Greene it was an accident." He shook his head. "I don't like it. Simons saw the body; he should have noticed those bruises around Greene's throat."

"So either they're covering up a crime," Jonas said, "or the sheriff is incompetent."

"Regardless, wouldn't you think the undertaker would have mentioned it to someone?"

"One would hope."

"He didn't want me to see the body, then he warned me not to tell anyone that he'd let me, like he was afraid." Tyler turned to look at his assistant. "What the hell is going on?"

"I told you right off, Ty, that I didn't trust Boothe."

"I'd hate to think I misjudged my partner. Boothe is a respected businessman in this town. I can't imagine him doing anything so vile as to commit murder."

"I'm not sure I'd go so far as to accuse him of murder," Jonas cautioned. "I'm only saying that what you overheard sounds highly suspicious."

Tyler nodded. Maybe he was reading too much into the conversation he'd overheard. Perhaps he should give Boothe the benefit of the doubt. Nevertheless, it wouldn't hurt to pay the sheriff a visit.

Wilbur Simons reported to Boothe's office first thing the next morning. "You wanted to see me, Mr. Boothe?"

"Did you talk to Mrs. Greene?"

"No, sir," he said dejectedly. "She seems to have left town."

Boothe leaned back, his fingers laced over his vest. "What do you think that means?"

"Maybe she was grieving so bad she went to visit relatives or something."

Boothe pondered the matter a moment. "I hope that's the case—for both our sakes."

"We've got another problem," the sheriff told him. "McCane came to see me this morning. He was asking questions about Greene's death like he suspects something."

"What did you tell him?"

"I told him I'd already investigated, that Greene had gotten drunk and fell in the river. But McCane said he hadn't smelled any liquor on the body."

"The body was in the water all night. Of course it wouldn't smell like alcohol!"

"He wanted to know if I'd had a good look at the body. He said he saw marks around Walter's neck, like he'd been strangled."

Boothe leaned forward, his eyes narrowing. "When did he see Greene's body?"

The sheriff nervously shifted his weight from one foot to the other. "McCane's men found it. McCane was there when it was pulled to shore."

Boothe's long fingers curled like talons. "You really bungled this, Wilbur."

"I told you I didn't like the situation," the sheriff complained. "What did you expect me to do? I've never had to dispose of a body before!"

The banker simmered silently. Why was Tyler McCane so concerned about a man he didn't know? "How did you leave it with McCane?" he snapped.

Simons peered hesitantly from under his bushy brows. "I said I'd look into it some more."

"Let's hope that puts an end to it."

"Did Cee Cee make the payment?" the sheriff asked.

"No. But I'm not taking any chances. Keep a watch on Grand Avenue coming in from Mt. Vernon. Simington could be delivering the money to Claire in person."

The sheriff glanced at him uneasily. "What do you want me to do if I see him?"

"Take him to the jail and hold him."

"On what charge?"

"Use your head, Sheriff!" Boothe snarled. "I need him out of circulation until four o'clock, when the bank closes."

"What if McCane comes back asking more questions?"

Boothe reached for his cigar. "I guess we'd better have some answers."

For hours that morning Claire paced the hallway, glancing at the tall case clock on the wall. Eleven o'clock! Where was Roger Simington? She didn't want to think that something had happened to him, but the circumstances of Walter Greene's death still worried her.

Agitated, she stepped outside. The sky was cloudy, as though more rain was on the way. Much more would damage the crops, and that would mean disaster. Crossing the lawn, she saw a buggy coming up the road and she heaved a sigh of relief. But as the buggy drew closer, Claire saw that it was Tyler driving and not Roger Simington.

"Morning," he said with a friendly nod, pulling the buggy to a halt.

"Morning," she returned, blushing when his gaze moved appreciatively over her. "Did you pass anyone on River Road heading this way?"

"Didn't see a soul."

With a worried frown, Claire turned to gaze back up the road. "I don't understand it. Something must have happened to him."

"Who? Your fiancé?" Tyler said, in a clearly irritated voice.

Surprised by his tone, Claire swung around. His features seemed harder than usual, his expression almost angry. "A friend of my father's," she told him, and almost instantly he seemed to relax. Had he been worried, or was she just indulging in some wishful thinking? She started for the house. "I'd better hitch up the buggy and see if I can find him."

"I'll take you," Tyler offered.

"Thank you," Claire called, "but I couldn't put you out."

"You're not putting me out. Climb in."

He had a brown booted foot propped on the front of the buggy, his dark hair was ruffled by a warm breeze, and his gaze was fixed on her with that fierce intensity that made Claire's stomach jump with excitement. How could she refuse?

Tyler leaned over and offered Claire a hand into the buggy. He didn't know why he had volunteered to take her back to town. He had brought out the blueprints to review for last minute changes on his new house. Was he turning as soft as Jonas?

But when he glanced over at Claire and saw the dark circles of worry under her beautiful eyes, he felt damned good about helping her. Perhaps he had a conscience after all. Tyler rubbed the side of his jaw, unsure of how he felt about that.

"This is very kind of you," Claire said. "I know you must have other plans."

"Nothing that important. I'm having a house built on my land," he found himself telling her. "They're going to start construction next week."

She turned to look at him with some amazement. "I didn't know you were building a permanent home here."

Tyler shuddered inwardly. He didn't like the word "permanent." "A *winter* home," he explained. "Just a place to stay when the river is unnavigable. I'll show you the plans sometime." For some reason, he was suddenly eager to share them with her.

"You'll be living next door to me, then."

Guilt stabbed him hard. He wouldn't be living next door to her, because she wouldn't be there. As if Claire had realized her mistake, her smile faded and her eyes shifted to some point in the distance. Tyler knew she was thinking of the foreclosure, and for the first time he found himself wondering where she would go—though he couldn't ask without giving himself away. He dreaded the moment when she learned he was in partnership with Boothe.

Damn—why did he have to develop a conscience

now? And when had he let down his guard long enough
for Claire to slip inside? He tightened his grip on the reins.
If he wasn't careful, she'd wind herself around his heart
like a constrictor and destroy his plans. Then she'd slink
away as stealthily as she came, leaving his life in ruins.
He couldn't let that happen again.

They turned onto Grand Avenue, and Claire had him
drive north to the edge of town. He pulled the buggy off
to the side while she stood, shading her eyes with her hand,
staring up the empty road. She seemed to grow prettier
each time he saw her. Trim figure, curves in the right
places, pleasing profile, even temper, a woman any man
would be proud to call his wife—

"You can head back," Claire said with a sigh, sitting
down again. "I don't see him."

—*If* a man was in the market for a wife. Which he
wasn't. "Back to Bellefleur?"

"I suppose so. No—wait. Would you stop by the telegraph office?"

Back in town, Tyler parked the buggy on Grand and
came around to help Claire down.

"I'm going to wait here for the reply," she told him.
"I'll walk back."

The rational thing to do was to drive away, yet that
irrational part of him, which Claire seemed to bring out in
full force, didn't want to leave her. "I've got a better
idea," Tyler found himself saying. "The *Lady Luck* isn't
far. Have the reply delivered there. You can sit under the
canopy on the upper deck, have a lemonade, and watch
for your visitor."

Claire's brow wrinkled as she pondered his idea. He
clenched his jaw so hard that it ached, hoping she didn't
refuse.

"If you're sure it will be no trouble," she said.

"I wouldn't have offered if it were."

"Then I accept." She smiled at him as he handed her
down. The gratitude shining in her beautiful eyes made

him feel as though he could single-handedly slay a dragon for her. The only problem was that he was the dragon.

While Claire was in the telegraph office, Tyler leaned back in the buggy to observe the people passing by. It surprised him how good he felt about helping her. Of course, he fully expected to be rewarded for his help, and not just with grateful looks. But he had to admit that it would be real easy to get accustomed to feeling needed and being appreciated.

He began to whistle a tune he'd learned as a boy. He couldn't remember the last time he'd felt like whistling—and he certainly wasn't accomplishing what he'd set out to do that day. Yet when Claire settled beside him once more, Tyler clicked his tongue at the horse and began to whistle again.

Wilbur Simons watched from the doorway of the bank as Claire rode off with Tyler McCane. He didn't like seeing his Cee Cee with another man—especially that damned McCane. She was too sweet and gentle for his likes. If she kept it up, he'd have to speak to Boothe about it.

The sheriff crossed the street and walked into the telegraph office. "Ned, how're you doin' today?" he asked with a friendly nod.

"Just fine, till you walked in," the old man snapped.

"You got something for me?"

"No! I got something for Boothe." Ned Barry shoved Claire's telegram through the opening with a scoff of disgust.

"Thanks, Ned," Simons called as he left. He tucked the telegram in his pocket and headed for the bank, still bothered by the thought of Claire being with McCane. Was McCane sweet on her? Could his little Cee Cee be taken with that cur?

Still muttering to himself, he walked into Boothe's office and handed over the telegram. The banker read it and wadded it up with a muttered curse. "I knew it! She's expecting Simington. Go back to the telegraph office and wait for the reply. I want to see it before it goes out to her—*if* I let it go out."

When Wilbur Simons lumbered into the telegraph office for the second time that day, Ned Barry swore under his breath. "What do you want now?" he snarled.

"When a reply comes back for Claire, Mr. Boothe wants you to give it to me." The sheriff hitched up his pants over his belly. "Understand?"

Ned gave him a furious scowl. Ignoring his dirty look, the sheriff pulled a wooden stool up to the front window, leaned his back against the side wall, propped his feet on the window ledge, and folded his thick arms across his chest. In a matter of minutes, his eyes drifted shut. Ned went back to his work, keeping a watch on the sheriff. He'd be danged if he'd be a whipping boy for Boothe.

The telegraph machine clattered into life, waking the sheriff with a jerk.

"Don't worry," Ned said crossly, as he bent to his work. "It ain't the reply you're after."

Simons rubbed his eyes, adjusted his stool, and was soon snoring softly. Ned finished typing up the incoming telegram, then quietly let himself out the back door. He'd show Boothe and that fool sheriff a thing or two. Slipping around to the street, he motioned to the twelve-year-old boy who ran deliveries for him. "Billy, take this over to the *Lady Luck*," he said in a low voice, pointing toward the docks. "Give it to Claire Cavanaugh. If anyone stops you, don't tell who it's for, got it?" Shoving two coins in the boy's palm, Ned scurried around to the back of the office and let himself inside. The sheriff was still sleeping peacefully on the stool.

From the window, Ned could see down the docks to where the *Lady Luck* was moored. He watched Billy deliver the message and waited until he saw Claire leave, then he gave Simons's shoulder a hard shove. "Hey! Here's your danged telegram."

Simons looked confused for a moment, then took the envelope containing a copy of the original and left the shop.

Claire placed her chair at the rail on the upper deck so she could watch the street. She had a good view of approaching vehicles, but it did little to calm her nerves. She had wired Roger Simington's feed shop, hoping the reply would come back that he was on his way. He knew the bind she was in. She couldn't imagine anything preventing him from coming.

Unless, her frantic mind whispered, *someone tried to stop him.* Claire's heart began to race. What if Roger had been murdered? What if Reginald Boothe had killed him to prevent him from bringing her the money? Feeling the first signs of panic, she forced herself to take slow, deep breaths until it passed. She could not let her fears overcome her good sense. Boothe had no idea she had gone to see Roger, and he had even less of an idea that Roger was supposed to be on his way to Fortune to help her out. She just had to keep praying that Roger would show up soon.

Tyler came up onto the deck and walked toward her carrying two tall glasses. Claire accepted one with thanks and took a long, thirsty drink of lemonade as Tyler pulled a chair up beside hers.

"So who is this friend of your father's?"

"Roger Simington. He used to live here. Now he owns a store in Mt. Vernon."

As the church bells tolled the noon hour, Claire spotted the telegram delivery boy running up the dock. "There's my reply," she said, and hurried to the gangway to the lower deck. She met the boy at the ramp and tore open the envelope.

SEND TO: CLAIRE CAVANAUGH/BELLEFLEUR,
FORTUNE, INDIANA
SIMINGTON SHOULD HAVE ARRIVED BEFORE
10:00 A.M. STOP.
PLEASE ADVISE FURTHER NEWS. STOP.

Claire stared at the message. Roger should have arrived
two hours ago.

"What's the word?" Tyler asked, coming up behind
her.

"Something has gone wrong. Mr. Simington should
have been here long before now."

"Maybe his buggy broke down."

"I hope that's all it is." Claire shoved the wire in her
pocket. Roger could be anywhere between Fortune and Mt.
Vernon. She'd have to start looking for him at once. She
had to find him quickly. She had only four hours until the
bank closed.

"I have to leave," she said, starting toward the ramp.
"Thank you for all your help."

Seeing the panic in her eyes, Tyler's newly awakened
conscience gave him a sharp jab. "Claire!" he called,
striding after her. "Why don't we take a ride toward Mt.
Vernon and see if we can find out what happened?"

"I couldn't take advantage of you. It's not your concern."

He pulled her to a stop. "I'd really like to help."

She hesitated a moment, then gave a nod, her eyes warm
with gratitude. "You've done so much already. I don't
know how to thank you."

I know a very good way, Tyler thought. But that would
come later. He stopped to let Jonas know what was happening, then escorted Claire to the buggy.

Watching from the rail, Jonas pondered Claire's situation. There had to be a way to help. He couldn't sit idly

by while she and Emily lost their home. He cared too much about them. But if he helped them save Bellefleur, he would hurt Ty. What he needed was a way to help them all.

Claire was exactly the kind of woman Jonas had always wanted Ty to marry. If he could just convince Ty of that, then everyone's problems would be solved. Ty would have a wife, Claire and Emily would be taken care of, and Jonas would have peace of mind. Dilemma solved.

But first things first. They needed a place to go if the bank foreclosed.

Suddenly, an idea came to Jonas that was so simple he wondered why he hadn't thought of it sooner. He'd simply bring Claire, Emily, and Mrs. Parks onto the *Lady Luck*. He'd even give them his cabin. And if Ty didn't like it . . . Jonas considered the ramifications for a moment and finally shrugged. If Ty didn't like it, that was *his* problem.

Reginald Boothe's eyebrows lifted as he read the telegram from Mt. Vernon. "Well, well. What do you know? Something must have happened to Simington on his way to Fortune." He glanced at Simons with a sly grin. "Sheriff?"

"No, Mr. Boothe, I didn't do anything wrong," Simons was quick to reply.

Boothe scowled. Simons never did anything *right*, and what he did do had to be spelled out for him first. The man was becoming a liability and Boothe couldn't afford any more liabilities. Unfortunately, he still needed the sheriff—for a while. "Keep an eye out for Simington," he said, in an irritated voice. "Same instructions as before. If he comes into town, hold him at the jail until the bank closes."

"Should I take the telegram to Cee Cee?"

"Of course. She might get suspicious if she doesn't receive an answer. But why not wait a bit—say an hour or so, to see if Mr. Simington arrives first?''

The road was dry and dusty as Tyler and Claire traveled east toward Mt. Vernon. When he thought of all the things he should have been doing, Tyler had to grit his teeth in frustration. Yet he wasn't so much angry with himself for offering to help as he was dismayed by how easily Claire had made him care despite his best efforts.

Well, maybe not my best efforts. In fact, not caring was a whole lot harder than Tyler had imagined it would be. Never before had he had problems separating his need for a woman with his feelings for her. Usually there weren't any feelings to contend with. Now, just a glance at Claire made his heart turn over.

Damn it, he could *not* give into his feelings. Claire would only use them against him. His mother had certainly done a fine job of that, telling him how much she loved him and then leaving him with his uncle. She'd said she was doing it for his own good, and that she'd be back. And he'd been foolish enough to believe her.

Tyler could still see himself as that frightened five-year-old boy, clinging to her, begging her not to leave him with strangers.

"Please, Mama, please don't leave me here. I need you."

"You need someone who can give you a decent home. I can't do that."

"Don't you love me, Mama?" he'd sobbed.

"Sure I love you, Cutie. That's why I have to do this. But I'll come back and see you."

The lessons Tyler had learned had been long-lasting: don't trust women, and don't let yourself feel. If you use your head and not your heart, you won't have any pain.

He wanted Claire's land to accomplish his plans and he

wanted her body to satisfy his lust. There could be no more than that.

"It's too bad about Walter Greene," he commented.

"Yes, it is. I hope to pay his widow a visit this afternoon, after I—take care of some business at the bank." Claire glanced at the watch pinned to her bodice and her heart began to pound. It was almost one o'clock.

"Did you know the Greenes well?" Tyler asked.

"Not really." Claire nibbled her lip. Should she tell him about Anna's warning? Tyler had been so kind—perhaps talking to him would ease her fears. "I saw Mrs. Greene yesterday, after she discovered her husband's disappearance. She knew something happened to him, and now she thinks she's in danger, too." Claire paused. "She told me to be careful."

"Why would she say that?"

"Because Mr. Greene was on his way to see me when he disappeared."

"How would that put you in danger?"

"I had tried to sell him some jewelry, but he said he couldn't buy it. In truth, Reginald Boothe told him not to. Then Mr. Greene felt bad and wanted to set things right, but he never made it to Bellefleur." She leaned closer. "Boothe could have murdered Mr. Greene to stop him from buying the jewelry."

Tyler gave her a skeptical look. "Why were you selling jewelry?"

Claire felt a hot blush creep over her cheeks. "I'm having some difficulty meeting my mortgage payment."

A muscle in his jaw twitched. "You think Boothe would murder Greene to get Bellefleur?"

"It's no secret that Reginald Boothe hated my father, nor that he wants Bellefleur."

Recalling his earlier conversation with Jonas, Tyler frowned. He didn't like to hear that Claire had to sell off her jewelry to pay her bills or that she might be in danger. Still, he had to give Boothe the benefit of the doubt. "I doubt you're in any danger. Reginald Boothe is an astute businessman who wouldn't jeopardize either his reputation or his career. I'm sure Mrs. Greene will see things more rationally once the shock has worn off.''

Claire gazed at him for a moment, her eyes troubled. ''I hope you're right.''

So did Tyler.

They rode for an hour, past farms and through hilly forests, before he spotted the overturned buggy along the side of the road. As they approached, a man climbed up the grassy incline to the road and waved his arms. He was disheveled and dusty, but didn't appear injured.

''Hello,'' the man called, a look of relief on his face. ''A little help here?''

As soon as Tyler stopped the buggy, Claire climbed down and hurried toward him. ''Mr. Simington, are you all right?''

''Claire! I'm so sorry about the delay. My horse got spooked by a fox and tipped the buggy. I've been waiting over an hour for someone to come along.'' He stopped as Tyler walked over.

''This is Tyler McCane,'' Claire offered, ''a—friend of mine.''

''Glad to meet you, McCane. Can you give me a hand righting the buggy?''

The two men worked together to push the vehicle back upright. After checking to make sure it wasn't damaged, Simington took out his handkerchief to wipe his face and hands. ''Thanks for the help.''

''Can we give you a lift to Fortune?'' Tyler asked.

''I'd better wait here for my horse to come back.''

As Tyler walked to the buggy, Simington pulled a leather pouch out of his pocket and handed it to Claire. ''This is for you. I'll come out to pick up the jewelry in a few days. By the way, I thought you should know that after you left my store, Sheriff Simons came in looking for you. I didn't know what to make of it, so I told him you'd bought feed and left.''

Claire kissed his cheek. "Thank you so much. Are you sure we can't give you a ride?''

"No, but thanks for the offer. Good luck.''

Standing beside the buggy, Tyler handed Claire up, noting the look of relief on her face.

"I can't *tell* you how much I appreciate your help,'' she said gaily.

He hoped she *showed* her appreciation, as well. He deserved something for his trouble.

"Would you take me with you into town, please?''

Before Tyler could reply, she said, "You *were* going back to the *Lady Luck*, weren't you?'' He nodded.

"Oh, I'm so glad we found Mr. Simington,'' she bubbled. "I don't know what I would have done if we hadn't. Poor, dear man—all that trouble! I'll have to bake him something. If I didn't thank you before, Tyler, then I do now. You don't know *how* frightened I *was*. Do you realize you've come to our rescue once again? You truly are a hero, just like my father!''

Tyler gritted his teeth and kept driving. He'd found her father's friend and helped him right his buggy. If it meant so much to Claire, he wanted a kiss for it, not a damn knighthood.

"You've gone to so much trouble,'' Claire continued, seemingly oblivious to his testy mood. "I just don't know how to thank you.''

"You don't need to thank me,'' he replied. He meant exactly that, too. What he needed was a good, swift kick in the pants. His plan had been to seduce Claire, not to keep rescuing her. But his plan kept getting all twisted around, so that sometimes he wasn't sure what his motives were anymore. He was sure about one thing, however: he couldn't let her turn him into a hero. He was afraid he'd start to believe it. And the danger in believing it was that you then had to act it.

She put her hand on his arm. "I want to make it up to you."

At last! Tyler pulled up on the reins. It was about time she showed some *real* gratitude.

He turned toward her, his gaze targeting her lips, his manhood already thickening with desire. "How are you going to make it up to me?" he asked huskily.

Instead of falling into his arms, Claire stared at him with wide, amazed eyes. Her lips parted, as though silently mouthing the word, "Oh!" Drawing her hand back, as though his skin was suddenly too hot to touch, she blushed furiously and looked away. "I meant that I would invite you to dinner." She paused, and then asked nervously, "Why did you stop the buggy?"

Tyler felt his ears turn red hot. "I thought the horse was limping." He gave the reins an impatient flick. "I guess I was wrong." *About more than one thing*, he thought with a scowl. "What were you saying about dinner?"

"It won't be as fancy as the meals on your boat, but it will be the *best* home-cooked dinner you've ever had. Oh, it's so wonderful to be able to plan again!" Claire smoothed the pouch in her lap. "I can't wait to see the look on Reginald Boothe's face when I walk into that bank."

Tyler glanced at the pouch, then stiffened as a shock of comprehension ran through him.

Boothe was foreclosing today! Roger Simington's pouch must contain the money to stop the foreclosure.

And Tyler, unsuspectingly, had helped put the money right into Claire's hands.

His plans were in ruins.

All because he had let this woman into his life.

Chapter 10

The horse seemed to plod along at an agonizing pace. But maybe it was the racing of her heart that made everything else seem to move in slow motion. Claire wanted to hug the man sitting silently next to her, but he seemed very remote, as though he'd built a wall between them. She didn't take offense; she knew he must have his own concerns on his mind. All that mattered was she hadn't lost Bellefleur.

When they finally rounded the corner onto Grand, Claire could barely sit in her seat. At Grand and Main Street, she couldn't wait any longer. "I'll get out here. You needn't pull over." She turned with a grateful smile. "Thank you, Tyler. You have no idea what this means to me."

"Or to me," he muttered cryptically.

Claire started to press a kiss on his cheek, but Tyler turned at that exact moment, and their lips met. Electricity raced through her body, heightening her senses and obliterating the rest, until there was only the feel of his mouth, the taste of his kiss, and the rapid pounding of her heart. Claire abruptly drew back, staring into his hooded gaze. Tyler's eyes had darkened, reflecting her own desire.

Then the outside world intruded. People walked past, turning their heads to stare. Wheels clattered, horses neighed, and the church bell tolled the time: three forty-five. Still stunned by the encounter, Claire climbed down and hurried toward the bank. She paused at the door to look back, but Tyler had already driven away.

Spotting Charlie Dibkins sitting at his desk, she sailed across the lobby. "Charlie, I have to see Mr. Boothe. Is he in his office?"

He jumped to his feet. "Oh, no, you don't! I got into hot water last time I let you barge in."

"Please, Charlie, this is important! I know he'll see me."

"Then let me send a messenger upstairs—no, Claire, stop!"

Claire didn't have time for messages to be passed between floors. She hurried to the staircase, lifted her skirt and started up with Charlie close on her heels.

"Claire, please don't do this again. I'll be sacked for sure."

"Then go back to your desk, Charlie," she said over her shoulder. "Pretend you didn't see me."

At the door to Boothe's office, Claire looked back and saw that Charlie had taken her advice. Drawing a deep breath, she rapped sharply on the door.

"Who is it?" Boothe snarled. "I'm very busy."

"I promised you some money, Mr. Boothe." Claire marched across the room and slapped the leather pouch on his desk. "I keep my promises."

The look on Boothe's face was worth every bit of what she'd suffered the last four days. His thin lips all but disappeared into his face and his complexion turned an ugly red as he snatched up the pouch and pulled out the money. When he'd finished counting it, he slowly looked up, his slitted eyes glittering with malice. Claire shuddered at the hatred she saw there.

"Get out," he said, in a voice choked with rage. Claire backed away as he stood abruptly and started toward her. "You think you've won, don't you? But your troubles are just beginning. I'll see you and your sister and that old hag who lives with you out on the street yet!"

Claire was too stunned to reply. She turned and fled

from his office, her heart racing in terror. But once she was out on the street, her reason returned, and with it, a feeling of elation. Bellefleur was safe, at least for another year. She had beaten Reginald Boothe!

Boothe stared at the money in disbelief. With a roar of defeat, he swept every dollar of it off the desktop. That land should have been *his*. *His*, God damn it! But she had pulled it off, snatched victory from his hands.

Boothe's eyes narrowed as he watched Claire start down the sidewalk, her bearing that of a queen, reminding him so much of her mother. Marie Reneau had been dark-haired and slender, like Claire. And proud. Much too proud for a widow who needed money.

Boothe's fists tightened until his knuckles turned white. He had tried to humble Marie, tried to make her understand that he was the master and she his servant. But she had been the widow of a soldier, an *officer*, no less, and that had given her airs.

All Boothe had wanted from Marie was respectful sub-servience. She could have had anything she'd wanted, had she only given him the respect he'd demanded. Instead, she chose to flaunt her disrespect by running off and mar-rying Arthur Cavanaugh. Boothe always imagined how she and Arthur must have laughed about their triumph over him.

Now Marie's daughter was laughing at him. Boothe reached for his cigar case. It was quite apparent that stronger measures would be necessary to get what he wanted. He would have Bellefleur. It wasn't a financial matter anymore: it was revenge.

"Mrs. Greene?" Claire called, knocking on the door of the tidy cottage. Cupping her hands, she peered through the front window. "Mrs. Greene?" She rapped on the pane.

Deciding the woman must have gone to the pawnshop to start packing up the merchandise, Claire walked back to town, where she found the door to the shop standing open. When she peered inside, one of a group of workers noticed her and came over.

"Something I can do for you, little lady?" he asked, looking her over appreciatively. He smiled, revealing rotten teeth.

"I'm looking for Mrs. Greene. Has she sold the shop?"

"Don't know a thing about that. We was told to empty the place, is all I know. 'Course, if you'd care to share a mug with me tonight down at the Dockside Tavern," he said, reaching out to stroke a finger down the side of her face, "I might be able to find out something more for you."

Claire pushed his hand away and lifted her chin. "No, thank you." She marched out to his guffaws. Someone would know where Mrs. Greene was. She couldn't have just disappeared.

Tyler sat alone in the dark in his cabin on the *Lady Luck*, listening to the soothing lap of water against the side of his boat. His emotions were so tangled he felt dazed. He had been deceived. But who was there to blame? He had offered to help Claire; she hadn't asked. So she hadn't owed him an explanation.

Was he to blame Simington for helping Claire? How was the man to know that her salvation would be Tyler's downfall?

He supposed he had no one to blame but himself. He had been weak. He'd allowed himself to be distracted from his plans. Tyler raked his hand through his hair, digging his fingers into his scalp, wanting to feel something, anything. He had been so close to achieving his ultimate goal that he'd tasted it, smelled it, dreamed of it nightly. Now his goal had slipped away. The irony was that he'd provided the grease.

Closing his eyes, Tyler leaned his head against the back of the chair. Owning the *Lady Luck* wasn't enough for him. He needed an empire, for only something that big could fill the enormous hole inside him.

His head came forward with a jerk. He knew *exactly* who was to blame for this mess: Reginald Boothe. He had lied from the beginning about that land. It made Tyler wonder what else Boothe had lied about. Did he even have the money to buy more boats and build shops, or had he lied about that, too?

Tyler pushed out of his chair and strode to the door. It was time for a confrontation.

From her seat at the head of the dining room table, Claire contentedly surveyed the people around her. Everyone was in a joyous mood. Their home was safe. And only Claire understood how very close they had come to losing it.

As a treat for their celebration meal, Jonas had stopped at the butcher shop and bought a smoked ham, which they had polished off in short order. Claire had hoped Tyler would be able to join in their celebration, but Jonas hadn't been able to find him. For some reason, his absence took away some of Claire's joy.

Her happiness was further dimmed by the burden of knowing she had to come up with more money quickly. She couldn't depend on Jonas to keep them supplied with food until the tobacco was sold, and that wouldn't be harvested for at least six more weeks—so she would have to find a source of income until that time. Plus, she still had to pay Ben and the others their back pay, not to mention what she would need to keep them on through the harvest. And then there was next year's mortgage payment to worry about.

"Would you like some more bread?" Jonas asked Emily.

"I'd rather have pickled toads, if you don't mind," Emily replied.

"Would you like biscuits or crackers with that?"

At their silly banter, Claire laughed out loud. She was immensely grateful for Jonas's help, and Emily had found a friend she could trust. Claire knew Emily's trust wasn't won easily. She had certainly given Lance a hard time when he'd visited last summer.

At the thought of Lance, Claire's smile faded. Where was the letter he had promised? She had already sent him two since she'd received his telegram. Had he forgotten her? She'd write him again that very evening to share her good news. Surely that would prompt a note.

And thank goodness she had good news to tell him! Now they could begin to plan again, and hopefully, be married in the fall. Then she and Lance could work together to run the estate.

Claire glanced around the elegant dining room, remembering how proud her father had been of his house. Would Lance feel the same? Would he work hard to make Bellefleur profitable? Lance was charming and fun to be with, but did he have the drive, the ambition, and the fortitude necessary to run an estate?

With a frown, Claire pushed her fears aside. She was sure Lance would write soon and explain everything. And then she would feel silly for doubting him.

What a shame that only the three of them lived in such a big, elegant home. Bellefleur needed the warmth of people to bring it to life. Claire picked up her spoon to admire the delicate pattern on the handle. Her father had spared no expense to furnish the house. Why, there had to be at least twenty-four place settings—enough for a whole houseful of guests.

Claire's fingers suddenly tightened on the silver handle. Why hadn't she thought of it before? There were certainly enough empty rooms available—she could take in boarders!

She looked up when Mrs. Parks scooted back her chair and rose shakily, reaching for her cane. Jonas was quick to assist her.

"I'm sorry, my dears, but I'm feeling very tired," the housekeeper explained.

Claire, too, rose from her chair, alarmed by the woman's drawn features. "Can I bring you anything? A cup of tea?"

"Tea would be nice, dear."

"I'll see her to her room," Jonas offered.

When they had left, Emily reached for Claire's hand. "What's wrong with her, Cee Cee?"

"I don't know. She's very pale," Claire admitted.

"I hear her sighing all the time," Emily said, "like she can't catch her breath."

"I'll have the doctor check on her tomorrow." Claire gave Emily's hand a reassuring pat, though she felt far from reassured herself. "We'll take care of her, Em. Don't worry."

"I don't want her to die, Cee Cee."

Claire glanced at her sister. Her head was bowed and tears trickled down her small face. Claire wrapped her arms around Emily and held her close. "I don't think she's going to die, Em. I think she's just very weak. But we'll put her in our prayers and hope for the best."

When Jonas returned, Claire made tea and took it upstairs.

The housekeeper's room was in the far corner of the attic, made bright with rows of dormers for light and ventilation. The third floor had been divided into four large rooms, two on each side of the hallway. Mrs. Parks had occupied her room for as long as Claire had been there.

Colorful throw rugs on the wooden floor, crocheted doilies on the tables, a warm lap robe draped over the back of an old rocking chair, and an inviting patchwork quilt on the small bed all brought back wonderful memories. How many times had she sat on that bed watching Mrs. Parks wind her hair in curl papers at night? How many times had their housekeeper soothed her fears, rocking her in that very rocker?

Mrs. Parks was lying on her bed, propped up by pillows. She smiled as Claire sat down beside her and handed her the cup. "Thank you, dear. You've always been such a sweet child."

"I was just remembering how I used to come up here when I was frightened," Claire said. "I always felt safe up here. You made me feel safe."

Mrs. Parks reached out a trembling hand and put it over Claire's. "Such a timid little thing you were. Afraid of your own shadow. When you first came to us, you wouldn't let your father get near you. Of course, he wasn't your father then, so who could blame you for being hesitant? But how you carried on when he tried to comfort you." The housekeeper stroked Claire's cheek. "He told me once he was afraid that you would never get over your fear of him."

"I don't remember that."

"Oh, my, and how you'd tremble and then turn heel and run when one of the farmhands came around. We'd usually find you hiding under the dining room table. It took years for you to get over that fear."

Claire heard Mrs. Parks draw in a shaky breath as she pressed a hand to her chest. "Are you in pain?" Claire asked in alarm.

"It just seems these days I can't catch my breath. And sometimes I get so weak that I can barely stand."

"I'm going to send for the doctor first thing tomorrow," Claire told her.

The housekeeper set her tea on the round table beside her bed. "I'm getting along in years, Claire. Maybe it's my time."

"No, it's not," Claire said instantly, blinking back tears. "We'll get you fixed up, I promise."

Mrs. Parks patted Claire's hand. "Whatever happens, you'll be fine, dear. I didn't know your real father, but your mama told me how courageous he was. She used to say how much you reminded her of him—not just in looks, but in strength of spirit."

"I remember Mama telling me I took after my father," Claire said.

"Yes, dear, you were fortunate. You had two wonderful fathers. But then, Emily was fortunate, too. I can't even imagine what would have happened if Arthur hadn't taken your mama in. How would she have cared for an infant?" The housekeeper's eyes drifted shut. "Your poor mama," Mrs. Parks said wearily. "How she suffered because of that man . . ."

Seeing that she had fallen asleep, Claire tiptoed out. She'd forgotten that Mrs. Parks knew about Emily's parentage. But of course she would: she had been there when Emily was born. As far as Claire knew, Mrs. Parks was the only person, other than herself, to know the truth about Emily.

"Is she better?" Emily asked, when Claire returned.

Claire put her arm around her sister's shoulders. "She's sleeping peacefully. But I'll have the doctor take a look at her anyway."

"First thing after breakfast tomorrow morning, I'm going to go upstairs and read to her," Emily said. "She likes it when I read to her." Emily found the Braille book she always kept close by and left the kitchen.

"Poor little tyke," Jonas mused, handing Claire a clean plate. "It'll be hard on her if something happens to Mrs. Parks."

"I'm not going to think like that," Claire told him firmly. "I'm going to concentrate on good things. In fact, I've thought of a way to make money, and I'd like your advice."

"I'd be honored."

"I've been thinking about renting out rooms."

"Would you offer meals, too?"

"I'd like to. Of course, that would mean hiring a cook and a housekeeper." She paused to look at him. "What do you think?"

Jonas pursed his lips. "I think," he said, "that I'd like to be your first boarder."

Claire stared at him in amazement. "You would?"

"A man gets tired of having his bed sway beneath him. What a pleasure it would be to lie still at night."

"Do you think my idea will work?"

"Don't see why not. The inn in town is always full. You've got a lovely home and grounds, and it's not that far from town. I'd say you have a first-rate idea."

Claire beamed. "I'll stop by the telegraph office tomorrow to put out the word about more help."

"I'll see what I can do, too," Jonas promised. Somehow, he had to get Tyler and Claire together to get her out of this financial bind. It just wasn't right, having to take in strangers.

Tyler tried the heavy door to the bank but found it locked. "Damn!" he swore, then looked up and down the street. A block away, he saw Boothe getting into his fancy landau. "Boothe!" he called out sharply.

Boothe swivelled around. "Wait just a moment," he told his driver.

Tyler waited for two vehicles to pass, then crossed the street and strode rapidly toward the carriage, anger simmering inside him like a pot ready to boil. He opened the door and climbed inside, sitting on the bench opposite the banker. "I need to talk to you."

"We'll have to meet another time, I'm afraid. I have an appointment to keep right now."

Tyler clenched his jaw. "Unless it's with God, your appointment will have to wait."

Boothe lifted an eyebrow. "Rather than take offense by that remark, I'll assume your ill temper is due to the most recent hitch in our plans."

"No, no," Tyler countered. "A hitch is a *temporary* situation."

"My point exactly. This is merely a minor roadblock."

"How about a major breach of trust? You lied to me from the beginning about that land."

"Not true," the banker retorted. "I *had* that land right here," he said, tapping the center of his palm. "There was no way Claire could come up with that much money."

"But she did, didn't she?" Tyler ground out. "*Now* what have we got? Nothing!"

"You're wrong there. I've got builders lined up, supplies ordered. I've even contacted a shipyard about building more boats."

"But you don't have the land, damn it! You *assured* me you would."

"Look here, McCane. I've handled hundreds of foreclosures over the years. I know how they work. Sometimes people manage to pay off the bank, but then they're strapped. They have no money to pay for food, supplies, or help. Perhaps they struggle for a while, but eventually they have to give up the fight. Trust me. It may take another month or two, but I'll *get* the land."

Tyler couldn't help but remember how excited Claire had been when she'd received Simington's money. Plotting to take away her home now left a very bad taste in his mouth. "Find another property," he said. "I don't want to use the Cavanaugh land anymore."

Boothe's features hardened. "You don't understand how valuable that land is, McCane. Believe me, I've done my research. Everything about it is perfect—size, location, topography, access to roads and town. And you've already got the plans for your house. Are you prepared to give that up to move miles up river, *if* I can find something else?''

Tyler's common sense battled with his conscience. He knew Boothe was right about the land. Damn it! Why did Claire have to be so stubborn? Why couldn't she just sell Bellefleur and move into something she could afford? It would certainly solve problems on both sides. He rubbed his jaw. Maybe he could convince her it would be the best thing to do. It was time he took matters into his own hands.

''I'm willing to wait another thirty days to see what happens,'' he told Boothe. ''If nothing is resolved in that time, I'm going to dissolve the partnership.''

By the flinty look in Boothe's eye, Tyler knew the banker was far from ready to admit defeat and very close to anger. Yet he exhibited none of his ire when he began speaking.

''I think you're being far too hasty,'' Boothe responded in a matter-of-fact voice. ''As I've told you all along, that property *will be mine*. But if that's your intent, I suppose I have no choice but to abide by it.''

''That's my intent.'' Tyler stepped down from the carriage and closed the door. ''Keep me informed.'' He strode across the street without looking back.

''Drive,'' Boothe ordered. He sat rigidly still as the vehicle moved away, his mind working furtively. Because of that Cavanaugh bitch, McCane didn't trust him. Now he had just thirty days to get the land or lose everything he had worked so hard for—and he would never allow that to happen.

He needed a way to force Claire into vacating Bellefleur, something that would impress upon her the importance of leaving—if not for her own sake, then for her sister's. The fact that his blood ran in the child's veins made no difference to him.

The driver stopped in front of a small cottage a safe distance from town. As Boothe stepped down, the front door opened and Daphne Duprey came out. But even the sight of his mistress's lush body failed to dull his rage. If there had been any way to obtain a gambling license on his own, he'd drop Tyler McCane instantly. Unfortunately, even with all his financial resources, he hadn't been able to buy one. He'd made too many enemies.

But that was a small price to pay for great wealth. In the end, he'd win anyway.

"Cee Cee," Emily said, making her way into Claire's room later that night, "Simple Simon brought a telegram for you this afternoon." She held it out sheepishly. "I forgot about it."

Claire read it, puzzled. It was the same telegram she had received in town. "That's odd."

"What does it say?" Emily asked.

"That Mr. Simington was supposed to be here by ten o'clock." Claire frowned. "I don't understand why Mr. Barry sent this message twice."

"That's easy. Simple Simon just wanted an excuse to come see you."

"How did he know I was waiting for a reply?"

"That's easy, too. He's spying on you."

Claire huffed in exasperation. "All right, Miss Know-It-All, tell me why Mr. Barry gave him a wire I'd already received."

Emily pondered the matter briefly. "I have it! To send you a secret message that the sheriff is a spy."

"You certainly don't lack for imagination, Em."

Yet, as far-fetched as it sounded, what if Emily's guess was right? Ned Barry was extremely efficient. He wouldn't have sent that message twice unless he had a very good reason to do so. But why would the sheriff want to spy on her?

She knew one way to find out.

At the telegraph office the next morning, Claire posted her new help-wanted notice, then turned to Ned Barry with a smile. "The oddest thing happened yesterday. I received a telegram while I was here in town, and then the sheriff brought me the same message later in the afternoon.''

He eyed her warily. ''What's your question?''

''Why did I receive it twice?''

With a shrug, Barry turned and went back to his work table. ''I didn't know you did.''

''But you must have printed it out twice.''

''I don't remember doing it, but it could've happened, I s'pose.''

Claire waited for him to elaborate, but he seemed absorbed in a newspaper. She couldn't imagine Ned Barry having any reason to lie to her, so she had to assume he was simply growing forgetful. ''Did you see that the pawnshop is being closed down?'' she asked.

''Yep. Too bad about that,'' Barry replied noncommitally.

''Have you heard if Mrs. Greene has sold the shop to someone else?''

''Haven't seen or heard from her since the day Greene died.''

Claire found his lack of concern puzzling. Ned Barry had always gotten along well with Walter. For years, she had seen them eating lunch together across the street by the docks. ''I stopped by to visit Mrs. Greene yesterday,'' Claire told him. ''I wanted to offer my condolences, but she wasn't there.''

''Too late for that,'' he said without looking up. ''She's gone.''

''Gone where?''

Barry shrugged. ''I don't ask those kinds of questions.''

''Well, I do,'' Claire retorted, peeved by his uncaring manner. ''Someone in town has to know something about her.''

The telegraph operator put down his pencil and came over to the cage. ''I wouldn't go nosing around, if I were you,'' he said in a low voice. ''Some folks will get mighty testy if you do.''

"Mr. Greene was a kind man. Everyone liked him," Claire retorted, as the doorbell tinkled. "Who would be upset if I asked after his widow?"

Ned Barry lifted his head and scowled at someone over Claire's shoulder. "Sheriff Simons," he spat out.

Claire turned with a jerk as the sheriff walked up behind her. She glanced back at Ned, who was watching the sheriff with a baleful eye. Had Ned answered her question, or was he just greeting the sheriff?

"Morning, Ned," Simons said with a stiff nod. "Morning, Cee Cee. I saw you in the window as I passed and thought I'd stop to see how you were doing."

"I'm doing well, thank you," Claire said. Thinking back to Emily's remarks on the sheriff's behavior, she had to admit that he did seem to turn up at the telegraph office whenever she was there. And he'd followed her to Roger Simington's. Whatever the reason behind it, his behavior was becoming worrisome.

"Thank you for your help, Mr. Barry," Claire said, and left the office. She was dismayed to find the sheriff right on her heels.

"Can I buy you a glass of iced tea at the hotel?" he asked hopefully.

"Actually, Sheriff, I'm looking for Mrs. Greene so I can offer my condolences."

"That's mighty kind-hearted of you, Cee Cee, but Mrs. Greene left town after her husband's accident."

"Do you know where she went?"

"It appears she didn't tell anyone." Simons shrugged his thick shoulders. "Maybe she went back to Germany."

"Without waiting for her shop to be sold? That's very odd."

"They were odd people," the sheriff replied, rubbing his full moustache. "Don't concern yourself with them. So what do you think about that glass of tea?"

"Perhaps another time," Claire told him. Another *lifetime*.

* * *

Watching Wilbur Simons talk to Claire outside the office, Ned Barry snickered when he saw Claire turn and sashay down the street alone. A minute later, however, he scowled when the sheriff opened the door to the telegraph office and stepped back inside. He was mighty sick of the sheriff giving him orders, and he was especially sick of who those orders came from. But as long as Reginald Boothe owned the building, he had to be careful.

"What did you tell her, Ned?" the sheriff demanded.

"Tell who what?" the telegraph operator snapped peevishly.

"You know who. Claire Cavanaugh. She thanked you for helping her. I want to know how you helped her."

"Aw, it ain't nothing that concerns you. She's takin' in boarders and needs to hire a cook and a housekeeper, if it's any of your beeswax."

"You sure that's all?"

"I ain't gonna do or say nothin' stupid, Sheriff."

"You'd better not, Ned. Mr. Boothe wouldn't like it one bit." Hitching his pants up over his belly, the sheriff sauntered out.

Ned Barry watched him go, then spit in his brass spittoon in disgust. "You're the one who's gonna do somethin' stupid, Sheriff. Then you're gonna see how Mr. Boothe likes that!"

After the *Lady Luck* finished its last trip of the day, Tyler retreated to his cabin to take care of his ledgers. When he'd finished, he checked the time, then looked up with a frown. Where was Jonas? They always met at eight o'clock to have their customary nightcap.

"Sorry I'm tardy," his assistant said with a guilty grin, as he stepped inside the cabin. He didn't offer a reason and Tyler didn't ask for one. He knew where Jonas had been.

His assistant went straight to the built-in sideboard where Tyler kept the whiskey decanter and tumblers, poured them each half a glass, and handed one to Tyler.

"I'd like to make a toast," Jonas offered. "To the future." He touched his rim to Tyler's.

"Let's hope it's better than the present," Tyler added sourly. "I suppose you know Claire stopped the foreclosure."

Jonas reddened as he settled in a chair. "Yes," he said. "I know."

"So you helped them celebrate," Tyler said peevishly. "But why wouldn't you? *Your* plans weren't destroyed."

"I hope you understand how very awkward this situation is for me, Ty."

"You put yourself in that situation, Jonas. You knew what my plans were before we arrived in Fortune."

"But then I didn't know the people involved."

"I tried to warn you," Tyler reminded him, "but as usual, you ignored my advice."

"Can you honestly say you're sorry Claire was able to keep her home?"

Tyler didn't want to answer that. He was too irritated to be honest. "Boothe hasn't given up on getting that land, you know. He says Claire won't be able to earn enough to run it. He's seen this kind of thing happen before."

"And just what kind of 'thing' is that?" Jonas asked. "A young lady trying to hold onto her home?"

Tyler gave him a scowl. "If you really want to help Claire, then help me convince her to sell while she can still make a profit."

"Sell to whom? Reginald Boothe?" Jonas sniffed in disgust. "She detests the blackguard."

"It doesn't have to be Boothe."

"Even if there was someone in the area with enough

money to buy Bellefleur, do you honestly think Boothe would let anyone outbid him?''

Tyler was silent.

Jonas swirled the contents of his glass. ''You may be interested to know that Claire has devised a plan to make money. She's going to take in boarders until she can get back on her feet.''

Tyler scoffed. ''Boarders? In that grand old home?''

''It's no different than turning the house into an inn,'' Jonas reminded him. ''Anyway, I think it's a bloody shame. Imagine all the work involved, not to mention putting up with the demands of the men who will want to room there.'' He paused to take a sip of whiskey. ''Claire is quite comely, after all.''

Tyler frowned, picturing Claire being pursued by drooling, lustful men. ''It's a foolhardy idea. She should just sell the estate and be done with it.''

Jonas shook his head. ''She's too attached, almost obsessively so.''

Tyler ran a fingertip around the rim of his glass as he thought over what Jonas had told him. Convincing Claire to sell was going to be harder than he thought.

''Of course, there is another solution,'' Jonas said, ''and one I believe would solve your problems, as well as hers.''

Tyler eyed him skeptically. ''I'm waiting.''

Jonas set his glass aside and looked straight at Tyler. ''Marry Claire.''

Chapter 11

"Marry Claire?" Tyler almost choked on his drink. "Other than putting me in debt, ruining my partnership with Boothe, shackling me to a wife, and spoiling *her* life in the process, what the hell would that solve?"

"You're looking at it all wrong, Ty." Jonas sat forward on his chair, his eyes twinkling. "In the first place, as Claire's husband, you'd be able to put the land to its best use. Second, Boothe would have no reason to continue harassing her; you'd already have the land. Third, you wouldn't be shackled if you made the marriage a business arrangement. In fact, you'd be free to come and go as you pleased. And last but not least, with your financial aid, Claire, Emily, and Mrs. Parks would get to live in their house. That would make them very happy indeed."

Tyler drummed his fingers on the glass. Jonas's reasoning was sound. If Claire was dead set on keeping Belle-fleur, he could think of only two sure ways, other than by natural disaster, that anyone would ever gain control of her land: either through marriage or death—which, in Tyler's eyes, were one and the same. But as a business arrangement, a marriage with Claire might just be tolerable. In fact, the more he thought about it, the more the idea made sense.

Jonas eyed Tyler as he swirled the liquid in his tumbler. "There is one hitch, however. Claire is still engaged."

"You know my philosophy on hitches, Jonas." Tyler folded his arms behind his head and leaned back against the chair. "So *if* I decide to take your suggestion, an absentee fiancé won't stop me."

"Nothing stops Tyler McCane!" Jonas said, smacking his fist against an open palm.

Tyler grinned, catching his enthusiasm. "Nothing!"

"And you do love a challenge, don't you?"

"I do indeed!"

"Then I say, go after her, lad! If anyone can win her over, it's you!"

"You're right!"

With a triumphant gleam in his eye, Jonas drained his glass and rose, leaving Tyler with the distinct feeling Jonas had maneuvered him into a corner.

"You're turning in so soon?" Tyler asked in surprise.

"No, actually, I've got to pack."

"Pack? Are you going on a trip?"

"I'm moving in with Claire and Emily. I'm their first boarder."

Tyler was dumbfounded. "What about your cabin? What about our nightcaps?"

"I thought it would be pleasant to sleep in a house for a change. And you're quite welcome to come to Bellefleur for a nightcap. I'm sure the other boarders will be gathering in the parlor in the evening to enjoy Claire's company." Jonas smiled innocently.

Tyler couldn't believe his ears. Jonas, his assistant, his right hand, his best friend, was leaving him? Who would he discuss the day's business with? Who would help him make plans for his empire?

"I'm not moving across country," Jonas went on. "I'll still make the daily runs upriver and back. I just won't be here in the evenings. But like I said, you can come to Bellefleur anytime."

"It won't be the same."

"Change is good for us. As my clever mum used to say

to my dad, 'You may be on the right track, dearie, but if you don't start moving, you're going to get run over.' "
Jonas shrugged. "Well, I'll be off now. Have a good night. See you in the morning." Touching his finger to his temple in salute, he sauntered away.

Tyler stared at the empty doorway. Had Jonas been putting him on? He could never be sure. As he finished his whiskey, he noticed Jonas had left his glass sitting on the table. Tyler set his own glass down with a bang. *So that's how it's going to be, is it?*

He couldn't believe Jonas had deserted him to live at Claire's. Neither could he believe Claire had decided to run a boarding house in her home. If she was willing to take in boarders, she would do about anything to keep Bellefleur.

Tyler suddenly had a mental picture of Claire playing hostess to a passel of renters, some of them men hungering for a beautiful, available woman. His nostrils flared as the green-eyed monster struck. He wondered if Claire's fiancé knew about the situation. Tyler knew *he* certainly wouldn't like what Claire was doing if she were *his* intended.

Tyler's blood began to boil. And why had Rancid Lanced left Claire in the lurch? What kind of man was he? And why the hell was Claire so enamored of him, when he seemed so indifferent to her problems? Realizing that he was clenching his jaw and tightening his fists as though he was about to throw a punch, Tyler forced his body to relax.

Should he seriously consider Jonas's suggestion and marry Claire? Or should he leave Claire to struggle until she collapsed under the sheer weight of her responsibilities?

Tyler pondered as he stripped off his shirt and pants. Turning down the wick of his lamp, he lay down on the bunk and crossed his arms behind his head. If he decided to follow through on Jonas's idea, then it might be beneficial to rent a room for himself at Claire's. That way he'd also be able to prevent any wayward male boarders from harassing her. Tyler smiled in the dark, imagining how grateful she'd be. And he'd be around all night to accept her gratitude. *All night, every night, till death do us part.*

With a shudder, Tyler sat up and went to the commode to splash water on his face. He'd had a long day. His thinking was irrational. He'd see things differently after a good night's sleep.

The next day passed in a hectic whirl for Claire. She started at dawn in the kitchen, giving every surface a good scrubbing. By noon she had worked her way through the back parlor, the dining room, the front parlor, and the front hallway. Standing back to survey the results of her labors, she smiled. Finally, the house was beginning to show its former beauty.

Dr. Jenkins arrived just as Claire and Emily were finishing their noon meal.

"Good to see you, Claire," he said, shaking her hand. Samuel Jenkins, a tall, strapping man in his late thirties, looked more like a woodcutter than a healer. He wore plaid shirts with black suspenders and pants and a heavy black beard, and had red cheeks and a bass voice. His father, Henry Jenkins, had been the town physician for forty years until his death.

After showing the doctor to Mrs. Parks' room, Claire sat at the kitchen table polishing a pair of tall, brass candlesticks from the mantelpiece in the parlor. Emily sat across from her, her small fingers moving carefully across the pages of her book. Both waited anxiously for the doctor to finish his exam.

At the sound of footsteps on the stairs, the sisters rose and went to the front hall. "How is she?" Claire asked.

"Is she going to die?" Emily piped in.

"Mrs. Parks has a weak heart, I won't tell you otherwise," the doctor said. "If you can get her to take it easy and not overwork herself, she should have some good years left. But I'd think about setting up a room for her down here. That climb certainly isn't helping any.''

"She can have the back parlor. It sits unused now anyway," Claire said. "I've been looking for someone to take over Mrs. Parks' duties, Doc, but I haven't had any luck so far. Do you know of anyone who needs work?''

Jenkins scratched his bushy beard. "I know a lady who may be able to help you out. She worked for Ed Crane until his wife died. Now he's moved in with his children, so I suspect she could use a job. She's a hard worker, but she takes some getting used to.''

"If she can do the work and will accept what I can pay, I don't care if she has three eyes," Claire admitted.

"As long as she doesn't smell," Emily added.

Doc Jenkins laughed. "I'll send her out. You can decide for yourself. In the meantime, see that Mrs. Parks takes the tonic I left her. I'll stop back in a week and see how she's doing.''

Claire followed the doctor out to his buggy. "I haven't had a chance to speak to you since my father's funeral,'' she said, glancing over her shoulder to be sure Emily hadn't followed. "I wanted to ask you a few questions.''

"I'll tell you what I can," he said, climbing into the old black buggy his father had used.

"Could an argument have caused my father's stroke?''

"If it was upsetting enough and if conditions were right, I suppose it could have.''

"Had he come to see you about any health problems?'' she asked.

"No, but he might have seen my father before I took over two years ago.''

Claire doubted that he had. Arthur Cavanaugh had always been as fit as a fiddle. She was more sure than ever that the argument between her father and Boothe had caused the stroke.

*   *   *

"So she's taking in boarders, is she?" Reginald Boothe drummed his fingers on the desktop and stared at the sheriff sitting across from him. "You realize if you had succeeded in wooing her, you'd be making wedding plans right now."

"I've tried, Mr. Boothe. Cee Cee always finds a way to hold me off."

Boothe studied him. It wasn't surprising that a woman as pretty as Claire would turn down Simons's advances. Remembering how Claire's mother had turned down *his* advances, his eyes narrowed and his hand curled into a fist. Haughty bitch. He'd taught Marie Reneau a lesson, however, one she'd paid for until the day she died. Now it was Claire Cavanaugh's turn to pay. "Has her fiancé turned up yet?"

"No."

"Then you still have a chance."

Simons toyed with his hat in his lap. "To be honest, Mr. Boothe, I think your partner has his sights set on her."

"McCane?" Boothe resumed his drumming. McCane was shrewd. Perhaps he'd decided marriage was the best way to get control of the land. "I don't really care who marries her, Wilbur, as long as we get that land."

The sheriff jumped to his feet. "You told me I could marry her!"

"What do you want me to do, *order* her to marry you?"

Simons's lower lip jutted out in a pout as he hung his head. "No, sir."

"Then I suggest you forget about her." Boothe watched the sheriff lumber out, then swivelled to look out the window. So Claire was taking in boarders to pay her living expenses, was she? Well, there were ways to put a stop to that.

*   *   *

Jonas arrived late in the afternoon, while Claire was beating a braided rug on the line in the back of the house. The upstairs rooms were now ready for renters, and Mrs. Parks was comfortably settled in the back parlor. Squinting through a dust fog, she waved at him cheerfully.

"Brought you a surprise," he called, holding up a sack. He removed a plucked chicken and held it up. "I'll even start it roasting."

"How kind of you, Mr. Polk!" Jonas had truly been a life-saver for them. Instead of sailing with the *Lady Luck* today, he had posted notices for boarders and picked up supplies for the pantry. She finished her task, rolled up the heavy rug, and carted it back to the house. Jonas met her at the door and helped her put it down on the bedroom floor.

"You've done wonders in the house," he told her as they returned to the kitchen. "And you're looking a bit worn out. Why don't you run upstairs, clean up, and put on a pretty frock, while Em and I finish preparing tonight's supper?"

Claire was too exhausted to argue. When she came down to the dining room later, she found that he and Emily had already set the table and had even lit the tapers on the sideboard. "Another celebration?" she asked.

"In honor of all your hard work," Jonas proclaimed.

After a delicious chicken dinner, Jonas surprised them with scones he'd had the *Lady Luck*'s cook prepare. As they were feasting on the delectable, buttery confections, the buzzer rang at the front door.

"Sit still," Jonas insisted, when Claire stood. "I'll get it."

A few moments later, Claire heard Tyler's deep voice in the hallway. Her heart raced as she jumped up from the table and hurried to greet him, smoothing wisps of hair away from her face. She should have worn one of her other frocks. The deep rose with white sprigs suddenly seemed frumpy.

She arrived just in time to hear Tyler say to Jonas, "I'll come back another time."

"Good evening," she said breathlessly. Just the sight of him made her cheeks grow warm. She saw his eyes darken with admiration, and blushed harder.

"I was just telling Ty that our dinner ran a bit late," Jonas said, giving Tyler a look Claire didn't understand.

"Won't you join us in the dining room for dessert?" Claire asked.

It almost seemed as though a curtain fell behind Tyler's eyes. "No thanks. I didn't mean to intrude."

"Oh, you aren't intruding at all," Claire said instantly, and just as quickly regretted her eagerness. It wasn't ladylike to seem eager for a man's company. It wasn't proper for an engaged lady to *be* eager for another man's company.

"Tell him we've got a special dessert," Emily called from somewhere close by.

"You don't want to hurt the tyke's feelings, do you?" Jonas chided. "Even though she is eavesdropping again— aren't you, Emily?"

Tyler gave Jonas a look that clearly showed his annoyance at being put on the spot. "I'd be happy to join you," he told Claire.

In the dining room, Tyler greeted Mrs. Parks and took a seat across from Emily as Jonas pulled out a chair for Claire. "Too bad you couldn't have come sooner," Jonas remarked. "We had such a wonderfully plump and juicy roasted chicken, and potatoes." He patted Claire's shoulder. "Your boarders are going to love it here. Home cooking is a rare treat for men without wives."

Claire stared at him perplexed. Jonas was making it sound as though *she* had prepared the meal.

"If you'll excuse me," Mrs. Parks said, rising slowly, "I'll leave you young people to talk. I'm feeling a bit worn out."

Jonas immediately jumped up. "Let me assist you,

Mum. Emily, perhaps you'll bring your book and read to Mrs. Parks a bit.''

As the three left the room, Claire glanced at Tyler, who appeared to be very uncomfortable. She immediately suspected that Jonas had coerced him into coming to Bellefleur. Obviously he hadn't thought of it on his own, or he wouldn't look so miserable. "Would you like some coffee?" she asked Tyler.

"That's fine."

Tyler waited until she had poured it, then gingerly picked up the dainty china demitasse, feeling like the proverbial bull in the china shop. He hadn't expected to walk in on such a homey domestic scene. It was painful for him to do so, a reminder of what he'd never had. He'd always told himself he didn't want this kind of life. Yet here he was, not only feeling sorry for himself, but also wanting it very much.

He glanced at Claire as she poured his coffee. She seemed glad to see him, which made him feel better. She sat down and picked up her own cup, sipping steadily, as though she didn't know what to say. He stared at her slender hands and wrists as she lifted the cup to her mouth.

Ah, how he remembered the taste of that mouth. Tyler felt the telltale signs of arousal as her lips fitted themselves to the contours of the cup. He watched her smooth throat move as she swallowed, and then saw her eyes focus on him. For a moment, their gazes locked and he knew she was remembering, too.

The coffee sloshed in her cup. Claire set it in the saucer with a clatter. "Would you care for a scone?" she asked quickly, reaching for the plate in the center of the table.

Tyler took one so he'd have something to do besides stare at her. Yet he found himself watching her still as he chewed a buttery mouthful. It was moist and tender and just a bit sweet. Like her kisses.

"Tyler," she said hesitantly, "why were you asking questions about the Greenes the other day?"

He swallowed the bite of scone and took a sip of coffee, trying to get his thoughts away from matters of the flesh. "I wondered how well acquainted you were. I thought you might know if Mr. Greene was much of a drinker."

Claire sat forward, her eyes instantly alert. "Would it make a difference if he were?"

"The sheriff is blaming Mr. Greene's death on alcohol," he told her. "But I was near the body when they loaded it into the wagon and I didn't smell any alcohol. I was just curious as to why he would be so quick to use that as an excuse."

Claire searched his gaze intently. "What do you think happened to him?"

Tyler rubbed his jaw, trying to decide how much to tell her about Greene's death. He didn't want to spread rumors, but he did want her to be aware that there was a murderer on the loose. "I suspect there's more to the story than Greene's getting drunk and walking into the river. My gut feeling is that he met with foul play." Tyler saw her eyes widen in alarm.

"Did you know that Mrs. Greene left town immediately after her husband's death?" she asked.

At that moment, Jonas and Emily came down the hall toward the dining room. Tyler stood up. He didn't want anyone intruding on their privacy. "Why don't we step outside for some fresh air?"

"There's a cool breeze tonight," Claire replied. "We can sit on the porch swing and talk."

Painted dark green, like the two rocking chairs near the door and the two giant flowerpots bordering the steps, the wooden swing hung at the far end of the deep porch. A pink, white, and green crocheted lap robe lay over the back. Tyler leaned against it and stretched his arm out. Claire sat beside him, her hands folded gracefully in her lap, her head turned, staring out at the river in the distance.

"What did you hear about Mrs. Greene?" he asked.

"The sheriff said she left without a word to anyone. He

thinks she went back to Germany. She didn't even stay to see the shop closed or the furnishings sold. I find that very disturbing. I don't think she would have done that willingly.''

''If it will put your mind at ease,'' Tyler told her, ''I'll see what I can find out.''

Claire smiled at him, her relief evident in her lovely eyes. ''Thank you,'' she said softly.

Just looking at her made Tyler's pulse race. Lord, how he wanted her. But he couldn't rush things. He knew better. ''Jonas tells me you're going to rent out rooms,'' he said casually.

Claire looked down at her hands, as though she was embarrassed about it. ''Yes, I am.''

''Seems kind of a shame,'' he said with sigh, glancing around, ''having all those strangers in your home.''

''It won't be so bad. The house feels empty without my father here. It will be pleasant to have people around.''

''Strangers,'' he corrected. When she said nothing, he added, ''Maybe having a few friends among the strangers would help.''

Claire turned to look at him. ''What do you mean?''

Tyler moved his hand to lift a strand of black hair away from her neck, brushing the satiny skin of her throat lightly with his fingers. ''I wouldn't mind being able to keep an eye on my property across the road while my house is being built.''

He saw her eyes widen. ''You want to stay here?''

''If you have the room.''

''Oh, yes! Yes, I do!'' she exclaimed happily. ''And as you say, having friends here would help.''

''I can move in tomorrow.''

''I don't have a housekeeper yet, or a cook.''

''That doesn't bother me.''

A smile spread across her face. ''Then tomorrow will be fine.'' Claire sat back with a sudden frown, nervously smoothing her skirt. "I suppose you're wondering why I'm taking in boarders."

Tyler didn't know how to answer, so he said nothing. She continued, "I'm in somewhat of a financial bind at the moment. The tobacco won't be harvested for another six weeks, so renting out rooms will give me enough income to get by until then."

"Maybe you should consider selling Bellefleur and finding something you can comfortably afford."

She turned with a jerk, her eyes wild with something that looked like fear. "*Never*. This is my home. I'll never leave it." Abruptly, she stood and walked across the porch.

Tyler was stunned by her quick, almost desperate response. Jonas was right: Claire wasn't about to be budged. He followed her over to the steps, where she stood rigidly by the railing, her back to him, one arm wrapped around the column that rose to the porch ceiling.

"I'm sorry," he said. "I didn't mean to upset you."

She rubbed her arms, as though suddenly chilled. "I can't explain my feelings about the house. I don't always understand them myself. I just know that this is the only real home I've ever known and I'll die fighting for it." She glanced at him over her shoulder and then looked down in embarrassment. "Sometimes I think I must be mad."

Tyler put his hands on her shoulders and gently turned her to face him. "I've felt that way about myself many times."

"You?" Claire searched his eyes. "You're not mad," she said softly.

"Neither are you." His gaze dropped from her eyes to her mouth, so soft and inviting. Dear God, how he wanted to taste those lips again. He put his finger under her chin and tilted it up, then ran his hand slowly, caressingly, along her jawline, enjoying the silkiness of her skin. He saw a warm blush color her cheeks, and her breasts rose and fell as her breathing quickened. He smiled, knowing she was as aroused as he was.

Bending his head, he kissed her—a light, feathery touch of his lips to hers. Fire coursed through his veins as Claire closed her eyes and leaned into him, her mouth supple and sweet. Pulling her into his arms, he kissed her harder. Her breasts were soft and yielding against his chest. Her thighs brushed his swollen groin, stoking the fire inside him to even greater heights. As he ran one hand down her back to her firm, round bottom, his manhood pulsed against the restraining clothing, pressing into her curves until he thought he would explode.

Suddenly Claire pushed away, breathing hard. "I can't kiss you like that," she said, turning her back on him.

Tyler gritted his teeth. That damn Lance again. The thought that she was so committed to the louse made Tyler see red. "Why can't you kiss me like that?" he asked. "Are you afraid your fiancé will object? It's hard for him to do that when he's not here, isn't it?"

He saw Claire's back stiffen. "He'll be here," she said in a curt voice.

"When, damn it? He should have been here for your father's funeral. What kind of fiancé deserts his bride-to-be at a time like that? And where was he when you were fighting to save your home?"

"I don't know where he is," Claire said through gritted teeth. She swung to face him, and for the first time Tyler saw anger in her eyes. Her fingers curled into fists. "I've written him again and again and he hasn't replied once. All I've had is one brief telegram. I don't know if something happened to him or if he's just"—she fought hard to keep from cryin—"forgotten me."

Tyler grabbed her shoulders and brought her close, his eyes blazing with fury. "No man in his right mind would forget you." He covered her mouth with a passionate kiss, oblivious to her cry of protest. She pushed against him, but he held her tightly until he felt her arms wind around his neck and her mouth soften and heard a low moan of desire in her throat.

Lance could go to hell. This woman was his.

Chapter 12

For a long time after Tyler had gone, Claire stood on the porch, running her fingertips over her lips. The powerful feelings his kisses evoked filled her with guilt. How could she profess to love Lance and still have such overwhelming feelings for Tyler? To complicate matters further, Tyler would soon be living in her home, where she would be in daily contact with him.

Her anger at Lance grew sharper. His absence and their long separation were to blame for her weakening loyalty. Tyler was right: Lance should have been there to support her at such a critical time in her life. Why wasn't he?

It seemed an eternity since she'd last seen him. They'd spent so many enjoyable afternoons together at college, walking the paths that crisscrossed the campus, studying in the quiet gloom of the library, picnicking in the park. Yet it was getting more and more difficult to remember Lance's face. When she closed her eyes very tightly and tried to call it up, another face always popped into view—Tyler's.

Claire was still standing on the porch when Jonas opened the door behind her and stepped out. "Did Ty leave?" he asked.

"A little while ago." Claire turned to look at him. "Tyler is going to rent a room here."

"Well, well! Will wonders never cease?" Jonas asked, one corner of his mouth twitching.

Claire planted her hands on her hips. "Did you put Tyler up to this?"

"I truly didn't know he was even contemplating it."

"How fun!" Emily said from inside the house. "Jonas *and* Tyler will be living with us."

"Emily, how many times must I tell you not to eavesdrop?" Claire asked in exasperation, turning toward the door. "You know it isn't polite. And by the way, isn't it your bedtime?"

"You're a stick-in-the-mud, Cee Cee," Emily griped as she began to climb the stairs. "Thank goodness fun people will be living here."

"Excuse me, won't you?" Claire said to Jonas. "I want to make sure Emily goes to bed—and stays there!"

Jonas chuckled. "I'll say goodnight, then. And goodnight to you, too, Emily."

" 'Night, Jonas," Emily called over her shoulder. She waited until Claire caught up with her, then said, "Won't Rancid Lanced be surprised when he finds out you're taking in boarders—*if* he ever comes here?"

Claire didn't even bother to reply this time. Lance didn't seem real to her now. And the life she had left behind at college was nothing more than a distant, faded memory. It almost felt like it had all happened to another girl, a girl she didn't know anymore. She wasn't sure she even loved Lance.

Claire stopped her thoughts before they could go further. As long as she was engaged to Lance, she had to be loyal to him, no matter how strong the attraction was to Tyler McCane, no matter how much she enjoyed his kisses. Remembering the desire he had stirred on the porch, she only hoped she was strong enough to resist him.

Tyler stood at the prow, watching the moonlight glimmer on black water. What had he been thinking? His passion had overtaken his common sense, something he never allowed to happen. Control was too important. His plan was to convince Claire to marry him for practical reasons, not emotional ones.

He understood now what that premonition had meant. But Claire could destroy him only if he fell in love with her. For that to happen, he would have to open his heart and expose that frightened child inside, that boy who was so impossible to love that his mother had left him. He couldn't take that risk. He couldn't go through the pain of abandonment twice.

Just as she finished her breakfast the next morning, Claire was startled by a heavy knocking on the front door.

"Good morning!" a woman declared in a cheerful, booming voice when Claire opened the door. "Doc Jenkins told me you were looking for a housekeeper. Well, here I am!"

Claire stared at her in astonishment. From her henna-colored hair, deep red lips, and streaks of rouge on her wide cheekbones, down to the red leather shoes showing beneath her full, blue-and-red striped skirt, she was a most outrageous sight. Tall, large-boned, and buxom, she had the exuberance of a young girl, though Claire guessed her to be in her early fifties. "Won't you come in, Mrs.—?" Claire stammered, holding open the door.

"Lulu will do, thanks." The woman snatched up the large satchel at her feet, scooped up a small pine chest, and swept into the hallway. Dropping the bag with a loud thud and depositing the chest beside it, she stood with arms akimbo, a pleased look on her face. "Grand place you have here! It'll do just fine. Where do I put my things?"

Lulu's presumptuousness stunned Claire so much that she was struck speechless. For heaven's sake, the woman didn't even know if she'd been hired!

Lulu laughed. "You're not sure you want a crazy ol' gal like me working for you, are you, sweetie pie?" Stooping, she yanked open her bag and pulled out some papers. "Here's letters from previous employers. Doc's letter is on top. I'll work hard for you and I'll keep the place as neat as a pin. All I ask is that I have a decent room, three meals a day, coffee when I need it, and Saturday evenings and Sunday mornings to myself."

Claire glanced at the papers. "Don't you want to know about the wages?"

"You pay me what you can and what you think I'm worth. I've never been cheated yet out of a day's wage."

Although her bold manner and loud voice intimidated Claire, there was something inherently likable about Lulu. Claire gave a cursory glance at the letters and handed them back. "I really need someone right away. How soon would you be able to start?"

"Right now." Lulu stuck out a broad hand and shook Claire's enthusiastically. "You won't be sorry, sweetie pie. Who's the little angel hiding behind the parlor door?"

Claire turned around in surprise. "Emily?"

A sheepish Emily came out, using her cane for guidance, and stood close beside Claire. "How did she know I was there?" Emily whispered. "Is she a witch?"

"This is my sister Emily," Claire said, giving her sister a discreet nudge.

Lulu looked at Claire and pointed to her eyes, silently asking if Emily was blind. Claire nodded. "So, angel!" Lulu boomed, "you like to eavesdrop, do you?"

Emily's voice came out in a squeak. "Yes, ma'am." Claire had to smother a chuckle; she had never seen her sister intimidated before.

Lulu's laughter echoed up the hallway. "Little pitchers have big ears, my ma always said. Come here, angel, and give Lulu a hug. Tomorrow we're going to work on those manners."

Claire was surprised to see her sister give the woman a shy hug.

Lulu was delighted with her accommodations, a large,

airy room on the third floor. Claire gave her time to settle in, then showed her the rest of the house and explained her duties. The woman seemed unfazed by the magnitude of her responsibilities, and when she found out that Claire hadn't yet found a cook, she even offered to prepare their meals.

As Claire walked through the house later that afternoon, she could hear Lulu singing, "While Strolling Through the Park One Day," at the top of her lungs while she worked in the kitchen. Claire couldn't help but hum along. For the first time in weeks, she felt optimistic. Bellefleur was coming back to life!

Shortly afterward, Jonas and Tyler arrived, carrying some of Tyler's belongings. Claire showed them to the room she had selected.

"Who's the alto downstairs?" Jonas asked, setting down one of Tyler's bags.

"My new housekeeper," Claire replied. "Her name is Lulu. She's cooking for us tonight."

"Lulu?" Jonas made a face. "Sounds like one of the puppets my parents used in their act."

Tyler had half-turned toward the door to listen. "What's the name of that song?" he asked.

" 'While Strolling Through the Park One Day,' " Claire replied. "It seems to be Lulu's favorite. She's been singing it ever since she got here."

"It reminds me of something," Tyler mused, rubbing his jaw.

"Think I'd better go down and make sure she's not destroying the kitchen the way she is that song," Jonas commented with a wink.

Claire leaned against the doorframe as Tyler inspected his new quarters. He exuded such confidence and strength, such easy, masculine grace. With all his attributes, she wondered why he'd never married. "Do you like the room?" she asked.

He opened the wardrobe and glanced inside. "It'll take some getting used to."

With a puzzled frown, Claire gazed at the walnut chest of drawers, the huge, burled walnut wardrobe filled with fragrant sachet packets, and the big, sturdy, brass bedstead covered with a fine handmade quilt. "You don't like it?"

Tyler held his arms straight out from his body and braced his legs. "It doesn't rock." With a devilish grin and twinkle in his eyes, he walked over to her. "Where's *your* room?"

Claire swallowed hard, her stomach aflutter. Why was she suddenly imagining him tiptoeing into her room, peeling back the quilt, and sliding in beside her, his nude body warm and hard against hers? A shiver of excitement raced down her spine. What would it be like to spend the night wrapped in those strong arms? Feeling suddenly weak in the knees, Claire replied in a faint voice, "Two doors down."

He braced his left arm to one side of her. "Whose room is in the middle?"

"No one's—yet."

Tyler put his right arm on the other side and stared deep into her eyes. "Is there some reason you didn't put me there?" His low, husky voice caused Claire's heart to skip a beat.

A very good reason. You'd be too close to me, just like you are now. She could feel the heat from his body as he moved closer still. Another inch and she'd feel the hard contours of his chest and thighs. She began to tremble inside, partly from nervousness, but mostly from anticipation. Would he kiss her right there where anyone could see them? The danger of it excited her.

Suddenly Lulu began calling her name. "Claire, sweetie pie, are you up there? You've got a customer. Claire?"

Tyler lowered his head, but instead of kissing her, he put his mouth near her ear. "Don't answer," he whispered, nibbling his way down her throat.

Delicious shivers of ecstasy traveled from his mouth to the juncture of her thighs, causing a deep, pleasant throbbing, a yearning for something she could only guess at.

"Claire? Can you hear me?" Lulu called.

"I have to answer," Claire said breathlessly. "She'll come looking for me if I don't." Ducking under his arm, Claire forced herself to walk away from him. At the top of the staircase, she paused to take a steadying breath and fan her face before she went to meet her new boarder.

Goodness! I have three boarders! And to think her biggest worry had been that no one would come.

"There you are, sweetie pie!" Lulu called. "Come meet your new boarder, Gunther somebody, from Switzerland." She stepped aside, revealing a very blond and very handsome young man carrying a bag in one hand and his derby in the other.

"Gun*ter*," he corrected, in a charming accent. He bowed as Claire came down the staircase and walked toward him. "Gunter Jenssen. From Sweden."

"Claire Cavanaugh." She stared at the stranger in awe as he took her hand and kissed it. She'd never met a Swede before, nor had she ever seen a man so exceptionally good looking.

"How do you do, Miss Cavanaugh?" he said politely, his vivid blue eyes sparkling with undisguised delight. "I am very pleased to make your acquaintance. I was just asking this lady if you still had a room to rent. I will need it only for four weeks."

"Oh, yes! Indeed I do. Right this way, Mr. Jenssen."

From the top of the stairs Tyler saw the complete stupefaction on Claire's face as she stared up at the stranger. Scowling, he started down the steps as she came up with the stranger following behind. She paused briefly to introduce them.

"Hello," the stranger said politely, reaching out to shake his hand.

Tyler made a quick assessment of the man. Though the

Swede was marginally good looking, Tyler assured himself that Jenssen was much too immature to attract Claire. Yet when he reached the bottom of the staircase, he stopped, thought about it, and started back up.

Pausing at the top to listen, Tyler walked softly down the hallway to the room Claire had given her new boarder. Just as he suspected, it was between his and Claire's.

With growing annoyance, he walked to the end of the hallway and back, checking the rooms one by one. There were plenty of other rooms available at the far end of the hall.

Why had she put the Swede in the room next to hers? Was this a game? Was she purposely trying to make him jealous? Or worse, could she actually be attracted to the oaf?

He simmered when Claire laughed at something the Swede said.

"Oh, there you are, Tyler," Jonas called from the top of the stairs.

Tyler put his finger to his mouth, striding quietly away from the room where Claire was finding the newcomer so hilarious. "Do you have to bellow?" he snapped.

"My, my, we're rather testy today." Jonas followed him downstairs. "It wouldn't have anything to do with that dapper fellow I met in the hall, would it?"

Tyler turned and nearly smacked into him. "You're beginning to vex me, Jonas."

"Could it be I've struck a nerve?" Jonas exclaimed. "Could it be that the fair Claire was taken with him? He's quite a handsome chap, after all."

"That piece of Swiss cheese?" Tyler strode out onto the porch with Jonas on his heels.

"Actually, he's Swedish."

"Shut up, old man," Tyler growled, untying the horse's lead. He didn't care that it was illogical to be upset if Claire was attracted to other men. It was also illogical to be so protective of her—yet he couldn't seem to stop himself from coming to her rescue.

Tyler felt like he was turning into someone he didn't know, and he didn't like the change.

"All I can say is that your taking a room here is a good idea," Jonas continued, as Tyler climbed into the buggy, "especially if you decide to marry her. I suspect Claire will have her hands full once all the eligible men in town discover she's renting out rooms. By the by, where are you off to in such a hurry?"

"To town."

"I'll tag along, if you don't mind. That *lady* in the kitchen, and I use the term advisedly, has ordered me out of her way. Can you imagine *her* ordering *me* out of the kitchen, as if *I* were the interloper?" Jonas sniffed, as he climbed in beside Tyler. "Why are we going to town?"

"I promised Claire I'd look into Mrs. Greene's disappearance."

"Is this part of your plan to sweep her off her feet?"

Tyler ignored the gibe. "I've suspected there was something wrong with this whole Greene matter since we found the body, and apparently Claire thinks so, too."

"And investigating it will certainly help you win her away from her negligent fiancé."

'That's the idea."

"So you've decided to marry her?" Jonas asked casually.

Tyler ignored that, too.

"Hey, there, Limey!"

Tyler turned to see a brightly garbed lady waving to them from the porch.

"Of all the nerve!" Jonas hissed through his teeth.

Tyler couldn't help but chuckle at the expression on Jonas's face. He'd never seen him so riled. "Is that Lulu?" he asked.

"In person," Jonas said in an angry whisper. "Now, I

ask you, what ninny would purposefully call herself by the name of *Lulu*?''

''What can we do for you, ma'am?'' Tyler called.

''We're nearly out of cornmeal,'' Lulu replied. ''Can you bring us a sack from town?''

''Be glad to.'' Tyler glanced at Jonas, whose face was still red with indignation. ''Won't we, Limey?''

''If we're going to call names,'' Jonas said sarcastically, ''what would you call a man who lets a lady believe he has only her best interests at heart, when he's merely acting on his own selfish behalf? A cad?''

Tyler shot him a glowering look. ''We've had this conversation before.''

''Remind me how it ends.''

''The selfish cad fires his assistant,'' Tyler retorted, ''and lives happily ever after.''

''Or,'' Jonas countered, ''the selfish cad discovers he has a heart after all when he falls in love with the lady, and *then* he lives happily ever after.''

''I'll stick with my version.''

Once they got into town, Tyler dropped Jonas off at the general store, then parked the buggy in front of the sheriff's office. He found the sheriff sitting at a battered rolltop desk, playing solitaire.

The office was nothing more than a square, sparsely furnished room with a scuffed wooden floor. A low divider separated the front of the office from the back, where the sheriff's desk sat. Several straight-backed chairs sat against the near wall. There was a gun cabinet against the back wall, and wanted posters hung on one of the side walls. A doorway at the back led to what Tyler supposed was the jail.

''Something I can do for you, McCane?'' the sheriff asked in an unfriendly tone.

Tyler opened the hinged wooden gate and walked through. ''Just wondered how the Greene investigation was coming.''

Sheriff Simons gathered the cards and began to shuffle them. "No one saw Greene that night. I don't have any witnesses or evidence, so I'm calling it a dead end."

Why is he giving up so quickly? Tyler turned a chair around to face the desk, straddling it to better see the sheriff's face. "Did Greene have any enemies?"

"None that I know of."

"Did you confirm that with his wife?"

The sheriff began laying out his cards. "She left town."

Tyler raised an eyebrow, pretending not to know. "Just like that?"

"Just up and left," Simons replied, carefully straightening the piles. "Must have gone in the night, too, because no one saw her go."

"Don't you find that strange?"

"They were strange people."

The sheriff wouldn't meet his eye. Tyler could always tell when a person was lying by the way they moved their eyes. Maybe that's why the sheriff wouldn't look at him—maybe he wasn't a very good liar. "So why do you think he was murdered?"

"You keep asking that, McCane, but we don't have any proof he was murdered."

"What about the strangulation marks around his neck?"

The sheriff's motions halted. "I don't recall seeing any marks," he answered sharply. "Even if there were, it don't mean nothing. Those marks could have happened before the murder. Maybe Greene got into a fight that night."

"Was he the kind of man to get into fights?"

"You know how those foreigners are," the sheriff grumbled, returning to his game. "Always ready to throw a punch."

"Then unless he was a shadow boxer," Tyler said dryly, "there would have to be another person involved, wouldn't there?"

"It's possible."

"Possible?" Tyler was growing more irritated by the

minute. "Is there some reason you don't want to know what happened to Mr. Greene?"

The sheriff looked straight at him then, and Tyler saw a flicker in his eyes that looked a lot like panic. "That's a fool thing to say."

"Then if I were you, I'd start asking around. Somebody is bound to know if there was a fight." He moved a black queen to a red king. "It's worth checking into, isn't it?"

The sheriff blinked, as though he had to think it over. "Yeah, I suppose I could do that."

"Let me know what you find out." Tyler strode toward the door.

"McCane," Simons called. "It ain't your business, you know."

Tyler smiled cannily. "I know, but I promised a friend I'd look into it, and I like to keep my promises."

He left the sheriff's office and found Jonas waiting by the buggy. "Find out anything?" Jonas asked.

Tyler unhitched the horse and climbed in the buggy. "The sheriff is dragging his feet on this murder, Jonas. In fact, he refuses to call it a murder. He had the gall to suggest those marks around the man's neck happened sometime earlier in a fight. I don't know if he's truly that ignorant, or just lazy."

"Or hiding something," Jonas added, as they drove through town.

"That's still a possibility."

"Maybe he's the murderer," Jonas suggested. "Or he knows who the murderer is."

"Let's suppose he knows who the murderer is," Tyler said. "If the sheriff is covering for someone, he has to have a reason to do so. My guess would be that he's either taking a bribe or someone is blackmailing him."

"I agree."

"The question is, how do we find out?"

"I don't think it's wise to go poking around in the sheriff's affairs, Ty. It could get sticky, especially since you're going to be running a business from this town.''

"I promised Claire I'd look into it.''

"Which you have done,'' Jonas reminded him.

"I don't think she'll be satisfied with the answers. I know I'm not. I keep remembering how agitated the sheriff was, that day he passed me in the hall on his way to see Boothe. They were discussing Greene's death as though they were mapping out a strategy.''

"Are we back to thinking that Boothe may be involved?''

Tyler rubbed his jaw. "I sure don't want to think so.''

"I wouldn't put anything past the bounder,'' Jonas said. "You know he went to see Claire's father the morning he died, don't you?''

"You never told me that.''

Jonas sniffed. "I tried. You weren't in the mood to listen.''

"Well, I am now.''

"It seems that Boothe and Claire's father had a terrible row that morning, probably over the foreclosure. From what I gather, Claire is holding Boothe responsible for his death.''

"Having an argument is not reason enough to convict a man.''

"No,'' Jonas admitted, "but in Claire's eyes, it's enough to hate him.''

And even more reason not to let Claire find out that he and Boothe were partners. Tyler turned the buggy around and headed back to town.

"Where are we going?'' Jonas asked.

"To the general store to ask some questions.''

After spending half an hour chatting with the store clerks, Tyler and Jonas headed back for Bellefleur. "That was a waste of time,'' Jonas commented. "They're as stumped as we are. No one can figure out why Mrs. Greene left everything behind.''

"*Would* she have left it behind?'' Tyler posed.

''What are you saying? That she might have been murdered, too?''

''We have to consider it.''

''What could these two people have done?'' Jonas asked. ''From what I gathered, Walter Greene was a frugal man who ran a tidy business and always paid his bills on time. No extravagant spending, no bad habits. He seems to have been an ordinary man who lived a frugal, boring life.'' He shrugged. ''Perhaps it was just a robbery that turned into murder.''

Tyler pondered the matter for a few minutes. ''I suppose we'll just have to see what the sheriff turns up. In the meantime, Claire needs to be aware that there's still a murderer on the loose.''

Chapter 13

When Tyler stopped the buggy in front of the house, Lulu stepped out onto the porch. "I was beginning to think you two got lost!" she called.

"No such luck," Jonas muttered, glaring at the woman as he carried the sack of cornmeal up the steps of the porch and thrust it into her hands.

"Hello, cutie," Lulu cried, spotting Tyler. She shifted the cornmeal to her left arm and stuck out her right hand. "I haven't met you yet. I'm Lulu."

The name wasn't familiar, yet her voice had a quality to it that triggered something in his mind, though he was unable to put a finger on it. "Pleased to meet you, Lulu." He held out his hand and suddenly found it being shaken enthusiastically. "I'm Tyler McCane."

Her handshake faltered. Tyler automatically looked into her eyes and found the pupils wide, as though he had startled her. "Tyler McCane, you say?" she said, trying to keep a casual tone to her voice.

"That's right. Do I know you?"

She gave a stilted laugh. "I don't think so." She stared at him a moment longer, then turned. "Well, don't just stand there, Limey, come on into the house."

"The name is Polk," Jonas said with a haughty air, emphasizing each word. "Jonas Winthrop Polk."

"I caught it the first time," she told him, starting down the hallway to the kitchen. "Supper's in ten minutes, cutie,'' she called over her shoulder to Tyler.

Tyler heard voices coming from the parlor and went to investigate. Claire was sitting beside Gunter Jenssen on the sofa, watching Emily's puppet show. Emily was crouched behind a wing-backed chair opposite them, her rabbit puppet on one hand and a fox on the other.

Tyler cleared his throat noisily. ''Am I interrupting?''

''Oh, no!'' Claire replied, jumping up. ''Please, sit down.

''You're just in time,'' Emily called. ''The fox was about to eat the rabbit.''

With a smug smile aimed at Gunter, Tyler strode across the Turkish carpet and sat in the spot Claire had just vacated. Claire sat across from them. All three waited for Emily to continue.

''Oh, please, Mr. Hunter,'' the rabbit begged, ''don't eat me.''

''I've caught you now, Hare,'' the fox answered, in Emily's deepest voice.

''Here comes my hero to the rescue! Help, Wiler, help me before this sly fox eats me!''

Hunter, Hare, and Wiler—the sly fox, the innocent rabbit and the hero. Remarkably similar to Gunter, Claire, and Tyler. Coughing to cover his laugh, Tyler glanced at Claire just as she glanced at him. She quickly looked away, her cheeks turning pink. Obviously, she had caught Emily's coded message, too.

''Supper's on the table, folks,'' Lulu bellowed from the dining room.

''Thank you, Em, for entertaining us,'' Claire said. ''Mr. Jenssen, may I show you to the dining room?''

Tyler's jealousy simmered as Gunter took Claire's arm and escorted her from the parlor. He heard Emily clear her throat noisily, and turned to find her standing directly behind him. ''Is there something wrong with your throat?'' he asked.

"It worked for you," she said, putting out a hand for him to take.

With a laugh, Tyler tucked her hand through his arm. "Pretty clever puppet show. I have to admire the originality of your puppets' names."

"Jonas taught me everything I know."

"I have a feeling you've improvised some. All that listening at doors must come in handy."

"If I were allowed in adult conversations," Emily pointed out, "I wouldn't have to listen at doors."

"Do you ever stop to think that there might be a reason why you're not allowed to listen in on adult conversations?" Tyler asked her.

"Every night, right before I say my prayers."

Tyler looked at her earnest little face and burst out laughing. "You'd make one hell of a card player, Emily. We'll have to look into finding some Braille cards for you."

"Do you think so?" Emily cried in delight. "Oh, that would be grand! I knew right away I liked you, Tyler." She tugged on his shirt so he would bend his ear down to her mouth. "Now we have to find a way to get rid of that fox."

"You mean 'Hunter'? Why should I help you get rid of him?" Tyler teased, keeping his voice low. "Your sister needs boarders."

"She wouldn't if she had a husband to take care of her. You said you were interested in my sister."

"I said I *might* be interested," Tyler corrected. "Besides, Claire has a fiancé."

Emily made a scoffing sound. "A skunk always gives himself away by his odor."

"What's that supposed to mean?"

"You'll see," she replied knowingly. "And when it happens, you'd better be ready."

They walked into the dining room to find that Gunter had taken a seat to Claire's right at the head of the table.

Jonas had taken a seat as far away from Lulu as possible, which put him at Claire's left, leaving only the chairs in the middle open. Emily took one next to Mrs. Parks and Tyler took the opposite side, next to Gunter. Tyler shot an irritated look at Jonas, who was sitting in the seat he should have been in.

The meal proceeded much too slowly for Tyler's liking. He wanted to speak to Claire privately, but he hadn't been able to interrupt Gunter's boring monologue long enough to ask her. Jonas was no help, either. He was discussing an upcoming puppet show with Emily. Tyler caught Lulu studying him, and wondered again why she had acted so strangely when they first met.

"Lulu, is that your given name or a nickname?" he asked her.

"Just a nickname. But I've used it for so long I've forgotten what my real name is," she said, laughing heartily.

"Do you have any family in Fortune?" Tyler asked.

"I'm what you call a free spirit," she said, laughing again. "I can't stand being tied to one place for very long."

"I know the feeling," Tyler replied.

"Oh, I hope that doesn't mean you'll be leaving us soon, Lulu," Claire said, interrupting Jenssen's oration.

"Don't you fret that pretty head, sweetie pie," Lulu reassured her. "I'll be here as long as you need me. Anyone for more corn? How about mashed potatoes? Emily, my angel, you need to eat more. You're as thin as a rail."

Tyler wasn't about to let Lulu slip off the hook that easily. "Where do you come from?" he asked, spooning more mashed potatoes onto his plate.

"Mr. Crane was the last man I worked for."

"I meant originally."

"Let's see," Lulu said, pursing her bright red lips. "Illinois, somewhere. You know, my parents traveled around so much I'm not sure I know. But wherever it was, it couldn't have been as exciting as Switzerland, right, Mr. Jenssen?"

"That's Sweden," Gunter corrected. "Fredriksberg, Sweden."

"Isn't that up by the Alps?" she asked.

"You would be thinking of Switzerland," Gunter told her.

"They all sound the same to me," Lulu said, once again filling the room with her booming laughter, which made everyone else laugh, too, except for Tyler. He didn't know what her game was, but he knew one thing for sure: there was much more to Lulu than met the eye.

The evening meal had not turned out to be the congenial social gathering Claire had hoped it would be. She pondered the matter as she and Emily helped Lulu clear away the dishes. Mrs. Parks had seemed even quieter than usual and had eaten very little. Lulu had downed third helpings of everything, and had chattered ceaselessly. Jonas had conversed with Emily and ignored Lulu, except to glare at her every time she made a remark he considered rude. Gunter had monopolized Claire's attention with long, detailed stories of his homeland, and Tyler had spent his time sending Gunter dark glances and quizzing Lulu about her background.

"Wasn't that just the grandest time?" Emily asked afterward, perching on a kitchen stool.

"Angel, that was more fun than a barrel of monkeys," Lulu exclaimed. "And you, sweetie pie," she said to Claire, "were the belle of the ball. Those two handsome stallions couldn't keep their eyes off you."

Claire blushed. "I'm sure Mr. Jenssen is just the friendly type. And Mr. McCane and I are simply acquaintances. Besides, I'm engaged." Claire heard Emily snicker behind her.

"Oh, well, that's a different story entirely." Lulu

paused to tie on her apron. "So when do I get to meet your intended?"

"His name's Rancid Lanced," Emily quickly put in. "And you won't. He's in hiding."

"In hiding?" Lulu turned to Claire and whispered, "He's not on the lam, is he?"

"No. He's just—very busy. And his name is Lance Logan. Emily, I'll thank you to stop calling him that other name."

Emily scoffed. "Well, he *is* a skunk. He's so stinky he forgets to write!"

Lulu gave Claire a sympathetic look. "I feel for you, sweetie pie. I've been forgotten more often than the name of the Vice President. Men!" she said, shaking her head. "If they weren't so danged cute, I'd take my carving knife and cut off their—"

"Emily, aren't you going to read to Mrs. Parks?" Claire interrupted quickly.

Emily, who had been listening avidly, pouted. "You're trying to get rid of me again."

Claire put her sister's Braille book in her hands and turned her toward the doorway. "Go. Mrs. Parks will be waiting."

As soon as Emily had gone, Lulu put her hands on her hips and gave Claire a puzzled look. "Now what did you think I was gonna say?"

"Miss Cavanaugh?" Gunter called, poking his head into the kitchen. "Could I trouble you for a cup of tea?"

"I'll make that for you," Lulu offered. "Want me to bring it to the parlor?"

"Well, I have been sitting on the porch, but if you want me to sit in the parlor, I will."

Lulu laughed. "Sit where ever you want and I'll bring it to you. Maybe Claire would like to sit on the porch and keep you company."

"That I would greatly enjoy," Gunter gushed.

"See there?" Lulu said to Claire. "Now go on out and I'll bring your tea in a jiffy."

As Gunter left the kitchen, Claire turned around and gave Lulu a look of disbelief. "I told you, I'm engaged!" she whispered.

"Sure you are, sweetie. But think of this: Gunter is just a boy in a strange country who misses his home. You're being friendly, is all. There's nothing wrong with that. Don't worry, I'll finish up here."

Although she knew Lulu was right, Claire was not looking forward to spending her evening with Gunter. Passing the parlor, she saw Tyler and Jonas having a deep discussion and instantly wished she could trade places with Jonas.

As though they heard her thoughts, both men turned at that moment and spotted her. "Claire," Tyler called, striding toward her. "Are you busy?"

He moved with a confident, masculine stride that made her pulse race. With his intense gaze on her, Claire felt the sudden return of those annoying butterflies. "I was on my way to the porch to visit with Mr. Jenssen," she told him.

"Then I came along just in time, didn't I?"

The conceit of this man!—although, in fact, he was rescuing her once again. Nevertheless, Tyler really needed to be brought down a few pegs. "Actually, I find Gunter quite polite and charming."

"And about as exciting as a used match." Tyler took her arm. "Jonas," he called, "see to Mr. Jenssen."

Claire gave Tyler a disgruntled look. "Gunter's not a horse. You can't simply 'see' to him."

"Jonas," Tyler called again, "Entertain Mr. Jenssen. Ask him about himself." Tyler took her arm and led her down the hall toward the back door. "Better?"

Claire ignored the gibe. "Where are we going?"

"Somewhere private."

Claire felt those butterflies begin to flutter madly. "For what reason?"

"For reasons better discussed in private."

They silently crossed the backyard and headed for the stables. The light had faded to a pale mauve glow in the west, and it would be dark within half an hour. She glanced at Tyler from the corner of her eye, wondering what she should do if his private reasons included seduction. She wasn't sure she trusted her resolve to resist him. It might be safer to turn back. Yet something urged her to go on—a need to be daring, a desire to tempt fate.

When they reached the stables, Tyler said, "Wait here," then disappeared inside, returning a moment later with a woolen blanket. He spread it on the ground behind the building and sat down. "Will you join me?"

Claire's heart beat wildly as she sat and carefully arranged her skirts about her, trying to hide her nervousness. "What is this about?" she asked, in as calm a voice as possible.

He leaned back on his elbows, watching her closely. "What do you know about Lulu?"

Claire was stunned—and disappointed. "I know she comes highly recommended by Doctor Jenkins."

"Is that all?"

Claire looked down, embarrassed now that she hadn't paid more attention to the matter. "Lulu had other letters with her, but I only glanced at them."

"You need to read them thoroughly."

She searched his face, alarmed by the serious tone of his voice. "Why? What do you think I'll find?"

Tyler paused to pluck a blade of grass and slip it between his teeth. "Maybe nothing, or maybe an indication that she's not who she pretends to be. Lulu is hiding something, Claire. I could tell by her answers at supper. That makes me wary."

"Doc Jenkins wouldn't send her to me if he thought something was wrong," Claire argued. "Perhaps she's hiding something personal about herself, such as a divorce."

"She evaded my questions about where she was born, about what her full name is, and about whether she has any family in the area. And she was very clever at shifting the subject away from herself. Wouldn't you say that was slightly suspicious?"

"Even so, Lulu seems to be a very warm-hearted, capable person. I don't believe that she presents any danger to us."

Tyler threw down the blade of grass. "People aren't always what they seem on the outside. Take my word for it."

Claire studied him for a long moment. "Are you what you seem on the outside?"

He shrugged casually. "Depends on what you see, I guess."

"Do you want to know what I see?"

Tyler seemed to distance himself from her without moving an inch. "No, I don't."

His answer surprised her. Lance had always loved flattery. Claire thought all men did. "It's nothing bad," she assured Tyler. "In fact, it's very good."

He broke off several long weed stems, one by one, and tossed them away, his movements quick, almost angry. "That's why I don't want to hear it."

"You don't like compliments?"

Tyler looked away. "I don't trust them."

"*Them*, or the person who gives them?"

He turned, looking at her as one stranger might another, and then the hard lines of his features softened. Reaching out to run his fingers down her cheek, he said, "The problem is that you trust everyone."

Shaking her head, Claire replied, "You're wrong. I trust carefully." She gazed deep into his eyes. "I trust you."

Tyler had difficulty holding her gaze without flinching. Claire's trust made his marriage plan all the easier to carry out, yet it also made his fledgling conscience take another painful step toward maturity. Could he live up to her trust?

The word *obligations* suddenly came to mind. If he carried out his intent to marry Claire, like it or not, he would be obligated to take care of her. Did he want that burden?

Tyler's jaw tightened in resolve. What he wanted was his dream. To fulfill it, he would undertake the obligations of a husband, as long as Claire understood his need for freedom. If he could fashion the marriage as he liked it, he'd enjoy having Claire as his companion. His gaze moved down over her shapely form and up again to focus on her mouth. He'd enjoy it very much. At once, he felt the deep surge of power in his groin.

He looked up to find Claire still gazing at him with large, trusting eyes. "I appreciate your faith in me," he said uncomfortably. "But there's something else I need to talk to you about."

"Oh," she said, a look of disappointment on her face.

Tyler realized Claire had been hoping for some kind of reciprocal statement. Feeling awkward, he decided it was a good time to change the subject. "I believe Walter Greene was murdered."

Claire blanched. "Murdered!"

She rose and paced to the corner of the building as her mind filled with frightening thoughts. Anna Greene's suspicions had been correct, and now Anna herself was missing. Claire remembered her warning. *"Miss Cavanaugh, pass auf! Watch yourself! You may also be in danger."* Claire put a hand to her throat. Was she next on the killer's list?

Tyler walked over to her. "Are you all right?"

"I just can't believe someone would kill him." Claire looked at Tyler. "Does the sheriff have any idea who did it?"

"If he does, he's not saying."

"And now Anna has disappeared," Claire said worriedly.

"Jonas and I went to the general store today to see what we could find out," Tyler told her. "Mrs. Greene didn't take anything with her, not even the clothes in her drawers. Would you go on a trip without clothes?''

"Do you think she was murdered?''

"It's a possibility.''

Claire twisted her fingers together anxiously. If she was in danger, then Emily could be, also. "What do we do?''

"Wait for the sheriff to investigate.''

"But the man who murdered them is out there somewhere. What if he—'' The thought was so frightening Claire couldn't finish it.

Tyler put his hands on her shoulders and stared directly into her eyes. "Listen to me. Whoever is responsible is not going to take any more risks. He's probably on the run, afraid that he'll be caught at any moment. But regardless, I'm not going to let anyone hurt you.'' Tyler put his arms around her, drawing her close. "I'll be here every evening, and so will Jonas. And you'll have plenty of company during the day. You'll be safe.''

Comforted by the strong arms around her, Claire blinked back a sudden film of tears. She was so grateful for everything Tyler had done. How could she ever repay him? Her heart swelled as she leaned back to gaze up at him. She knew now that what she felt for him was so much more than gratitude. It was love.

Tyler bent his head toward her and Claire knew he was about to kiss her. Should she refuse him? For a brief moment, she thought she should. But when Tyler's lips touched hers, she knew better.

Chapter 14

Their mouths came together in a fervent clash of desire. Claire wound her arms around Tyler's neck as he pulled her against him, ravishing her with hungry kisses. They broke apart, breathing hard, then came together again. Claire yearned for more, kissing him eagerly, letting him explore her mouth with his insistent tongue, besotted by his taste and touch.

A far-off cry caused her to break their kiss.

"Claire? Sweetie pie, are you out there?"

Tyler pressed her to his chest as he caught his breath. "Don't answer."

Claire wanted so much to comply, but couldn't. "I have to," she said with regret. "Something might have happened." Reluctantly, she moved away from him, away from the safety of his arms. "I'd better go back alone."

Without looking at him, she turned the corner of the building and started across the yard. Her heart pounded and her body still trembled from the tremendous force of her desire. She heard Lulu call again, and knew she should be grateful for the interruption. Her passion had been so overwhelming that she doubted she could have controlled it. How would she have lived with herself? "I'm coming," she called dispiritedly.

Lulu stood on the back porch, squinting into the darkness. Spotting Claire, a smile of relief spread across her face. "I was beginning to worry, sweetie pie. I'm sorry to bother you." She opened the back door and they went into the big kitchen together. "There's a lady here to see you about renting a room. I wasn't sure if I should take it upon myself to give her one."

By the tone of Lulu's voice, Claire knew there was something questionable about the late caller. She also was surprised that a lady would be out at that hour looking for a place to stay so far from town. "I'll take care of it. Thank you, Lulu." Starting briskly up the hallway, her step slowed when she saw who was at the door.

The lady smiled arrogantly from beneath the wide brim of her hat. "Hello, Claire."

Claire stared at her former schoolmate in surprise. Daphne Duprey was the daughter of the town council president. Her mother was a bastion of social functions. They lived in a large house two blocks off of Grand Avenue, but Daphne also had her own residence on Eleventh. Why would she need a room at Bellefleur?

Daphne removed the large, pearl hat pin from her hat, swept the hat from her head, and patted her thick copper-brown ringlets. "I understand you're taking in boarders."

"Yes, I am," Claire replied, perplexed.

"I'm having my house painted inside and I can't abide the fumes. I'll need a room for two weeks." She paused. "You do have a room available, don't you?"

"Yes," Claire replied automatically. She heard Lulu come up behind her and turned. "Will you take Miss Duprey upstairs? Either room at the end of the hall will do."

Lulu plucked Daphne's traveling case from the floor. "Right this way, Miss Duprey. Why, that rhymes, doesn't it? I'm a poet and you didn't know it." Her booming laughter echoed in the stairwell as she led Daphne up to her room.

Perplexed, Claire watched them go. She and Daphne had been adversaries for years. Coming into the school at the age of ten, Claire had been unaware of Daphne's prestigious social position. But Daphne had taken swift and cruel measures to correct that and had never missed an opportunity to remind Claire of her humble beginnings. Why didn't Daphne stay with her parents, or at the hotel in town? Oh, well—she needed money and Daphne was a paying customer.

Hearing a slight creaking sound, Claire turned as Emily stepped out from behind the parlor door. "What is Daffy doing here?" her sister asked.

Claire sighed in exasperation. "Emily!"

Her sister puckered her mouth. "She smells so sweet my teeth hurt."

"Daphne's house is being painted. She needs a temporary place to stay."

"Hah! That's what she's telling you. *I* think it's because Tyler McCane is here. You know what everyone says about Daffy being a loose woman. She's probably set her sights on him."

Claire gasped. "Emily! Where did you ever hear that?"

"Sh-h-h! Here comes Tyler." Emily felt her way along the wall to the stairs.

Claire looked around, but saw no sign of him. "Just a minute, young lady!"

" 'Night, Tyler," Emily called.

"Goodnight, Emily." Tyler opened the front door and stepped inside. His gaze moved from Emily's retreating form to Claire, and immediately she felt the blood rush to her face. He walked over to her, stopping inches away, gazing down at her as though he were ravenous. His hand came up to stroke the side of her face. "What was the emergency?"

Claire stared up at him, wanting to drown in his gaze. "I have a new boarder."

He cupped her chin in one strong hand and ran his thumb over the contours of her lips. "I'm sorry Lulu interrupted us."

Claire had to fight her conscience not to agree with him.

Hearing Lulu's heavy footsteps overhead, she stepped back. "I have to say goodnight to Emily."

Tyler's gaze darkened as he stared down at her. "Hurry back," he said in a husky voice. He dropped his hand as the housekeeper started down the stairs. " 'Evening, Lulu."

"Well, isn't this a pleasant surprise? Hello there, cutie." She stopped to pinch Tyler's cheek as though he were a little boy. "I've been saving a surprise for you in the kitchen—an apple tart with your name on it."

"An apple tart." The thought of it made Tyler's mouth water. He knew exactly what it would taste like, too. "I haven't had one since I was a boy."

She gazed at him for a moment, a sadness in her eyes. "Then it's time you had another." Giving him a pat on his cheek, Lulu turned to Claire. "Miss Duprey is all settled in. I told her there were refreshments in the parlor, and I took Mrs. Parks some chamomile tea earlier to save you the bother." She leaned close to whisper, "I figured you were busy." Straightening, she started toward the kitchen. "Come on, cutie, before that old limey buzzard finds your dessert."

With a wink at Claire, Tyler obediently started after Lulu.

Claire watched him go, his tall, handsome form stirring her blood, making her yearn for what she couldn't have. With a resolute sigh, she headed upstairs to tuck her sister into bed. Daphne's cloying fragrance lingered in the stairwell, reminding her of what Emily had said. *Had* Daphne come to Bellefleur because of Tyler? Claire caught herself growing jealous and frowned. She had no claims on Tyler.

Still, she couldn't help hoping that Emily was wrong.

Seated at the kitchen table, Tyler bit into a bite of juicy apple tart. "Delicious," he said through a mouthful of flaky crust.

"I knew you'd like it." Lulu propped her chin on her hand and leaned toward him, scrutinizing him closely while he took another bite and chewed it. As though satisfied with what she saw, she sat back with a smile. "Tell me about yourself, Tyler McCane."

"What do you want to know?"

"Tell me what you're like."

He swallowed the food. "I don't know how to answer that."

"Are you quick tempered? Easy going? Shy?"

Tyler's eyes narrowed as he studied her. "Why do you want to know?"

"I'm curious. Just like you were curious about me at supper this evening."

Tyler grinned, sensing he'd met his match. "You know one thing about me already. I'm curious. And I'm cautious."

"I could tell." She leaned back in the chair. "What are your dreams?"

"My dreams?"

Lulu smiled. "You have dreams, don't you? Everyone has dreams."

Tyler cut another bite of the tart with his fork. He'd thought having dessert with her would be a good opportunity to find out more about the woman. It seemed she had the same idea about him. "I suppose I do. What about you? Do you have dreams, Lulu?"

She laughed heartily. "Me?" For just an instant, her gaze shifted beyond him and an incredible sadness stole across her features. "I used to," she said quietly. Her gaze focused once again on him, her jovial face back in place. "And you?"

"Sure, I have dreams. Big ones."

Lulu grinned. "I kind of figured that. So what are these big dreams of yours?"

Tyler finished off the tart and sat back. "They're still in the works."

With a knowing smile, she studied him. "You're awfully private, aren't you?"

"I could say the same about you."

With a chuckle, Lulu stood up and took Tyler's empty plate to the sink. "Maybe we're just two of a kind."

Tyler watched her as she washed the plate. He had a sense of knowing her, yet he was sure he didn't. And whatever Lulu was hiding, she was very good at it. But there was something so comforting about her that he decided Claire was right. She presented no danger to them.

"I think I'll turn in now," Lulu told him. "It's been a long day. Sleep tight."

And don't let the bedbugs bite, Tyler thought to himself. When had he last heard that old saying? Surely not since he was a boy. "Thanks for the dessert," he called out.

"It was my pleasure," came her reply.

Tyler wandered down the hallway toward the parlor, hoping to find that Claire had returned. He found Jonas there instead, listening to one of Gunter's boring stories. "Excuse me," he said. "Jonas, I need to speak with you."

He caught a movement from the corner of his eye, and turned around. A young woman uncurled a remarkably sensuous body from her chair and rose, gazing at him with a lazy smile.

Jonas walked over to him. "Ty, there's someone I'd like to introduce to you. Tyler McCane, this is Daphne Duprey. Miss Duprey is Claire's newest boarder."

She held out a well-manicured hand. "Pleased to meet you, Mr. McCane."

Tyler took her hand, gazing at her with interest. Daphne's hair was a burnished copper, her eyes were the color of golden topaz, and her tawny brown eyebrows arched up over them to give her the look of an exotic jungle cat. Even her dress matched her coloring. "I'm pleased to meet you, too, Miss Duprey."

"We were just listening to one of Mr. Jenssen's fascinating stories," Jonas said. "Why don't you join us?"

"Yes, why don't you, Mr. McCane?" Daphne echoed, flashing her golden cat eyes at him. "You can sit beside me on the sofa."

Tyler smiled. Daphne was anything but subtle. "I'd love to, but another time, perhaps."

Daphne's mouth formed into a pretty pout. "I'll hold you to that."

"I'm sure you will." Tyler glanced at his assistant. "Jonas?"

"Coming. Goodnight, all."

The two men retired to Tyler's room, where he produced his decanter and two glasses. "So who is Daphne Duprey?"

"Luscious, isn't she?" Jonas watched Tyler pour a measure of whiskey into each glass. "And definitely dangerous. The spoiled, unmarried daughter of one of the town's best families. On the hunt for a mate, too, is my guess. Seems her house is being painted." Jonas accepted a glass and took a sip. "Ahhh! Much better. If Jenssen had gone on any longer I would have begun to snore. Nice chap, but he does tend to rattle on."

"What is Jenssen doing in Fortune?" Tyler asked, turning a desk chair to straddle it.

Jonas removed his shoes and lounged on the bed, his back against the headboard. "He represents some wealthy investors in Sweden who are eager to get in on some oil speculating. Apparently there are rumors that this area is ripe for development. He was sent to find out if they were true. If so, he has the authority to buy into them."

"Think there's anything to the oil rumors?" Tyler asked.

"I haven't the foggiest." Jonas sipped his drink thoughtfully. "I wonder if those wealthy Swedes would be interested in investing in a fleet of riverboats."

Tyler studied his assistant, pondering the idea. "It might be worth looking into."

Jonas sat forward, swinging his legs off the bed. "Think

about it, Ty. You could end your affiliation with Boothe. You wouldn't need his money if you had theirs.''

Tyler frowned thoughtfully. "You may be on to something, Jonas. I've been thinking of cutting loose from Boothe anyway. I don't trust him anymore, not after the lies he's told me. I don't know to what lengths Boothe would go to get Bellefleur from Claire and that worries me, too. If I could get the financial backing from someone else, I could develop this property without Boothe. Then I know she'd be safe because the land would be in my control.''

"I take it you've definitely decided to marry her.''

For a moment, Tyler swirled the whiskey in his glass, watching it color the sides. "It looks like I'm heading in that direction.''

"And how was your little rendezvous with Claire this evening?''

Tyler finished his drink and stood up. "Productive.''

"Think she'll accept your proposal?''

"I'm sure of it. Would I take no for an answer?''

They both looked up as Gunter appeared in the open doorway. "I heard voices. I'm sorry if I'm interrupting.''

"No, you're not interrupting,'' Tyler said, jumping to his feet. "In fact, we were just talking about you. Come on in and have a seat. Would you like a glass of whiskey?''

"Yes, thank you. I would very much like that.''

Tyler poured him a glass and offered him the desk chair. "I understand you represent some businessmen who want to get in on some oil speculating.''

"That is my purpose here, yes.''

Jonas sat forward excitedly. "Do you think they'd be interested in investing in a big riverboat operation?''

"I could ask them. If it will make money, I'm sure they would want to hear about it.''

Tyler exchanged a satisfied grin with Jonas. He found a pencil and paper and began to jot down some numbers. If

Jonas's idea worked, Tyler could get rid of Boothe and make Jonas a full partner. It was time he was rewarded for his years of faithful assistance.

Reginald Boothe arrived at the bank early the next morning to find the sheriff waiting for him outside. "Is something wrong?" he asked, using his key to open the thick, wooden door.

"McCane came to see me yesterday." Simons glanced around nervously, adding in a low voice, "He's still asking questions about Greene's death."

"*Damn* it! I was afraid this might happen. Come inside." Their shoes echoed on the polished oak floor as he led Simons upstairs to his office. "All right. Tell me what happened."

"McCane asked about the marks on Greene's neck again." Simons took out his handkerchief and mopped his face. "He knows it was murder, Mr. Boothe."

"Don't panic, Sheriff. He doesn't know who the murderer is. What did you tell him?"

"I said maybe Greene had gotten into a fight that night. Now he wants me to ask around to find out who he fought with."

"Well, then I think you should do just that."

Simons stared at him in disbelief. "But there isn't going to be anyone."

"Of course there is."

"I don't understand. You want me to blame Greene's death on an innocent man?"

"Unless you can find a guilty one to blame," Boothe remarked sarcastically.

Simons squeezed his red handkerchief in his big hands. "But I know most of the men in town. I can't blame a murder on one of my friends."

Boothe gritted his teeth. He despised the word *can't*, and never tolerated it in his underlings. "I'm not suggesting you blame it on one of your friends. There's a man boarding at the Cavanaughs' place—he's a foreigner, and he was renting a room from me over the pawnshop at the time of the murder. He's the perfect suspect."

Simons stared at him unhappily. "Mr. Boothe, this isn't right."

"Look here," Boothe said, losing patience, "if McCane is nosing around, sooner or later others will be, too, thanks to your bungling. And the townsfolk aren't going to be too happy if there's a murderer on the loose, are they? They'll be clamoring for you to find the killer. So I feel very strongly, Sheriff, that Mr. Jenssen may have been in the vicinity the night Greene was murdered. Go down to the Dockside Tavern and find a couple of men who heard him come in afterward, bragging about the killing."

Simons kept shaking his head. "It's not right, Mr. Boothe. This young fella is gonna hang for something he didn't do."

Boothe lifted one eyebrow. "Better a stranger than you or me—isn't that right, Wilbur?"

With a sick feeling in his stomach, Simons turned and headed for the door. It seemed to him that they might be saving their necks, but they were certainly selling their souls to the devil.

That afternoon, Claire sat at the table with Lulu and made out a list of all the supplies they would need to finish stocking the pantry. The house was quiet and a gentle breeze wafted through the open windows, bringing with it the sounds of chirping birds. Emily had taken her book outside to read to Mrs. Parks on the porch. Tyler and Jonas were out with the *Lady Luck*. Daphne and Gunter had both risen early and left after breakfast.

"Well, I think that should about do it," Lulu announced. "Want me to go for the supplies?"

"No, thank you. I need to go to the post office anyway and check for mail."

"Still waiting for that letter from your fiancé?" Lulu asked, her voice heavy with sympathy. "From what your sister tells me, you'd be better off setting your sights on Tyler."

"Don't believe everything Emily tells you," Claire cautioned. "She never liked Lance."

"How do you feel about him? Do you love him?"

"He's my fiancé," Claire answered automatically.

Lulu watched her closely. "But do you love him?"

Claire opened her mouth to reply, but closed it again. She didn't love Lance—she knew that now. But she was still committed to him.

Lulu leaned across the table towards her. "If you can't answer that one, then answer this: how do you feel about Tyler?"

Claire felt herself blush. "I don't think that matters."

Lulu stared intently into Claire's eyes, for some reason reminding her of Tyler with his probing gaze. Then she leaned back. "So why doesn't Emily like Lance?"

"I wish I knew. She got to know him last summer when he came to meet my father. Lance was very pleasant to Emily, but she didn't even try to get along with him."

"That's young'uns for you," Lulu said, with a shake of her head.

"Do you have children?" Claire asked.

The question seemed to catch Lulu off guard, but she quickly recovered. "Do I look like the type of person who'd want babies hanging all over her?" She gave a bark of laughter "Not me. I wasn't cut out for that kind of life. You, now, sweetie pie, you look like the type."

"I do hope to have a family some day," Claire said with a sigh. "I hope to have a *wedding* someday."

"Maybe that letter will come today," Lulu told her, patting her hand.

Claire hitched up the buggy, and Emily decided to go along, chattering nonstop all the way.

Seeing her sister so content was a great relief, but Claire wasn't sure what to do about school. Would she have enough money to pay Emily's tuition along with all the other expenses? She wouldn't be able to make plans until she sold the crops and knew what her budget would be. Yet, even if Emily had to stay home, Claire reminded herself, at least she had a home to stay in.

Half a block from the general store, Claire parked the buggy and helped Emily down. They proceeded along the wooden sidewalk and were just about to turn into the store when a man stepped out in front of them. Claire grabbed Emily's arm and pulled her back as she stared up into the haughty countenance of Reginald Boothe.

For a moment, he too seemed taken aback, as he stared at Emily. But when Claire pulled her farther away from him, shielding her sister from his hideous gaze, he gave her a smirk and tipped his hat.

"Good afternoon, ladies."

Claire could feel Emily trembling. Keeping a firm hold on her sister's arm, Claire stepped around Boothe without replying. She watched through the window until Boothe had disappeared from sight, then she turned to her sister, who was pale and quiet. "Em, are you all right?"

"It was him, wasn't it?" her sister whispered. "It was The Snake."

"It's all right, Em," Claire assured her. "He's gone."

Emily shivered. "He smells evil, Cee Cee. He frightens me."

"I know. He's an intimidating man, but he can't hurt us. Let's pick out some candy to take back with us, all right?" Claire smoothed back her sister's hair, waiting for her to answer, but Emily still seemed shaken by the encounter. "All right, Em?"

"Can I have some horehound candy?" she asked in a little voice.

''That sounds scrumptious.''

The clerk took their list and began to assemble their supplies while Claire and Emily went to the post office in the back to check for mail. Claire glanced at her sister uneasily. She'd never seen Emily so disturbed before. How telling it was, that Emily could sense the man's wickedness without even being able to see his face. And how sad that it was her own father.

Claire flipped through her mail, stopping in surprise when she saw a letter addressed to her in Lance's hand-writing.

Her heart skipped a beat. He had written at last.

Chapter 15

Claire could hardly contain her excitement as she headed back to Bellefleur. Finally she would learn why it had taken Lance so long to reply. As soon as she and Lulu had put away the supplies, she escaped to her room to read the letter in private.

"Cee Cee?" Emily called, as she made her way up the staircase. "Do you want a horehound drop?"

"No, thank you, Em." Closing her bedroom door, Claire opened the envelope, removed the single sheet of paper and sat on the edge of the bed to read it.

Dear Claire,

I hope this letter finds you in good health and a generous frame of mind. I have put off writing to you because of the unpleasantness of what I must say. Please do not think too unkindly of me. I have struggled with this decision for some time now.

Claire's stomach suddenly felt queasy. She knew intuitively what Lance was about to say, and did not want to read on. She went to her open window and took deep breaths. For several long moments she gazed out at the land that gave her strength. Then, holding the letter in her trembling hand, she forced herself to go on.

As you may know, my own finances are somewhat pre-carious, so rather than taking on additional burdens, I felt it was best to release you from our engagement.

He thought of her as a burden. Claire looked up, angry tears blurring her vision. She should have guessed there were money reasons involved, but she had refused to believe Lance was that shallow. Gripping the letter in both hands, she blinked to clear away the tears.

Please do not worry about me, Claire. Mary Taylor, who you must surely recall from our history class last semester, has kindly introduced me to her father. He has promised me a position with his company in Spring-dale. With my talent, I expect I shall do very nicely there.

Sincerely,
Lance

Claire read the letter again, sickened by the insincerity of it. *Please do not worry about me,* he had written. "Did you worry about *me*, Lance?" she cried, flinging the letter to the floor. "Did you wonder how I was coping with my father's death? Did you think of me *at all*?"

With deliberate movements, Claire picked up the letter and slowly crushed it. Of course she recalled Mary Taylor, who had flirted shamelessly with Lance right in front of her. As far as Claire was concerned, Mary was welcome to him. They deserved each other.

Dropping the crumpled letter in her wastebasket, Claire stared out the window. She had struggled to keep her commitment to Lance while he obviously had felt no such loyalty to her. How had she so misjudged him, when Emily had seen through him all along? Why had she believed that he loved her, when he'd only wanted to use her?

Tears of fury and pain ran down her cheeks. Feeling

suddenly trapped by the four walls, she flung open her
door, dashed down the stairs, and fled the house, holding
her skirt so she wouldn't trip as she ran down the long
slope to the river. There she collapsed onto the grassy bank
and wept.

Emily listened to the fading footsteps, then quietly
stepped from behind the door across the hall and entered
her sister's room. Feeling along the top of the bed, then
the small writing desk, and finally the wastebasket next to
it, she found what she was looking for. She smoothed out
the wrinkles and took it downstairs.

"What do you have there, angel?" Lulu asked, as Emily
made her way into the kitchen.

"Cee Cee's letter from Lance. Will you read it to me?"

"But that's private, sweetie pie."

"Please, Lulu!" Emily begged. "That Rancid Lanced
wrote something that made her go running out of the house
crying."

Lulu took the letter reluctantly. "I don't know about
this, angel. I don't like prying."

"She'll never know," Emily assured her.

"What if she comes back and catches us at it?"

"I'll hear her coming. Please, Lulu?"

Lulu pulled out a chair and sat down. "All right—but
I don't like doing this."

"I don't like seeing my sister cry, either," Emily replied.

They both gasped when they heard the front door open.
"Who's there?" Lulu called.

"Jonas Polk."

"It's just the limey," Lulu said. "He won't come back
here. He hates me." She began to read the letter aloud,
but stopped in surprise when Jonas walked in. She quickly
stuck the paper behind her back.

"What do you have there?" he asked suspiciously.

Lulu lifted her chin haughtily. "None of your business, Limey."

"It's all right, Lulu," Emily said. "Jonas is my friend and Cee Cee's, too. He should hear what it says." She turned her head in the direction of Jonas's voice. "Where's Tyler?"

"He saw your sister running down toward the river and followed her. She appeared to be in distress." He looked from Emily to Lulu. "What's going on? What should I hear?"

Lulu pulled out the letter. "The reply from Rancid Lanced."

Tyler paused at the top of the rise, shading his eyes with his hand. Spotting Claire sitting near the river's edge, holding her hands to her face, he started down. As he drew nearer, he heard her weeping. The sound made his stomach knot.

At the soft fall of his footsteps on the grass, Claire looked around. Her eyes were swollen and red and her lower lip trembled. Tyler knelt down and instinctively put his arms around her. "What happened, Claire?"

Turning her face to his shoulder, Claire sobbed out her story—but all Tyler could make out were the words *letter* and *money* and *Lance*.

"Has Lance written to you for money?" he asked.

"No!" she sobbed, lifting her head. "It's off!"

"What is?" he asked, smoothing wisps of black hair away from her face.

"Our—" she hiccuped, "—engagement!" She buried her face in his shoulder once again and wept harder.

Elation filled his soul: Lance Logan was out of the picture! Now there was nothing to stop Claire from marrying him. The only question was whether Claire would be amenable to the idea. But he was a master at strategy; he knew which cards to play and which to keep up his sleeve.

With renewed confidence, Tyler gazed out over the vast spread of land. At last he could see his plans completed. He stroked his hand over Claire's hair. "You don't need Lance," he assured her. "He didn't love Bellefleur like you do. You need someone who respects the land, someone who has vision. Lance isn't that man."

Claire lifted her head to look at him, her eyes sparking with anger. "Lance didn't love me. All that time I believed he cared, but he only wanted my father's money. He *used* me. How could I have been so naive? How could I have trusted him?"

"Lance is a fool, Claire." But even as he said it, Tyler felt a sharp inner jab. Was he any better than Lance? Wasn't he using Claire to get her land?

This was different. He did care about her; and besides, Claire had as much to gain from the marriage as he had.

Claire turned to stare out at the river and Tyler could see the tension in her face. "Lance has already found someone else," she told him in a flat, controlled voice. "He's been seeing her since I left school. Maybe even before. I can't believe I was so blind."

Her anger nearly hid her pain, but Tyler recognized it. How many times had he done the same thing? He put his arm around her shoulders and drew her against his side. "Lance is the one who's blind. No one has to offer what you have. You're a good woman, Claire. A kind, decent woman." His words came out without thinking, and Tyler realized he meant them. "You deserve more than what Lance could give you."

Claire leaned against Tyler, letting his comforting words smooth the sharp edges of her anger. She wiped her eyes with the backs of her hands. He was so different from Lance. He had strength, kindness, and above all, integrity. "Thank you," she told him. "You're very kind."

"I meant every word I said."

"I feel like such a fool."

Tyler drew her back into his arms, tucking her head

beneath his chin. "Lance is the fool. Remember that."

In the safety of his embrace, the deep ache of Lance's betrayal began to ease. Claire let herself absorb Tyler's strength and his comforting words. When she thought back to all the pleasant times she and Lance had shared, it was clear to her that they had never really been in love—not the kind of deep abiding love her mother and father had shared.

Now she doubted that they had even been friends. What kind of person would use and betray a friend? Perhaps she had merely been infatuated with Lance's charm and popularity. Perhaps for Lance, there had never been anything more than an attraction to her father's money. If she hadn't been called home prematurely, she might have married him and found out too late that there was no love between them.

When she was ready to go back, Tyler rose and held out a hand to assist her. Standing beside him, Claire gazed across the river. It was a view she had thought to share with Lance someday. "It's beautiful, isn't it?"

"Yes, it is." Tyler turned her by the shoulders and stared deep into her eyes. "And so are you." Bending his head down, he put his mouth lightly on hers, tasting her lips in a tender, reassuring kiss. He leaned back to look at her, his strong hands cupping her face. "You're going to be all right, Claire."

She slipped her arms around his ribs and hugged him tightly. His caring words and gentle touch were the perfect medicine to heal her wounds. She *was* going to be all right.

Conversation at supper that evening was a bit different than it had been the prior evening. Jonas watched Tyler and Claire carefully. Whatever damage the letter had inflicted, the end result was good. Indeed, they seemed hardly to notice anyone else. It gave Jonas hope that Tyler's heart was softening. To help things along Jonas had given

Ty his seat at Claire's left, and had cautioned Emily and Lulu to pretend they knew nothing about the letter. Thank goodness, they were behaving admirably. Mrs. Parks, bless her heart, knew nothing about it anyway. Daphne had not returned for the meal.

Jonas glanced at Lulu, who was chatting amiably with Gunter. Prickly as she was, Lulu seemed genuinely concerned about Claire's welfare. And he had to give her credit in the work department; she was no slacker. She was also a damned good cook.

"Would you pass the beans, please?" he asked her.

"Here you go, Jonas," she said, handing him a big dish of green beans cooked with bacon.

That was another benefit from the letter: Lulu had stopped calling him "Limey."

He sat back with a satisfied grunt. It looked like Ty's plans were going to work out, after all. Jonas had a few plans of his own, and it seemed they were going to work out, too. Then again, how could Ty not fall in love with Claire? Even a cautious heart would open up to her.

Reginald Boothe strode quickly up the back path to Daphne's house. He had come in from the alley so as not to be seen, since Daphne was supposedly not living at home.

As usual, she was waiting at the door to greet him. "Evenin', darlin'," she said. Her long hair was loose and she wore only a silk wrapper, as was evident by her hardened nipples. He knew it was an expensive silk wrapper—he had purchased it for her himself.

Without saying a word, he went to her bedroom, sat on the edge of her bed, and waited. In a moment Daphne appeared, garbed in the manner he demanded—wearing a black wig, the long, silky locks hanging down her back, just as Marie Reneau's had.

Her sultry gaze fixed on him, Daphne untied the sash

and let the garment slide slowly over her shoulders and down her lush body, pooling in a silken puddle at her feet. Boothe's eyes moved up her golden flesh, pausing at the tawny triangle between her thighs, rising to her heavy breasts. She walked toward him, her hips swaying provocatively.

Boothe ran his hands down her body and up again. "Did you do as I asked?"

"I always do as you ask, darlin.'" She dropped her head back as he pleasured her.

"Claire was willing to rent you a room?"

"Oh, yes," she moaned.

"And that Swede is still there?"

"Yes," she panted. "And so is—McCane—and his—assistant."

"McCane?" Boothe decided he'd have to ponder that situation later. He was too aroused to think about it now. "Anyone else?"

Daphne was barely able to answer. "Some old crone—by the name of—Lulu." She clutched his shoulders and let out a scream of pleasure.

Boothe grabbed her around the waist and tossed her on the bed, face down. "Good girl," he told her as he took his own pleasure from her. "You're such a good, obedient girl." He smiled down at the beautiful body beneath him, imagining not Daphne, but Marie.

But even acting out his private fantasy wasn't enough to satisfy his lust for revenge. Only having Bellefleur could do that. *Soon*, he assured himself. *Very soon, it will be mine.*

Throughout the next day, Claire moved steadily away from her broken dreams and focused on building new ones. She now felt grateful that Lance had finally broken their engagement, even though she was still angry at herself for being so naive and trusting. Indeed, she was hesitant now to put her trust in anyone. Yet Tyler had demonstrated his strength of character—she knew he wouldn't let her down.

The hours seemed to crawl by as she waited to see him again. Tyler and Jonas had left before sunrise to sail on the *Lady Luck* and wouldn't be back until late in the day. Daphne had slipped out after breakfast and Gunter had left mid-morning. Claire spent the morning walking the fields to check on the crops and talk with the farmhands. She was encouraged by the weather: the rain had finally moved on and the crops were doing well.

That afternoon, Claire finally faced the painful task of packing her father's belongings. When she had done as much as she could for one day, she went downstairs, where Emily was entertaining Gunter with a puppet show.

As Claire stood in the parlor doorway watching, a heavy knock sounded on the front door. She glanced through the window and saw the sheriff and a deputy on her porch.

"Good afternoon," she greeted them.

Simons gave her a solemn nod and in a business-like tone said, "Afternoon, Cee Cee. Do you have a fellow here by the name of Jenssen?"

Claire's stomach tightened in sudden foreboding. "Yes; why?"

"I've come to arrest him for the murder of Walter Greene."

Chapter 16

~⌒⌒⌒~

Claire nearly laughed. Gunter, a murderer? She couldn't believe he was capable of *any* crime, let alone such a heinous one. Stepping outside, she closed the door so she wouldn't be overheard. "Sheriff, what on earth would make you think Mr. Jenssen killed Walter Greene?"

"I have witnesses," Simons replied. "Several fellows down at the Dockside Tavern heard him talking about the killing the next day."

His proof sounded like nothing more than rumor. "Talking about a killing is very different than confessing to it, Sheriff. I'm sure all the men at the tavern were talking about it."

Flustered by her logic, Simons's face grew red. "Cee Cee, I only told you as a favor. Now I'm going to have to ask you to get Jenssen for me."

"What are you going to do with him?"

"Take him down to the jail."

Claire stared at him in dismay. Poor Gunter, locked in a jail cell! "Can't you just question him here? I'm sure once you talk to him, you'll find out for yourself that he's innocent."

Simons took a step toward the door. "Cee Cee, if you won't go get him for me, I'll have to get him myself."

Backing away, Claire stepped inside and closed the door. Her stomach knotted as she hurried to the parlor.

"Gunter," she said apologetically, "the sheriff wants to see you outside."

"The sheriff?" Gunter looked bewildered as he stood. "He wants to see me?"

Emily popped up from behind the chair as Claire started out of the room after Gunter. "What happened, Cee Cee? Why does Simple Simon want to see Gunter?"

"This is Gunter's business," Claire replied, pausing at the door. "I want you to stay in the house, Emily."

"No! I want to go with you."

Claire's nerves were ready to snap. "Stay here, Em!" she ordered. She hurried to the door and stepped outside just as the sheriff clapped handcuffs on Gunter.

"But I did not do anything!" Gunter was protesting. He turned to Claire imploringly. "Miss Cavanaugh, they are arresting me for murder!"

"The sheriff just wants to ask you some questions, Gunter," Claire assured him, giving Simons a furious glance. "You'll be fine. Just answer honestly."

As the sheriff and his deputy escorted Gunter down the front porch steps, Lulu came rushing out the door, followed by Emily, who had obviously gone to get her. "What's going on here?" the housekeeper demanded loudly, starting down the steps.

"They're arresting Gunter for the murder of Mr. Greene," Claire told her.

"Hogwash! You release that boy," Lulu demanded, following the sheriff and Gunter to the wagon parked in front of the house. When the sheriff ignored her, she stepped between him and the frightened Swede. "You listen to me, *Mister* Simons! This boy is no more capable of murder than I am! Release him now, or you'll have me to deal with!"

The sheriff nodded to his deputy, who grabbed Lulu's arms from behind. "Let go of me, you big lummox!" Lulu cried, trying to wrestle free.

Claire ran toward Lulu as the sheriff climbed into the

wagon with Gunter. Holding on to the porch rail for guidance, Emily started after Claire, screaming, "Let them go! Let them go!"

Claire grabbed Emily's arm and pulled her back as the sheriff picked up his rifle and aimed it at Lulu. "Stand back or I'll arrest you, too!" he barked.

Lulu froze. The deputy released his hold and climbed into the front of the wagon, taking up the reins. Lulu glared at them, but stood where she was as the wagon pulled away. "You're a bigger idiot than I thought, Wilbur Simons!" she yelled.

Claire watched mutely as the wagon drove down the road. Emily clung to her. "What's going to happen to Gunter, Cee Cee? Will they hang him?"

"I don't think so, Em."

"Is he a killer?"

"No, angel." Lulu came up the steps and ran her hand over Emily's head. "Gunter is no killer. That sheriff is an idiot and always has been. Everyone in town knows it." Shaking her head, she looked down the road where only a cloud of dust marked where the wagon had been. "Poor Gunter. Poor, scared boy."

"Tyler will be here soon," Claire said. "He'll know what to do."

Gunter sat mutely on one of the side benches in the back of the wagon as they made the trip back to town. Simons, sitting opposite him, could feel the Swede's eyes boring into him, but he refused to look back. He stared out at the passing countryside, too ashamed of his role in this deception to meet Gunter's perplexed gaze.

He took Gunter out of the wagon in the alley behind the jail and ushered him in the back door, placing him in one of the four small cells.

"Why are you doing this?" Gunter asked in a bewildered voice, as his handcuffs were removed. "What evidence do you have?"

"We have men at the Dockside Tavern who heard you talking about the killing."

"They are lying!" Gunter cried desperately. "Take me to them. They will not be able to say such a thing to my face!"

"You were living above the pawnshop. You had the perfect opportunity to follow Greene that night and kill him."

"It isn't true!" Gunter protested. "I'm not the killer. I was Walter's friend!"

Simons glanced nervously over his shoulder. "Can you prove you're not the killer?"

Gunter started to speak, then pressed his lips together and looked down. After a moment, he slowly shook his head. "No," he said desolately.

"Then be quiet."

Morosely, Gunter sat on the wall-hung wooden bed and glanced uneasily around his confined quarters. "What will happen now?"

"You'll have to appear before the judge." Simons walked out of the cell and locked the door. "He'll look at the evidence and then decide if there will be a trial."

"A trial?"

At the sight of the young man's frightened face, Simons gut twisted, imagining what was in store for the young man. He turned away with a frown. "I'll see about getting you some chow."

At six o'clock, Claire, Emily, Lulu, and Mrs. Parks sat down in the dining room to the delicious meal Lulu had prepared, but no one seemed to have an appetite for it. Conversation was stilted and forced. Claire watched the clock, waiting for Tyler to come home. The mantel clock ticked along with her thoughts. *Hur-ry. Hur-ry.* She couldn't get the image of Gunter's frightened, bewildered face out of her mind. She was certain he was innocent.

At the sound of wheels on the gravel in front of the house, Claire jumped up in relief. "They're home." She ran to the front door and stepped out on the porch, twisting her fingers together as Tyler and Jonas climbed down from the buggy.

Tyler knew something was wrong immediately by the look on Claire's face. He strode forward, mounting the steps two at a time. "What is it?"

"Gunter's been arrested. The sheriff says he murdered Mr. Greene."

"Faugh!" Jonas scoffed, as Lulu and Emily came out onto the porch.

"Did the sheriff say what proof he had?" Tyler asked her.

"Yes, but it's just rumor. He has witnesses who say they heard Gunter talk about the killing the day after it happened."

Tyler tried to remember if Gunter had ever said anything the least bit suspicious. He could read people pretty well, and there had been nothing in Gunter's face or behavior that had alerted him to any danger. Basically, Gunter seemed to be a harmless young man whose major crime was that he liked to talk too much. He didn't seem the type to murder anyone in cold blood. But that didn't mean he couldn't have killed the pawnshop owner in a fit of rage.

"Will you help Gunter?" Emily asked, tugging on Tyler's sleeve.

"I'm not sure what I can do for him, Emily."

"You don't think he did it, do you?" Emily asked.

Tyler looked at Claire as he answered. "I think I'd better talk to him." He turned to Jonas. "Want to come along?"

The three women stood on the porch watching anxiously as he and Jonas pulled away.

"They're certain Jenssen is innocent, aren't they?" Tyler remarked to his assistant.

"Women seem to have an instinctive feel for these things," Jonas replied. "What do you think?"

Tyler settled himself more comfortably on the seat. "If it's possible to bore a person to death, then maybe the sheriff has a case against him. My gut feeling is that the sheriff needed to find a killer and Gunter, being a foreigner, was a convenient suspect."

Daphne drew her buggy up to Reginald Boothe's imposing home and stopped. Boothe put his hand on her knee. "Same time tomorrow?

"Whatever you say, darlin'."

Boothe watched her pull away, then turned to find the sheriff sitting on the brick wall that edged his shrubbery. As Boothe walked up to the house, Simons stood and removed his hat.

" 'Evening, Mr. Boothe."

"Sheriff, how did it go?"

"The Swede is down at the jail now."

Boothe unlocked his door and stepped inside. "Did he put up much of a fight?"

"No, I think I took him by surprise. But the women sure did object."

Boothe motioned for Simons to follow him. Closing the door, he walked into a sumptuous drawing room and opened a lead-glass fronted wine cabinet to remove a bottle of Cabernet. "Did you see McCane?"

"No, sir. He left on his riverboat early this morning. He wasn't back yet when I went out to the house."

"With all the questions he's been asking, I expect he'll be down to see you when he returns. I trust you have the story straight."

With a frown, the sheriff lowered his eyes. "Yes, sir."

"Don't look so grim, Wilbur. You know this is necessary.'' Boothe uncorked the wine, poured two glasses, and handed one to Simons. ''Remember this, Sheriff: you're lying to save your job *and* your neck—because if I'm ever discovered, you'll hang right alongside me.''

Tyler strode into the sheriff's office with Jonas close behind. The young deputy seated at the rolltop desk jumped to his feet, startled by their sudden entrance.

''Where's Jenssen?'' Tyler demanded.

The deputy motioned over his shoulder, edging closer to the gun cabinet. ''In the back.''

Tyler went straight to the door that separated the jail from the front office. ''Open it.''

''I can't let you in there.''

''Why not?''

The deputy looked rattled. ''Well, because the prisoner is in there.''

Tyler saw the man's eyes shift nervously from him to Jonas. ''Look, I'm not going to try to break him out of jail,'' Tyler assured him. ''I want to ask him some questions. My assistant can stay out here if you'd like.''

''How long you gonna be?''

''A quarter of an hour, no more.''

The deputy looked from one man to the other. ''All right,'' he said finally, taking out the ring of keys, ''but I'll be out here watching through the window.''

Tyler shrugged. ''Suit yourself.''

He walked through the door held open by the deputy and heard it shut firmly behind him. In the dim interior, he saw four jail cells, two on either side of the short hallway. A lone man in the first cell on the right rose from a wooden bed and came to the bars. ''Mr. McCane!''

''Jenssen, what happened?''

Gunter's grip tightened on the bars. ''I am being blamed for Walter Greene's death! You must believe me, Mr. McCane, Walter was my friend. I would not hurt him.''

"You knew Greene?"

"Yes. I was renting a room above his shop. His wife is half Swedish, you know. They were very good to me. Often they invited me to eat dinner with them." Gunter held up his hands in a shrug. "Why would I want to hurt them?"

"Do you know where Mrs. Greene is?"

"No." Gunter shook his head adamantly. "I do not know where she is."

Pulling a stool up to the bars, Tyler took a seat. "What kind of proof does the sheriff have against you?"

"People who heard me talking about killing Walter. But that's not true: I never go to taverns."

"Never? Are you sure?"

Gunter started to reply, then paused. "Well, maybe once, when I first came to this town."

That was bad. Tyler knew witnesses could be bribed to forget exactly when they saw him at the tavern. "Could anyone have seen you leave the pawnshop after Mr. Greene went out the evening he was killed?"

"No! I did not go out at all that evening."

Gunter's eyes clearly reflected his fright, but they also showed something more. "What *did* you do that evening?" Tyler asked.

Gunter began to rub his temples. "I think I read. Or maybe I wrote a letter to my family in Sweden. I can't remember. My mind is twisting and turning so." He looked up plaintively, reminding Tyler of a frightened little boy. "The sheriff told me I have to see a judge. Do you know if this judge is a fair man?"

"I don't know him, Gunter. He's a circuit judge and only comes to Fortune once a week. I imagine there will be a hearing for you the next time he comes through." Tyler put the stool back. "I'm going to see about getting you a lawyer."

Gunter stared forlornly at Tyler. "Thank you for your help, Mr. McCane."

Tyler reached through the bars and patted his shoulder. "Rest easy, Jenssen. We'll do our best to get you out of this." He signaled to the deputy who was watching from the tiny square window in the door. "Where's Sheriff Simons?" he asked, as he exited the dark hallway.

"He's not on duty tonight," the deputy replied, "so he's probably at home."

"Where does he live?"

The deputy looked outraged. "You can't just go knocking on his door this late at night!"

"I'm right here, Lyle."

Tyler and Jonas turned as the sheriff came in the front door carrying a package wrapped in butcher paper. Lumbering across the wooden floor, he opened the swinging gate. "Take this grub to the prisoner," he told the deputy. Then he said, "You need to see me, McCane?"

"You bet I do, Sheriff."

"Pull up a chair." The wooden swivel chair creaked as Simons sat down and turned it to face Tyler. The deputy returned and took up a station nearby, watching every movement the two visitors made as though he expected trouble at any moment.

Seated in a narrow, straight-backed chair next to Jonas, Tyler folded his arms across his chest and eyed the sheriff skeptically. "You honestly believe Gunter Jenssen killed Greene?"

"Would I have arrested him if I didn't believe it?"

"You tell me, Sheriff. From what Jenssen says, you don't have much evidence."

Simons opened a drawer and took out several sheets of paper. "I have the testimony of two people who heard Jenssen talk about the murder and saw him carrying a wad of money."

"May I?" Tyler asked skeptically, holding out a hand.

The sheriff handed him the papers. Tyler looked at one and gave the other to Jonas. The only thing written on the paper was a single line that read, "I swear I heard Gunter

Jenssen talk about killing Walter Greene and saw the money he had stolen from him," with a signature Tyler didn't recognize. "Who are these witnesses? Where did they hear him say this?"

The sheriff filed the papers away. "At the Dockside Tavern. They're dock workers."

Conveniently for the sheriff, dock workers didn't always live in town. The men would have to be found and questioned thoroughly. "What about this so-called wad of money?"

"Jenssen was carrying money on him when we arrested him. We think he stole it from Greene."

"In other words," Tyler said, "you believe Gunter's motive for killing Greene was to steal his money. Then you know for sure that Greene was robbed?"

The sheriff shifted uncomfortably in his chair. "Well, not for sure."

"Mr. Jenssen represents wealthy investors, Sheriff," Jonas said with a haughty sniff. "He carries *their* money with him."

"That's what he *says*," Simons countered.

They were getting nowhere. "When is the hearing?" Tyler asked, rising from his chair.

"Judge Crawford will be coming through on Tuesday."

"We'll see you then, Sheriff."

Simons watched them go, then immediately pulled out his handkerchief and mopped his forehead. He'd had a bad feeling about this right from the start. He still didn't understand why his boss had to murder Greene—he was a harmless fellow. Simons also didn't understand why Boothe was so determined to get the Cavanaugh land. But he knew better than to ask questions.

He hadn't wanted to arrest Gunter, but Boothe had ordered it, and he dared not go against an order. Now the sheriff had to hope that the judge would release Gunter for lack of solid evidence, and that the matter would be dropped. He knew one thing for sure: he didn't want to hang for Boothe's crime.

Heading back to Bellefleur, Tyler shook his head in disgust. "This whole situation stinks."

"You know why they're blaming Gunter, don't you?" Jonas snorted. "He's a foreigner. I should be grateful that Gunter was here to take the blame. Otherwise, it could have been me."

Tyler was silent. He hadn't cared for Gunter from the beginning, but now he realized that it had nothing to do with the man himself. It was only because Claire had taken such interest in him. "You know, Jonas, before I spoke to Gunter, I was hoping he was guilty."

Jonas stared at him in shock. "For God's sake, Ty! Not out of jealousy, I hope."

"Certainly not! But if Gunter didn't kill Greene, that means we have a murderer on the loose and an innocent man in jail."

"I see your point."

"We're going to have to get him a lawyer."

"Of course. I'm certain the lad's innocent."

"He's also our link to those wealthy investors," Tyler reminded him.

"Ever the pragmatist, aren't you, Ty?"

"Always."

As though they had not moved an inch from the time Tyler and Jonas had left, Claire, Lulu, and Emily stood on the porch watching the buggy pull up to the house.

"Did you see Gunter?" Claire called.

Tyler hitched the horse while Jonas went up to talk to them. "Yes, we did. Or rather, Ty did."

"Is the boy all right?" Lulu asked.

"He's a little nervous, but not harmed," Tyler replied,

walking up the steps. "He's going to need a lawyer."

"Is it that serious?" Claire asked him, searching his face.

"Serious enough that I don't want to take any chances. Jonas will go into Mt. Vernon tomorrow. He'll be able to find a good attorney there."

"Oh, that poor boy," Lulu moaned. "I'm going to bake him a pie. Angel, come help me."

Claire paced to the end of the porch and gazed out at the field of tobacco in the distance. Jonas gave Tyler a pat on the back. "You go talk to her. I'll leave you alone," he whispered.

As Tyler approached, Claire turned. "You talked to Gunter. Do you think he did it?"

Tyler shook his head. "No, I don't."

"Then how can the sheriff think so?"

"He needs to catch a murderer. Otherwise, he's not doing his job and folks will complain. So his solution is to find a likely candidate, and unfortunately, Gunter fits the bill: he lived above the pawnshop; he had a large sum of money on him; he supposedly talked about the killing at the Dockside Tavern; and he's a foreigner. People are usually suspicious of foreigners anyway, so the sheriff is using that to his advantage."

"I didn't know Gunter lived above the pawnshop."

"He was renting a room there. Gunter says the Greenes befriended him. There's enough circumstantial evidence to make it important that he gets a good lawyer."

Claire twisted her fingers together anxiously. "I feel like this is my fault."

"How is it your fault?"

"Everything I touch goes bad."

Tyler put his arms around her and drew her close. "You're touching me. Nothing bad is happening."

As Claire gazed up at his handsome face, a shiver of apprehension raced up her spine. It was only a matter of time until something did.

Chapter 17

⤜⟡⤛

Claire sat hunched over the desk in her father's den the next afternoon, working and reworking figures for a budget. She paused when she heard the front door open, then, recognizing Lulu's heavy tread, went back to her calculations. Lulu had gone to the jail after lunch, taking Gunter the peach pie she and Emily had made.

Claire looked up in surprise when Lulu came storming in. "Look at this!" she exclaimed, slapping her hand against the front page of the Fortune *Globe*. "How dare they print this hogwash!"

In large, bold print, the front page headlines screamed the news: WALTER GREENE'S KILLER CAUGHT!

"Oh, no!" Claire groaned. "They've already decided he's guilty!"

"Read it out loud, Cee Cee," Emily called, making her way into the den.

Claire reluctantly began to read.

Sheriff Wilbur Simons has announced the arrest of the man suspected of murdering pawnshop owner Walter Greene. A hearing on this matter will be held on Tuesday. The man, who goes by the name of Gunter Jenssen, stated that he is from Sweden and is here on business.

Claire looked up, her anger simmering. "He *goes* by the name of Gunter? They make it sound like he's using a false name!"

"What else does it say?" Emily asked.

Jenssen has been renting a room at the late Arthur Cavanaugh's home, Bellefleur.

"Well, isn't that just dandy?" Lulu said, shaking her head.

Too disgusted to read the rest, Claire gave the paper back to Lulu and returned to her calculations, only to be interrupted again half an hour later. Harry Weysel, the newspaper's sole reporter, stood on her porch, notepad in hand.

"Afternoon, Miss Cavanaugh. It is still *Miss Cavanaugh*, isn't it?"

Claire gave him an icy look. Harry, who stood five feet five and was so thin he'd been nicknamed "Slats," had a sly way of asking personal questions without actually seeming to do so. He was doing that now, fishing for information about Lance, whom the whole town had known about after his visit last summer. "Have you heard otherwise, Mr. Weysel?"

He grinned. "No, miss, I guess I haven't."

"Why have you come here?"

"I want to ask you a few questions about Gunter Jenssen."

Claire stepped outside. "Good. I want to set the newspaper straight on a thing or two."

"So do you think he's guilty?" Harry asked, pulling a pencil from behind his ear.

"No, and I resent your newspaper making it sound like he is. That's completely unfair. Gunter hasn't even had a hearing yet."

Sticking his tongue out of the corner of his mouth in

concentration, Harry wrote down her answer. "Did you get to know him while he stayed here?"

"Yes, I did, and I found him to be a perfect gentleman. He was very polite to all of us."

"What did he talk about?"

"Sweden, mostly. And that brings me to another point. Just because he's foreign doesn't mean he's a criminal."

Harry paused to write down her answer. "Do you trust foreigners, Miss Cavanaugh?"

"Of course, unless I know of a good reason not to. I would certainly give them the benefit of the doubt before I jumped to any conclusions. I'm renting to a British man right now."

"Is that right? So you're saying you would rent out rooms to any foreigner who came through town?" He watched her closely.

Claire saw the trap and knew she had already fallen into it. "I wouldn't refuse them just because they came from a different country."

Harry scribbled again, then looked up. "This is certainly a beautiful home. It's been in the Cavanaugh family a long time, hasn't it?"

Claire gave him a wary look. "Yes."

"Why are you renting out rooms?"

As Claire stared at him, wondering how to answer the question without embarrassing herself or Emily, she heard a buggy approaching. Over Harry's shoulder, she saw Daphne step down. The reporter turned, watching with obvious interest as Daphne sashayed up to the porch, hips swaying in her fawn-colored dress. She stopped directly in front of Claire.

"I need my bill, if you please." She lifted her chin haughtily. "I'm moving out."

Puzzled, Claire took her to one side to keep Harry from hearing, "Aren't you staying the full two weeks?"

"And have my reputation besmirched by residing in a house that caters to criminals?" Daphne replied louder than was necessary. "I should say not!" As though she had just noticed the little man gaping at her from less than a yard away, she turned to give him a sultry smile. "Why hello, Slats. What are you doing here?"

"Interviewing Miss Cavanaugh. Say, can I ask you a few questions, Miss Duprey?"

"Why, I'd be delighted!" She gave Claire a chilly look. "Let me know what I owe you."

Claire glowered as Daphne made a production out of arranging herself on the swing, while Harry Weysel crouched at her feet, his notepad on one knee. She cringed to think what Harry would put in his article about her. And now that Daphne had announced she was leaving, there would be even more fodder for town gossip. Things were going from bad to worse.

Now she had only two rooms rented. That income barely covered their food. If others felt as Daphne did, and no one would rent a room from her, how would she pay her bills?

Less than a month ago she had been at school, blissfully happy that she was about to graduate and return home to Bellefleur. She had been on the brink of beginning a new life as Lance's wife. Now she dreaded waking up in the morning, afraid of what the day would bring.

Papa, I miss you so! Claire had never felt more alone.

When Daphne sashayed into his office just before closing that afternoon, Boothe jumped up in dismay and quickly shut the door behind her. "Why did you come here?" he asked through gritted teeth. "I told you never to do that."

"Relax, darlin', I came on bank business." Daphne took off her tan gloves and hat and sat in the chair in front of his desk. "Everything went exactly as you planned, even to the timing of Harry's arrival. When I left, that house was in a turmoil."

Boothe sat in his chair and took a cigar out of the humidor. "Good," he said, clenching the cigar between his teeth. "Now, go before someone notices you."

"My, you're nervous today." Daphne rose, her glittering cat eyes on him. She walked around the desk, swivelled his chair so the back was facing her, and began to massage his shoulders. "Doesn't that feel good?"

"Nice," Boothe admitted reluctantly. "But I'd feel even better if you left."

With a huff of annoyance, Daphne gave up. Retrieving her gloves and hat, she walked to the door and yanked it open.

"Same time this evening?" Boothe asked.

Daphne eyed him coldly. "I'm busy this evening," she said, adding pointedly, "*darlin'.*"

Seated at his desk near the staircase, Charlie Dibkins watched Daphne stamp out the door. She hadn't asked if she could go up to Boothe's office, which was what the customers were supposed to do. Instead, she had walked right past Charlie like she owned the building.

The young clerk frowned thoughtfully. He'd heard rumors that his boss's carriage had often been seen outside Daphne's house late at night. Now it seemed that Daphne and Boothe had just had a little spat. Charlie made a note to mention the incident to his mother. She was a member of the Fortune Ladies' Society, and so was Daphne's mother. Wouldn't she love to find out that her precious daughter was carrying on with a man more than twice her age? And what would her father have to say?

Charlie tapped his chin thoughtfully. Steven Duprey doted on his little girl. Nothing was too good for Daphne, and no man good enough. When he found out about Boothe, Charlie hoped he was around to see it.

*   *   *

At supper that evening, Tyler heard all about the news-paper reporter's visit and Daphne's untimely exit from Emily, who had just happened to overhear their conversation. As Emily described the man she had nicknamed "the hairy weasel," Tyler glanced at Claire, who was obviously worried. It bothered him to see the lines around her eyes, yet the timing couldn't have been better. It would make his marriage proposal even more attractive.

"I have some good news to report," Jonas announced. "I found an excellent attorney today in Mt. Vernon, a Mr. John Oldham, who comes highly recommended. He promised he would come out to see Gunter soon."

"Well, that *is* good news!" Lulu exclaimed. "We'll show that idiot sheriff up yet."

After the meal, Tyler sat in the parlor reading the news-paper, killing time until Claire was free. When she came into the parlor, he stood. "Feel like some fresh air?"

Claire's heart turned over as she gazed up at him. "I'd love some fresh air."

Sitting beside her in the swing, Tyler gave her hand a gentle squeeze. "I know you're worried, but this is going to work out, Claire. You'll be all right."

"I'm afraid of what that newspaper article is going to say," she admitted. "Harry Weysel likes nothing better than to make a story as sensational as possible. I'm sure he'll use everything Daphne told him. That article could very well keep potential boarders away."

Tyler put an arm around her. "You're worrying need-lessly. I'll be here to help you."

Claire gazed at him, her gratitude evident in her eyes. "I appreciate that, Tyler, but I can't keep counting on you to come to my rescue."

Though Tyler was still uncomfortable in the role of a hero, at the moment, it was useful. He leaned down to nuzzle her ear. "You can always count on me, Claire. I want to help." They heard Lulu's voice nearby, and Claire quickly moved away.

Tyler rose and held out his hand. "Shall we take a walk?"

As they had done before, Tyler spread a blanket on the grass behind the stable and stretched out on it, his arms folded behind his head. Claire sat beside him, taking care to keep her limbs covered with her long skirt. The sky was nearly dark and the stars were already visible. It was a beautiful night for seduction.

"What do you think Gunter's chances are of going free?" Claire asked.

Tyler didn't want to talk about Gunter. His thoughts were on more immediate matters, such as what a beautiful profile she had. "I think they're good," he replied.

"You do? Really?"

"Really." He liked the way her eyes lit up when she was excited. "He's got a good attorney now."

"Thanks to you." She turned to face him, lying on her side, her head propped up on one hand.

Tyler smiled. He put his hand on the back of her head and drew her closer, raising his head to meet her mouth. His loins throbbed in anticipation of the pleasures to come.

As they kissed, Tyler shifted his body above hers, his kisses growing hotter and deeper, leaving Claire too weak with desire to think clearly. Somewhere in the back of her mind she knew she was behaving brazenly, but his passionate response sent currents of electricity surging through her body. She put her hands on either side of his face, reveling in the feel of his skin, the rough stubble of his beard beneath her fingertips.

As Tyler's lips moved down her throat, his fingers worked open the buttons of her blouse. She knew she should stop him, yet she wanted him to go on. His hand slipped beneath the thin fabric, under the lace edges of her corset, until it reached the soft mound of her breast.

Claire drew in her breath as his bold touch kindled a throbbing heat between her thighs. He peeled back her blouse and slipped the strap of her corset cover over her shoulders, baring her flesh to his hungry eyes. Cupping her breasts, he captured her mouth in an intense kiss, then blazed a trail down her throat. Claire gasped as his mouth found a nipple, then she shuddered with pleasure as his tongue ran around the tip and his lips pulled it into sweet, wet warmth.

She whimpered softly as he suckled, her enjoyment so great that she made no protest when he ran a hand down her clothed thighs and up again. His hand lingered at their junction as though forgotten as he continued the delicious assault on her breasts, then she felt the light pressure of his fingertips once again, stroking, then massaging, her sensitive folds until she writhed beneath his touch. When he gathered her skirts and pushed them above her knees, she made no protest.

He rolled to his side, leaving his hand free to slide up the inside of her thigh. The touch of his fingertips made her quiver, and when he dared to explore her secrets, she could only gasp and thrust her hips forward in a heated, pounding rhythm that came as naturally as breathing. She felt herself sliding into oblivion as her passion built, and then—there was nothing. Her body throbbing with desire, Claire opened her eyes to see Tyler unfastening his pants, leaving no doubt as to what his intentions were. But as much as she desperately wanted to give in to her passion and let him sweep her away on it, she couldn't.

Claire sat up, pushing down her skirts and fastening the buttons of her blouse with shaking hands.

Tyler looked at her in puzzlement, his eyes still clouded with passion. ''What's wrong?''

''I can't, Tyler.'' She released a shaky breath. ''I'm sorry.''

Tyler crouched down, his gaze piercing, intense. ''You're not engaged anymore.''

''We're not married, either. It's not right.''

Tyler gritted his teeth in frustration. His arousal was so fierce he thought he would explode. But he was coherent enough to realize he had blundered. If he proposed now, it would look as though he was saying it just to finish making love to her. He should have proposed first, and then made love to her. Cursing silently at his own impatience, he got to his feet.

Claire looked contrite as she stood and smoothed out her clothing. "I didn't mean to entice you. I know that's unfair."

Seeing her bent head, Tyler couldn't help but put his arms around her. "You do stir my passion, Claire. I won't deny that."

He saw her tense features soften. She reached up to run her hand along the side of his face. "Neither can I deny that you stir mine. But I can't go against my conscience."

Her face radiated her strength and determination. Rather than being angered, Tyler found himself envying Claire's restraint—one more reason not to let her see the real Tyler McCane. That man would have taken whatever she had offered and never looked back.

He walked Claire to the house and said goodnight to her on the porch. Sitting on the front steps, he stared out at the river. He would have to find another opportunity to present his proposal. He wanted everything in place well before Boothe's thirty days were up.

A movement at the side of the porch caught his eye. Turning his head, he saw Jonas coming toward him. "Where were you?" he asked his assistant.

"I walked across the road to take a look at your property. How did it go with Claire? Did you pop the question?"

Tyler frowned into the darkness. "The timing was wrong. I didn't ask her."

"Still think she'll say yes?"

"Do I ever take no for an answer?"

"That's my lad."

*   *   *

Emily moved silently away from the front door and started up the staircase. When she reached the third floor, she felt her way to Lulu's room and knocked softly. "It's me, Emily."

"What is it, angel?" Lulu opened the door. "I thought you were asleep."

"Can I come in? I have a secret to tell you."

"You do? Well, sure you can come in. I can't wait to hear it."

Emily felt her way to the bed and climbed up on it. "Guess what I heard?" she asked, nearly bouncing up and down in her excitement. "Tyler is going to ask Cee Cee to marry him."

"That's the best news I've heard in a long time. When is he going to ask her?"

"He almost did tonight, but he said it was the wrong time."

"Probably because of all the worries on Claire's mind," Lulu agreed. "We'll have to have a big celebration. Isn't it lucky that I showed up at just the right time?" She laughed loudly, then hushed herself. "You'd better get to bed. We've got a lot of planning to do tomorrow."

"Should we tell Cee Cee?"

"And ruin Tyler's proposal? Not on your life! We've got to keep it hushed up and not let on like we know a thing."

Emily sighed glumly. "I suppose."

Lulu chucked her under the chin. "That'll be half the fun! It's always fun keeping secrets."

"You keep secrets, don't you, Lulu?"

The housekeeper stared at her in surprise. "How did you know that, angel?"

"I know lots more than people think." With a yawn, Emily slid off the bed and made her way to the door. "G'night, Lulu."

Lulu kissed the top of her head. "Goodnight, my precious angel. Sleep tight." Closing the door, she glanced at the small, locked chest on the floor beside her bed, then shook her head. Emily couldn't open the lock, and even if she did, she couldn't see what was inside. But just to be on the safe side, Lulu pushed the chest under the bed. No sense taking chances.

Chapter 18

For the next two days, Claire tried to keep busy so she wouldn't think about the forthcoming newspaper article. She walked the fields, inspected the drying barns to see that they were ready for the tobacco harvest, and made daily trips with Lulu and Emily to visit Gunter.

The *Globe* came out twice weekly, on Tuesdays and Saturdays. On Saturday morning Claire drove to town early, wanting to buy a copy of the paper without Lulu and Emily being there. As she walked down the street toward the general store, she heard the whispers of people passing by and saw their covert glances. Keeping her head high, Claire marched into the store, bought a copy of the paper, and left.

Several women passing by noticed her and raised their eyebrows in silent reproach. She heard them whispering about her, their heads close together, and could only imagine what terrible things Harry Weysel had written. Claire hurried to her buggy, her stomach twisting with dread. As soon as she pulled up to the house, she hitched the horse and headed straight for her bedroom to read the newspaper in private.

The story was on page one, right in the center. Nibbling her lower lip, Claire read it quickly, then threw the paper aside. Just as she had feared, Harry Weysel had found a way to make it seem like she was running a house of ill repute.

Sickened, Claire stared out her window. No one would want to rent from her now—except for the kind of men the article had insinuated were already living there.

"Claire? Sweetie pie?" Lulu called from downstairs. "Are you going to town with us?"

"No, thank you," Claire called back. "I have a headache."

She paced her room until she saw the buggy pull away, then she left the house, walking rapidly down the slope to the river to sit and think. Already their food supplies were low, and soon the plow horses and milk cows would need more feed. And how long could she expect the farmhands to work with no pay? Or Lulu? Where would she find the money to pay for everything?

Her heart began to race, and she started breathing rapidly. Clenching her fists, Claire forced herself to take slow, deep breaths, trying desperately to ward off her mounting hysteria. But the old terrors were always there, just at the edge of her consciousness. With an anguished cry, she pressed the heels of her hands against her temples, trying to drive out the ugly memories.

Suddenly a voice broke through the blackness of her misery—Tyler's voice, calling her name. The ugly visions shattered into fragments, leaving her drained and shaken. Claire hugged her knees to her chest as Tyler came striding down to the river's edge.

"Here you are! No one was in the house. I was beginning to worry."

When Claire didn't answer, Tyler crouched down to study her face. He could tell she was terribly upset, and he had a hunch what had caused it. "You've seen the newspaper article?"

She nodded slowly. "I'm going to lose my home. No one will rent from me now. I still have five weeks to go before the tobacco can be harvested, and then another two while it dries. I don't know what I'm going to do."

"Marry me."

Claire turned her head. "What did you say?"

The words had slipped out involuntarily. He'd imagined a very different scenario for his proposal, but now that he'd done it he felt almost exhilarated, and most definitely relieved. He got down on one knee, took her hand and held it between his own. "Marry me, Claire."

"That's what I thought you said."

Tyler brought her hand to his mouth and kissed it, gazing into her eyes. "Will you?"

Claire's heart seemed to triple in size as she gazed at his handsome face. He wanted to marry her! It seemed incredible, and yet . . . she hesitated. His proposal was so sudden. She needed time to think about it. Lance's betrayal had shaken her faith in her ability to make a sound decision. "I—I don't know," she stammered.

"What can I say to convince you?"

She ran her hand lovingly along the side of his face. "Please understand, Tyler. I trusted Lance and he betrayed me. I don't want that to happen again." She got to her feet and walked several yards down the riverbank to ponder.

Tyler came up behind her and put his arms around her waist, pressing soft kisses against her neck. "Claire?" he said softly. "Did you love Lance?"

She was silent for a long time, and then she slowly shook her head. "No. I was infatuated with him."

"Are you just infatuated with me?"

Claire sighed. She loved Tyler; there was no doubt in her mind about that. But she had just lost her fiancé. How would it look to gain another so quickly?

"What will people say about my getting engaged to another man?" she asked him. "Everyone in town thinks I'm to marry Lance this fall."

"Do you really care what others say?" Tyler asked, his voice husky and low in her ear. "You know they would have learned about Lance eventually anyway."

His voice, his touch, were so reassuring that Claire was

tempted to throw caution to the wind. But she had to consider her sister's welfare, too. "I don't want vicious gossip to hurt Emily."

"Once we're married, what can they say? We'll be a family. Isn't that better for Emily? And you won't need to run a boarding house. That should stop the gossipers dead in their tracks."

He was right. Moreover, Emily had been the one to recognize Lance for what he was—and Emily liked Tyler. He had proven himself a good, dependable man, a man of integrity like her father. But was he simply coming to her rescue yet again? After all, he had never said he loved her, and she didn't want to make the mistake she had made with Lance. She turned to face him, searching his eyes for answers. "Why do you want to marry me?"

Tyler knew that what he said now was crucial to her accepting his proposal. Yet he could not bring himself to tell her he loved her. He could say honestly that he desired her, that he needed her land, that he cared about her. But he could not say what she wanted to hear.

The important thing was to convince her to say yes before she went back to the house. If he gave her time to consider, he ran the risk of losing her.

Tyler cupped her face. "There are so many reasons," he said, gazing intently into her eyes. "Your beautiful smile, for one, and that pert nose." He kissed her lips, then the tip of her nose. Then, still holding her face between his hands, he kissed her eyelids. "And these astonishingly lovely eyes." He ran his hands down her arms. "Your beauty, your gracefulness, your sweet, gentle ways." Slowly he pulled her close, dipping his head to kiss her deeply until he could feel the rapid beat of her heart against his chest.

He broke the kiss to whisper huskily against her ear, "Your passion stirs me, Claire. I want you by my side and in my bed. We can have a good life together. Just say you'll be my wife."

Drugged by his words, his taste, his touch, Claire tried to pull together her scattered thoughts. She knew Tyler would be good to her and to Emily. They would be a family once more, and her future would be secure. Tyler was right. What did it matter if people thought it was too sudden? It was her life. She had to do what was best for all of them.

She leaned back to look up at him, searching his eyes. They were honest, intelligent eyes, in a face she could trust. She gave him a quick nod. "I'll marry you."

Tyler began to laugh, as though he was greatly relieved. Claire gasped when he suddenly threw his arms around her, nearly toppling them both over. She laughed with him, gasping again when he grabbed her face between his hands and kissed her hard. He smiled broadly, a rare sight. "This is wonderful!" he exclaimed.

Holding hands, they started back up the slope towards the house. "When shall we set the wedding date?" Claire asked.

For a brief moment, he seemed to falter. "I hadn't thought about it."

"How about after the harvest?" Claire's mind began to fill with plans. "We can have a big feast and invite the farmhands and their families . . . We'll have to start making preparations soon—thank goodness we have Lulu! And of course Emily can be my maid of honor, and Jonas can be your best man—or perhaps he should walk me down the aisle." She paused to take a breath, then turned excitedly. "Won't everyone be surprised?"

"I don't think Emily will be surprised at all," Tyler replied. "She's hinted to me about our getting married on several occasions."

"Why, that little stinker!" Claire cried.

"You have to admit, she had a great idea." Tyler stopped to draw her close, gazing down at her with suddenly solemn brown eyes. "Let's seal our agreement with a kiss."

Claire closed her eyes as he bent his head toward her. She felt the warm brush of his lips against hers, felt his strong hands on her back and knew an immense sense of security. Yet something about his words bothered her. *"Seal our agreement...."*

It almost sounded like he was making a business deal.

Claire made Tyler promise not to tell the family right away, but to save it for a surprise. As they sat down with Lulu, Emily, Jonas, and Mrs. Parks for supper, Claire urged Lulu to tell them about their visit with Gunter.

"Well, the poor boy is doing as well as he can," Lulu told them, "considering he's sitting in a cold, damp cell. Isn't that right, angel?"

Emily took a drink of milk to wash down her food. "He sends his best to everyone and he wants to know if you'll send a wire to his family, Cee Cee."

"Of course." Remembering the whispers and looks she'd received the last time she went to town, Claire felt that sting of humiliation all over again. By now, they'd probably pegged her as a loose woman.

Suddenly she felt Tyler's hand on hers under the table. Then he flashed one of his rare smiles, and Claire couldn't help but smile back.

"All right, you two!" Lulu boomed. "What's going on? Ever since you came in, sweetie pie, you've looked like that sly cat who swallowed a canary."

Claire met Tyler's gaze and raised her eyebrows questioningly. At his nod, Claire broke into a wide smile. "Tyler and I are going to be married."

Everyone seemed to jump up at once. Lulu nearly squeezed the breath out of her, while Emily wrapped her arms around Claire's waist and hopped up and down, squealing, "I knew it! I knew it!" Jonas gave her a fatherly peck on the cheek and Mrs. Parks reached for her hands, pressing them between her own.

"Your father is smiling down on you, dear," the elderly woman said. "He would be delighted. Such a fine young man you're marrying. My warmest congratulations to you both."

"When is this momentous event to take place?" Lulu asked.

Claire glanced at Tyler. "After the harvest."

"Let's drink a toast to the happy couple," Jonas suggested. "Is there any wine in the house, perchance?"

"Mrs. Parks, didn't my father keep bottles of wine in the cold cellar?" Claire asked.

"Why, yes, dear. I believe he did keep some for special occasions."

"If this isn't a special occasion, nothing is!" Lulu declared. "I'll go down there right now and see if I can find it."

"Why don't you let me look for it?" Tyler said, jumping up.

Jonas got up, too. "I'll help you, Ty. Ladies, sit still and we shall return shortly."

Tyler climbed down the narrow steps into the cellar, holding a lantern in front of him. Jonas followed behind. "I take it Claire was amenable to your plan?"

"You saw her tonight. Didn't she look happy?" Tyler spotted several bottles on their sides on a high shelf and turned to hand Jonas the lantern.

"You didn't tell her everything, did you?" Jonas asked reproachfully.

Tyler grasped one bottle by its neck and brought it down with a shower of dust. He brushed off the bottle and looked at it. "This will do." He glanced at his assistant and saw the accusation in his eyes. "No, I didn't, Jonas."

"For God's sake, Ty—you're the one who's insisting on certain conditions. Don't you think it's only fair to tell her about those conditions before she agrees to the marriage?''

"It's too late to worry about that now, isn't it?" Tyler snapped.

"No one outside the family knows. She can still decline without too much embarrassment."

Tyler gave him a cold look. "It took some doing to convince her that marrying me was the best thing for her. I wasn't about to jeopardize that. Besides, she had just read the article in the paper and she was very upset. It wasn't the right time to begin naming my conditions. What would you have done?"

"Been truthful."

"You weren't there." Tyler paused. "I just didn't have the heart." What he couldn't admit was that he also didn't have the courage. He had been too afraid Claire would say no.

"So when are you going to tell her?"

Tyler started up the steps. "Soon. Very soon."

Claire, Emily, Mrs. Parks and Lulu made the trip to town on Sunday morning to attend church. Lulu went reluctantly, and only to appease Emily, or so she said. But her enthusiasm as she gustily sang the hymns hinted otherwise.

They sat in a pew at the rear of the sanctuary where Claire felt there would be fewer eyes watching her. She tried to concentrate on the sermon, but her thoughts kept drifting back to Tyler and his surprising proposal. As happy as she was, had she responded too hastily? She had made a mental list of all the reasons she should marry Tyler, and they far outweighed the reasons she shouldn't. In fact, there were only two reasons she was hesitant to marry him. Unfortunately, they were big ones.

Did she trust her own judgment? Claire couldn't help but doubt herself. And in all the reasons he had given for wanting to marry her, he had never said the one she most wanted to hear: that he loved her.

Yet there were so many benefits to marrying Tyler, was love truly the most important reason for getting married? He cared about her; he desired her; he would take care of Emily. Wouldn't that be enough?

After the service, they stopped to visit Gunter.

" 'Morning, ladies," Wilbur Simons said, his gaze fixed on Claire. "Come to see the prisoner?"

"He's got a name," Lulu insisted. "Why don't you use it?"

"What do you have there?" he asked.

"A buttermilk cake," Lulu said defiantly. "Want to poke your fat fingers into it to see if I hid a hacksaw in the middle?"

Giving her a disgruntled look, the sheriff nodded to the deputy to open the door. As the women filed past him, he said to Claire. "How are you getting along, Cee Cee? I'm sure you weren't pleased about that story in the paper."

Claire stopped to let Emily go around her. "It was a very unfair article."

"Like I mentioned before," he said in a lowered voice, "what you need is a man around the house to take care of you."

"And she's going to have one real soon," Emily said smugly, standing inside the doorway. "She's engaged to Tyler McCane."

Simons stared at Claire, his confusion evident. "But you already have a fiancé."

Claire felt a blush color her cheeks. "Mr. Logan and I have parted ways, Sheriff."

For a long moment Simons said nothing, but Claire saw his hands curl into fists at his sides. She glanced at his face and was stunned by the look of outrage in his eyes.

He nodded toward the door. "You'd better get in and see the prisoner. You've only got ten minutes."

Until that moment, Claire hadn't taken his courting seriously. Now she realized that he must have been hoping all along that she wouldn't marry Lance so he could ask her himself. She was immensely grateful Tyler had asked her first—she wouldn't have wanted to hurt the sheriff's feelings.

Wilbur Simons grumbled all the way to Reginald Boothe's house. People were staring at him, but he didn't care. He had every right to be angry. He had distrusted that McCane right from the beginning; he knew a scoundrel when he saw one. To think his Cee Cee was planning to marry that womanizing riverboat gambler!

He pounded on the front door of the elegant brick home. "Mr. Boothe?"

After a few minutes, the door opened and Boothe stepped outside, pulling it shut behind him. He wore a dressing robe, odd for that time of day.

"What is it, Sheriff?" Boothe said sharply. "I'm rather busy at the moment."

"Mr. Boothe, that scoundrel McCane is gonna marry Cee Cee!"

The banker looked bored. "Well, you guessed that might happen."

Simons balled his hands into fists, shifting restlessly on his feet. "I don't want it to happen—that's the problem."

Boothe leaned against the doorjamb and folded his arms across his chest. "And just what is it you want me to do about it?"

"Can't you talk to McCane? He'll listen to you."

"And tell him what? That he should step aside for you? Would you do the same if the situation were reversed?"

Wilbur Simons blinked rapidly. "Well, no, I guess not."

"I've told you before, I don't care who marries the little bitch as long as we get her land."

Simons was perplexed. Hadn't he always helped Boothe out, even when his conscience told him he shouldn't? He couldn't understand why the banker wasn't willing to do the same for him. "But, Mr. Boothe," he began.

Boothe stepped into the house. "Sheriff, I am not interested in your love life or lack of it. Now you'll have to excuse me. I have company." With that, he shut the door in Simons' face.

Stunned, Simons lumbered toward his buggy. Boothe and McCane were *both* just using Cee Cee to get what they wanted. McCane didn't care about her. But Wilbur cared. He'd known Cee Cee most of her life, and he wasn't going to let her be hurt any more than she already had been. He knew he had hurt her himself, in an effort to please Boothe, but this was where he put his foot down. He couldn't let Cee Cee sacrifice herself for that good-for-nothing gambler. It was time to tell her the truth about the man she had agreed to marry.

Chapter 19

$\backsim\!\!\!\smile\!\!\!\varnothing\!\!\!\bigcirc\!\!\!\smile$

Daphne Duprey turned from the window. "Wasn't that precious? Who would have thought that Wilbur would be attracted to a mousy nobody like Claire Cavanaugh?"

Boothe lifted an eyebrow. "Mousy? She may not be as striking as her mother was, but she certainly has some very appealing qualities."

Letting out a loud huff, Daphne stalked into the bedroom and began dressing with quick, angry motions.

"Leaving so soon?" Boothe asked from the doorway, a glass of wine in his hand.

She gave him a frosty look in the mirror as she carefully put on her hat. "My parents are expectin' me for Sunday dinner."

"You're in rather a feisty mood today."

"Maybe I'm just tired of you reminding me how beautiful and desirable Claire Cavanaugh is." She picked up her bag and walked toward the doorway, pausing in front of him to add, "Maybe I want to hear you say how beautiful and desirable *I* am!"

"Well, of course you are."

She gave him a look of pure distrust, then marched down the wide, marbled hallway to the front door. "I'm surprised you didn't court Claire yourself. Then you and the sheriff could both look like fools!" She slammed the door before he could reply.

Boothe laughed as he poured more wine. She'd be back. She liked his expensive presents too much to stay away for long. Sipping his wine, he stood at the window gazing down the street. So McCane had actually proposed, had he? That certainly made things a lot simpler. All he had to do now was sit back and wait. As soon as the marriage had taken place, he and McCane could begin their plans in earnest.

Wilbur, Wilbur! Boothe thought with a shake of his head. What a fool. Didn't he realize a woman of Claire's beauty would never marry him? For a moment, he thought back to what Daphne had said about pursuing Claire himself. But that would have been utterly ridiculous—Claire was too common to be the wife of Reginald Boothe.

He let the wine roll around on his tongue, savoring the smoky taste and dry texture. Ah, how he enjoyed the finer things in life. All he really lacked was Bellefleur, and that had just come within his reach.

That afternoon, with Tyler and Jonas out on the *Lady Luck* and the weather mild, Lulu decided the ladies should have a picnic down by the river, under the big oak trees. Blankets were set up, food was carried down, and they all ate lunch feeling lazy and contented. Only Mrs. Parks was absent; the trek down the slope was too arduous for her.

"Are we all going to live here together after you're married, Cee Cee?" Emily asked.

Claire leaned back on her elbows, enjoying the warm sunshine. "Of course we will. Tyler seems to love Bellefleur almost as much as we do, Em."

"But what about the house he's going to build?"

"He might sell it, I suppose."

"Will he keep his boat?"

Claire pondered the question. There was much she didn't know about her future husband. "I would think so. It's his pride and joy."

"Is Lulu going to stay and work for us?"

Lulu reached across the blanket to pat Emily's hand. "I never plan that far ahead, angel."

"You can't leave!" Emily cried, scooting over to hug her. "Cee Cee, tell Lulu she can't!"

Claire's gaze met Lulu's over Emily's head. "We do want her to stay, Em, but that must be Lulu's decision."

At the clatter of wheels on the dusty road, they turned. Claire stood to look up the slope toward the house. "It's Sheriff Simons. I wonder what he wants now?"

"Want us to go back to the house with you?" Lulu asked.

"No, I'm sure it's not important. I'll be back shortly." Claire started toward the house at a fast stride, her irritation growing. Though at first she had been annoyed at Emily for letting the sheriff know about her engagement, she had decided it was for the best. With Tyler around, the sheriff would have to stop pestering her. So what did he want now?

"Hello, Sheriff," she called as she came up the driveway.

He was standing on the porch, getting ready to knock. He turned in surprise. "Oh, hello, Cee Cee." Doffing his hat, he watched her come up the porch steps. "I hope I'm not interrupting. There's something I need to talk to you about—urgently."

Claire frowned in concern. "Is it about Gunter?"

"Oh, no, ma'am. Nothing like that. It's kind of personal, though." He looked around and spotted the swing. "Can we sit down?"

Claire seated herself on the swing, which sagged as the sheriff settled his bulk. "What is it you want to talk about?"

He crumpled the brim of his hat in his hands, staring at the floor. "Well, this is kind of embarrassing, Cee Cee. I'm not sure how to say this without—" He paused, groping for words. "I guess the best thing to do is just to say it flat out.'' He took a deep breath and let it out. "It would be a serious mistake if you married Tyler McCane.''

Claire nearly laughed. He was jealous! "And why is that, Sheriff?''

"I know you're thinking I'm just looking out for my own interests, but you've got to believe me. It's more than that, Cee Cee. I've been watching what's been going on for some time.''

Emily had been right again—the sheriff *had* been spying on her.

"I have to say this 'cause I'm partial to you,'' Simons went on. "The only reason Tyler McCane is marrying you is to get your land.''

Claire gave him a look of disbelief. "Sheriff, Mr. McCane bought the property next to mine. He has land.''

The sheriff was growing frustrated. "But that property doesn't go down to the river. He needs your land for his plans. He and Mr. Boothe want to put in more docks. They're gonna buy a whole fleet of riverboats and run 'em from here. And they're gonna turn your house into an inn!''

"An inn?'' Claire felt as though someone had poured ice water through her veins. The sheriff had to be mistaken—or lying. Yet she knew he wouldn't make accusations against Reginald Boothe unless he knew they were true.

"Yes, ma'am. An inn to house the visitors the boats would bring in.''

She sat numbly staring at him, her hands clasped tightly together in her lap. "Then Tyler and Boothe are partners,'' she stated in a flat voice. At his nod she looked away, feeling as though a dagger had been driven through her heart. She had been betrayed again.

"If you don't believe me, ask McCane yourself. Or ask that man of his. He's in on it, too.''

"Jonas!'' Claire whispered. The man who had befriended Emily had misled them, too.

"I'm sorry if this hurts you, Cee Cee," the sheriff told her. "I thought you ought to know who you were marrying."

Claire rose on wooden legs. "Thank you, Sheriff, for being honest with me."

He rose, too, and looked at her with sympathy. "Are you gonna be all right?"

Claire nodded, unable to speak.

He stared at her for a moment, then put on his hat. "You know where to find me if you need me."

Claire couldn't look at him as he lumbered out to his buggy. She stood staring out at the river, holding onto the porch post for support. Docks, boats, an inn—at Bellefleur! Had Tyler planned this from the beginning? Was that why he had come to town to see Boothe? And to think she had tried to warn Tyler about Boothe's character! The thought of him working with that evil man made her sick to her stomach.

Claire suddenly remembered what Tyler had said to comfort her after she had received Lance's letter. *"You don't need Lance. He didn't love Bellefleur like you do. You need someone who respects the land, someone who has vision."*

She hadn't guessed that Tyler had been talking about himself. *He* was the one who had vision—of turning her home into an inn, and putting her land to use harboring his boats—with Reginald Boothe as his partner.

"Lance didn't love me," she had told Tyler. *"All that time I believed he cared, and he only wanted my father's money. How could I have been so naive? How could I have trusted him?"*

"He's a fool, Claire. No one has to offer what you have."

Claire pressed a hand to her aching heart. No one had to offer what she had, and what Tyler and Boothe needed: valuable riverfront land. Everything Tyler had said to her suddenly made sense. And everything he hadn't said suddenly became too much to bear. He didn't love her. He was simply using her.

"You're a good woman, Claire. A kind, decent woman." And an extremely gullible one, she thought bitterly. At least Tyler had never pretended that he loved her, as Lance had. But each time Tyler had come to her rescue, she had assumed it was because he felt something for her—a feeling she had mistakenly believed was love. She had even endowed him with her father's heroism. Now she knew those rescues had only been to further Tyler's own selfish interests.

Claire recalled suddenly what Tyler had said to her just after he proposed. *"Shall we seal our agreement with a kiss?"* His words had struck her as odd at the time. Now she understood: to Tyler, this was business.

The sound of Emily's laughter drew Claire's attention back to the river. She knew they were waiting for her to return, wondering why the sheriff had come—but what would she tell them? Claire started down the slope, her mind numb. Should she tell them the truth? Should she say she'd just found out that Tyler was a liar? That he was using her? That Reginald Boothe was back in their lives, trying to take over their land?

Claire pressed her lips together. She would say nothing until she had time to sort out her thoughts.

Only three things were clear: she could not marry a man who was partners with Boothe; she could never trust Tyler again; and—she would never stop loving him.

Tyler strode down the ramp with Jonas, whistling a carefree tune. It felt good to be going to a home where a family awaited him. It would feel even better when he had a luscious female body to snuggle against at night. His desire flared as he pictured Claire with her long hair unbound, dressed in only a thin night robe.

"What's that you're whistling?" Jonas asked.

Tyler paused and frowned thoughtfully. "I don't know the name of it. I think it's something I learned as a boy."

"Isn't that the song Lulu always sings?"

"Is it?"

"I'm sure it is." Jonas began to sing in his baritone, "*While strolling through the park one day, in the merry, merry month of May, I was taken by surprise—*"

"And you accused Lulu of destroying that song?" Tyler quipped. "By the time you're through, a miracle couldn't save it."

"I've been told I have a rather charming voice," Jonas said haughtily.

"To a snake, maybe."

Jonas sniffed. "A member of the English court told me that, if you must know."

"Who? The jester?"

Jonas cast him a dour look. "Jesters have been out of vogue for quite some time. But I wouldn't expect *you* to know that, being from the *Colonies*. I keep forgetting they don't teach history in schools here—only readin', writin' and 'rithmatic."

Tyler laughed. "Touché, Jonas."

His assistant gave him a wary look. "What has your funnybone twitching today?"

"I've been thinking—"

"That's encouraging."

"—That maybe Claire and I should get married aboard the *Lady Luck*."

"Is that right? I'll grant you that would be nice, but you might want to consult Claire. Females usually have pretty strong feelings about their wedding plans."

"I hope she doesn't want anything fancy."

"If she does, you'd better smile and tell her you'll do whatever pleases her. Remember, Ty, she's still getting over the shock of losing her fiancé, and he was quite a selfish bastard. You don't want to appear as though you were cut from the same cloth." Jonas hoisted himself into the buggy and took up the reins. "When are you going to break the news to Boothe?"

"Tomorrow," Tyler replied, climbing in beside him.

"How do you think he'll react to losing not only his partner, but also his plans for Bellefleur?"

"Calm on the outside, but inside he'll be boiling mad. Not that I blame him; I'd feel the same way. The real question is what he'll do with that anger."

Jonas turned to look at him. "What are you thinking?"

"We still don't know if he had a hand in the Greene murder. If there's any chance he did, then he bears watching, especially where Claire is concerned."

As they headed back to Bellefleur, Tyler said, "I've been thinking about those plans for Claire's house. There's no reason why we can't build an inn on my land, instead."

"That's a marvelous idea." Jonas said. "It will certainly make Claire and Emily happy. Which brings me to another topic: when are you planning to have that little chat with Claire?"

"I was thinking about after supper tonight."

Jonas patted his shoulder. "Good luck, lad. You're going to need it."

Jonas worried too much. Claire had already accepted his proposal; once she understood how much she stood to gain by their marriage, there was no way she would change her mind.

The sounds of female chatter and childish laughter gladdened Tyler's heart as the buggy pulled up to Bellefleur. When he walked into the dining room, he was met by Emily's and Lulu's cheerful faces and the salty, crisp aroma of roasted pork. Tyler looked at Claire, hoping for a smile from her, but she seemed preoccupied with putting the food on the table.

They started the meal with a prayer, as was Claire's custom. Tyler couldn't help watching her as she bowed her head and closed her eyes, her hands folded serenely under her chin. Claire would make a fine mother. He'd never thought much about having a family; now he began to wonder what it would be like to sit at a table with his wife and children.

"Dear Lord," Claire began, "we come before you tonight to thank you for this delicious meal and for allowing us to be a part of your beautiful world. We ask that you keep us in your grace and make us healthy and honest. We know how much you value honesty." She cast a quick glance in Tyler's direction. "And thank you, Lord, for giving us the strength and courage to fight to keep our wonderful home. You know how much this home means to us. Amen."

Claire picked up the dish of roasted potatoes and passed them to her right. Tyler watched her, baffled by her odd behavior.

"And what did you ladies do this beautiful afternoon?" Jonas asked, forking a slice of juicy pork from the platter.

"We had a picnic!" Emily exclaimed.

"And we visited Gunter," Lulu added. "Poor boy—his spirits are so low. I hope your fancy lawyer comes to see him tomorrow."

"He will," Jonas assured her.

"Oh, and one other thing happened," Emily said with a snicker. "The sheriff paid another social call on Cee Cee."

Tyler looked at Claire, but she said nothing. "What did he want?"

"Well, he *is* still sweet on her, you know," Emily explained. "And I even told him about your engagement."

"Emily, that's enough," Claire said tersely.

Tyler glanced at Claire again, but she said no more. By the tense set of her features, he could tell something was bothering her. A nice stroll along the river might be just what she needed. Tyler was confident that he'd find a way to distract her from her troubling thoughts.

When the dishes were done, Tyler suggested the idea of a walk to her and Claire agreed, though she didn't seem too excited about it. They walked down to the river in silence, then stood side by side, watching a barge go past. "Looks like rain is coming," he remarked, glancing at the sky. When she said nothing, Tyler turned toward her, picking up her hands. "You're awfully quiet this evening."

Claire's gaze finally lifted to his, revealing the same spark of determination he'd seen the first time they met, yet she said nothing.

Hoping to draw her out, he said, "I've been thinking about our wedding." He still avoided using the word *marriage*, though he kept reminding himself that it wasn't going to be the typical "till death do us part" arrangement. "It might be fitting to have the ceremony on the *Lady Luck*. But whatever you decide is fine with me," he quickly offered, remembering Jonas's warning. "I want you to be happy. I know how important these things are to females." He put one arm around her shoulders and drew her close, hoping to prompt a kiss.

Grinding her teeth together, Claire moved away from him and began walking. His condescending attitude was almost worse than his lies. "I appreciate your consideration," she forced herself to say.

"I think this will work out well for both of us," he said. "Think about it: no more boarders, no more fears of losing your home."

Claire looked at him sharply. How could he say such things when he planned on turning Bellefleur into an inn? Did he think she would stay to run it? "And how will it work out well for you, Tyler?"

"I'll have a nice winter home and—"

Claire stopped abruptly. "A *winter* home? What about the rest of the year?"

It looked like the time for this discussion had arrived. "I'll be on my boat a good deal of the time. You have to understand, Claire: I'm used to coming and going as I please. I won't be tied down to a place.''

Or a person? Claire rubbed her upper arms. Even if Boothe weren't in the picture, she was chilled by the prospect of marrying a man who didn't love her and, in fact, didn't even want to live with her.

She couldn't tolerate Tyler's dishonesty and manipulation any longer.

Chapter 20

❝**I** haven't told you yet why the sheriff came to see me this afternoon,❞ Claire began.

Tyler glanced at her, puzzled. ❝I thought Emily said he was still trying to court you.❞

❝I let her believe that.❞ Claire watched Tyler's face. ❝But that wasn't his reason.❞

As though he sensed what was coming, Tyler's gaze grew wary. ❝Then what was it?❞

❝He was concerned about me.❞ Claire turned to look straight at him. ❝He told me all about your plans, Tyler. He told me that you and Boothe are partners.❞

For a long, tense moment, Tyler said nothing. And then he let out his breath slowly. ❝I didn't want you to find out about that.❞

Anger and hurt raged inside her, but Claire refused to let it show. ❝I can understand,❞ she said with brittle calmness, ❝why you wouldn't want me to know that you'd decided to turn my home into an inn, and take my land— and let's not forget that you made my enemy your partner!❞ She struggled to control her emotions. ❝What I can't understand is why you pretended to care. Why did you keep coming to my rescue if you didn't care?❞

Tyler's jaw tensed. He didn't like the way she was misrepresenting his behavior. ❝I wasn't pretending; I do care! And I helped you because I wanted to.❞

Tears rolled down her cheeks and she dashed them

away. "Don't lie to me, Tyler. You're asking me to believe you wanted to help me, and at the same time you were planning to take away my home. Is that what you call caring?"

"Those plans were made before I knew you."

"And once you knew me, did you stop them?"

"Look here, Claire, Boothe said the bank was going to foreclose," he answered tersely. "There was nothing I could do about that."

"Boothe has been my father's enemy for twelve years, Tyler! Of course he would say that. And now that the bank can't foreclose, you have to marry me to get the land."

"You're looking at it all wrong, Claire," he insisted. "I didn't see it right away, either, until Jonas explained it to me."

She gaped at him in shock. "This was *Jonas's* idea?"

Tyler could tell that he'd said the wrong thing. But she'd asked for the truth. "Jonas has been concerned about you and Emily since we first met you. He didn't want to see you lose your home, yet he knows how I feel about— getting married." He clenched his jaw to keep from shuddering. "So Jonas came up with a plan to benefit us both and make the idea of *marriage* palatable. I can put your land to its most profitable use and at the same time see my plans accomplished; you'll no longer have to fear Boothe; and with the money I make from my business, you and Emily will always be able to live comfortably in your house."

Claire balled her hands into fists and glared at him. "Do you honestly think I would go along with any plan that included Reginald Boothe?"

"You don't need to worry about that," Tyler quickly assured her. "I intended to end the partnership anyway. In fact, I'd planned on doing it tomorrow. The only reason I went into partnership with Boothe in the first place was because he had the money to invest and I didn't. But now it looks as though Gunter's employers may be able to provide the financing.''

''And what about the inn?''

''As a matter of fact, I just talked to Jonas about that. I've decided to build an inn on my land. So you see, it will all work out for the best for both of us.'' He tried to draw her close, but she pulled away, turning her back toward him.

''Claire,'' he said, moving around to see her face, ''I wouldn't marry you to hurt you. You'll have your home, your sister can go back to school, and I'll be able to run my business from Bellefleur.'' He picked up her hands, and this time she didn't pull away. ''Trust me, Claire, this is the best thing for everyone. And I didn't lie when I told you how much I cared, and how much I desire you.'' He lifted her chin to stare into her eyes. ''I want you beside me, Claire.''

It was too much for Claire to absorb. She had questions that needed answering, but her thoughts were in such turmoil that she couldn't begin to frame them. ''I need time to think.''

Tyler took her by the shoulders and stared down into her eyes, his own burning with the fierce intensity that once made her throb with desire. Now it merely broke her heart.

''Claire, I've given this serious thought. It's the best solution. You must know in your heart that I would never do anything to hurt you.''

''It's too late for that, isn't it, Tyler?''

''When I proposed, you had just read that newspaper article and you were distraught. I didn't want to upset you further by telling you about my partnership with Boothe. I didn't want to take the chance of losing you.'' He added softly, ''I still don't, Claire.''

She looked up at the handsome, earnest face of the man she loved and wanted desperately to believe him, almost as much as she wanted him to say he loved her. But now she knew that Tyler would tell her what he thought she wanted to hear, if it would further his cause. "I need time to think," she said again, and walked away from him.

When she got back to the house, Emily was putting on a puppet show for Jonas, Mrs. Parks, and Lulu. Claire joined them in the parlor, a smile pasted on her face, but she didn't hear a word. Doubts and fears tumbled though her mind, until she wanted to scream for them to stop. With a muttered apology, she left the room and hurried upstairs to her bedroom.

Lulu watched Claire go, then glanced at Jonas, who was frowning in concern. When Emily finished her show, Lulu shooed her upstairs to get ready for bed, then said quietly to Jonas, "Something must have happened."

"I'll go find Ty," Jonas volunteered.

"I'll go talk to Claire." Lulu helped Mrs. Parks to her room, then started toward the staircase. It was times like this that she wished she had more mothering experience.

Tyler was sitting on the porch swing when Jonas stepped outside. After a quick glance at the sky, Jonas started toward him. "Starting to drizzle, I see."

"I hadn't noticed."

Jonas sat beside him. "I wondered where you were when Claire came back alone."

"She wasn't feeling too well."

Ignoring Jonas's knowing glance, Tyler leaned his head against the back of the swing. "You know why I like poker? There's little talk and no women. You make all your plans yourself; you don't ask anyone's opinion; and if you make a mistake, you're the only one who gets hurt."

"So Claire didn't like the plan, eh?"

Tyler shot him a dark look. "She didn't like *your* plan, old man."

"I suppose you told her it was my idea."

"I thought it would help."

"What would have helped was to tell her the plan *before* you proposed, *before* she started to get the impression that you loved her." Jonas sighed. "Ah, well—as you say, it's too late to fret about that now." He glanced at Tyler's scowling face. "Or is it? Did she change her mind?"

"I don't know. All she would say is that she had to think."

"That's to be expected, I suppose. You did give her a lot to think about." He slapped Tyler on the knee. "To be on the safe side, you'd better start thinking of another way to get her land."

"That's not amusing."

"That's your goal, isn't it? Isn't that why you're marrying her? Or is there another reason?"

Tyler's scowl deepened. He knew what Jonas was driving at. He wanted to hear Tyler say he loved her. "There's no other reason."

"For your sake, Ty, I hope Claire doesn't need another reason." Shaking his head sadly, Jonas rose. "I shall leave you to your ruminations. I'm going to turn in now. It's been a long day."

"No nightcap?" Tyler asked, with little enthusiasm.

"I don't really feel like it tonight."

Tyler watched Jonas go inside, letting the swing sway beneath him. Love? He didn't know what it meant. So if that was what Claire needed to hear, she was out of luck.

Tyler sat forward with a frown. What if Claire did change her mind? He didn't even want to think about what it would do to his plans—or to him. Jumping up from the swing, he strode out to the buggy. He needed to get away for a while. Maybe he'd stay on his boat tonight. Maybe he'd sail off and never come back.

As he drove down Grand, he saw a woman strolling along the sidewalk, holding an umbrella over her head. He couldn't see her face, but thought he recognized her sensuous walk. Pulling up alongside her, he waited until she looked in his direction and then he nodded at her. "Evening, Miss Duprey."

A smile spread across her face. "Why, hello, darlin'," she said in her soft drawl.

"Kind of late for you to be out alone, isn't it?"

"I was just walking home from my parents' house. But I could always use a lift."

Tyler pulled the horse to a stop. "Climb in."

He watched her lift the hem of her brown skirt, revealing a glimpse of ecru lace drawers and a slender ankle. "Turn at the next corner," she directed, settling herself beside him.

Tyler clicked his tongue and the horse pulled away.

"Where are you off to?" she asked. "Surely it's too late for a run on the river."

"I was just going down to check on my boat. Which way to your house?"

"Drive down another two blocks and turn right," she told him. "If you're in no particular hurry, I'd like to invite you in for a drink."

Tyler regarded her as she smiled invitingly, flashing her golden cat eyes at him. "I think I'd like that," he said with a smile.

Claire sat at her dressing table, brushing out her hair, her thoughts churning in angry confusion. Why did she fall in love with men who didn't love her? What had Lance seen when he looked at her? A gullible woman with a wealthy father? She already knew what Tyler had seen. Her father was the only man who had never betrayed her trust. She wouldn't consider their financial problems a betrayal. She knew he hadn't meant his investments to affect them negatively, but rather to make more money for them. If her father hadn't argued with Reginald Boothe, everything would have been fine.

At a knock on the door, Claire tensed, praying it was not Tyler. "Who's there?"

"Lulu," came the quiet reply.

"Come in."

The housekeeper stuck her head around the door. Seeing Claire sitting at the dressing table, she came all the way in and closed the door. "I didn't want to interrupt you."

Claire began brushing her hair again as Lulu came up behind her. "May I?" the housekeeper asked, holding out her hand. She ran the brush from the crown of Claire's head to the ends. "It's something I've always wanted to do, but I never had a daughter. You'll probably do this for your own little girl someday."

Claire closed her eyes, thinking only about how good it felt to have her hair brushed. "My mother used to brush my hair."

"Was your mama beautiful, like you?"

"She had black hair like mine." Claire sighed despondently. "But my mother was lucky. She knew the love of two good men who adored her."

"You're lucky, too, sweetie. You have Tyler."

Claire opened her eyes to stare at her reflection in the mirror. She didn't have Tyler's love—and that was what she wanted. "That's enough brushing."

"You know, sweetie, I'm not very good at this," Lulu said, following her to the window. "But I know there's something troubling you deeply. I wish you would tell me how I can help."

"How are you at mending broken hearts, Lulu?"

Lulu patted her bosom. "You see this big chest of mine? You know why it's so big? Because of all the times my heart's been broken and stuck back together again. It doesn't fit so well anymore."

Claire knew exactly what she meant. It was just how her own heart felt, except that it was still in tiny pieces, and she wasn't sure it could ever be mended. Her eyes welled with tears and she put her hands over her face as she began to weep. Lulu held her as sobs wracked her body. Too much had happened in a short time. She had lost her father; she had nearly lost her house; she had been betrayed by her fiancé; and her plans for the future had been ruined. Now her heart was broken yet again.

Lulu stroked her hair as she crooned sympathetic words. "You're gonna pull through this, sweetie pie, whatever it is that's causing your grief. We're strong creatures. We can bear a lot of pain. And my shoulders are extra wide if you want to share some of that pain."

"Tyler doesn't love me," Claire wept brokenly. "He only asked me to marry him because he wants my land."

"Is that what he told you tonight?"

Claire nodded. "The sheriff came to warn me about him. He told me that Tyler and Reginald Boothe were partners."

Lulu gasped. "Tyler's in cahoots with that money grubber?"

"I asked him about it tonight and he couldn't deny it. But he said he'd decided to end his partnership. He said the marriage would benefit us both." Claire sniffled. "And he said Jonas was the one who came up with the idea. Getting married wasn't even Tyler's idea!"

"There, there, now, sweetie," Lulu said, rubbing her back. "There's no sense crying your eyes out over any man. They're just not worth it. What you need is a good night's rest."

"I don't think that's likely to happen tonight, Lulu."

"Then I'll make you one of my hot toddys. That'll put you right off to sleep." She gave Claire a final pat. "Things are gonna look much brighter tomorrow—you'll see. Now, you wash that pretty face and slip into your night robe. I'll be back in a bit."

Lulu shut the door quietly behind her and hurried down to the kitchen to heat some rum. As she put the pan on the stove, Jonas walked in.

"Did you talk to Claire?" he asked.

"I did. And right now I'd like to take a strap to that boy for hurting her, and to you for coming up with such a cockamamy plan."

"The idea was to get those two married and let nature take its course," Jonas countered.

Lulu planted her hands on her hips. "That's not good enough for Claire. She doesn't want to go into a loveless marriage, and I can't say that I blame her."

"Unfortunately," Jonas said, "it will have to do for now. Ty doesn't believe in love, or marriage, for that matter."

"Hogwash!"

"I'm serious. And I'm convinced it's because he's never experienced love, and, if the truth be known, doesn't want to. I hate to say this about Tyler but, basically, he's a coward when it comes to love."

Lulu made a disgusted face. "How do you know he's never experienced love? What about his folks? They loved him, didn't they?"

"I hardly think so. They abandoned him."

Lulu turned to the stove to stir her concoction. "Maybe they had their reasons."

"Whatever their reasons, the outcome was that he's afraid to let himself fall in love. Ty fancies himself a ladies' man, because of all the females who flock to him. But he's never had one special lady. He's never let himself get close to anyone for fear of being jilted. In fact, until he met Claire, Ty wouldn't even utter the word *marriage*. It seems his parents' disastrous union left a bitter taste in his mouth. So he tells himself he's marrying Claire for business reasons, because that makes him feel safe. One uses one's head for business, you see, and not one's heart. If Ty admitted he was marrying for love, then he could get hurt, and he doesn't want that to happen."

Lulu's features hardened. "He'd better wise up, or he'll lose Claire. She loves that boy, and she knows he doesn't love her. She's hurting real bad." Lulu shook her head as she added honey to the pan. "I still can't believe Tyler was working with that varmint Boothe to get her land."

"I hope she told you that Ty has decided to end their partnership. He doesn't trust Boothe any more than Claire does, and he wants Claire to keep her house. He has all the right intentions. He just has to let himself fall in love with her."

Lulu poured her tonic into a mug and turned toward Jonas. "So what can we do?"

"There's nothing we *can* do to make Tyler realize he loves Claire, but we can make sure they both get to the altar. I truly believe they're good for each other, and I—" Jonas heard a slight sound coming from the dining room and paused for a moment to listen. "—I didn't mean to keep you. Is that drink for Claire?"

"Yes, and I've got to get it up to her right now so she can get some sleep." She started out of the room, then stopped. "I appreciate your confiding in me, Jonas."

"You're quite welcome, Lulu. We need to work together on this for everyone's sake."

Emily flattened herself against the wall in the dining room as Lulu walked past. For the first time in her life, Emily wished she hadn't listened in on a conversation, because now she had lots to worry about. She liked Tyler; she didn't want to be angry at him. But she didn't want him hurting her sister, either. Chewing a finger, Emily tried to think what she could do.

"So this is where you're hiding," Jonas said.

Emily gasped and turned toward the sound of his voice. "I—I didn't mean to hide. I was coming down to get some warm milk and I heard you talking to Lulu."

"And why didn't you let us know you were here?" Jonas asked.

Emily heard the sound of the housekeeper's footsteps on the stairs. "Sh-h!" she whispered. "Don't tell Lulu.

I'll go straight upstairs and I won't say a word about it, I promise."

"It's a deal."

Holding the rail, Emily climbed the steps as fast as she could, thinking about what she had heard. She had promised not to *say* anything, but she hadn't promised not to *do* anything.

Holding a glass of bourbon, Tyler wandered around Daphne's house, noting the costly oil paintings, the crystal lamps, the expensively furnished rooms. Daphne had left to change out of her clothes, which were damp from the drizzle.

Hearing a rustle of silk behind him, Tyler turned, his gaze immediately drawn to the shimmering coffee-colored silk wrapper that cloaked her voluptuous curves. He knew instantly that she wore nothing beneath it, and his body responded accordingly. He watched in fascination as her gaze left his face and traveled downward to where his arousal bulged against his trousers. She smiled cagily and moved toward him, her hips swaying. He saw her tongue run around the outside of her lips and he quickly took a sip of the drink.

"Enjoying my bourbon, Mr. McCane?" she purred, taking his glass.

He grunted, unable to form a coherent reply. It had been too long since he'd enjoyed the pleasures of a female. Much too long. She bent to set his glass on a table, giving him a delicious view of her rounded bottom. Slowly she turned to face him, her fingers untying the sash.

"How would you like to enjoy this, Mr. McCane?" she asked, holding her wrapper open.

Tyler let out his breath between his teeth as his manhood pulsed and throbbed, heavy with desire. He couldn't form a single thought but one: he wanted her.

Chapter 21

Daphne led Tyler through an arched doorway into a bedroom decorated in deep burgundy and gold. Candles winked invitingly as she pulled him toward the bed. He groaned in pleasure as she kissed him deeply, inching him backward onto the bed, until she was lying atop him. Tyler's desire raged like an angry inferno. He gazed into her eyes and saw his own lust reflected back—fierce, demanding, and selfish—and for some reason it made him pause.

Lust was all he'd ever wanted before—but now he remembered the warmth and admiration in Claire's eyes when she'd kissed him, and he wanted that, too.

As Daphne stroked him through the material of his pants, he kissed her again, trying to convince himself he could use her to satisfy his passion and then go back to Claire. But for some reason, the thought soured his stomach and killed his desire.

Tyler rolled her off him and sat up. Daphne was immediately at his side, rubbing his back, kissing his neck, running her fingers down his chest to his groin. "What's wrong, darlin'?"

He gently but firmly placed her hand on her knee. "I made a mistake. I'm sorry—I don't mean you any disrespect."

She tried to smile. "Mistake?"

"I'm getting married, Daphne. I shouldn't have come here."

Daphne laughed dryly. "Darlin', whoever the lucky woman is, I won't tell her. You don't have to leave."

He stood up and straightened his clothing. "Yes, I do."

With a pout, Daphne closed her wrapper. "I thought you found me desirable."

Tyler tilted her face up. "You are an extremely desirable woman, Daphne. There's no mistake about that."

She followed Tyler to the door. "So who is the lucky woman?"

"Claire Cavanaugh."

Daphne stood frozen to the spot as he strode out the door. Claire Cavanaugh. How she hated Claire Cavanaugh! Reginald Boothe couldn't stop thinking about her, and Tyler McCane, the most eligible man in town, was going to marry her!

She stamped her feet in anger. Somehow she had to get back at that mousy, common little tramp who passed herself off as Arthur Cavanaugh's daughter. First thing in the morning, she was going to see Reginald. If she was clever, she might be able to get him to help.

The next morning there was a soft tap on Claire's door. "Sweetie pie? Are you up yet?"

"Yes, Lulu. Come in."

"I thought you might need something to eat." Lulu put a tray of food on the bedside table. "Did you sleep all right?"

"The hot toddy helped. Thank you." Her stomach growled, surprising her. Claire eyed the plate of scrambled eggs, toasted bread and jam, and crispy fried pork and suddenly felt ravenous. Sitting on the edge of the bed, she picked up a fork and dug in. The steaming eggs were salty and buttery, and the toast was crisp, evenly browned and sweet with strawberry jam. "Thank you, Lulu," she said, swallowing a mouthful of food. "This is wonderful."

"Have you been thinking any more about what you're going to do?" Lulu asked, sitting beside her.

Claire nodded as she chewed a bite of pork. "I've made up my mind. I'll do whatever it takes to keep Bellefleur. If that means marrying a man who doesn't love me, then so be it, as long as he has no more connection to Reginald Boothe."

Lulu patted her shoulder. "You know, there's lots of women who don't get to pick their husbands. And even in those arranged marriages, they often learn to love each other. I think in time Tyler will come to love you as much as you love him."

Claire gave her a grateful smile. "I'd like to think that, Lulu, but I won't count on it."

Lulu stood up. "You finish your breakfast. Emily and I are going to town to visit Gunter. That lawyer is supposed to meet with him today, and I want to make sure the sheriff doesn't give him a hard time about it."

"I'd like to go, too."

Lulu beamed. "Good for you: you're not going to sit and mope."

"No, I'm not," Claire said with determination. "I'll bring the tray down when I'm done."

Emily was quiet during the ride to town, but when asked, all she would say was that she was thinking. Lulu gave Claire a puzzled look, but Claire could only shrug.

By the time they arrived at the sheriff's office, Mr. Oldham, the attorney, was already meeting with Gunter. When he came out, Claire stood to introduce herself. John Oldham appeared to be in his late fifties, a distinguished looking gentleman with a trim white beard and moustache, wavy white hair, and long sideburns. He wore a striped suit and black top hat and carried a gold-tipped ebony cane.

"Ah, Miss Cavanaugh," Mr. Oldham said, after she'd introduced the others, "you're exactly who I wanted to see." He looked around at the deputy with a scowl. "Let's go somewhere we can talk in private."

When they left the office, Lulu took Emily down to the general store while Claire and the attorney crossed the street to the dock side. Several benches had been placed under large maple trees along Grand and they stopped to talk there.

"I'd like to go over the facts of this matter as you understand them," the attorney began, taking a large notepad out of his leather case. "If you wouldn't mind, tell me what you know from when you first heard the news of Mr. Greene's disappearance."

After Claire told him all she knew, she asked, "Do you think it will go to trial?"

"If the evidence is as weak as it now appears to be, I'd say in all likelihood we won't. However, I must caution you that I have witnessed firsthand how these small town sheriffs operate. They want their suspect tried and convicted quickly and with no fuss. Therefore, we must be prepared for the worst."

"Poor Gunter!" Claire said softly.

"Ah, but that is where I come in," he told her. "If that possibility should come to bear, I will create the fuss. Tomorrow, we'll try to get the case dismissed. I'm confident that once the judge sees the evidence, he'll grant the dismissal. If by chance he doesn't, then we'll start to work in earnest." He patted her hand. "Have faith, Miss Cavanaugh. Gunter has hired the best."

Reginald Boothe watched from his window as Claire sat talking to a man who seemed very familiar to him. He sent for a clerk and motioned him over to the window. "Do you see that gentleman in the black suit sitting on the bench? Find out who he is. And hurry. He's leaving."

Charlie Dibkins scooted down the staircase and out of the bank, glad for any excuse to be outdoors. He looked both ways, then dashed across the street, but the bench where Claire and the gentleman had been sitting was vacant. He glanced up at Boothe's window and saw the banker watching him.

"I'd better find her," he muttered aloud, and began to make his way through the people on the sidewalk. He finally spotted Claire with her sister, climbing into their buggy.

"Claire!" he called, waving. He was out of breath when he caught up with her.

"Good heavens, Charlie, what is it?" Claire cried in concern.

"Hello—Emily. Hello, ma'am," he panted, acknowledging the others. "That—gentleman—you were—with, Claire. Who—is he?"

"He's an attorney from Mt. Vernon, Charlie. Why?"

"Mr. Boothe—wanted to know. *Don't* glance at his window, Claire. He's watching us."

"In that case, you can tell Mr. Boothe that the man was Mr. Oldham, a very well-known attorney from Mt. Vernon, who is representing my boarder, Mr. Jenssen. But I imagine you already know about Mr. Jenssen from the paper."

Charlie blushed uncomfortably. "I'm sorry, Claire. I know what they wrote isn't true about you. Anyone with an ounce of brains in his head knows that it was just ol' Slats doing what he does best."

"It still makes me angry," Claire admitted. "But why is Mr. Boothe so interested?"

"Who knows what that old codger is thinking?" Charlie grinned. "I'll give him your message, Claire, exactly as you told me." He gave her a wink, pinched Emily's cheek, and started down the street at a jaunty stride, hands in his pockets.

When Charlie returned, Boothe was pacing his office. "Well?" he snarled.

"The gentleman is Mr. Oldham, a very well-known attorney from Mt. Vernon."

"What's he doing here? Did you find out?"

"He's representing Gunter Jenssen."

Boothe's eyes narrowed as he strode to the window. Claire was just driving past the bank, her head held high. "Damn her," he whispered.

Charlie couldn't help but grin. "Will there be anything else, Mr. Boothe?"

"Send for the sheriff. I need to talk to him—now."

At the quick rap on his door, Boothe looked up, expecting to see Simons. Instead, Daphne sashayed into the room and flopped down on a chair opposite his desk.

"What are you doing here?" he asked bluntly.

Regarding him with a coy smile from beneath the brim of her brown hat, Daphne slowly removed her gloves, drawing them carefully from each finger, then placing them across her lap. "I have news for you, darlin'."

"Couldn't it have waited until this evening?"

Her gaze hardened. "No, it couldn't. Claire Cavanaugh is marrying your partner. What do you think about that?" With a gloating smile, she sat back to wait for his reaction.

He leaned back in his chair with a scowl, his fingers tapping impatiently on the leather arms. "I already knew."

Her smile dissolved. "What are you going to do about it?"

"Why should I do anything? This is the best thing that could have happened. Once McCane marries her, her property is ours to do with as we like."

"What if Tyler decides he doesn't need you anymore?"

Slyly lifting one eyebrow, Boothe said, "He needs my money."

With a frustrated huff, Daphne grabbed her gloves and

rose. "You'd better hope he doesn't find a way to get money on his own."

Boothe watched her march toward the door in an obvious fit of temper. Whatever her reason for coming to see him, he had thwarted it. "Daphne," he called, just before she turned the corner. "Regular time tonight?"

As she scowled at him over her shoulder, he opened his drawer and took out a slender black velvet case, letting it dangle temptingly between his fingers.

Her scowl slowly turned to a canny smile. "Whatever you say, darlin'."

"Oh, excuse me, ma'am!" Sheriff Simons exclaimed, as he nearly collided with her in the doorway. He backed away, tipping his hat, and sidestepped into the office. "You sent for me?"

Boothe took out a fresh cigar and clipped the tip. "Sit down, Sheriff."

Glancing at him uneasily, the sheriff settled into the chair Daphne had just vacated. Boothe lit his cigar and puffed on it until the end glowed red. "You seem nervous, Wilbur."

Balancing his hat on one knee, the sheriff shook his head quickly. "No, sir. I'm not nervous. What did you want to see me about?"

"I've just learned that Attorney Oldham from Mt. Vernon will be representing Mr. Jenssen. You know what that means, don't you?"

"Yes, sir. I'd better be extra cautious."

"Do you have your witnesses lined up?"

"Yes, sir."

"Have they been coached properly?"

"Yes, sir, and I promised them they would each get one hundred dollars if they had to testify."

"Good. Any news on Mrs. Greene?"

"No, sir."

Boothe frowned. "That worries me somewhat, but I

suppose no news is good news. Did you deliver my gift to Judge Crawford?''

"Yes, sir," Simons replied unhappily. "He's very appreciative."

Boothe blew out a ring of smoke. "All right, Sheriff. It seems everything is under control. Just remember, we can't afford for anything to go wrong, can we?"

"No, sir."

"You may go now, Sheriff." With a smile of satisfaction, the banker swivelled to face the window. Judge Crawford would make sure Jenssen hanged for the crime. After all, Boothe was making it possible for him to retire in comfort. He puffed contentedly on his cigar. There was always a way to win.

The *Lady Luck* docked a half hour before the bank's closing time. Tyler was the first to disembark, striding rapidly down the ramp and along the pier toward Grand Avenue. He entered the bank, stopping at the desk of the young, redheaded clerk. "I need to see Mr. Boothe."

The clerk hopped up. "I'll check, sir. Just a minute."

Tyler waited impatiently as the young man dashed up the wide staircase to the second floor. Tyler had been anticipating this meeting all day, knowing it wouldn't be pleasant. But it was important that the partnership be ended quickly.

"He'll see you now, sir," the clerk said breathlessly.

"Thanks." Tyler took the steps quickly and strode into Boothe's office without knocking. The banker rose with a smile. "McCane! Good to see you. Sit down. May I offer you anything? Tea? Cigar?"

"No, thanks." Tyler took a seat as Boothe resumed his.

"I hear you have good news," the banker said, leaning back with a smile.

Tyler was amazed he knew so quickly. "Where did you hear it?"

"I don't recall. That certainly simplifies the property ownership." The banker sat forward, reaching for the lid of his humidor. "So when do you expect we can start to work on the docks?"

"That's what I came to see you about. I've decided not to go ahead with our plans."

Boothe's hand froze and his eyes narrowed as he stared at Tyler. "You've decided *not* to?"

"That's right. Claire wants to keep her house intact."

"What about the docks?"

"No immediate plans there, either."

His gaze never leaving Tyler's face, Boothe removed a cigar, clipped the tip, stuck the cigar in his mouth, and lit a match, slowly drawing in the smoke and puffing it out again until the end glowed. His actions were completely unhurried, but his eyes were cold and calculating. "And our partnership?"

Tyler crossed one booted foot over his knee. "There's really no need for a partnership anymore."

Boothe took the cigar out of his mouth and leaned forward. "What about your plans to build more riverboats? Where will you get the backing for them?"

"I'll worry about that when the time comes."

The banker swivelled to face the window. With his back to Tyler, he stared out the window, smoking his cigar. Tyler could only guess the thoughts going through his cunning mind.

"Do you have your copy of the agreement handy?" Tyler asked.

For a long moment there was no reply, then Boothe slowly turned his chair to face Tyler. His features seemed molded from stone, but his eyes glittered dangerously. Tyler almost expected him to pull a pistol from his desk drawer—but that wasn't Boothe's style. The banker looked through a drawer of files and removed a paper, sliding it across the desk. "There it is."

Tyler took his own copy out of his vest pocket. "I have mine here." He tore it in half.

Boothe watched him, squinting through the haze of smoke. Finally, he placed his cigar on an ashtray and reached for his own copy. Meticulously, he folded the paper, tore it into small squares and let it fall into the waste basket beside his desk.

With a great sense of relief, Tyler rose. "I'm sorry this didn't work out for both of us. I wish you success on your next venture."

Boothe rose and extended his hand in a gesture of goodwill. Only his eyes betrayed the angry inferno raging inside. "Good luck on your marriage."

After Tyler had gone, Boothe sat down again and slowly puffed on his cigar. He would have success on his next venture, all right. But Tyler's luck was about to run out. Boothe stubbed out his cigar in the crystal ash tray, took the black velvet case from his drawer, tucked it in his coat pocket, and rose. No one betrayed Reginald Boothe without paying the price.

Chapter 22

Jonas was waiting in front of the bank in a buggy. Tyler strode around to the other side and climbed in. "Let's go pay a visit to Gunter."

"How did it go?" his assistant asked, nodding toward the bank.

Tyler rubbed his jaw. "Not as badly as I'd anticipated, but Boothe was definitely not happy about it."

"But the partnership is dissolved?"

"Completely. We each tore up our copy of the agreement."

Jonas sighed in relief. "Well, I'm certainly glad that's over. I think Claire has good reason to mistrust that man."

"We still have to get Gunter's employers' backing, you know. Without it, I can't build my docks."

They stopped at the sheriff's office, where Tyler went inside. He found Gunter sitting on the wooden bed, staring desolately at the floor. "Mr. McCane!" he said, jumping up. "It's so good to see you!"

"Has the attorney been here?"

"Yes, he came this morning. A very able man, this Mr. Oldham is. If anyone can get me out of this jail cell, it will be him."

"Jonas says he's quite capable. I'm sure you'll be out in no time."

"I have to go to court tomorrow. I hope to be able to go home then."

"I hope so, too." Tyler pulled up the stool and sat on it. "Do you remember our conversation about building boat docks on the river at Bellefleur?"

"Yes, you expressed an interest in speaking with my employers on the subject."

"Do you think you can wire them when you get out of here?"

"I would be happy to." Gunter gave a lopsided grin. "Of course, I would be even happier just to get out of here."

"If they were to agree to back me, how long would it take before we could work out some kind of deal?"

Gunter scratched his temple. "Perhaps a month. There would be much paperwork to sign first, of course."

"That's no problem." Tyler rose and shook the Swede's hand. "Well, good luck tomorrow. We'll talk more when you get out."

Tyler related the conversation to Jonas on the ride back to Bellefleur. "The only problem with using Gunter's employers is that Claire will still need money to run the farm until their money comes through. I suppose I'd better plan on using the *Lady Luck*'s profits for a while."

Jonas gave him a curious glance. "That doesn't bother you, does it?"

Tyler rubbed his jaw. "I've never had to worry about supporting anyone but myself."

"Ah, that's it. You're frightened."

Tyler threw him a cold look. "Don't be ridiculous."

"It's not ridiculous. You're taking on not just a wife, but a family as well. Let's face it, Ty, you've led a selfish life until now. That's hard to give up."

"I don't like being called selfish, old man."

Jonas sniffed. "Then how does the word *parsimonious* sit with you?"

"How does the word *unemployed* sit with you?" Tyler shot back.

"Overused," Jonas retorted.

They rode in silence the rest of the way home. As they pulled up in front of the house, Tyler saw Emily sitting alone on one side of the house. He walked over to see what she was doing while Jonas drove to the stables.

"Hi, Tyler," she said, before he'd even opened his mouth.

"Hi, Em." He crouched down on the blanket, marveling at her extraordinary ability to recognize a person. "Playing with your puppets?"

She scoffed at the notion. "I'm too old to play. We were rehearsing."

Tyler glanced around curiously. "You and who else?"

"Me and Hare and Wiler, silly!"

Tyler smacked himself on the forehead, causing Emily to giggle. "Of course! What are you rehearsing?"

"A new play." She wiggled her hand into the rabbit's cloth body. "But Hare is very sad today. I'm having a hard time getting her to cooperate."

"Anything I can do?"

Emily sighed, her small face contemplative. "Perhaps if you listen to her story, that will make her feel better."

"All right." Tyler made himself more comfortable.

"Once upon a time," she began, "a little bunny named Hare lived with her mom in a mean farmer's field. Oh, I forgot to tell you that Hare didn't have a father. He was killed by a fox when Hare was a baby. Anyway, one day the farmer caught Hare's mother in a trap and threw her and Hare out of the garden into the dark, scary woods. Hare's mother had to find food for them, so she left the little bunny alone while she went looking in other gardens for something to eat. Poor Hare was so frightened. She had no home and no food, and she was left for days all by herself."

Tyler watched the emotions play across Emily's face. He knew she was telling a story about Claire, but he wasn't sure why.

"Finally, a big, strong jackrabbit discovered Hare and

her mother and felt sorry for them. He took them to his warm den in the ground to live, and he fell in love with Hare's mother and they got married. Poor Hare was very sad when her beautiful mother died, but she still loved it there in the den. Then one day the jackrabbit died and she was alone again and frightened, especially when the mean farmer tried to buy the field where the den was, so Hare wouldn't have a home. But then another jackrabbit came along. He didn't love Hare, but he wanted to help her. She fell in love with him and they got married—but they didn't live happily ever after, because what Hare really wanted all along was someone to love her.''

Emily sighed again and turned her head toward Tyler. ''That's all.''

It was more than enough. Tyler wished he could assure Emily that the tale would turn out happily ever after without love, but he knew she wouldn't accept it. She wanted a fairy tale ending. ''Thank you for the story, Emily. I hope Hare will feel better now.''

''Me, too,'' she replied wistfully. Suddenly, she cocked her head to one side, listening intently. ''Here comes Jonas.''

Tyler turned as his assistant trudged toward them. ''Why, if it isn't my old chum, Emily!'' Jonas exclaimed. ''Did I miss a show?''

''A story,'' Tyler corrected.

''I love stories.'' Jonas took a seat on the blanket. ''Will you tell me?''

Standing beside the open window in her bedroom, Claire watched the scene in the yard below. She found it odd that Tyler should take the time to sit and talk with Emily. Her first thought had been to warn her sister to beware of Tyler; that he was not the man she thought she knew. Yet Claire had to admit that Tyler had always been patient and kind to Emily. For her sake, marrying Tyler was probably the right thing to do. But what kind of marriage would it be?

Morosely, Claire turned away from the window. How difficult it was to love someone and not have that love returned. How she yearned to share her thoughts and dreams with Tyler. How she longed to be close to him, to know his deepest fears and greatest triumphs. How she desired to share her body with him. Claire had always dreamed of a marriage in which two people pledged their undying love to each other. But if one of those people didn't share the love, wouldn't their vows be a mockery? Wouldn't their marriage be, as well?

Lulu had insisted that people could learn to love each other. Claire knew she would be foolish to count on that happening. The question she still had to answer was, could she live in a marriage without love? Or, more important, did she want to?

Tyler left Jonas and Emily and returned to the house, feeling oddly unsettled by Emily's little tale. He hadn't known the details of Claire's early life, and in truth, hadn't really cared to know. He'd always felt sorry for himself for having a rotten childhood. He hadn't even considered that anyone else might have had a rough go of it.

He now knew Claire had been orphaned, and that Arthur Cavanaugh wasn't her birth father. What Tyler wasn't sure of was Reginald Boothe's role in the story. Had he been the farmer who had not only coveted the den where Claire lived, but who had also trapped her mother and thrown her out? Emily's tale seemed to imply so. If that was true, Tyler could understand Claire's hatred of the man.

He saw Mrs. Parks sitting on a rocking chair on the porch, knitting contentedly, and decided she was just the person to ask. After glancing through the screen door to make sure no one else was nearby, he walked over to the elderly housekeeper.

"Afternoon, ma'am."

"Why, hello, Mr.—" She looked puzzled for a moment, then her face brightened. "Mr. McCane! Are you back so soon?"

"It's nearly time for supper," he said, hunkering down near her chair.

"Oh, dear. I seem to have lost track of the time."

"Sitting here in the shade of the porch on such a beautiful day, I imagine it would be easy to lose track of time."

"You're very kind to say so, Mr. McCane."

"I'll bet you've seen many summers come and go from this porch."

"Oh, my, yes!"

"I'll bet you remember when Claire and her mother arrived, too."

Mrs. Parks' hands stilled and her eyes grew wistful. "Such an exciting time that was. This house needed a family, and so did Claire. Poor child, she was frightened of her own shadow when she first came to us. But it was quite understandable. She'd been subjected to all sorts of horrors, living in terrible conditions while her mother tried to find work. It was years before her nightmares stopped.

"And then there was poor Mr. Cavanaugh," she continued, "who'd been alone for so long. Then he found Marie and fell head over heels in love with her." Mrs. Parks sighed. "Such a beautiful woman was our Marie, so sweet-natured and kind. It was easy to see why he fell in love with her." The elderly lady shook her head as she resumed her knitting. "I'll never understand why that horrible man treated her so cruelly."

Tyler had a hunch who she meant. "You're speaking of Reginald Boothe, of course."

"Oh my, yes. Marie worked for him before she came here, you see." Mrs. Parks' face suddenly took on a stony look. "He hurt her in ways beyond belief. They never spoke of it again, Marie and Arthur. But the reminder was always there."

Claire heard voices coming from the porch and stopped

by a window to listen. Catching enough of the conversation to realize what it was about, she dashed to the front door just as Tyler spoke again.

"What reminder was that, Mrs. Parks?"

Mrs. Parks turned as Claire came out of the house. "Hello, dear. Is it suppertime yet?"

"Nearly. Why don't you come in now, and I'll help you get ready?"

"Why, thank you, dear." She folded up her knitting and put it in the basket alongside the chair.

As Tyler stood up and moved aside, Claire cast him a quick, questioning glance. "Supper will be on the table shortly, if you would be so kind as to inform my sister and Jonas." She helped Mrs. Parks up and walked with her into the house.

Tyler watched her for a moment, wondering if Claire had overheard the conversation and had purposely interrupted them. Now he was all the more curious.

At the supper table that evening, Claire had the distinct feeling that everyone was watching her and not really concentrating on the conversation. She ate hastily and was the first to rise at the end of the meal.

When the dishes were done Claire walked quietly up the hallway, intending to slip upstairs where she could be alone to think. But Tyler was waiting for her in the front hall. He was wearing black boots and pants, and a white shirt that stood out like snow against his tanned neck. Just seeing him made her heart ache.

He pushed himself away from the door and walked towards her. "Would you join me for a stroll? I have some good news."

His husky voice still had the power to send shivers of excitement up her spine. Claire nodded and followed him outside. He held out his arm, and after a moment's hesitation she took it. His eyes held hers for a long moment, as though he were trying divine her thoughts. Claire looked away, fearing he would see the love there.

They strolled down to the riverbank.

"I met with Boothe today," Tyler began. "We dissolved the partnership." He pulled several scraps of paper from his pocket and showed her. "This was our agreement. I figured you'd want to see some proof."

Claire opened one of the folded pieces, glanced at it, and handed it back. "I'm relieved," she admitted.

"I understand."

Claire glanced at him sharply. "What do you understand?"

"Why you despise Reginald Boothe."

Claire's heart began to pound in dread. Could Tyler have learned the secret of Emily's birth? Claire had hoped she'd interrupted their conversation before Mrs. Parks had revealed that. "And why do I despise Boothe?" she asked, watching him carefully.

His brows drew together, as though he was puzzled by her question. "Mrs. Parks told me he hurt your mother."

Claire let out her breath in relief. "Why were you asking questions about us?"

Tyler shrugged nonchalantly. "I was curious. Emily told me you had come to Bellefleur as a child. Is it true?"

Claire nodded. "My father died when I was a baby. He was a soldier. To support us, my mother took jobs cooking and cleaning. Her last employer was Reginald Boothe. He—dismissed her after two months. Then my father, or rather, Arthur Cavanaugh, hired her and they fell in love. They married shortly afterward. Emily was born the following summer."

"Was she born blind?"

"Yes. My mother caught rubella when she was carrying Emily."

Tyler shook his head sadly. "That's a pity."

"In truth, it bothers others more than it bothers Emily. She's a remarkable child." Claire glanced at Tyler as they strolled along. "Now that you know about my history, I think it's only fair you tell me something about yours."

"There's not much to tell. My father left home when I was five years old. My mother took me to live with my uncle in New Orleans. I spent the following fifteen years working on my uncle's riverboat until I had saved enough money to buy my own." Tyler shrugged. "That's about it."

"Why did your mother take you to live with your uncle?"

Tyler rubbed his jaw hard, as though the question disturbed him. "She was having a hard time raising me. I guess I was a pretty bad kid. Anyway, I was glad to go."

"Did she visit you?"

"What for?"

Claire frowned in bewilderment. "Why would any mother visit her child? Because she loved him. And to see how he was doing."

She saw his eyes go flat. "I never saw my mother again. I saw my father once, when his drunken body turned up in the water near the dock where my uncle's boat was moored."

For a long moment, Claire was too astonished to speak. She remembered vividly how it felt to be abandoned; yet for her, it had only been for a matter of hours. "I'm terribly sorry," she finally said.

"Don't feel sorry for me," Tyler said tersely. "I didn't miss them."

"You were five years old. Of course you missed your parents."

"*I didn't miss them.*" Tyler's jaw tightened, and Claire could feel the tenseness of his arm muscle where her hand rested. She knew instinctively he was lying to himself. How it must have hurt when they didn't come back for him. How lonely and unloved that five-year-old child must have felt. At least she had been sure of her mother's and father's love for her.

"Anyway," he finished, "it taught me a good lesson: never to depend on anyone but myself."

Perhaps that explained why he didn't love her, Claire thought. Perhaps he had decided never to risk loving anyone again.

She wondered if she could accept that.

At nine o'clock the next morning, Claire, Lulu, and Emily watched the hearing from the first row in the fire station's meeting room. In front, Mr. Oldham sat on Gunter's left.

The prosecutor, Lawrence Jamieson, sat on the right. Only three years out of law school, Jamieson had become popular with the citizens because of his even temper and friendly nature.

When the judge entered, everyone rose. Judge Crawford was a short, portly, red-faced man dressed in linsey-woolsey and a broad-brimmed hat. He strode to the table at the front, took off his hat, adjusted his chair, and pounded the gavel twice.

"The court is now in session," he announced, holding the lapels of his coat. "What is the business of the day?"

Jamieson rose and introduced himself to the court, and then Oldham followed suit. After each side gave their opening statements, Claire listened confidently as Oldham made his case for dismissal. Jamieson's accusations were so farfetched that she nearly laughed. And when the judge finally rapped his gavel to announce his decision, Claire was positive the case would be dismissed.

"It is the judgment of this Court," Crawford began, "that the motion for dismissal is hereby *denied*. Furthermore, the defendant shall remain incarcerated *without bail* until the trial."

Claire gasped and Lulu spluttered in outrage, while the rest of the room broke out in loud chatter.

"Cee Cee, what does 'incarcerated' mean?" Emily asked anxiously, tugging on her sleeve.

"Gunter has to stay in jail until they have a trial," Claire explained, still in a state of shock. "The judge won't let him go."

"They're not going to hang him, are they?"

"Don't even think that—Gunter is innocent!" Claire looked around at Gunter, who was sitting slumped over in his chair, his head in his hands. Sheriff Simons, standing at one side of the room, looked almost as distraught as Gunter did.

As she watched, Gunter slowly turned his head to look at the sheriff. For a long moment, the two men stared at each other, then the sheriff dropped his gaze, a look of shame on his face. Claire burned to know what was behind that shame.

Chapter 23

⟨∿⟩

The judge rapped his gavel sharply until the noise died. "As a courtesy to the defense," he said with a short nod to Mr. Oldham, "I will expedite these proceedings and allow for a swift trial date of one month hence. Trial will commence at nine A.M. sharp in exactly thirty days. The Court will make itself available for any pretrial motions or discovery requests. The Court further orders that the defendant be held in an adjoining city where the facilities are more adequate for a longer incarceration. There being no further business before the Court, we stand adjourned."

"What does he mean?" Emily demanded, as the chattering crowd began to file out. "Where are they taking Gunter?"

Claire was too upset to reply. "Stay here, Em. I need to speak to Mr. Oldham. I'll be right back."

Emily turned to Lulu, but she was engaged in an angry discussion with the people in the row behind them. Frustrated, Emily decided to get some answers for herself. Using her cane, she made her way to the front of the room where the judge had been standing, only to find that no one was there. Listening intently, she heard his voice coming from another room. She felt her way past the table and along the front wall until she reached a doorway. The door was partly closed, so she stood at one side, listening to the conversation inside.

"Judge, I'm not comfortable talking to you without Mr. Oldham being present, but the truth of the matter is, I don't have enough evidence to try this case, and I don't want the defense to know."

Emily recognized the voice of the attorney, Mr. Jamieson.

"Regardless, son, you *will* try this case."

"But, Judge, these witnesses aren't reliable." Emily heard the rattle of papers. "These witness statements won't hold up in front of a jury. What if Mr. Oldham wants to take the witnesses' depositions before the trial?"

"He'll have a hard time doing that. The sheriff tells me they can't be located at this time."

"Then how will I be able to put them on the stand?"

"You're not listening to me, son. I said, *at this time*. Do you understand?"

There was a long pause, and then Emily heard the attorney say in a sad voice, "I understand."

"Good. Then I'll see you same time next week. Say hello to your wife Sarah for me."

Emily stepped away from the door. She heard the judge coming toward her a moment later and pretended to be disoriented.

"Child, what are you doing up here?" the judge asked.

Emily tapped her cane on the floor, holding a hand in front of her. "I've lost my way."

"Where's your mama?" he asked curtly.

"I don't have a mama, and my papa died just a month ago." She sniffled. "I'm an orphan."

"Then why are you here, child?" he asked more kindly.

"Because that mean sheriff arrested my friend. You know my friend, Gunter Jenssen?"

His voice grew gruff. "In that case, I think you'd best find yourself a new friend."

Emily waited until he had walked away, then muttered, "Awful man!" She made her way toward the sound of her sister's voice. "Awful Crawful, that's what I'm going to call him."

She stood behind Claire, listening as her sister talked with Gunter and Mr. Oldham.

"How can the judge hold Gunter?" Claire demanded. "You said yourself they don't have good evidence."

"I stand behind that statement, Miss Cavanaugh," Mr. Oldham replied. "There's chicanery afoot here. But never fear: I shall have these so-called witnesses tracked down so I can take their depositions. I think under a thorough questioning, we shall uncover some lies. Once that's done, I intend to speak with the prosecutor to find out exactly what's going on. In the meantime, I'm afraid Mr. Jenssen will have to go to Mt. Vernon."

Claire looked at Gunter, who was staring forlornly at the attorney as though he still couldn't believe what was happening to him. "Gunter, don't worry," she said, putting her arms around him. "We'll come to visit you. And Mr. Oldham will take care of everything." She gave the attorney a pleading look.

"I shall do my utmost," Oldham assured them as the sheriff walked toward them.

"Let's go, Jenssen," Simons said.

Outraged by the blatant injustice she had witnessed, Claire stepped in front of Gunter. "I don't believe for one minute that this man is guilty, Sheriff, and I don't understand why you do. You know better than anyone here that the evidence is flimsy."

"I'm just doing my job, Cee Cee," Simons said stiffly.

"Your job is to protect us from murderers, Sheriff—not to accuse innocent men because they are foreigners."

Simons gazed down at her for a long moment, conflicting emotions playing across his face. But all he said was, "I'll see that he's treated fairly in Mt. Vernon."

Claire put her arm around her sister as the sheriff led Gunter away. She glanced to the right and saw Daphne Duprey sitting at the back of the room, watching her with a smug grin. Lifting her chin, Claire took Emily's arm and marched over to Lulu. "Let's go home. This room is beginning to smell."

The closed landau was waiting in the alley behind the fire station. Looking over her shoulder, Daphne quickly opened the door and stepped inside.

"Well?" Reginald Boothe said impatiently. "What happened?"

Adjusting her hat and gloves, Daphne gave him a coy glance. "Hello, darlin'. How are you today?"

Boothe didn't have time for games. "Peachy," he replied snidely. "Now, what happened in there?"

"The judge is sending Mr. Jenssen to the jail in Mt. Vernon until the trial."

Boothe smiled in relief. "Good. Very good."

Daphne regarded him skeptically. "I don't understand why you're so interested in this case."

"I hate to see crime go unpunished." He paused as his eyes slid up her curves. "Or good behavior go unrewarded."

Daphne sidled up against him. "Was I good last night?"

"Excellent," he murmured against her ear. "And didn't you like your little gift?"

Daphne pulled back the sleeve of her blouse, revealing a diamond bracelet. "It's lovely."

"There's one more thing I want you to do for me," he told her, "and then you'll get another little bauble to match that one."

She smiled invitingly. "Whatever you'd like, darlin'."

"I'm going to send the judge over to see you this evening. I trust you'll do your best to *entertain* His Honor?"

For a moment, Daphne's smile faltered and her eyes narrowed slightly, as though she found his request distasteful. But Boothe knew her greed would win over any scruples she might have suddenly acquired. "Shall I tell him to be there about seven o'clock?'' he asked.

Daphne let out a sigh, then forced her smile back in place. "Whatever you say, darlin'."

"Wonderful. I'll see you tomorrow, then. Same time as usual." He tapped on the side and the landau came to a stop. Daphne climbed down, paused to glance back as though she were about to say something, then gave him a fleeting smile and walked away.

Boothe leaned out the window to speak to his driver. "Would you take me to the jeweler's, please?" He leaned back with a sigh of contentment. How he loved deciding people's fates. He felt like a supreme puppet master, controlling his own little section of the world. When a puppet stopped dancing for him, all he had to do was cut its strings and watch it collapse.

As the landau rounded the corner, Boothe caught sight of Claire and Emily climbing into their buggy. A sly grin crossed his face. Ah, how he would enjoy cutting their strings!

Tyler and Jonas listened quietly as the ladies reported on the hearing at supper. Tyler watched Claire's eyes, envious of the concern he saw there. Would she feel the same concern if he were in trouble?

A week ago, he would have answered yes. But since he'd told Claire the truth about his reasons for marrying her, she'd been distant and cool. When she'd looked at him before, he'd seen warmth and admiration in her beautiful eyes. Now he saw only mistrust, and he didn't like it. What if she decided not to marry him?

Tyler gave himself a mental shake. Since when did he, who loved a challenge, become so doubtful? What had happened to his confidence? Had he ever gone after something and not attained it? If Claire decided not to marry him, he'd just forge ahead in a different direction. He'd find land somewhere else, and a new backer as well. As his uncle used to say, there was more than one way to skin a polecat.

Yet as Tyler glanced around the dining room, he couldn't help thinking of all he'd miss if they didn't marry—the comforts of this beautiful, stately home, a ready-made family to come home to, the beautiful riverfront property that seemed so well suited for his docks. His gaze came back to Claire, and he realized with a jolt that what he'd miss most—was her.

With a scowl, he reached for his glass of cider. Attachments only made the eventual separation more difficult. Each time he looked at her, he wondered how long it would be before she grew tired of him. A month? A year? It had taken his mother five years. He doubted Claire would be that tolerant.

Yet as he saw her concern over a man she barely knew, Tyler hoped that maybe she would find something in him that everyone else had missed, and that she would need him enough to stay with him. He only knew that he didn't want to lose her.

Realizing that Jonas was watching him, Tyler felt his ears grow warm. Had he been staring at Claire? Were his feelings written on his face? He forced his attention back to the conversation.

"Jonas, what do you think about Gunter's case?" Lulu asked.

"Well," Jonas said, leaning back, "I'd like to believe that Mr. Oldham has a fighting chance, but from what Claire says, he's beginning to wonder if there's something shady going on."

Emily squirmed in her chair, as though she was bursting to tell a secret.

"What is churning in that pretty head of yours, angel?" Lulu finally asked.

Emily pressed her lips together. "I can't say. Cee Cee will be angry."

Claire's eyebrows lifted in surprise. Lulu winked at her

as she leaned close to Emily. "Why don't you whisper what it's about in my ear?"

Emily cupped her hand to the woman's ear and said a few words. Lulu's eyes widened and she sat up straight. "Angel, you need to tell that to everyone. Trust me, Claire isn't gonna be angry."

Emily looked sheepish. "Cee Cee, promise you won't scold me."

"It's about Gunter," Lulu told her.

"I promise, Em," Claire said. "Go on."

"It's just that you were busy talking to Gunter and Mr. Oldham," Emily explained, "and Lulu was talking to the lady behind us, and no one was listening to me. So I decided to ask Awful Crawful why he was sending Gunter away."

"Awful Crawful?" Jonas asked, giving Claire a puzzled look.

"Judge Crawford," Claire explained. "Go ahead, Em."

"I went up to the front of the room and heard Awful Crawful talking to that nice lawyer, Mr. Jamieson, in another room. So I thought I'd better wait until he was done." She took a breath and let it out. "That's when I heard Mr. Jamieson say that he doesn't have enough evidence and that he doesn't want to go ahead with a trial, but Awful Crawful said he had to, and not to worry about the witnesses being missing now. They'd show up in time for the trial."

Tyler glanced at Jonas, frowning. "I think Mr. Oldham needs to know about this conversation."

"I agree." Jonas turned to Emily. "Em, will you tell Mr. Oldham what you heard?"

At Emily's nod, Tyler said, "I'll take her to Mt. Vernon first thing in the morning. Jonas, will you take charge of the *Lady Luck* for me tomorrow?"

"Of course."

"I'd like to go with you," Claire said to Tyler.

He met her steady gaze, hoping to see something more

than concern there, wishing to see the warmth that had been missing lately. He was disappointed. ''We'll leave at seven in the morning.''

''We'll be ready,'' Claire replied, looking at her sister.

The law offices of Oldham and Meade were in a narrow three-story building. The downtown area was much larger than Fortune's, and much busier. The roads were crowded with buggies, wagons, food carts, and men on horseback. Ladies with their parasols unfurled scurried to cross to the other side of the street. Women with small children moved in and out of the various shops along the broad sidewalks, and men in black suits and hats dodged children and dogs as they made their way to their offices. Claire tried to describe it all to Emily, but there was too much to see.

''How may I help you?'' Mr. Oldham asked, after they had been shown into his office.

''We have some information we think you'll find highly interesting, and hopefully of some help,'' Tyler explained. He put his hand on Emily's shoulder. ''This young lady overheard a conversation between Judge Crawford and the prosecutor after the hearing yesterday.''

Oldham's heavy white eyebrows rose. ''Just between the two of them?''

''Mr. Jamieson said he didn't like talking to the judge without you present,'' Emily explained, ''but he had to.''

''And why was that?''

''He said he didn't have enough evidence.''

''Did he now?'' Oldham dipped his pen in the inkwell and began to write on his notepad as he spoke. ''Emily, why don't you start from the beginning and tell me everything they said, exactly as you remember it.''

He continued to write as Emily related the events, stopping her several times to ask her questions. When she had finished, he wrote for another minute, then put his pen in its stand. ''Well, well,'' he said, glancing over his notes, "it appears I was right: there is chicanery afoot. It looks like I'd better have a little meeting with the prosecutor."

"You won't tell him about Emily overhearing him, will you?" Claire asked.

"Absolutely not." His frank gaze moved from Tyler to Claire. "I'll try to get down to Fortune in the next day or two and meet with Mr. Jamieson. I shall let you know the outcome as soon as I do."

"Is there anything we can do?" Claire asked, glancing anxiously at Tyler.

Oldham tugged at his short beard. "I've already hired a man to track down the two witnesses, and I hope to hear something from him soon. However, it wouldn't hurt if you, Mr. McCane, went down to the tavern where Mr. Jenssen made his alleged confession and put out the word that you have it on good authority that these so-called witnesses will have to testify under oath in a court of law. And you might remind them that there are penalties for lying under oath, such as going to prison."

"What do you think that will that do?" Claire asked.

"Hopefully, it will put the fear of God in them. If they're as phony as I suspect, they'll never agree to testify. And with no witnesses, the prosecutor doesn't have a case. The judge will have no choice but to dismiss it."

"That's wonderful!" Claire exclaimed.

"Let's not get ahead of ourselves," Oldham cautioned. "I suggest we take things one step at a time." He rose, signaling the close of their meeting. "I'll be in touch."

The mood wasn't quite as cheerful on the way home. Before leaving Mt. Vernon, they had stopped to visit Gunter in his new quarters, assuring him that Mr. Oldham was doing a fine job and that everything would work out. But privately Tyler wasn't convinced it would, and he could tell Claire wasn't, either. For Emily's sake, neither of them mentioned their fears.

*   *   *

With several hours to kill before the *Lady Luck* returned, Tyler decided to take Mr. Oldham's advice and visit the tavern situated near the docks. He ordered a beer, then sat at the bar, exchanging stories with a group of friendly dockworkers who had finished for the day. But when he mentioned Gunter Jenssen, the men around him grew silent.

"It's a damn shame," Tyler went on, taking a swig of his beer, "when some poor devil is railroaded so a fat, comfortable moneybags doesn't have to soil his fancy clothes sitting in a jail cell. To think that wealth means a murderer gets off scot free, while the poor scapegoat has to put his neck in a noose."

"How d'ya know the Swede was railroaded?" a big, burly worker asked.

"The only evidence the state has is statements made by two men in this very tavern who swore they heard Jenssen confess to the crime." Tyler shook his head sympathetically. "I'd hate to be in their shoes now."

"Why's that?" another man wanted to know.

"They're going to have to testify in court, *under oath,*" Tyler told them. "And that Mt. Vernon attorney, John Oldham—he's a tough old bird—will be asking the questions." Tyler leaned closer to the men, cupping his hand around one side of his mouth as though to share a confidence, "I've heard he can make a mute talk."

While the men murmured among themselves, Tyler took another drink of beer. "Eventually Oldham will get it out of the witnesses that they lied. And then . . ." He shrugged, letting them fill in the blanks.

"They'll go to prison?" the burly man asked stupidly.

"More likely they'll hang. Like I said, I wouldn't want to be in their shoes. I hear Oldham's got an investigator working on finding those witnesses right now." Tyler drained his beer and stood up. "Nice talking to you fellas." He left, grinning to himself as the men gathered behind him to discuss the situation.

At five o'clock, Tyler was waiting at the dock for the *Lady Luck*'s return. Pacing up and down the pier, he finally saw the riverboat round the bend, and as always, his heart swelled with pride. He had worked long and hard to buy that boat, and he had turned it into something magnificent. Now he longed to do that with six boats, all new and shiny white, with black trim and red letters. He already had ideas for their names, too. Tyler grinned, imagining Claire's surprise when she saw a riverboat with the name *Lady Claire* on the side. Maybe he'd even name boats for Emily and Lulu.

He watched the crew dock the riverboat and waited until the passengers had disembarked before starting up the ramp. After checking in with his pilot, he inspected the daily log, then went to find his assistant. Jonas caught sight of him and strode down the deck toward him.

"How did it go in Mt. Vernon?" he asked.

"Oldham agrees with us," he said as they walked down the narrow hallway to his cabin. "Something fishy is going on. Now I'm more certain than ever that someone is setting Gunter up."

"That's what we were afraid of," Jonas said sadly.

Tyler sat in one chair and Jonas the other, both men stretching their legs out in front of them. "According to Oldham," Tyler reported, "it looks as though the judge and the prosecutor are in on it. Whoever the man is behind all this, he has a lot of power. I can't help but wonder if he isn't the same person who murdered Mr. Greene."

"The name Reginald Boothe comes to mind," Jonas said dryly. "I hate to be pessimistic, but it seems Gunter's chances of going free are pretty slim."

Tyler's jaw twitched angrily. "Not if I can help it."

Jonas glanced at him curiously. "What are you thinking? Do you have a plan?"

"I've already put it in motion, Jonas. Now we have to sit back and wait for Mr. Oldham's report."

"I don't mean to sound callous," Jonas admitted, "but

you do realize that your financial backing may be jeopardy, depending on the outcome of Gunter's trial.''

"I realize it."

"Just to play devil's advocate, Ty, without the backing, you won't be able to carry out your plans for new docks and boats. And that means you won't need Claire's land." He paused to glance at Tyler. "My question is, in that event, will you still marry Claire?"

Tyler rubbed his jaw. He hated to consider the possibility that his plans would fall through, but Jonas had made a good point. What reason would there be to get married, if not to secure the use of the land? "I don't know," he said somberly.

"You don't have feelings one way or the other?" Jonas queried.

Tyler glanced at him with a scowl. "Why are you hounding me about this?"

Jonas went to the cabinet, took out the whiskey decanter, poured a swallow in a glass, and handed it to Tyler. "Here. I think you're going to need this after I tell you what I learned today."

Tyler narrowed his eyes as he settled back in his chair. "What the devil did you learn?"

"We had a passenger on board today, a fellow by the name of Thomas. Hank Thomas, I believe. It seems he did some work for Arthur Cavanaugh sometime last year."

"And how did you come by that information?"

"I gave him a few glasses of whiskey," Jonas said with a sniff. "The bloke has been working out in the fields, you see, and had just seen his first newspaper in weeks. I suppose that's where he saw the Cavanaugh name mentioned. Anyway, when he learned we were stopping in Fortune, he brought up the fact that he knew Arthur Cavanaugh, so naturally I *encouraged* him to talk. After a few whiskeys, he was quite willing. He's a wildcatter, I found out. Arthur called him out to talk to him about the possibility of drilling for oil on his land, and the bloke never got paid for his services.''

"So he wants his money.''

"Yes. In fact, he's going out to see Claire tomorrow. But that's not all.'' Jonas resumed his seat in his chair and leaned forward, warming to his story. "Arthur wasn't simply speculating, Ty. He found oil.''

Tyler sat forward. "You're joking.''

Jonas made an "X" on the front of his shirt. "On my mother's grave, Ty.''

"Your mother is still alive," Tyler reminded him with a scowl.

"Barely. Anyway, Arthur never followed through on it. That oil is just sitting there, waiting to be brought up.''

Stunned, Tyler leaned back, raking his fingers through his hair. Claire was sitting on a fortune! "You know what this means?'' he asked excitedly. "We won't need Gunter's employers to back our boat docks. All we need is to bring up that oil and let the money start pouring in.''

"You know what else it means?'' Jonas asked. "It means Claire doesn't need you anymore.''

Chapter 24

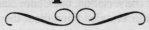

Tyler stared at Jonas open-mouthed. He was right! If Claire had money, she wouldn't need to marry him. The thought of losing her made his gut clench. He stood up and walked to the other side of the cabin. "I can't let that happen."

"Then you'd better make sure she has a damn good reason for marrying you, and you'd better do it before she finds out about the oil."

Tyler swung around, his jaw twitching in frustration. "And just how do I make sure she wants to marry me?"

"You know how: by giving her something money can't buy."

Tyler ground his teeth together. "We're back to that again."

Jonas got to his feet. "Yes, we're back to that again! For God's sake, Ty, why don't you just admit you love Claire? You *do*—I know you do. If you weren't so bloody afraid of getting hurt, you'd say it and save us both a lot of bother."

"Watch your tongue, old man."

"You watch yours too bloody much!" Jonas snapped. "If you lose her, it's your own damn fault." He stalked to the door, yanked it open, and let it slam behind him.

Tyler stared at the closed door. Jonas was wrong: he couldn't love Claire; he wouldn't take that chance—yet neither would he let her go.

*   *   *

Supper that evening was a strained affair. Jonas made a few attempts at conversation, but Claire could tell his heart wasn't in it. Tyler brooded throughout the meal, and Lulu tried to make up for their lack of conversation by supplying a constant stream of stories. Emily and Mrs. Parks seemed the only ones who were oblivious to the tension.

As soon as supper was over, Claire offered to help Lulu with the dishes. Emily had decided to read to Mrs. Parks on the front porch, and Tyler and Jonas had headed in separate directions.

"Something's going on with those two fellas," Lulu commented, as she scraped dishes and set them in a pan of sudsy water.

"I think they're both worried about Gunter," Claire told her. "I know I am."

"Me, too, sweetie pie. It makes me sick to think that someone's railroading that poor boy." Lulu finished washing the plates and started on the pots. "What about you? Are you coming to terms with this marriage idea?"

Claire thought about it as she dried a plate and put it in the cupboard. "I suppose I am. Tyler and Emily get along very well, and it is a relief to think that I'll have someone to help me with the farm expenses. And then there's the rumors that are being spread about me. I don't want Emily to be hurt by gossip. I just wish . . ." She let her sentence trail off. There was no sense wishing for the improbable.

"I know what you wish," Lulu assured her. "It's what we all wish for, from time to time—that there's one special someone out there who will love us all to pieces." She sighed loudly. "I used to wish it myself."

"Have you ever had that one special person in your life?" Claire asked.

Lulu chuckled dryly. "I thought I did once. I was just a young, foolish girl then. I didn't ever think he'd stop loving me. But he found another love."

"Did he run off with her?"

"I guess you could say that. Her name was Demon Rum." Lulu shook her head sadly as she pumped water into the coffee pot. "There I was—no money, no husband, a kid, and just a kid myself. I fairly lost my mind."

"You had a baby?" Claire asked in surprise.

The pot suddenly slipped from Lulu's hands and water splashed all over the floor. "Oh, gracious! I'll take care of it," she said, as Claire rushed to sop up the spill. Lulu got down on her knees and began to wipe it up. "*I* was a kid. I was alone and scared. That's all I meant."

Claire let the subject drop. "You've never fallen in love since then?"

Lulu stood up and wiped her skirt. "Wouldn't want to take the chance."

"You sound like Tyler," Claire scoffed.

The housekeeper paused. "I do, don't I?" she said in some amazement. She finished filling the pot with water and put it on the stove to heat. "Don't use me as your example, sweetie pie," she said, turning to Claire. "No matter what Tyler says, I believe he cares a great deal for you. He's a good man down deep." She patted her chest. "I know it in here. Give him a chance."

Claire put away the last plate and hung the linen towel to dry. "Thanks for the advice, Lulu."

Tyler nearly collided with Claire in the kitchen doorway. He grabbed her shoulders to steady her, staring down into her startled face. For a long moment their gazes locked, and his heart turned over at the sight of those beautiful eyes. Glancing up, he saw Lulu watching. She gave him an encouraging wink.

Tyler smiled at Claire. "Would you take a walk with me?"

With a nod, Claire put her hand through his arm, and they proceeded out the back door. Tyler led her toward the stables so that no one would overhear their conversation. He'd thought long and hard about what Jonas had said, and he was still angry at the insinuation that he was a coward. He was simply cautious.

Still, Tyler understood what Jonas was saying. If Claire didn't need him for support, he'd better give her another reason to marry him. Perhaps he could convince her that she was important to him, not just for her land, but for herself—which was the truth. Until he'd faced the possibility of losing her, he hadn't realized how much he looked forward to being with her. He hoped that would be enough for her, because it was all he could offer.

Tyler retrieved the woolen blanket from the stables and spread it on the ground. Claire sat, smoothing out her skirts as he made himself comfortable beside her.

"Nice evening," Tyler said, glancing at the sky.

"Yes, very." Claire swatted a bug away.

Tyler cleared his throat, keeping his gaze fixed on the heavens. "There's something I want to say." He glanced at her and saw a flicker of hope in her eyes that made him pause. Was she hoping that he would say he loved her?

Tyler suddenly grew nervous, and everything he'd planned to say flew out of his mind. Damn that Jonas; this was all his fault. He licked suddenly dry lips, knowing Claire was waiting. "I'd like to know if you've decided where you want to get married," he blurted. "Whatever you decide is fine by me."

Claire stared at him. Thank God she'd been smart enough to let Tyler talk first. She'd planned to make a little speech about how she hoped love could develop in a home where both people were committed to making their marriage succeed. Clearly, it would have been a mistake to mention the word *love*. For Tyler, this was still a business arrangement. Hiding her disappointment, she toyed with a loose thread in the blanket. "I haven't decided. But I think you're right about it being a practical solution for us both."

"Yes. Absolutely." Tyler felt a stab of remorse. He knew he should tell her about the wildcatter; it wasn't fair that she didn't know, and he didn't like deceiving her. But if Claire were to find out now that he knew there was oil on her land, she would think that was his reason for marrying her. He certainly hadn't given her any reasons, besides purely practical ones, for her to think otherwise.

Yet the simple truth was that he wanted her. Knowing he'd be coming home to Claire made him feel less lonely, less empty. She seemed to fill that deep void inside him. Not only that, but he had made a commitment to her when he proposed, and he wasn't going to back away from it now.

But he'd save that for another time—it never hurt to have an ace up his sleeve. "Did you still want to wait until after the harvest?" he asked her.

"I hadn't really thought about it," she replied.

"I've been thinking that maybe we should get married sooner."

"I see."

"It might be best to have it before Gunter's trial," Tyler explained, "since the harvest will begin soon afterward; you'll be busy with that for another couple of months."

"That's true." With a thoughtful frown, Claire rubbed her forehead. "When were you thinking?"

"Whenever you say. Tomorrow, if you'd like. In fact, I can go round up the justice of the peace right now."

Claire lifted her astonished gaze to meet his. "Right now?"

Tyler gave her a crooked grin to let her know he was joking. She smiled back, breaking some of the tension between them. For the first time in days, he saw a glimmer of warmth in her eyes.

That was what he had missed! Tyler's pulse quickened as he stared into those pools of cobalt blue. His gaze dropped to her mouth, lusciously smooth and inviting. He remembered how sweet it had tasted, and how her skin had felt beneath his fingers, and how she had aroused him so with her kisses. His instinct was to kiss her now, hard and long.

Claire watched wide-eyed as Tyler leaned toward her. His hand came up to cup her face, then he dipped his head until his lips met hers. She closed her eyes, unsure of what had prompted the kiss, but enjoying it nevertheless. He tasted of coffee and smelled of clean soap; a day's growth of whiskers scratched her chin. The effect was intoxicating. Kissing him harder, Claire slid her hand around to the back of his neck, the feel of his thick hair between her fingers intimate, arousing. As he held her tenderly in his arms, she couldn't help but believe he felt something for her. Could he kiss her with such feeling if he didn't?

Perhaps Lulu was right. Perhaps love could grow, and was blossoming right now.

Claire let him lower her to the blanket, his kisses growing hotter, hungrier. His hand ran up her ribs to her breast, his thumb seeking the nipple, circling it until it puckered and tingled. Claire moaned deep in her throat, which only made him kiss her with more fervor.

As Tyler's lips moved down her throat, his hand slid across her belly, down to the junction of her thighs, pressing through the material, his fingers knowing just where and how to touch her. Closing her eyes, Claire moaned again and arched against his hand. Her blood coursed heavily through her body, pooling where his fingers stroked. She wanted more and she wanted to stop, yet the intense pleasure made it difficult to do anything but gasp.

Tyler kissed her again as he grasped the hem of her skirt and bunched it around her hips. His desire was inflamed beyond bearable limits. He had resisted Daphne for this woman. Now, at last, she would be his.

As he slid a hand beneath her drawers, Tyler raised his head to gaze down at Claire, searching again for what he had missed in Daphne's lustful glances. But what he saw made him hesitate. She was breathing fast, staring at him with large, questioning eyes. There was no warmth in her gaze now, or admiration, but there were plenty of misgivings. She was struggling to trust him, but he could see she hadn't quite made it. And Tyler suddenly realized he needed that warmth and trust more than he needed to relieve his lust.

He gently straightened her skirt, then rolled away and sat up. His conscience had taken a giant leap forward and he wasn't overly happy about it. Hearing her rise, Tyler got to his feet. "I guess I got a little ahead of myself."

She looked down, clearly embarrassed. "So did I."

"I think we were talking about a date for our wedding."

"I seem to recall that." Claire paused, then said hesitantly, "Would two weeks from Saturday be all right?"

Two weeks! Tyler swallowed hard. Suddenly he didn't think two *years* would be enough.

Then Tyler's gaze slid over Claire's delicate features, from her passion-swollen lips to those blue eyes that could capture a man's heart—if he wasn't careful. At that moment, two *minutes* was too long.

He picked up her hand and kissed it. "Two weeks it is."

Two weeks! Claire shook her head as she took her freshly laundered bedding out to the yard and hung it on the line the next morning. What had she been thinking? Two weeks weren't nearly enough time to prepare for a wedding. She would have to go into town today and see if she could have a proper dress made in such a short time.

She paused, a wooden clothespin between her teeth. Tyler's passion had swept her along in a tidal wave of desire, until she had nearly lost all reason. With a shiver, she realized she would have lost more than just reason if Tyler had not stopped them from going further. But his restraint had impressed her. And now that she'd had time to think about it, it heartened her as well. Perhaps Lulu was correct after all: perhaps Tyler truly did care about her.

It seemed all the more logical when she realized that Tyler's chances for getting the money he needed from Gunter's employers seemed doubtful. What benefit would Tyler gain by marrying her if he couldn't carry out his plans? Yet he had said that he still wanted to marry her. Perhaps there was hope for them, after all.

Claire looked over the line to see Lulu trudging toward her, carrying a basket of wet clothing. They had gotten a late start on the laundry that morning. Claire, Lulu, and Mrs. Parks had spent a good part of it discussing the details of the wedding. They had finally decided a quiet ceremony at the church would be best, with just family, a few friends, and the farmhands and their families in attendance. Afterward Lulu was planning on roasting a hog, so that their guests could come by for a buffet meal outdoors.

"I'll have to go to town after lunch to see if I can have a dress made quickly," Claire informed Lulu as she pinned a sheet to the line.

"Didn't your mama have a wedding dress you can use?"

Claire's forehead wrinkled in thought. She remembered her mother's wedding day clearly. The dress had been ivory satin, with an overlay of ecru lace set with seed pearls. She doubted her father had given it away. "That's a wonderful idea!" she exclaimed. "I'll look for it today."

They both turned at the rapid clop of horse's hooves on the dirt road, and watched as a man rode up to Bellefleur. Claire finished pinning the pillowcase to the line and started for the house.

"Want me to go?" Lulu called.

Claire shook her head. "I'll see to it." She studied the man as she approached. He was of medium build and lanky, with a battered yellow broad-brimmed hat, sharp, tanned features, and a leather vest. He reminded Claire of pictures she'd seen of cowboys.

He nodded as Claire walked up to him. "Howdy, ma'am. Are you Miss Cavanaugh?"

"Yes, I am."

"Your pa was Arthur Cavanaugh?"

Claire studied him curiously. "Yes."

He stuck out a weathered hand. "Name's Hank Thomas. I was here last fall doing some work for your pa. I've been out of the area for awhile, doing some drilling down in Texas. I was traveling through the other day and heard that he had passed on." He shook his head. "A tragedy, ma'am. I was sorry to hear it."

"Thank you, Mr. Thomas. But surely you didn't come all this way to pay your respects."

"No, ma'am, that wasn't my sole purpose. I'm a wild-catter by trade. Your pa had me come out to see about drilling some oil wells for him. He didn't pay me at the time, because he didn't have the money. He told me he'd contact me in a few months, but that was more than half a year ago. Since's he's passed on, I figured I'd better collect what was owed me."

"I'm so sorry for your trouble," Claire told him. "You see, we're having some financial problems and—"

"Then your pa didn't tell you about the oil?"

Claire stared at him, perplexed. "What oil?"

Hank grinned, white teeth showing against brown skin. "Your oil, ma'am. You're sitting on an oil field."

Chapter 25

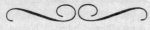

Claire put a hand over her mouth, her eyes wide with shock. They were sitting on oil! At last she knew what her father's surprise was. She looked at the man, who was watching her with some amusement. "Mr. Thomas, I'm just so surprised I can't think clearly. Where did you find the oil?"

"Come on. I'll show you."

He took her down the road to a rocky area that had never been farmed. Staring down at the rough terrain, he walked around it, moving some rocks with the toe of his heavy boot, then bent down. "Here it is. See this seepage of oil between these rocks? You've got an underground reservoir in this area."

"What do I need to do to bring up the oil?"

"Depends on how you want to handle it," he said. "Your pa wanted to do it all himself, but he didn't have the money to hire the roughnecks and lease the rig, so he told me to hold off until he could raise it. Most people just sign a mineral lease and let an oil company bring in the well. The company would pay you about one-eighth of the value of each barrel of oil they produce."

Only an eighth? Claire frowned in thought. Her father had never trusted anyone to handle his finances. Should she follow his example? "How much money would it take to do it myself?"

Hank looked at her skeptically. "I don't know that

you'd want to tackle that yourself, ma'am. It's an awfully big undertaking. You'd need to hire a crew of roughnecks and lease the rig, and neither the men nor the machinery comes cheap.'' Hank scratched his sideburn. ''Give me a piece of paper and a pencil and I'll calculate it for you.''

Claire took him back to the house and showed him to her father's study. While Hank worked at the desk, Claire paced, one hand rubbing her forehead as she contemplated what an oil strike would mean. Now she understood why her father had thanked his forefathers for buying the land! And now she understood why he hadn't wanted anyone to know. If Boothe had found out, he would have moved heaven and earth to foreclose on Bellefleur.

Oil! Claire still couldn't believe it. She was rich! She wouldn't have to fear losing her home or going hungry. She would never have to depend on anyone ever again!

Claire came to a sudden halt as another startling thought occurred to her. She wouldn't have to marry Tyler. The oil would be her security.

The thought of never again seeing that handsome face, nor hearing that deep, husky voice, broke Claire's heart. Yet now she had so much to consider—so much more at risk. As her husband, Tyler would be entitled to use the oil money at his discretion. There was no law to protect her from that. What kind of security would she have then?

The question was one of trust.

Claire pressed her lips together. If she married him, she'd have to trust him.

''Here's what I come up with,'' Hank said, breaking into her thoughts.

Claire walked to the desk and took the paper, her eyes widening in shock. Hank pointed to the first number. ''That's what your pa owed me from last year,'' he explained. ''The next figure is what it would take to hire a crew for two months' work. And the third is the cost of leasing the rig. You understand, these are all estimates. Equipment breaks down and has to be fixed, and that can cause delays. Sometimes you pay for men to sit and wait.'' He paused to point to the last figure. ''There's your total amount, and that's just for starters.''

Claire slowly shook her head in amazement. No wonder her father hadn't been able to afford it! ''That's a lot of money, Mr. Thomas.''

''Yes, ma'am, it is—but you could get it back a thousand times over. Of course, you can take the worry out of it and sign a mineral lease.''

The thought of sitting on so much wealth made Claire dizzy. Her instincts told her to hire a crew and bring up the oil herself, but how would she raise enough money? ''Will you be in town for a few days so I can get back to you?''

Hank scratched his sideburn again. ''Tell you what, I'll stay in town for another day. If I haven't heard from you by then, I'll leave an address where you can wire me.''

Claire walked him to the door. ''Thank you so much, Mr. Thomas, for coming back.''

He lifted his hat and was on his way. As Claire stood on the porch, watching him ride off, Lulu came up the walk carrying the empty basket. ''Who's the cowboy?'' she called.

''Hank Thomas. He's an oil driller.'' Claire heard the screen door squeak and turned as Emily stepped outside. Her little face was tense with worry.

''Cee Cee, what's going to happen to the crops?'' she asked.

''Nothing, Em, why?''

''Won't all that oil ruin them?''

''Were you eavesdropping again?'' Claire shook her head in chagrin. ''No, Em, the crops are fine. The oil is down too deep to hurt them.''

''Oil?'' Lulu cried. ''You found oil?''

Claire laughed at the expression on Lulu's face, then gasped as she found herself enveloped in a big bear hug.

''Sweetie pie, this is your lucky day!'' Lulu cried, kissing her on the forehead. "Come here, angel!" she called, pulling Emily into the fold.

"Claire?" Mrs. Parks asked, standing at the door. "Did I hear you right?"

"Yes, Mrs. Parks. We're going to be rich!"

Shortly before noon that day, John Oldham walked into the cramped office of the prosecutor and looked around. The office was in an old building that also housed the town treasurer and clerk's office. A young man came out of a back room. "Did you want to see Mr. Jamieson?"

"Yes, sir. Tell him John Oldham is here to see him about the Jenssen matter."

Before the young clerk could relay the message, Lawrence Jamieson came out, a startled look on his face. "Mr. Oldham!" he said, holding out his hand. "This is a surprise."

Oldham shook his hand. "How are you, Jamieson?"

"Fine, thank you, sir. Please come in and sit down."

Oldham followed him to an even smaller room crowded with books, stacks of files, legal pads, and transcripts. While Jamieson sat at his tiny desk, Oldham took the only other seat available—an old ladderback chair, the type normally used in kitchens. Jamieson, obviously awed by the senior attorney's presence, seemed embarrassed by his humble surroundings.

"I appreciate your seeing me on short notice," Oldham began, trying to put the younger man at ease. "I didn't have a chance to talk with you in court the other day. You seemed to have disappeared after the hearing." He paused to let the prosecutor squirm a bit. "This case troubles me, Mr. Jamieson. I hope you appreciate the enormous responsibility I have in representing Mr. Jenssen. His freedom, as well as his life, may well be at stake here."

"I do appreciate that, sir. But I'm not sure what it is I can do for you."

"For one thing, produce those witnesses, so I can take their depositions. I've had my investigator trying to locate them, but they seem to have vanished into thin air, if they ever existed at all."

Jamieson pushed to his feet, looking flustered. "You're not trying to tell me that I made the whole thing up, are you?"

"Now, now, Mr. Jamieson," Oldham soothed, holding up his hands, "take it easy. I realize you're not the one who developed this case, but ultimately you're going to have to prosecute it. And in doing that, you're going to have to produce those witnesses. Right?"

Jamieson stared at him for a moment, then slowly sank down, a look of misery on his face. The truth of the matter had finally sunk in. If he didn't have witnesses, he didn't have a case.

"Here's what I suggest," Oldham explained. "Talk to the sheriff and find out what this is all about, and then you and I can meet again and start our discovery in earnest. All right?"

At Jamieson's nod, Oldham rose. "Good. Let's meet in, say, a week." He walked out, a satisfied smile on his face. That young prosecutor had a long career ahead of him. Oldham was betting on the fact that he wouldn't do anything to jeopardize it.

At four o'clock that afternoon, Wilbur Simons burst into Reginald Boothe's office, breathing heavily. Boothe looked up in surprise. "What is it, Sheriff?"

"Trouble, Mr. Boothe," he said, panting. "Lawrence Jamieson came to see me today. He has to produce the witnesses who gave those statements about Jenssen."

"Well then, find them, Sheriff, and bring them in."

"I tried. They won't come."

"What do you mean?" Boothe demanded angrily.

"You told me they were all lined up. You paid them, didn't you?"

"I told them I would pay them if they had to testify. Now they're saying there's not enough money to get them to testify."

"Well then, if they won't do it, find others who will, damn it!"

Simons shook his head. "I'll try, Mr. Boothe, but I don't think it will work. Something has scared those men."

"Or someone," Boothe muttered. "Go back down there, Sheriff, and try again. And find out who that some-one is."

He waited until the sheriff had gone, then he slowly swivelled his chair toward the window. Money would get those men to cooperate. Greed always won out.

It was dark when Tyler pulled the buggy to a stop in front of the house. He let Jonas out and led the horse back to the stables. His assistant hadn't said a word to him all day, beyond what was absolutely necessary, and it was starting to wear on Tyler's nerves. Bone tired, he rubbed down the horse and gave her some feed, then headed back to the house. He had been looking forward to coming home to Bellefleur all afternoon, but delays on the river had stretched his day well into the evening hours.

As he came around the front of the house, he saw Claire sitting on the swing, her feminine form outlined by the glow of lamplight through the parlor windows. He smiled to himself. It felt good to see her waiting for him.

"Hello," he said, coming up the porch steps.

"Hi." She gave him a tentative smile as he walked to-ward her. "I have some news."

"About Gunter?" he asked, sitting beside her. When he saw the sparkle of excitement in her eyes, however, he knew it wasn't about Gunter. She had learned about the oil.

"A man came to see me today—a wildcatter."

Tyler raised his eyebrows, pretending surprise. "What did he want?"

"My father discovered an oil seepage last fall and hired Mr. Thomas to investigate," Claire said, barely able to contain her excitement. "We're sitting on an oil field! My father wanted to set up an oil rig and bring up a well, but he didn't have the money."

"Don't landowners usually lease their land to oil companies and let them do it?"

"My father always had to do everything himself," Claire replied. She took a deep breath. "Now I have a decision to make: I can lease the land, and only make a profit of one-eighth of every barrel of oil brought up, or I can hire a crew and equipment and do it myself."

"How much money will that take?"

The excitement in her eyes faded. "Thousands of dollars. I have the figures inside. But that's not my only money problem. My father never paid Mr. Thomas and he's asking for his money. And the farmhands have to be paid, too. I probably should lease the land, even though it goes against my better judgment."

Tyler studied her anxious face. Claire was not asking him for help, so why did he feel obliged to be her hero again? The problem was, other than a small savings account, he didn't have any money, either. All he had was his boat. He rubbed his jaw as he pondered the matter. "Would you mind if I took a look at the figures?"

"Of course not."

Tyler watched Claire hurry into the house, then he stood up and walked to the railing. He hated pretending he didn't know about the oil, but if Claire discovered otherwise, she would never trust him again.

Hearing the door hinges squeak, Tyler turned as Claire swept across the porch, her pale blue dress glowing almost white in the moonlight. "Here," she told him, handing him the paper.

He let out his breath. Damn! That was a whole lot more than he was expecting.

Claire clasped her fingers together anxiously. "What do you think?"

As Tyler looked at her, the stories about her childhood popped into his mind. Claire was counting on the oil to secure her home, as well as her future. He tilted her face up to stare deep into her eyes. "I think it's a lot of money—but we'll find a way to do it."

His reward was the warmth shimmering in her eyes. She was willing to accept his help. She was starting to trust him again.

"There's only one condition," Claire told him, her face suddenly serious. "Whatever you do, I don't want Reginald Boothe involved in *any way*."

"Agreed. I'll go talk to Jonas and see if he has any ideas." He started to walk away, then returned to give her a resounding kiss. Her amazement made him grin, and the pleased look in her eyes warmed him all the way to his toes.

Inside, Tyler knocked twice on Jonas's door. "Are you in there, Jonas?"

"Sorry, he's not available," came the snide comment.

"Jonas, this is important."

There was a long pause, and then a reluctant, "Very well. Come in if you must."

Tyler walked in and shut the door. Jonas was sitting against propped pillows, absorbed in a book. Straddling a chair, Tyler waited for his assistant to look up, and finally said irritably, "All right, Jonas, I apologize."

Jonas snapped the book shut. "What do you want?"

"I have a problem. Claire wants to bring up the oil herself, and I offered to help."

"You don't have any money."

"I know that." Tyler raked his fingers through his hair. "She's counting on me, Jonas."

"I take it she still wants to marry you?"

"Yes. I talked to her yesterday evening. We've set a date in two weeks."

"However did you pull it off?" Jonas asked dryly.

Tyler put his finger to his lips to warn Jonas not to speak, tiptoed to the door, opened it quickly and looked out. Emily was nowhere in sight. "We decided it was in our mutual best interests," he said quietly.

Jonas opened his book, looking extremely perturbed. "I see."

"How am I going to come up with the money?"

"Don't look at me," Jonas said. "I have a little saved, but certainly not enough to finance an oil rig. Ask the bank for a loan."

"What would I use as collateral? All I have is the *Lady Luck*."

"I suppose you'll have to use that," Jonas said with a sniff.

Tyler shook his head. "Never. Not my boat. You know how I feel: that boat is my life."

"And what is Claire?"

"That's not a fair question."

"Perhaps not—but it's one you're going to have to answer sooner or later."

Tyler paced across the room. What if it turned out there was no oil field, or just a small pocket of oil? They could drill ten wells and come up dry. Could he risk his boat?

He paused at the window to look across the rolling land to the river, where moonlight glistened on the water. He understood Claire's love for Bellefleur; he felt the same way about the *Lady Luck*. But this was her big chance to secure her future. Could he disappoint her?

"Maybe there's a way to help Claire without risking my boat," he told Jonas. "She has the option of leasing the land to an oil company. She'd only get a percentage of the oil profits, but she also wouldn't be taking any risks. If I can convince her that's the wisest course, I'll only need to help her out with the driller's costs and the farmhands' wages.''

"And where will you get that money?''

"I have some cash put aside in a bank in Mount Vernon,'' he said.

"All right—I'll take the *Lady Luck* for you tomorrow so you can work on business here at home.''

Tyler leaned against the window frame and watched the light play across the rippling surface of the water. Home.

It *was* beginning to feel like home.

The hour was late when Tyler walked down the hall to his room. Seeing a faint light beneath Claire's door, he paused. Should he let her know now what he and Jonas had discussed, or wait until morning? He pictured her opening the door in her nightdress, her long black hair unbound, and his blood pulsed hot and thick. He tapped softly.

In a moment, the door opened. Claire was hastily pulling on her wrapper, covering her diaphanous white nightdress, but not before he'd had a tempting glimpse of rose-colored nipples and the dark shadow between her legs. His groin tightened as his gaze swept up to her face. A pink blush tinged her creamy cheeks, and her silky hair fell gracefully around her shoulders. He met her cobalt blue gaze and swallowed hard. His hands clenched to keep from reaching for her. "I just wanted to tell you that Jonas and I discussed your situation.''

She moved back into her room. "Come in.''

Tyler stepped inside and looked around. Her dresser against the near wall was lined with framed photographs of her family. The lamp next to her bed cast a soft, golden glow on the pink and green wallpaper. The pale green bedcover was turned down invitingly and her pillows were propped against the tall, wooden headboard. A book lay open nearby. She had been in bed.

Tyler's eyes met Claire's. All he could think of was how

much he wanted to lay her down on that bed and make love to her.

"What did Jonas think?" Claire asked eagerly.

Tyler swallowed again, his throat so dry he had to clear it to speak. "There's risk involved. We may find only a small pocket of oil. A lot of money could be spent drilling for little profit."

Claire's eagerness turning to dismay. Her brows knitted and her fingers twisted together. "Do you think that's likely?"

Tyler hadn't meant to alarm her and now hastened to put her fears to rest. "I'm not the expert—Mr. Thomas is. But my policy has always been to minimize risk. That's what I'm suggesting you do."

"You're right," she said, before he could elaborate. "I have to minimize the risk. Why involve an oil company if there's only a pocket of oil? This is something I have to do myself."

That wasn't what he meant at all. Tyler started to explain, but the utter determination in Claire's face stopped him. He knew exactly how she felt and what a lonely position it was. She needed his support. Gently, he gripped her shoulders. "We'll do it together."

Claire's features softened and her eyes filled with love. "Thank you," she whispered.

Tyler's heart twisted in agony. If only he could return that love.

He ran his palms slowly, sensuously, along the soft line of her jaw to her temple. With growing desire, he traced her eyebrows with his fingertips, then threaded his fingers in her hair, feeling the heavy, silken texture of it. Lifting an ebony lock to his nose, he closed his eyes and inhaled the soft rose scent that clung to it.

When he opened his eyes again, there was a tortured look on Claire's face that squeezed his heart. Suddenly he wanted to show her that he cared about her, that he desired her. He could give her that much.

His hands moved down her long, slender neck to cover her breasts, feeling the firm, supple mounds with their hard buds beneath his palms, their taste and texture still vivid in his memory. Claire's pupils widened and Tyler expected her to pull back in alarm, but then he saw a spark of desire flicker to life in her eyes. His blood coursed through his veins, thickening his manhood. It would be so easy to lock the door and make love to her, to teach her what real passion was.

Cupping her face, Tyler brought it to his, kissing her gently, then with deepening urgency. He pulled Claire against him, melding her soft contours to his as he coaxed her lips open. Plunging his tongue into the sweet, wet warmth of her mouth, Tyler knew he had to have her.

Claire struggled against the tide of passion that swept her along, but Tyler's sensuous assault on her mouth broke down her defenses. Her skin tingled where his fingers touched, her breasts swelled, her body throbbed, her desire flared white hot—and her heart overflowed with love. She wound her arms around his neck, standing on tiptoe, pressing passion-hardened nipples against his solid chest as Tyler slid his hands down the curve of her waist, over her hips, to cup her bottom. Leaning against him, Claire felt the evidence of his arousal and her own spun out of control.

He quickly closed the door. Then, with a primal growl that made her body throb, Tyler swept her up and carried her to the bed. Untying the sash at her waist, he parted her robe and unfastened the buttons of her nightdress. Claire shivered as the cool air touched her heated flesh, then she gasped when his mouth covered her breast. As he teased one nipple and then the other, he raised her gown and ran his hand between her thighs until they parted. Claire's eyes closed and her back arched as he stroked her faster and faster, until she gasped and cried out for relief.

Leaving a trail of hot kisses down the smooth plane of her stomach to her inner thighs, Tyler further inflamed her passion by sampling her feminine mysteries, leaving Claire panting with need. At first scandalized, she soon abandoned herself to the wanton sensations, until her thoughts were as uninhibited as his actions.

Quickly, Tyler shed his clothing and covered her with his body. His hot, turgid flesh burned the tender skin of her belly. She felt him probe her slick folds, seeking entrance. Imagining the feel of him inside her, Claire lifted her hips to welcome him, but suddenly tensed. Should she give Tyler her most precious gift—a gift that by rights should be given to her husband? Did she trust him? Her instincts warned her not to, but her heart said otherwise. Tyler had pledged his help, knowing the risks. Surely that meant he loved her.

Claire met Tyler's expectant gaze and opened her arms—and her heart—to him. She felt him gently ease inside her, holding her until she adjusted to his size. Slowly, he stroked her, gradually increasing the rhythm until her pulse beat in time to it; until every muscle, every nerve, every thought was focused on their joining. Her fingers dug into his back as the tension built. He captured her mouth in a powerful kiss, and Claire moaned as the pressure built. As it exploded into a thousand shock waves of pleasure, she cried out.

For a long moment she held him tightly, afraid to let him go, fearing that her soul-shaking experience had been one-sided. But when Tyler lifted his head to gaze at her, Claire was sure that what she saw in his eyes was love. He kissed her tenderly, then got up and pulled on his clothing.

As Claire donned her nightdress and smoothed her tousled hair, Tyler came up behind her and put his arms around her. "I'll see you tomorrow," he murmured in her ear.

For a long time afterward, Claire sat at her window remembering every moment of their lovemaking. She had been right to trust her heart.

*   *   *

After a quick breakfast, Claire sought out Hank Thomas at the Good Fortune Inn. She found him lounging on the front porch talking with the inn's owner, a potbellied, talkative man in his early fifties named Cyrus Haines.

"Good morning, gentlemen," Claire said, climbing the steps to the long porch.

"Miss Cavanaugh," both men said, rising.

"Mr. Thomas, we have some business to discuss."

"Yes, ma'am."

After Cyrus excused himself and left the porch, Claire sat on a wicker chair next to Thomas. "I've decided I'm going to finance the oil rig myself."

Thomas raised his eyebrows. "You sure you want to do that?"

"Definitely. My fiancé, Tyler McCane, is going to help me get the financing."

"Is that the fellow who owns the riverboat?"

Claire smiled. "Then you know him."

"Not personally, but I met his assistant, Polk, on my trip here to Fortune." Thomas's eyebrows knitted in bewilderment. "We talked at some length about the oil on your land. I'm surprised he didn't tell you."

Stunned, Claire could only stare at him. If Jonas had known about the oil strike, then so had Tyler. Yet he had pretended not to know.

A sharp pain sliced through her heart. She had given herself to Tyler believing he loved her.

Once again, she had been played for a fool.

Chapter 26

Tyler's gut clenched as the loan officer explained the terms of the mortgage. Despite his promise to help Claire, now that the papers were in front of him, he couldn't sign. Breaking into a cold sweat, he rose abruptly, nearly knocking over his chair. "I've changed my mind."

Ignoring the bemused look on the banker's face, Tyler strode out into the fresh air. There was too much risk. He couldn't do it. He'd have to tell Claire to lease the land.

Stopping at Mr. Oldham's office, Tyler received some good news: the two witnesses hadn't been located, and the prosecutor was growing nervous.

"I'm certain Mr. Jamieson will want the case dismissed rather than risk the embarrassment of trial," Oldham explained, "but there is always the possibility that those men may come forward. It would help our case enormously if Gunter had a witness. What's more," he said, "I think Gunter knows more than he's telling."

Tyler studied the attorney's somber face. "What makes you think that?"

"I've gone over the events of the night of the murder with him several times. The first time, he said he never left his apartment above the pawnshop. The second time, he said he left late that night for a brief walk, just to get some fresh air. The last time, he said he left to run an errand, yet he won't specify what the errand was for. I'd like to take you across the street to the jail. Perhaps you

322

can impress upon him the importance of being truthful.''

"Let's go.''

At the jail, the two men were shown into a room the size of a pantry, furnished with a small table and three chairs. In a few moments, Gunter was brought in, his hands cuffed. His eyes were lifeless and he had lost weight. Tyler took a seat across from him.

"Gunter, are you holding back any information that would help your case?''

Gunter shook his head adamantly. "I have no more information!''

"Your stories aren't holding up. Why are you lying?''

The Swede clasped his hands together in supplication. "Please, Mr. McCane, do not ask me. I cannot say anything. I have made a vow.''

"To whom?''

Gunter dropped his head into his hands. "I cannot say.'' He raised his head, his eyes alarmed. *"I cannot say!* Do you understand?''

"Do you understand that you may be found guilty?'' Tyler grasped his arm. "Do you know what that means, Gunter? You may hang.''

The Swede broke into tears, laying his head on his arms. "My family! What will they think? Will they believe I am a murderer?''

"For God's sake, help yourself!'' Tyler pleaded.

"I promised her she would be safe!''

Both men sat forward. "Who, Gunter?'' Tyler demanded.

He sighed heavily. "Anna Greene.''

Oldham stared at him in surprise. "You know where Anna Greene is?''

Gunter nodded ashamedly. "She is hiding. I took her to the train station in the middle of the night. She was so afraid she would be murdered in her bed that she took nothing, only some money.'' He looked up at Tyler, his eyes lifeless once again. "I cannot betray her.''

"Would she want you to hang for her, Gunter?"

His chin quivered as he shook his head. "I was like a son to her."

"She'll be safe here in Mt. Vernon," Oldham offered. "I'll even keep her at my house. Then she can testify for you."

Gunter's eyes came to life and he sat forward expectantly. "Would you do that?"

"Absolutely. Now tell me everything you know."

Later, as the two men left the jail, the attorney clapped Tyler on the back. "At last we have a fighting chance!"

Reginald Boothe heard nothing from the sheriff all day. By the time the bank closed, he could stand it no longer. When he strode into the sheriff's office, Simons jumped up from his desk, a guilty look on his face.

"Well?" Boothe snapped. "Did you get witnesses?"

"No, Mr. Boothe. No one down at the Dockside would take the money."

Boothe's nostrils flared and his eyes glittered dangerously. "So you've decided to just sit here and play cards."

"I don't know what else to do."

"Have you thought of trying somewhere besides the tavern?" Boothe snarled. "We have to have witnesses! Do you understand, Sheriff? Is your brain capable of comprehending that little fact?" He glared at Simons, wanting to choke the life out of him, then wheeled around and stormed out.

By the time Tyler returned from Mt. Vernon, supper was over and the dining room was empty. Wanting to avoid Claire, Tyler strode quickly to Jonas's room and let himself in. His assistant looked up in surprise, laying aside his book.

"Jonas, I have a problem."

Jonas merely lifted an eyebrow.

"Last night I tried to tell Claire that the risks involved in bringing up the oil herself were too great, but she misunderstood. She thought I was encouraging her to do it with my help."

"Naturally you tried to dissuade her."

"Well, I—she was in her nightdress, and—"

"Enough said."

"I even went to the bank this morning, with every intention of taking out a loan on the boat." Tyler's shoulders sagged. "I couldn't do it."

"You know I have little money. What is it exactly that you want me to do?"

Tyler sank down and buried his face in his hands. "Shoot me."

Lulu put away the last dish, doused the lamps, and started down the hall. As she passed the dining room, she saw Emily standing on a chair next to the window. "What in heaven's name are you doing, angel?"

"Sh-h-h!" Emily pointed toward the grate in the ceiling.

Standing beside her, Lulu could hear Tyler and Jonas talking in the room above. "Are you eavesdropping again?" she asked.

"This is important," Emily whispered. She craned her neck, listening intently.

"That's enough. Time for bed."

"They've stopped anyway." Emily obediently climbed down, seemingly satisfied by what she had learned. "Goodnight."

Shaking her head, Lulu followed her out of the room.

Standing outside Claire's door, Tyler rehearsed his speech. He had to convince her to change her mind. She'd just have to understand that he didn't have the money. Taking a steadying breath, he knocked.

When she opened the door, Tyler's speech froze in his throat. Claire's eyes snapped with anger; her features were stiff; her hands were clenched at her sides. Yet her voice was eerily calm when she said, "You knew about the oil."

Tyler's heart sank. "Claire, let me explain."

Her icy glare silenced him. "There's nothing to explain. You lied to me again, and I won't marry a man I can't trust. Goodbye, Tyler." Stepping back, she closed the door.

For a moment, he was too stunned to move. Then he swung around and strode to his room. As he packed his bag, Jonas walked in.

"Going somewhere?"

"Back to the boat. The wedding is off. Claire found out that I knew about the oil."

Jonas shook his head, his eyes full of sympathy, and for once he had no glib retort. "I'm sorry, lad."

"Maybe it's for the best. It wouldn't have lasted anyway." Tyler closed the bag, slung it over his shoulder and walked out.

When Daphne arrived at Boothe's house the next afternoon, he let her in, then went to the bedroom to wait for her to appear in costume, his manhood already stiff with need. Hearing the soft rustle of Daphne's silk wrapper, he looked up expectantly, then snapped, "Where's your wig?"

"We don't need that ol' thing today," Daphne purred, her body moving in a seductive sway as she approached him. She untied the sash of her wrapper, then freed her copper hair from its pins, sweeping the mass up in her hands and letting it cascade over her shoulders.

"Get the wig," he ordered through gritted teeth.

Daphne froze. With a chilly look, she closed her wrapper. "Whatever you say, darlin'."

Boothe fumed silently as she left the bedroom. Whatever had gotten into her? She knew the routine. He looked up a short while later when Daphne returned dressed in her street clothes.

"What are you doing?" Boothe demanded, getting to his feet.

She preened in front of his mirror for a moment, then turned to face him. "I'm going to my parents' house for dinner."

"Not yet, you're not," he said, gripping her wrist with his long fingers.

She jerked her hand loose. "I was going to tell you later, but since there isn't going to be a later, I'll tell you now. My daddy found out about us. He told me if I ever saw you again, he'd come after you with a shotgun."

"Then why the hell did you come here?" Boothe demanded, following her as she sashayed down the hall to his front door.

"I love danger, you know that. But if I were you, I'd start lookin' over my shoulder. It's all over town, darlin'— the old banker going after a sweet, innocent girl young enough to be his daughter." Daphne gave him a saccharine smile.

"You trollop!" Boothe sneered.

Daphne pressed one finger to her lips, as though deep in thought. "I believe there is *one* person who doesn't know about us—your former partner, Tyler McCane. Or if he did know, he didn't seem to mind once I took off my clothes for him."

She opened the door, pausing to look at Boothe over her shoulder. "Before I forget, here's another bit of news I'm sure you'll find interesting. Claire Cavanaugh struck oil on her property. She's going to be a wealthy woman." Daphne stepped out into the sunshine and smiled. " 'Bye, darlin'. It's been a pleasure."

In a near state of shock, Boothe watched Daphne stroll down the block, her parasol unfurled. He backed up and slammed the door, rattling his fine crystal. "It can't be true!" he said aloud. "That property was supposed to be *mine*!" Boothe shouted for his servant to bring the landau around. Who would know if it was true? Someone would have to know. The sheriff! Simons would be able to find out for him.

But he couldn't find Simons. Boothe's driver took him from the sheriff's office to his house, and then around town. Finally, they parked in front of Simons's cottage to wait. After more than an hour, the sheriff came lumbering up the street. Boothe jumped out of the landau and ran toward him, causing Simons to stop and stare.

Boothe grabbed his shirt front with both fists, his eyes wild. "What news have you heard about the Cavanaugh land?"

Simons leaned back. "I heard they found oil."

"Is it true?" Boothe hissed, leaning into his face. "Has it been verified?"

Simons watched him with growing unease. "I can't say. They're talking about it down at the general store."

"Then find out!" Boothe snarled, releasing the sheriff with a backward shove.

Simons scratched the back of his neck as his boss ran back to his carriage. He'd never seen the banker so rattled. He could understand Boothe's frustration at missing out on owning that land, but his behavior now was downright peculiar.

Simons let himself in his house, thinking about Boothe's latest orders. He'd go out to Bellefleur in the morning to see if the rumors were true. In the meantime, he was going to bed. He was tired of jumping to Boothe's commands.

On Monday morning, John Oldham strode into the prosecutor's office with a smile on his face. "I've got some news that will please both of us: I found Walter Greene's wife. Before I take her deposition, I thought I'd give you the courtesy of telling you what she's going to say." Oldham beamed. "Mr. Jamieson, your job is about to become much easier."

The prosecutor smiled back. "I can't wait to hear it."

Oldham pulled up a chair. "Anna Greene was with Gunter Jenssen on the evening the murder took place. I'm sure you'll agree there could be no finer alibi witness than the deceased's own wife. Moreover, she has a piece of evidence which will not only help clear my client, but which I believe points in another direction entirely. The man who discovered Greene's body found a pocketwatch and chain which he thought belonged to the deceased. He gave it to the widow, who identified it as a very unique timepiece which she herself sold to Reginald Boothe. I don't know what this means and I really don't care. All I know is that justice demands that my client be released immediately."

The prosecutor looked both astounded and relieved. "Sir, if these facts are true, I will personally file the dismissal and I will authorize the release of your client."

"Thank you, Mr. Jamieson. I was hoping you'd say that. Now I think we need to see the judge."

"He'll be here tomorrow morning, as usual," Jamieson told him. "I'll meet you right after the morning hearings."

John Oldham rode immediately to Bellefleur, doffing his hat when Claire answered the door. "Good morning, Miss Cavanaugh."

"Mr. Oldham! Come in, please. Good heavens, what brings you out here?"

"Two reasons. I have some wonderful news for you, and I was hoping I could rent one of your rooms for the night."

Claire had Lulu make a pot of coffee and then she, Emily, Lulu, and the attorney gathered in the parlor for an update on Gunter's case. Oldham told them about Anna's testimony, but omitted any mention of new evidence. That was strictly between him and the prosecutor for the time being. "So you see, ladies, Gunter has been exonerated, as we knew he should be."

"That's the best news I've had in a long time," Claire said with a rueful smile.

"When will Gunter be released?" Lulu asked.

"I'm hoping in a few days. We'll talk to the judge tomorrow."

"But who is the real killer?" Emily asked.

"That, my dear, is for the prosecutor to discover," the attorney explained.

Tyler rang the buzzer twice, waiting impatiently for someone to answer it. *Damn it, Claire, answer the door!* He knew she was home; he'd seen a light in her window.

Lulu finally answered it. "Hello, cutie," she said solemnly.

"I need to talk to Claire."

Lulu's eyes brimmed with sympathy. "She won't see you, Tyler."

"Tell her it's important." Seeing the hesitation on Lulu's face, he said, "Never mind. I'll tell her myself." He strode past the startled housekeeper and took the stairs two at a time, bursting into Claire's room unannounced. She swung around, a shocked, furious look on her face as he strode toward her. Opening his satchel, he held it out. "This won't make up for the pain I've caused you, but I want you to have it—no strings attached."

Claire glanced into the bag, then lifted her angry gaze to his. "I don't want your money."

"You need it. Take it."

She lifted her chin, her fierce pride tugging at his heartstrings. "I don't need anything from you."

Tyler wanted more than anything to pull her into his arms and hold her. He had no chance with Claire now—he didn't deserve one, after the lies he had told—but he knew how much Bellefleur meant to her. With this money she would have a chance to secure it forever.

Setting the bag on the floor, he strode from the room.

For a long moment Claire stared at the empty doorway, then slowly knelt before the bag. Bundles of fifty dollar bills lay inside—enough to pay her expenses, hire a crew, and bring up the oil. Claire picked up a bundle and stared at it.

"Are you all right?" Lulu asked, sticking her head in the doorway. With a gasp she came forward. "Lord have mercy!" she said, gaping at the satchel's contents. Emily followed her, sinking to her knees to explore the bag.

"Cee Cee, it's the money we need!"

"I can't accept it."

"Then how are you going to pay for everything?" Lulu asked.

"I'll find another way."

Lulu shook her head in awe. "I wonder where he got all this money."

"He's a gambler," Claire replied bitterly.

"No, he sold his boat." Emily piped in, stacking the bundles on the floor.

Annoyed, Claire began stuffing them back in the bag. "He wouldn't do that."

"Yes, he would."

Claire scoffed. "How are you such an expert, Miss Know-It-All?"

"You were eavesdropping again, weren't you, angel?" Lulu asked. "I found her in the dining room the other night listening through a grate in the ceiling."

Emily stuck out her lower lip. "I wasn't eavesdropping. Their voices just came through. They were discussing how to raise the money to help you. Jonas said he had none, and Tyler said all he had was his boat. He said he'd have to m-morg-"

"Mortgage it?" Lulu prompted.

"Yes, mortgage it. But he said it would be too big a risk."

"Looks like he decided to take that risk," Lulu told Claire. She hunkered down to stare into her eyes. "You know what this means, sweetie pie: you mean more to him than that boat does."

Claire finished packing the money and closed the satchel. She refused to believe Lulu could be right. "I'll put it in the safe until I can return it."

On Tuesday, Judge Crawford finished his last case of the morning, then called John Oldham and Lawrence Jamieson into the private room at the back. "Gentlemen, since you've both asked to see me, I trust this has to do with the Greene case."

"It does, Your Honor," the prosecutor replied. "The state has no witnesses and no evidence to back its case. And the defendant now has an ironclad alibi witness."

"And evidence that directly implicates another party as the murderer," Oldham added.

Crawford lifted his eyebrows in surprise. "What evidence might that be?"

"A very distinctive and unique pocketwatch, Your Honor," Oldham replied. "The deceased's wife sold it to a man by the name of Reginald Boothe. The aforementioned watch was found on the person of the deceased after the murder."

"Your Honor," the prosecutor said, "in light of all this, I have a sworn duty to uphold the law. Therefore, I have to ask for a dismissal and a release of Mr. Jenssen."

Crawford slowly removed his black robe and folded it. Boothe had wanted a fast conviction on Jenssen; now it was apparent why. Under the circumstances, Crawford knew he now had no choice but to follow the letter of the law. But he sure would miss all those favors Boothe had given him.

With a resigned sigh, he looked up at both men. "Gentlemen, I appreciate the integrity you both have displayed, and I have no choice but to sign any papers you give me."

"I'll prepare them right away," Jamieson offered.

Crawford waited until both attorneys had gone, then he called in his bailiff. "Go get me Reginald Boothe. Tell him I want to see him immediately."

Chapter 27

Boothe sat at his desk, trying unsuccessfully to focus his thoughts on bank business. He shot out of his chair and paced his office for the twentieth time that morning. Bellefleur should have been his. What had gone wrong? He'd had everything planned so perfectly.

He jumped at a knock on the door. "Come in," he answered distractedly.

Charlie Dibkins peered around the door. "Mr. Boothe? There's a gentleman from the court here with a message for you. He says Judge Crawford needs to see you right away."

Boothe stared at him, his thoughts so scattered it took him a moment to realize what Dibkins had said. "Tell him I'm on my way." He picked up his hat and left his office. Why was the judge bothering him at a time like this?

Crawford was waiting for him in the empty meeting room, sitting at his chair behind the table, calmly reading the newspaper. Boothe strode impatiently across the long room, irritated by the interruption. "You wanted to see me? I'm rather busy today."

The judge lowered the paper to look at him, then slowly folded it and laid it aside. "I believe this is more important than anything on your schedule."

"Well then, tell me."

"First off, the witnesses that your friend the sheriff was supposed to produce seem to have disappeared."

"He's working on that."

The judge ignored the interruption. "Secondly, the witness I'm sure you hoped wouldn't appear *has* appeared."

"Who do you mean?"

"I'm talking about Mrs. Greene."

Boothe grew suddenly wary. "Why wouldn't I want her to appear?"

"Because she says she was with Gunter Jenssen the night of the murder. That means he couldn't possibly have done it."

"She was with him?" Boothe repeated, dazed. He turned away, staring blindly at the floor. "She was with him!"

"In all my days," the judge commented, "I've never seen a better alibi witness. It seems I'll have no choice but to dismiss this case."

"No!" Boothe shouted. "You can't! You told me there would be no problem with it."

Crawford held up his hands. "I was willing to help you because we've had a longstanding relationship. But at this point, I can be of no help to you because there is no case."

Boothe paced, raking his fingers through the thin hair at his temples. "You can't do this. I paid you to take care of it for me. You're going back on your word."

The judge rose angrily. "I'm going to say it to you once again, and I'm going to say it real slow, so there's no mistake. *There—is—no—case!* As soon as the prosecutor brings me the papers, I'm going to order the dismissal and the release of the defendant."

Boothe lunged across the table and grabbed the little man by his lapels. "You can't back out on me like this!" he said, baring his teeth.

"Take your hands off me right now and calm down. I haven't finished yet." Crawford glared at Boothe until the banker finally released his hold and straightened.

The judge brushed off his coat and straightened his collar. "It seems Mrs. Greene has a pocketwatch that was found on the deceased—which she claims she sold to you. Now, I'm not drawing any conclusions, but if I were a betting man, I'd say that you're in a heap of trouble.''

Boothe automatically reached for the watch, which had since been replaced. How could Simons have missed seeing the watch when he dumped Greene's body?

''I'm afraid this is where our friendship ends,'' Crawford announced, picking up his folded robe and his leather case. ''My advice to you is to hire yourself a good lawyer.'' He started to walk away, then stopped and looked back. ''And one other thing: out of respect for our past relationship, I will recuse myself from any further participation in this murder case.''

For several long minutes Boothe stood frozen at the front of the room. Woodenly, he walked out and started toward the bank, the judge's words running through his head.

Hire a lawyer? Because of a watch? What did Crawford know, fool that he was? No one would believe Reginald Boothe had committed a murder. He had a good name in town. He was respected, admired. His underlings at the bank emulated him.

Maybe that was the problem. Maybe they were jealous and had plotted against him. Maybe even now they were waiting for him to return so they could laugh at him.

''Hey! You! Get out of the street!''

Boothe looked up at the irate wagon driver and realized he was standing in the middle of Grand Avenue. He started across, then changed directions. He couldn't return to the bank. He couldn't stand to be ridiculed.

Thinking frantically, he walked rapidly without direction until he found himself at the pier, where the *Lady Luck* docked when it was in town. McCane had betrayed him, just as the judge had. And so had the sheriff, who had failed to produce witnesses.

What would he do if they charged him with murder? Boothe tugged at his collar, already feeling the tightness of a noose around his neck. He certainly was not about to allow that! He had money, power. He could buy his freedom. He would win this. He always won.

Boothe headed for home, his eyes narrowed, his hands clenched in fury. He knew where his troubles had begun. They had begun with Marie Reneau and continued with Claire Cavanaugh. Those two had brought this down on his head.

He'd had his revenge with Marie. Now it was time Claire paid.

The sun had set by the time Sheriff Simons got home. He trudged wearily up the steps to his front door and put his hand on the doorknob. Before he could turn it, an arm shot out of the darkness and gripped his wrist.

"Wilbur," a voice whispered hoarsely.

"What the hell?" he cried, jumping back. A figure separated itself from the shadows, allowing him to make out his boss's strained features. "Mr. Boothe! What are you doing here?"

"Wilbur, I need your help."

Boothe's voice was hoarse, his expression desperate. Wilbur stared at him, alarmed. "What do you want me to do?"

"Come with me." Boothe turned, sliding back into the shadows.

Wilbur followed him down the steps, around to the alley, where Boothe's landau waited. There was no driver. Boothe climbed up on the driver's perch and took the reins in hand, waiting. Simons climbed up beside him, glancing warily at the black cloak that covered Boothe's clothing. The night was hot and sultry—certainly not cloak weather. Boothe flicked the reins, guiding the horse into the street.

"Where are we going?" the sheriff asked in trepidation.

"You'll see."

They turned onto Grand and followed it to River Road.

As they headed toward Bellefleur, Wilbur grew even more wary. "What are you going this way for?"

Boothe's gaze was glassy. "Did you do as I asked? Did you find out about the oil?"

"No, sir. I really didn't have a chance."

"I think it's time we found out, don't you, Wilbur?"

"Tonight, Mr. Boothe? It's late."

"It's never too late to make things right," he said cryptically.

Wilbur knew there was something very wrong. "Mr. Boothe, let's head back to town. We can come out tomorrow. Tell you what, I'll come out for you."

"You've already bungled this too many times, Wilbur."

The hair rose on the sheriff's neck. "Bungled what? What are you talking about?"

"My plans. You bungled my plans, Wilbur, because of your stupidity. Now I'm forced to take action I didn't want to take. But it's the only way now. She has to pay."

Wilbur's gut twisted with fear. "Who are you talking about? You're not talking about Cee Cee, are you?"

"She could have been your wife, you know. But you bungled that, too." He pulled up alongside the road near one of the big black drying barns and got down. Wilbur swivelled to watch as Boothe took a large kerosene lantern from the landau and a rifle from the boot and started up the incline towards the barn.

"Where are you going?" Wilbur shouted apprehensively.

"Come on, Wilbur. We've got work to do."

The sheriff climbed down and started after him, his palms sweaty and his mouth dry. "Mr. Boothe, what have you got in mind?"

"You'll see." Boothe unlatched one of the huge barn doors and swung it wide. Inside, he stooped to light the lantern. "Where shall we start?" he said, looking around.

Wilbur stood just inside the doorway, his heart hammering against his ribs. "What are you gonna do?"

"We're going to have a celebration, Wilbur. We're celebrating the discovery of oil on my land. That's a cause for celebrating, isn't it? What do you say we invite the Cavanaughs?" Boothe kicked some of the straw covering the floor into a mound beside one of the walls, and took out a match.

"No!" Wilbur bellowed. "Stop! You can't do that!"

Boothe began to laugh. "What are you going to do, Sheriff? Arrest me?"

Wilbur stared at him, trying to think what to do. The man had obviously gone mad. He looked around and spotted the rifle nearby. "Yes, Mr. Boothe, I'll arrest you if I have to."

Boothe's smile dissolved instantly and he bared his teeth. "You take orders from me, Wilbur, remember?"

"No, sir, not on this. I draw the line here. You've done enough damage in this town. I won't let you hurt Cee Cee or any of her family." He bent to pick up the rifle, freezing at the sound of a gun cocking. Slowly, he straightened and turned. Boothe had a pistol leveled at him.

"People who work for me never tell me no," Boothe said with deadly calm.

"Then I don't work for you anymore."

"Don't you care about your own neck, Wilbur?"

"I can't stomach what you've done or what I've done to help you. So I guess I'll just have to pay the price. Now put that gun down and come with me."

Boothe laughed sharply. "Where, Wilbur? Are you going to lock me up?"

"If I have to." Simons reached for the gun again.

"Don't touch it! Get your hands in the air."

The sheriff shrugged his thick shoulders and obediently raised his hands.

"Now the party begins," Boothe said.

As he squatted beside the pile of straw to light the match, Simons dove for the rifle. At once two shots rang out. The first hit the sheriff in the shoulder. Simons turned in surprise as the second went straight through his heart.

"You see what happens when you disobey, Wilbur?"

With a gasp, Sheriff Simons collapsed as the life flowed out of him.

Claire opened the parlor windows to catch the faint night breeze. Lulu was teaching Emily a card game, using a pack of Braille cards Jonas had managed to find on one of his trips upriver. Mrs. Parks was crocheting, and Jonas had not yet returned from his run to Cincinnati.

At the sound of gunshots, all four stopped what they were doing and turned towards the window. "Good gracious, what was that?" Mrs. Parks asked.

"Sounded like a gun going off," Lulu replied.

Claire peered out the window. "It's too dark to see anything. I'd better go investigate."

"Oh, good heavens, dear!" Mrs. Parks exclaimed. "You mustn't take such a chance."

"It's probably just Ben scaring off a fox," Claire assured her. "They've been stealing his chickens."

"I'll go with you," Lulu volunteered. "Angel, you shuffle those cards real good."

The two women walked out onto the porch, moving silently down to the far end to look around the side of the house. Seeing nothing, they went around to the back.

"I don't see anything," Lulu said.

"No more shots, either," Claire noted.

"Let's go back," Lulu said nervously. "Tyler and Jonas can look around later."

Claire hesitated. "I'd feel better if I checked the horses." She started toward the stables, with Lulu fast on her heels. As they came up to the long limestone building, Claire saw a flickering glow in the sky above the barn. She stopped with a gasp, fear prickling along her spine. "Fire!" she cried. "It's in one of the barns! Lulu, go ring the bell behind the house. We've got to get the farmhands here at once!''

As Lulu ran toward the house, Claire headed for the barn. The huge wooden structure was engulfed in flame and she could see a line of fire moving in a narrow path toward the other barn, as though someone had connected the two. Claire dashed back to the stable for horse blankets as, in the distance, she heard the persistent clanging of their fire alarm.

Her heart thundering, Claire ran toward the second barn, the blankets clutched to her chest. Out of the corner of her eye, she caught sight of a figure running away from the barn. With no time to wonder, she threw blankets down over the trail of fire to smother it, stopping it in its tracks as flames from the first barn stretched high into the night sky. Claire knew it would be a matter of luck if the second barn didn't catch a spark and start a fire as well.

She heard shouts and the pounding of feet as their farmhands came running from nearby cottages. Each man knew his role and began forming a line from the well, hoping to wet down the second barn enough to ward off the flames. The first was hopeless.

Claire turned around and saw a glow through an end window in the stables. ''Oh, dear God!'' she cried. ''Ben! The stables are on fire!''

Without waiting to see if he had heard her, Claire gathered her skirts and ran as fast as she could. By the time she pulled the big door open, the horses were already wild with fear. Spears of fire had climbed the wooden posts to the ceiling, filling the room with smoke and heat. Claire ran to the back and flung open the stall door, leading the terrified beast outside, giving it a hard slap to send it running. The next horse reared when she tried to open the door, its sharp, heavy hooves nearly hitting her. Claire grabbed its blanket and threw it over the animal's head to keep it from seeing the flames so she could lead it to safety.

As she worked to draw out the next horse, Ben climbed the wall of the stall and got in behind the animal as the roof above them crackled with fire.

"Miss Cavanaugh, get out!" Ben shouted, as they struggled with the horse. "I'll manage."

"You can't do it alone!" Claire tried again to toss the blanket over the frightened mare's head, but the horse kept rearing, her teeth bared in terror. Claire stopped to wipe the perspiration from her eyes. It was growing difficult to breathe and she could no longer see the doorway.

"Claire? Are you in there?" Lulu cried.

"Stay out!" Claire shouted, coughing from the acrid smoke. Her eyes burned and watered, making it even more difficult to see. Ben finally grabbed the horse's neck and brought the head down so that Claire was able to get the blanket over the mare's face. Ben climbed on her back and Claire stepped out of his way as he rode the horse out of the building.

Hardly daring to draw a breath, Claire lifted the hem of her skirt to cover her mouth as she fought her way through the dense smoke. But she grew disoriented and suddenly didn't know which way to go.

"Claire?" Lulu cried anxiously from outside. "Sweetie pie?"

"Lulu," Claire called hoarsely. "I can't find my way."

"Listen for my claps," Lulu ordered, hitting her palms together.

Claire stumbled toward the sounds, emerging just as the other farmhands descended on the stables. She collapsed against Lulu, who half carried her away from the burning building, then set her on the ground. "Sweetie pie, you're gonna be all right," she said, rubbing her hands. "All the horses made it out."

Claire wiped her eyes with her skirt hem and looked

over at the stable, where men swarmed around it, doing their best to put out the blaze.

Lulu ran her hand down Claire's soot-blackened face. "I'm gonna give these fellas a hand. Will you be all right?"

Claire nodded, still dazed by the suddenness of the fire. As Lulu joined the team at the stable, Claire stood up slowly, drawing a shaky breath. What could have started it?

She suddenly remembered seeing a figure running from the barn toward the stable. Could the fire have been set deliberately? Had she seen the culprit? Claire turned to look at the house. Where was he now?

With a feeling of foreboding, she ran toward the house, her whole body filled with terror. Emily and Mrs. Parks were inside.

Claire opened the back door and headed for the front parlor. "Emily, Mrs. Parks! You've got to get out!" Breathlessly, she came to a halt as Mrs. Parks hobbled into the hallway. "I heard the fire bell. Are the barns on fire?"

"The barns and stable," Claire panted, holding her side. "I'm afraid the house may be next. You've got to get out." She looked around. "Where's Em?"

"She went upstairs to get her puppets."

Claire was already dashing up the staircase. A lamp on the narrow hall table flickered as she ran down the hallway to Emily's bedroom, calling for her sister. But there was no answer and her room was empty. Claire checked the other rooms, with no success.

Her breathing grew shallow as panic welled up inside. She took deep breaths and forced herself to think. She had to find Emily. Where could she have gone?

Lifting her skirts, Claire took the stairs to the third floor two at a time. At the end of the hallway, she could see the faint glow of a lamp. "Em!" she cried, standing at the top of the stairs. "Emily! Where are you?"

As she passed the first room, a tall black figure lunged

out of the doorway and a gloved hand clamped over her mouth, another hand gripping the back of her head. Then a face loomed out of sthe darkness, and Claire's eyes widened in terror as she recognized it.

Reginald Boothe grinned, his features ghoulish in the faint light. "Welcome to the celebration, Miss Cavanaugh."

Chapter 28

As the *Lady Lucky* docked, Jonas joined Tyler at the rail, where he stood staring upriver toward Bellefleur. "How are you faring, lad?"

"Just dandy," Tyler retorted irritably. All he could think about was Claire.

"You miss her, don't you?"

Tyler glanced at his assistant in surprise.

"You think I can't read the signs? You feel like your veins are wiggling and your nerve endings are standing up at attention. Your stomach is jittery and you have a longing for something you can't name."

Tyler frowned at him. "You make it sound like I'm sick."

"Oh, you are, lad. And you've got it bad. You're lovesick."

"Lovesick?" Tyler threw back his head and laughed.

"Go ahead—deny it. But you know it's true and I know it's true."

Tyler scoffed. "I've never been in love."

"Which is why you don't recognize those feelings. It's a rare and wonderful experience, Ty. Some never get to feel it. You're one of the lucky ones."

The thought of being in love made Ty want to sail away on the *Lady Luck* and never come back. And Jonas called that lucky? "I can't be, Jonas."

"You don't have a choice, lad. You're there."

"Well, I can't be *there*!" he ground out, turning his back on his assistant.

For a moment Jonas said nothing. Then suddenly, "Look at that glow in the sky. Something's on fire."

A shiver grabbed hold of Tyler's spine as he swung around. "My God, Jonas, it's coming from Bellefleur!"

Both men dashed for the buggy. Tyler sat on the edge of his seat, his heart in his throat. What if the house was on fire? What if Claire and the others were trapped inside? Tyler hadn't said a prayer in twenty-five years, but he began to pray now. *"Please, Lord, let them be safe."*

As they drew nearer, Tyler saw flames shooting into the sky from one of the barns. Another glow told him something else was burning. He saw the outline of the house high on the hill, but it appeared to be all right.

A landau was parked on the road near the barn. Tyler recognized it. "That's Boothe's carriage," he told Jonas.

"What's he doing here?" Jonas asked.

Tyler had a sinking feeling in the pit of his stomach. "Setting a fire."

The wagons and buggies of the volunteer firemen who had heard the alarm lined the road by the first barn, which was now a charred skeleton. A group of men were dousing the second barn with water.

"They need help down at the stable," someone cried.

There were at least twenty volunteers manning water lines and pouring water on the stable roof from ladders. Jonas joined in, while Tyler looked around for Claire. He spotted Lulu standing in the line of men. "Where's Claire?" he called.

Her face blackened from soot, Lulu passed a bucket to the next man and wiped her hand across her forehead. "Claire's working on the other side. I saw her a bit ago."

"Someone grab that ax!" a man called.

Tyler spotted the ax lying nearby, picked it up, and ran to help.

*   *   *

Claire's heart pounded in terror as Boothe forced her down the hallway. She clawed at his gloves, struggling to free herself, but he held her firmly, one arm around her neck. At the doorway of Mrs. Parks' old bedroom, he gave her a shove that sent her flying across the room. Claire landed in a crumpled heap beside the bed, too dazed to think. Before she could get to her knees, he pulled her up and tossed her backward onto the bed.

Claire scooted back against the headboard as he came toward her, a tall, menacing figure in a black cloak. Staring at him with wide, terrified eyes, she pulled up her knees. Her breathing grew rapid and shallow as panic set in. With a whimper, she raised up an arm to shield herself as he grabbed her wrist and tied it to the bedpost with a thick rope.

Suddenly Claire was ten years old again, hiding under the bridge. She began to shake, her teeth clattering so hard her vision grew fuzzy. The room wobbled and spun. She wanted to cry for help, but no sound would come out.

Boothe's thin, cruel lips drew back in a semblance of a grin. "Cat got your tongue?" He took matches out of his pocket and set them on the table. "Are you enjoying my celebration? You do know what we're celebrating, don't you? The discovery of oil on my land. Oh, pardon me, *your* land—at least for the next hour. By that time, this house ought to be in full blaze."

His words penetrated through her childhood terror, replacing it with the horror of the present. He was going to kill her, burn her alive in her own home.

But where was Emily? Had she made it out of the house? "Why are you doing this?" Claire cried, straining against the rope. "What have I done to you?"

The pupils of Boothe's eyes went black. "What have you done?" he sneered. "You, your mother, Arthur—*all* of you plotted against me from the beginning."

"Plotted against you? I just wanted you to leave us alone and let us live in peace!"

"This land should have been *mine*!" he raged. "But your *father* wouldn't give it up, not even after he lost all his money in that phony oil speculation. Rather ironic, isn't it, that he would actually discover oil?"

Claire's mouth opened in shock. Phony? Boothe must have set him up!

From the corner of her eye, Claire saw a slip of blue fabric beneath the storage closet door. As Boothe continued to brag about his clever trickery, the door opened an inch, and then she caught a glimpse of a small face through the crack. With a terrible sinking feeling, she realized it was Emily.

Dear God! If she didn't do something to stop Boothe, she and Emily would both perish. Somehow, she had to get her sister out before Boothe discovered her! She forced her stunned brain to think.

Make him angry. Distract him. "You set my father up!" she protested. "And then you tried to foreclose, yet we still beat you. We're smarter than you are, Mr. Boothe!"

Raising his hand as though he were going to slap her, Boothe took a threatening step forward. When Claire drew back with a gasp, he smiled smugly. "You *should* cringe, my dear. You should be absolutely terrified. You're going to pay the price of your parents' misbehavior."

"I'm not afraid of you! I despise you! You're a monster."

Boothe wagged a black-gloved finger at her. "Is that a polite thing to say? Didn't your mother teach you manners? Ah! How silly of me. I nearly forgot. Your mother didn't have any manners. She didn't know how to show respect."

"You don't deserve respect!" Claire shot back. "You tossed us out onto the streets with no money and nowhere to live!"

Boothe slowly removed his gloves, his eyes glinting with madness. "Your mother had to be punished." He sat down on the edge of the bed as though they were having a normal conversation. "She didn't know her place."

His back was to the closet. Claire knew she had to get Emily out now. But how could she signal to her? What words would make her understand? *Think, Claire, think!*

Her puppets!

"My mother's place was not as your *puppet*," Claire cried. "She hid from you at night—in a storage closet—because she couldn't stand the thought of you touching her. She had to escape from you, like a scared rabbit. Now!"

"Ah, but she *was* a puppet, just like you are. And I control the strings." He leaned over and tugged the rope around Claire's wrist. "See? I can make you do whatever I want."

Claire held her breath as the closet door slowly opened. Her heart pounded so loud she thought surely Boothe would hear it. She had to keep him from looking around as her sister crawled silently to the door.

"You're mad!" she cried. "I can see why my mother fled your house rather than stay another night under your roof!"

Boothe's body tensed and his eyes suddenly shifted to the right. Claire's heart skipped a beat. She was sure he had heard Emily!

But he merely continued talking. "Marie could have had anything she wanted if she had only shown me the respect I demanded. Do you doubt me? It's true! I was willing to make her my queen. She was quite regal, you know, in her ways. I would have given her the world. But she disdained me. She ridiculed me. Then she mocked me by marrying Arthur Cavanaugh."

"My mother loved Arthur Cavanaugh," Claire cried, yanking on the rope. "She hated you!"

"She thought she was too good for me!" Boothe sneered. "But I put her in her place."

"You sent her right into my father's arms."

"Well, I got even with your father, too, didn't I?"

"Murderer! You killed my father! Your foreclosure threats caused his stroke!"

Boothe laughed, a hollow, thin sound that made Claire shiver in repulsion. "I threatened him, all right, but not about the foreclosure. I told him I was going to take back my daughter. With you out of the way, I may still do that."

Claire was too shocked to speak. He knew about Emily! What her father had feared most had come true. Quickly, she glanced at the doorway. It was empty. Her sister had gotten out.

Tyler couldn't shake his uneasy feeling. Tossing down the ax, he circled the building, searching for Claire among the volunteers, calling her name. His gut twisted in apprehension. What if she was hurt? Could she have gone up to the house for first aid? He set off at a run; he wouldn't be of any help with the fire unless he knew she was safe.

As he came across the side yard, Tyler saw a small figure stumbling away from the house, her hands held straight out in front of her. He could hear her sobbing wildly.

"Emily!" he called out.

"Tyler!" she screamed, turning in the direction of his voice. "Tyler, you've got to help Cee Cee! Please!"

His chest tight with fear, Tyler grabbed Emily. She clung to him, sobbing. "Hurry, Tyler, hurry!"

"Where is she? What's happened to her?"

"Boothe has her up in Mrs. Parks' old room. He's going to kill her, Tyler. You've got to save her! Hurry, please!" she cried hysterically.

"Emily, can you find Jonas for me? He's out by the stables. Tell him I need his help."

She nodded, sobs wracking her body.

"Good girl. I'll go help Claire and you get Jonas."

Emily turned and stumbled on, screaming, "Jonas,

Jonas!'' as Tyler raced for the house. *Why* hadn't he told Claire he loved her? Why had he been so stubborn? What if he never got a chance to tell her?

Lulu heard Emily's cries first. Alarmed, she started toward her. "Angel, baby, what is it?"

Emily held out her arms, her teeth chattering so hard she could barely talk. "I went upstairs to get my puppets and I smelled him," she said as Lulu gathered her close. "I was afraid, so I hid in the closet. Then Cee Cee came upstairs looking for me and he grabbed her."

"Who, angel? Who grabbed her?"

"Mr. Boothe! Tyler went to help her, but he needs Jonas. We've got to hurry, Lulu! He's going to set the house on fire."

"Oh, Lordy!" Lulu ran back to the line of men, shouting for them to find Jonas and send him to the house. She led Emily to the shelter of a big weeping willow at the side of the yard. "Angel, you have to stay here. Promise me, now. Lulu has to go help them, too."

"Hurry, Lulu," Emily cried. "Don't let anything happen to my sister."

"I'll kill that dirty money grubber myself if he lays a hand on either one of them."

"Did you think I didn't know I had a daughter?" Boothe asked, eyeing Claire as he circled the bed. "You don't give me much credit, my dear."

"You raped my mother!" Claire ground out.

Boothe simply smiled. "She needed to be taught some respect."

Claire glared at him with all the hatred she could muster. "You got your revenge. Why are you doing this now?"

Boothe's smile vanished instantly, a look of pure malice replacing it. "Someone has to pay for what I suffered. How do you think I felt, knowing they were mocking me all those years? Knowing Arthur was raising *my* child as his own, rubbing it in my face.''

"He took us in after you tossed us out like garbage," Claire countered. "He loved us, and he raised Emily as his own because he loved her, too. He taught her right from wrong, which is something you couldn't do!''

One thin eyebrow lifted haughtily. ''You're awfully brave, for someone who's about to die.''

"I'm not going to die. Help is on its way right now. But you're going to hang for murder.''

"Good try." Boothe peered out the window. "But it seems everyone is concentrating on putting out those fires. I doubt that anyone will notice you're missing until it's too late.''

Claire nodded toward the closet. "Emily will tell them.''

Boothe swung around and saw the door standing open.

"She was hiding," Claire said with a triumphant smile. "She crawled out while you were bragging about your success.''

His expression changed, his eyes clearly reflecting the madness that had seized his mind. Claire saw him start for the matches on the table. "You killed Mr. Greene, didn't you?" she challenged, trying to distract him.

"People should not disobey me.''

Claire watched in horror as he struck a match and held it to the bottom of the curtain.

"Tyler guessed you were the murderer," she said, her voice shaking with fear. "That's why he ended the partnership.''

The match burned Boothe's fingers. He dropped it, swearing as he stuck the finger in his mouth. "McCane ended the partnership because he didn't need me any longer. He betrayed me like all the others did. But he'll pay, just like Greene. In fact, just like Wilbur did.''

"You killed him?" Claire cried, remembering the gunshots.

Boothe lit another match. As the curtain caught, he stepped back to watch the flames climb the thin fabric. "It's time to say goodnight and farewell, my dear. I trust you'll sleep well."

As he left the room, Claire worked desperately to untie the knot, using her fingers and teeth. Flames engulfed the curtain. Soon the ceiling and wall around it would start to blister. It wouldn't take long for the room to become an inferno.

Frantic, she tried again, her fingernails breaking and her fingertips starting to bleed. She slid the other end of the rope up to the top of the bedpost, but couldn't get it over the large ball.

Was she fated to die a prisoner in the home she'd worked so valiantly to keep? Tears rolled down Claire's cheeks. Who would take care of Emily? What would become of Mrs. Parks? She thought of Tyler and began to cry softly. She had so wanted him to love her.

Suddenly she heard Tyler's voice. "Claire!" he shouted.

She let out a sob of relief. "Back here! Hurry! The room is on fire!"

Tyler raced in and looked around for something to smother the flame. He grabbed a folded quilt from the rocker and beat the curtain until he could grip the material and yank it to the floor. Quickly, he threw the quilt over it and stamped it with his boots.

"Claire!" he said, turning to look at her, his heart in his throat. She was huddled on the bed, her eyes wide with terror. He slashed the rope with his pocketknife and clutched her against him. "I was so afraid I'd lost you!" Tyler whispered. His throat choked with emotion. "I love you, Claire."

Surely she hadn't heard him right—but it was in his eyes, shining out at her like a beacon. He loved her!

"What a touching finale."

Claire and Tyler turned to see Boothe standing in the doorway, his pistol pointed at them.

"How considerate of you to join our little celebration, McCane. Now I can settle two matters at once."

Tyler moved in front of Claire. "If you have something to settle with me, let's settle it like men. Cowards hide behind guns."

Boothe laughed. "Are you calling me a coward? How ironic. My definition of a coward is a man who's afraid to do his own dirty work. How long was it—two weeks, three at the most—that you asked me to do your dirty work for you? As I recall, you said something to the effect that I was to get Claire and her sister out of the house however I could, no questions asked."

Tyler felt Claire's accusing eyes on him. "But that was before I—"

"Before you found out you could get her land by marrying her?" Boothe leaned to the side to give Claire a sympathetic frown. "My dear, I hope you're not terribly hurt by this news."

"He told me why he wanted to marry me," Claire retorted, looking at Tyler. "I know he needs my land. He didn't lie about that."

Tyler stared at her in awe. She loved him, even believing the worst about him.

Boothe snickered. "Did he also tell you he was having an affair with my mistress?"

"What?" Tyler shouted.

"I'm sure you remember Daphne Duprey," Boothe said to Claire. "I believe she was renting from you for a while. Apparently, she preferred your fiancé's lovemaking to mine. At least that's what she told me this afternoon."

"That's a lie!" Tyler said, his intense gaze burning into Claire. "Don't believe him. I went to see Daphne once, but nothing happened. I didn't let it."

"At this point, does it really matter?" Boothe said, cocking the trigger.

Suddenly there was a blur of movement behind him as Lulu rushed in, wielding an iron poker, and brought it

down as hard as she could on his right shoulder. With a
bellow of pain, Boothe swung and fired, sending Lulu stag-
gering back into the hallway.

"Lulu!" Claire screamed. The woman clutched her
shoulder, a look of shock on her face as she slid slowly
to the floor.

Boothe swung back toward Claire and Tyler, but at the
sounds of men's shouts and heavy footsteps pounding up
the stairs, he panicked and fled into the room across the
hall.

In horror, Claire saw Tyler start after him. "Tyler, let
him go!" she cried.

Using his pistol, Boothe broke the glass out of the dor-
mer window. He was halfway out when Tyler lunged for
him. Running after Tyler, Claire held her breath as the two
men grappled for the gun. Jonas rushed in, followed by
several farmhands, but all they could do was watch help-
lessly.

Suddenly Boothe broke free and climbed through the
broken window onto the steeply sloped roof.

"No!" Tyler shouted, kicking the final shards of jagged
glass from the frame. He followed Boothe out onto the
slate roof. "You're not going to get away—not this time!"

Boothe turned his head to look at Tyler. His eyes were
steady, his voice calm. "Of course I'll get away. You see,
I always win." He leveled the pistol, his thin mouth curv-
ing into a triumphant smile.

"Tyler!" Claire screamed, pressing her hand to her
heart.

Boothe slowly squeezed the trigger, but his boot suddenly slipped on the shingles. The shot went wild, ringing
clear into the night. Tyler froze, watching in shock as the
banker fell three stories. He hit the ground with a soft thud
and lay crookedly on the lawn, unmoving.

Tyler climbed back inside just as Claire's knees buckled.
He caught her as she sank to the ground. "It's all right,
sweetheart," he said, pressing his lips to her temple.

"We're safe now." He carried her into the hallway as Jonas and one of the men lifted Lulu.

"We've got to get Lulu some help," Jonas told him as they headed for the staircase. "She took a hit in the shoulder. What happened to Boothe?"

"He fell. I'm sure he's dead."

Tyler followed them down the steps, holding Claire securely in his arms. He didn't even want to think how close he'd come to losing her. As he walked out onto the porch, he saw Emily and Mrs. Parks waiting anxiously on the lawn. Tyler glanced down to find Claire gazing up at him in confusion. "What happened?" she asked.

"You fainted."

"Boothe?"

"He's dead." Tyler felt the shudder ripple through Claire's body. He set her down near her sister as Jonas and the other man lay Lulu on the grass nearby.

"Cee Cee?" Emily called, stretching out her hands.

Tyler took Emily's hand and led her over to Claire. He stepped back as the sisters hugged. "I got your message about the rabbit," Emily said. "I ran as fast as I could."

Claire didn't know whether to laugh or cry as she stroked her sister's dark hair. "I knew you would, Em."

"I'll go get Doc Jenkins," Jonas told Tyler. "He's helping down at the stables."

"Is Lulu hurt?" Emily asked, raising her head as Tyler and Mrs. Parks knelt beside the unconscious woman.

"She fainted, Emily," Tyler explained. "She was shot in the shoulder."

Within minutes, Doc Jenkins and Jonas came on the run.

"Looks like the bullet missed the bone and imbedded itself in the muscle," the doctor told them, as he examined her arm. "Let's get her to the kitchen so I can remove it. Miss Cavanaugh, if you're up to it, I'll need your help."

For an hour, Tyler, Mrs. Parks, Jonas, and Emily waited in the parlor. When Claire finally walked in, she sank onto a chair, weak from fatigue. "Lulu's going to be all right.

Doc says there's not much damage. She's awake now. She's asking to see you, Em, and you, too, Tyler.''

Tyler looked surprised. He took Emily's hand and they left together. Claire glanced wearily at Jonas. ''How much damage is there from the fire?''

''One barn is completely gone, but they saved the other. The stable will have to be rebuilt. All that's left is a shell.''

''Thank God that's all.'' She closed her eyes and leaned her head against the back of the chair, but opened them when Tyler came back. Near exhaustion, Claire pushed to her feet. ''I have to go look at the damage.''

''Claire, you're about to drop,'' Tyler said. ''You can see it tomorrow.''

''I have to see it now.''

''Then I'll come with you.''

Tyler put his arm around her as they walked around the side of the house and headed for the stable. Men were still working, making sure there were no smoldering embers.

Claire stood still for a long while, watching numbly.

''We can rebuild,'' Tyler told her. ''The important thing is that we're all safe.''

''Yes. As much as I value the house, it would mean nothing if I lost the people I love.'' She reached up to touch his face, like hers, blackened from the smoke. ''I owe you my life.''

He covered her hand with his. ''Claire, you may think I'm brave, but I'm not. I'm a coward. I told myself that I wanted to marry you for business reasons, because I was afraid to love you. I thought if you found out what I was really like underneath, you'd change your mind. But when I saw the fire, all I could think of was that I hadn't told you how much you mean to me. All that matters to me now is that you know how I feel. I want to marry you— but whatever you decide to do, I'll always love you.''

Claire searched his eyes for a long moment and then brought his hand to her lips. ''I saw beneath your bravado from the start. But I didn't see a coward. I saw a good man who was too cautious to fall in love.'' She kissed his fingers. ''You will always be my hero, Ty, and I want you to be my husband.''

Tyler stared at her, unable to believe what she'd said. He remembered the premonition he'd had when they first met and was surprised to realize it had come true. She *had* destroyed him—or rather the wall he had built to shutter his feelings, to exclude love. He felt complete now, a whole man. The emptiness that had always been there was gone at last.

Pulling her into his arms, Tyler kissed her hard, his heart brimming with happiness. When they finally broke apart, Claire gave him a weary smile. ''Look at us,'' she said. ''We're covered with soot and bone tired. And here we stand, smooching in the dark.'' She nodded toward the men. ''We'd better go back to the house and get them some food and water. I imagine they'll need it.''

''Claire, you're exhausted. Jonas and I will take care of the food.''

She looked up at him as they walked back. ''We're partners. We'll do this together.''

Chapter 29

Lulu sat on the edge of her bed, holding her pine chest in her lap, waiting for daybreak. Her left shoulder had been bandaged, making it immobile. Although it had been two days since the fire, her body still ached all over and her throat and lungs were raw from the smoke she had inhaled. Yet she considered herself fortunate.

Her hands rested on the top of the chest as she stared at the floor. She had carried the precious container with her for twenty-five years. It held her most treasured belongings—a small oval locket with her mother's likeness in it, a hair ribbon her first beau had given her, a few letters from friends now gone—and her secret. But the time had come to share that secret. She owed Tyler the truth, though she dreaded the price she would pay for it.

Lulu ran her hand lovingly over the chest, dark now from years of travel and lemon oil polish. With a tremulous sigh, she glanced around the cozy room. She had grown to love the Cavanaugh home. But more than that, she had grown to love the people in it. She had never felt like she belonged anywhere until she had come to Bellefleur. Now she would have to leave. Once Tyler knew the truth, he wouldn't want her there.

Dashing away a tear, she opened the chest and selected one of the objects in it—a slender wooden soldier, perhaps ten inches tall, with a black rifle at his side and a black hat on his head. The paint of his bright blue uniform had chipped in places, and the black boots were scuffed from a small boy marching him across the floor. Lulu bit her bottom lip to keep it from trembling as she stood and placed the soldier on the bed. Beside it she put the letter she had written.

Picking up her satchel, Lulu paused at the door to look back at the soldier. Stifling a sob, she hurried down the stairs and let herself quietly out the door, heading toward town as the first rays of the morning sun appeared in the east. With a heavy heart, she paused to look back, then trudged slowly up the road. With any luck, she would be able to catch an early train out.

Claire awoke with a start, thinking she heard the clang of fire bells. She sat up, ready to bolt from the bed, then she realized she'd only been dreaming. With a relieved sigh, she threw back the cover and slid out of bed. Slipping on her wrapper, she headed for the stairs. The smell of smoke still hung heavily in the air, and she shuddered. She'd come so close to losing her home—but now she knew that even if she had, as long as her loved ones were safe, she could go on.

The other revelation to come out of the near tragedy was that Tyler truly loved her. Now, at last, Claire felt that her life was coming together.

She walked down the main hallway, expecting to hear Lulu humming as she made breakfast. But the kitchen was empty and the stove was cold. Thinking that Lulu had slept late, Claire put the coffee on herself.

"Morning," Tyler said, as he came into the kitchen a few minutes later. She smiled up at him as he bent to kiss her. Then he looked around with a perplexed frown. "Where's Lulu?"

"She must be sleeping in today. You'll have to take your chances with my cooking."

Tyler grimaced as he filled a cup with coffee. "Do I have a choice?"

"Cee Cee?" Emily said as she made her way into the kitchen. "Where's Lulu?"

"She's still asleep."

"No, she's not," Emily replied. "I just went to her room. She's not there."

"Maybe she went out to the garden for some fresh mint," Claire suggested. "She loves mint tea in the morning."

Tyler opened the back door and looked out. "I don't see her."

"Something's wrong, Cee Cee," Emily insisted.

"Let's check upstairs." Claire started down the hallway, with Tyler on her heels and Emily following behind. They met Jonas at the top of the stairs, adjusting the cuffs of his white shirt.

"Is there a parade?" he asked jovially.

"We're looking for Lulu," Emily told him. "She's missing."

"I'm sure she's here someplace, Em," Claire assured her. But when she spotted the letter on Lulu's bed, she knew better. "It's for you, Tyler," she said in some surprise.

With a puzzled look, Tyler silently skimmed the paper. As he read, his face grew stony and his jaw muscles tightened. He glanced at the soldier on the bed, then wordlessly handed the letter to Claire and walked out. Claire looked at Jonas in surprise.

"Why did Tyler leave?" Emily asked.

Jonas frowned. "I'm not sure, Em, but I think we'd better read the letter."

"Should we?" Claire asked doubtfully.

"I think he wanted you to," Jonas replied.

Claire sat down and began to read out loud.

Dear Tyler, First of all, I want to tell you how proud I am of you. You've proved yourself a good man—strong, honest and brave—and I only wish I could take credit for it.

Claire paused to glance up at Jonas, who seemed as bewildered as she.

I know I should say this to you face to face, but I was afraid of what I would see in your eyes when you learned the truth. You've probably figured out by now what I'm going to tell you; maybe you've even known all along deep down inside. I'm your mama.

"Bloody hell," Jonas said under his breath, meeting Claire's equally stunned gaze.

"Lulu is Tyler's mother?" Emily asked.

Claire nodded and kept reading.

You probably think I was a terrible mother, and you're right. I was young and alone and scared. I took the easy way out and left you with your uncle so you'd get a decent upbringing. But it wasn't easy at all—it was the hardest thing I've ever done. I don't regret doing it, though, not when I see how you've turned out.

I didn't plan on us ever meeting again, son, but now I'm glad I had the opportunity to get to know you as a man. I'm leaving you a gift, a little treasure I've kept because it reminded me of you. I only hope you can forgive me one day, and believe that I never stopped loving you. You were my sweet little boy, my cutie. I know you'll be a good husband to Claire, and some day you'll make a fine father, too. Take care of my little angel, Emily, and tell that old limey I'll never forget him.

I love you, my precious boy.

Your mama,
Louise McCane

Claire blinked to clear the tears from her eyes. Jonas's eyes were watery, too.

Emily's chin began to quiver. "She's gone for good, isn't she?"

Claire put her arm around her sister as she glanced at Jonas over her head. "Maybe not, Em. Maybe we can bring her back."

"I think you'd better talk to Tyler about that first," Jonas said with a doubtful frown. "Em, why don't you and I see if we can rustle up some breakfast?"

As Jonas and Emily headed for the kitchen, Claire picked up the wooden soldier, remembering the look on Tyler's face when he saw it. He was furious, but he had to be hurting, as well. His mother had left him again. Yet just as before, Lulu would not have left him if she hadn't believed it was the wisest decision. Now Claire had to convince Tyler to bring her back.

She found him sitting on the riverbank, skipping stones across the water. Wordlessly she sat down beside him, cradling the soldier. He glanced at her, then down at the object in her lap. She saw the muscles in his jaw clench.

He held out his hand. "Give that thing to me."

Claire tightened her hold on it. "You'll throw it away."

"Why shouldn't I?"

"Your mother wanted you to have it."

Tyler scoffed.

Claire sighed, wondering how to reach him. "Tyler, listen: Lulu obviously loved you. That's why she held onto this toy all these years."

He gave her a skeptical look. "She held onto a toy and let her child go? Is that how you'd show love to your child?"

"You read her letter. You know why she left you. She thought she'd do you more harm if she stayed."

"Or maybe she just didn't think I was worth loving." Tyler picked up another stone and sent it skipping out over the water. "She ruined my life."

"*Is* your life ruined? Have you been unhappy these past twenty-five years?"

He frowned as he tossed another stone. "You know what I mean."

"I'm afraid I don't," Claire retorted angrily. "Terrible things have happened to me, too, but they haven't ruined my life." She thrust the soldier in his hand. "Here, then— throw it away. You probably don't even remember it, anyway."

Tyler slowly closed his hand around the soldier's waist. Why not throw it away? Hadn't his mother thrown him away? Why hold onto an object that only brought back painful memories, things he'd worked for years to erase from his mind?

Tyler glanced down at the soldier's unsmiling face. He'd had four soldiers, all with different colored uniforms. Those soldiers had suffered right along with him as he'd lain awake at night, frightened and alone, holding his hands over his ears while his father swore and his mother cried and things crashed all around them. And the soldiers had listened, just as Tyler had, to the tirade of angry words his mother had poured out later, words his father had never heard because he'd always been passed out cold.

Then, one night, it was over. His father had left them. There was no more shouting or crying or loud crashes. But shortly afterward, Tyler had been bundled up with his few clothes and toys and taken to New Orleans. He'd had no idea what had become of the blue soldier. He'd always thought he'd lost it in the move.

Tyler pulled back his arm, ready to cast the toy far out into the river. Why had she kept the damn soldier if she never intended for them to meet?

The words in Lulu's letter jumped into his mind. *"I'm leaving you a gift, a little treasure I've kept because it reminded me of you."*

Tyler hesitated, then slowly lowered his arm. He didn't

want to believe she cared that much. He made himself remember that terrible day in New Orleans, the last time he'd seen her.

"Please, Mama, please don't leave me here. I need you."

"You need someone who can give you a decent home. I can't do that."

"Don't you love me, Mama?"

"Sure I love you, cutie. That's why I have to do this. But I'll come back and see you."

She had lied to him, then. How could he believe her now? He handed the soldier to Claire. "Do what you want with it. If you want to keep it, I won't stop you." He got up and started back to the house.

Claire jumped up and followed him. "Where are you going?"

"I'm going to town to see about getting lumber for a new barn."

She stared at him in bewilderment. How could he act like nothing out of the ordinary had happened? He'd just found his mother! "I thought that maybe you'd decided to go after Lulu."

"What for?"

"What for?" she cried, coming to a sudden stop.

Tyler halted, too, a look of exasperation on his face. "Yes, what for?"

Claire shook her head and started walking rapidly. "Damn you, Tyler McCane, do you know what I would give to have my mother back, or my father?"

"You weren't abandoned, Claire."

Infuriated, she stopped in front of him. "Wasn't I? Do you know what happened when my mother and I were thrown out of Boothe's house with no money and nowhere to go? We lived wherever we could find shelter—alleys, barns, under bridges—and during the day, when my mother was searching for work or food, I was left alone."

As the memories came back, Claire's breathing grew faster. She clenched her jaws to keep from trembling as she spoke. "Do you know the kind of men who live in those places? Horrible, disgusting men, filthy men who take pleasure in terrorizing children, especially young girls. I hid for hours under dirty woolen blankets, too afraid to move for fear of them discovering me. I'll *never* be able to forget that."

Claire closed her eyes and drew deep breaths, trying to ward off the panic. She was determined to tell the whole story, to purge herself of her guilty secret. "But they did find me. And they"—she gritted her teeth to get out the words—"touched me with their filthy hands."

Tyler put his arms around her, pulling her close. "I'm sorry, Claire. I didn't have any idea."

Feeling trapped, suffocated, Claire pushed away from him as the nightmare images flashed through her mind. She dragged each breath through a constricted throat, the pain of those memories so sharp it felt as though a knife were slicing through her heart. "My mother chased them off before—" Claire shuddered, unable to finish the sentence. "She was horrified at what almost happened, and took care to find a safer place to leave me after that, but—"

She pressed her hands against her temples as the words finally tumbled out, the guilt she had carried for years. "But I still hated her for putting me through that ordeal. I hated her for that until the day she died."

Tyler caught her to him and held her as she sobbed. "I'm so sorry," he whispered against her ear. "I know how you feel. You have every right to be angry. But believe me, it's going to be all right."

Tyler's words broke through the thick, smothering blanket of guilt and torment. He understood. "How could I have hated my mother?" Claire asked, wiping her eyes. "I was so ashamed of my feelings. She suffered so much more than I did."

"I doubt that's possible."

"Reginald Boothe raped my mother, Tyler. That's why she fled his house." Claire drew a shaky breath. "Emily is Boothe's daughter."

Tyler's face registered his shock, then darkened with fury. "The bastard!"

"Now you understand why my father despised him," Claire said. "He always feared Boothe would find out and try to get Emily back." She shook her head sadly. "I didn't learn the truth about Emily until my mother died. I never knew what Boothe had done to her. When I finally found out, I couldn't forgive myself for hating her."

Tyler cupped Claire's face. "You'll get over it. You just have to push it out of your mind."

"You can't push it away, Tyler. It stays there, festering like an open wound. When I read Lulu's letter, I suddenly realized that my mother, like yours, did the best she could. But it's too late for me to tell her I forgive her." Claire gripped his hands tightly. "Don't make that mistake, Tyler. Lulu may not have done what was right, but she did what she thought was best. Forgive her, please. It may be too late for me, but it's not for you."

Tyler's mind was so filled with confusion and anger, self-pity and pain, that he couldn't respond. He was amazed at Claire's resilience. He couldn't imagine the bitterness she must have felt whenever she was reminded of what Boothe had done to her mother, or the anger she had harbored toward her mother for her silent suffering. He ached for her; he wanted to do whatever he could to soothe away her pain. But what Claire was asking him to do was impossible.

Her mother had not handed Claire to a stranger. She had not relinquished her duties as a mother. Lulu had abandoned him and then suddenly appeared, twenty-five years later, asking for forgiveness. Tyler wouldn't absolve her for what she'd done. She deserved to suffer for the years of pain she had brought him.

And yet . . .

Tyler raked his fingers through his hair, digging them into his scalp.

Lulu was his mother.

Wracked with emotional pain, he bent his head and scrunched his eyes shut, wishing he could reach into his chest and rip out his heart. He knew Claire was waiting for his answer, but his throat was so constricted he could barely reply. "I can't forgive her," he whispered.

With a sorrowful heart, Claire watched him stride away. She had known by the look on his face that her words hadn't reached him. But it had taken her over four years to accept her own feelings. Indeed, until she read Lulu's letter, she hadn't realized she harbored such bitter feelings. She had buried them, believing she had no right to be that angry with her own mother. Now Claire understood that she did have the right to be angry. Terrible things had happened to her. And just knowing her feelings were justified, she could find it in her heart to forgive her mother.

Claire only hoped Tyler was able to come to the same conclusion before it was too late.

Tyler made the trip into town alone. In the distance, he heard a train whistle. For some reason he found himself wondering if Lulu would be on it, then angrily chided himself for thinking about her. She was gone—out of his life. What did it matter where she went or what she did? She meant nothing to him. No doubt she would find another job as a housekeeper. That was probably how she had supported herself all those years.

He shook his head, remembering how, as a boy, he used to lie awake at night, wondering where she was and how she was surviving. Christmases were especially hard. He used to imagine that she'd married again and had another child, one she truly loved. Now he suspected she'd spent the majority of her holidays as someone's hired help—part of a household, yet never part of a family. She'd had no family to go home to.

Tyler's jaw twitched angrily. Yes, she did have a family. She'd had him. It had been her decision to leave him behind. And for what? To cook and clean for other people's children instead of her own? Was that the dream she had referred to in the kitchen that one evening?

"Do you have dreams, Lulu?"

"Me? I used to. And you?"

"Sure I have dreams. Big ones."

"You're awfully private, aren't you?"

"I could say the same about you."

"Maybe we're just two of a kind."

She had known then who he was. Why hadn't she told him the truth? Was it her own guilt that had prevented her from being honest?

Tyler recalled the apple tart Lulu had saved for him. He had known exactly how it would taste before he bit into it—now he knew why. Lulu had made apple tarts for him when he was little. He'd help her roll out the dough, then she'd write his name in the crust with the tip of a knife. She'd had dark hair back then, and a thin, sad face. Yet he remembered times when the kitchen had been filled with her laughter, and her booming voice as she sang her favorite song.

Goosebumps ran up Tyler's spine. The song he kept whistling—it was her song. He could hear her young, hopeful voice as clear as a bell. *"While strolling through the park one day, in the merry, merry month of May, I was taken by surprise by a pair of roguish eyes. In a moment my poor heart was stole away."*

She couldn't have been more than twenty-two years old then, coping with a drunken, abusive husband and raising an unruly young child.

"Sleep tight, and don't let the bedbugs bite." Tyler had

to chuckle at that. She had recited that to him every night, just after he'd said his prayers, and she'd kissed him and hugged him and called him her precious boy.

He pulled the buggy to a stop. Why had he forgotten those memories? Why had only the ugly ones stayed with him?

A wagon passed him, and someone called out a greeting. Tyler answered remotely, thinking of what Claire had said about wishing she could tell her mother she forgave her. *"Don't make that mistake, Tyler. Lulu may not have done what was right, but she did what she thought was best. Forgive her, please. It may be too late for me, but it's not for you."*

The train whistled again. It was nearer now.

Tyler called to the horse and they started off at a trot. Over the trees he saw the spiraling column of smoke from the engine's stack. Was Lulu waiting to get on it? Would she find another job quickly, another family to live with?

His mind began to fill with other, long-forgotten images, things he had deliberately pushed to the back of his mind. Why had he wanted to remember only the bad times? Had he wanted to punish himself for driving her away?

The train whistle sounded again. On a sudden whim, Tyler turned the horse in the direction of the station. There was no harm in checking to see if she was there.

How ironic, that for years he had convinced himself he was bad and unlovable, yet these newfound memories told him that his mother had loved him deeply. She must have been overwhelmed by her situation. And when his father finally left them, even though she had surely been relieved, she also must have been terribly frightened to be on her own with a small child.

"She did what she thought was best."

And he had hated her for it.

Tyler heard the slow chugs of the engine and the screech of brakes as the train pulled to a stop. In a matter of minutes, the passengers would board and the train would depart.

"I only hope you can forgive me one day and believe that I never stopped loving you," Lulu had written.

With a racing heart, Tyler pulled up to the station and jumped down from the buggy. Quickly winding the reins around the hitching rail, he ran through the small wooden building and dashed out onto the platform. Coming to a quick stop, he looked around at the people milling about and spotted Lulu climbing the steps into a passenger car. In one hand she held her worn satchel. The other hand clasped a small pine chest to her bosom.

"Lulu!" Tyler shouted, dodging people and luggage. "Louise McCane!"

Lulu looked around in surprise. As Tyler ran toward her, she put her hand to her mouth, her face registering her disbelief.

"Mother," he said breathlessly, coming to a stop in front of her. "Don't go."

After Ty left, Claire unearthed her mother's wedding gown, and now stood in front of the tall cheval glass in her parents' room, studying her reflection.

"Does it fit?" Emily asked eagerly.

"It fits perfectly, Em."

"Describe it to me."

"It's shiny satin, the color of fresh cream, with an overskirt of ecru lace."

"And seed pearls," Emily added, her fingers moving deftly over the skirt of the dress.

"Yes, and there's a lace veil that covers my face to my chin, and falls down to the hem in the back."

"Oh, how I wish I could see you!" Emily stopped and turned her head to the window. "Someone's coming."

Claire ran to the window and looked out. "Emily! Tyler brought Lulu back!"

"Lulu!" Emily cried joyously, making her way as quickly as she could to the stairs.

"Wait, Em!" Claire called, struggling to get out of the dress. She couldn't go running downstairs in her wedding dress. It wouldn't be right for Tyler to see her. She managed to unbutton some of the tiny pearl buttons down the back, but couldn't reach the rest. "Drat!" she said in exasperation. Below, she could hear the happy cries of Lulu and Emily. "Drat, drat, drat!" she said, fumbling with the buttons.

"Can I help?"

Claire spun around with a gasp. "Oh, Tyler, you can't see me in this! Close your eyes!"

With a grin, he immediately scrunched them shut. "How can I help if I can't see you?"

"Keep your eyes closed," she commanded. She stood with her back to him. "Put out your hands and feel for the buttons."

He did as she asked. "I brought Lulu back," he told her.

Claire turned her head to look at him and found his eyes open. "I'm so glad."

"So am I," he said, adroitly freeing her from the gown.

"I'm not going to ask where you learned that skill," she said with a scowl.

Tyler laughed, and bent to nibble the delicate nape of her neck. "I asked Lulu to stay with us," he said. "I hope you don't mind."

A delicious shiver ran down her back. "Of course I don't mind. We're her family."

He turned Claire around and gazed into her eyes with the intensity that made her heart skip a beat. "You were right about forgiving. I decided that if you could forgive your mother, then I could forgive mine."

"Did you tell her that?"

He nodded solemnly. "She got kind of weepy."

With a laugh, Claire threw her arms around Tyler's neck. "I love you very much."

He leaned back to look at her, his heart overflowing with happiness. A month ago, he wouldn't have believed her. He'd thought that genuine, unselfish love was impossible. But two women had proved him wrong. Tyler smiled down at her, still amazed at the love he saw shining in Claire's eyes. He didn't want it ever to go away.

"Will you marry me?" he asked.

Claire tapped her finger against her lips. "Let me see— I'm not busy Saturday."

"It's a date." He bent his head and kissed her deeply, then began pressing teasing kisses down her jaw to her throat. "This isn't easy for me, you know," he murmured. "I'm not good at expressing my feelings. You're going to have to help me."

"I intend to."

"Then I think we should start now," Tyler said, slipping the satin gown over her shoulders.

Claire gasped as it pooled on the floor at her feet. "Tyler!"

"You taste so sweet," he murmured, trailing kisses down her shoulder. "How can I resist you?"

"You'll just have to," she told him on a sigh.

One hand slipped beneath her corset to gently massage a breast, until the nipple puckered and tingled. Claire felt herself weakening. She wondered if she had the patience to wait.

"Claire," he murmured in her ear, his voice husky with desire. "I want to make love to you. We can lock the door. No one will bother us."

Claire melted against him. What would it matter? They were almost married.

"Tyler? Claire?" she heard Lulu call. "Are you two up there?"

Why did Lulu always pick the most inopportune times

to interrupt them? "Don't answer," Claire murmured, repeating the line he had used several times.

"I have to." Tyler kissed her, then set her away with a wicked grin. "She's my mother."

A fantasy, a love story, a summer of change...

The China Garden

By LIZ BERRY

AVON
tempest

"Like a jewel box with hidden drawers and compartments, this finely crafted, multilayered novel holds many secrets...richly laden with mystery and suspense, in which the ordinary often masks unexpected interconnections and the extraordinary is natural to the story's wildly imagined terrain."
—PUBLISHERS WEEKLY ☆

CHN 0599

Dear Reader,

This month, two of your favorite series return! First, don't miss *A Rogue's Proposal* by rising star Stephanie Laurens. Her series about the scintillating Cynster clan continues with this, her first Avon Romance Superleader. Demon Cynster has seen love bring his brethren to their knees, and he's not about to fall into this trap—until he meets pert Felicity and falls under her spell.

And if you love Draycott Abbey, don't miss Christina Skye's latest, *The Perfect Gift*. A talented jewelry designer is invited to the abbey and discovers a connection to the past—and an exciting, passionate love in the present. It's a delightful love story, filled with sensuality and, of course, a touch of Christmas spirit.

Contemporary readers have been waiting for Michelle Jerrott's follow-up to her exciting debut, *Absolute Trouble*. Well, wait no longer, because here she is with *All Night Long*. A long, tall hero—a man of the land—finds unexpected romance with a woman who just can't settle down. Warning: this story sizzles!

Beverly Jenkins is historical romance's premiere writer of African-American historical romance, and her newest, *The Taming of Jessi Rose*, is an irresistible blend of western romance and historical tidbits that give her books that something special.

And if you love Eve Byron's unique heroines and fascinating look at Regency romance, you won't want to miss *My Lord Destiny*, the follow-up to *My Lord Stranger*. It's delectable!

So, until next month, happy reading!

Lucia Macro
Lucia Macro
Senior Editor

We've got love on our minds at

www.avonromance.com

*V*ote for your favorite hero in
<u>"He's the One."</u>

*R*ead monthly gossip columns,
"Happenings Around the House"
in <u>Announcements.</u>

*J*oin the <u>Avon Romance Club.</u>

*S*ubscribe to our monthly e-mail
<u>newsletter</u> to find out about all the
romance buzz on the web.

*B*rowse through our list of new
titles and read <u>chapter excerpts.</u>

*R*ead Mrs. Giggles' review
of an Avon Romance in
<u>One Woman's Opinion.</u>

RWS 0799